The

by Emma V. Leech

Published by: Emma V. Leech.

Cover Art by Victoria Cooper

ISBN-13: 978-1545218082
ISBN-10: 1545218080

****

Table of Contents

And on that cheek, and o'er that brow,
So soft, so calm, yet eloquent,
The smiles that win, the tints that glow,
But tell of days in goodness spent,
A mind at peace with all below,
A heart whose love is innocent!

She Walks in Beauty by Lord Byron.

Prologue

Roscoff. France. July. 1814

The old woman shifted her bird-frail bones on the thin pallet and coughed. The movement racked her fragile body, lea4ving her gasping and clutching at the ragged blanket that covered her. Her young charge ran to her and clutched at her hand, all wide blue eyes and desperation.

Old age was a curse and a blessing. Dying and leaving this God-forsaken place was no hardship, but leaving Céleste was hard indeed. The poor, sweet child. With both her parents gone, she had no one now and not a penny to her name. The last real money they'd had was spent years ago, on bribing the priest into giving her *Maman* a proper burial despite the fact she'd committed suicide. Since then their existence had consisted of grasping at life with frantic fingers, taking in washing and mending; the girl had even been driven to steal on occasion, though the risks were dreadfully high. Marie knew her own bones would be consigned to a pauper's grave but couldn't find the will to care about that. Her worries were over, but Céleste ... God alone knew how she would survive.

"Now, Céleste, go to the chest over there, quickly," she rasped, her voice barely audible, her skeletal fingers pointing towards the girl's only hope. "There are papers. Get them out."

She watched the young woman move and wished, as she had wished every day since they had fled their old lives, that things had been different. The Revolution had changed many things. Supposedly it would bring a better life to the poor and the needy, though she had seen little sign of it yet, with the wars that had followed on its heels. A new world born of such bloodshed ... how could that ever be justified? And Napoleon seemed just as grasping and power hungry as any monarch had ever been.

"These, Marie?" The girl held up a thick roll of parchment and the old woman nodded. Céleste ran back to sit beside her, the papers clutched in her hand.

Marie reached out and touched the perfect face with a bony finger, the calloused and ugly digit looking obscene beside her sweet countenance. "The picture of your mother, such beauty." The words were not happy ones though, for she well knew the kind of attentions the girl already attracted, a situation that would only get worse. She was seventeen now, almost eighteen, and did all she could to hide the gifts she'd been given, tucking her long hair under an ugly cap and wearing shapeless garments many sizes too big. But nothing could disguise those wide blue eyes framed with thick dark lashes, the porcelain skin, or the perfect bow of her pink lips.

"These papers," Marie said, dragging her tired mind back to the important matter she must deal with. "These you must guard and keep hidden until such time as you find someone you can trust, someone who can help you regain all you've lost."

Céleste shook her head and Marie felt a surge of anger. *"Oui*! You must and you will regain it. It is your duty, it belongs to you. You are Célestine de Lavelle, *La Comtesse de Valrey*. You are the last of your line. The title goes to you from your mother, and from her mother before her. You must ... *you must ..."* The old woman bent over as a cough shook her bones and chased away any remaining strength she had. "Promise me, Céleste," she whispered.

The girl looked up at her, eyes full of sorrow and fear, but she nodded. *"Je promets,"* she whispered and Marie sighed and laid her head down. She had done all she could, her time was up, and now the fates would take the girl where they would. She prayed they would be kind.

Chapter 1

"Wherein things go awry and the fates get tangled."

Roscoff. 25 February. 1815

Alex Sinclair, fourth Earl of Falmouth, regarded his men with satisfaction. It had been another good night's work and once the last of the cargo was away they could breathe again.

"Well, Mousy, how are you enjoying your first run?" he demanded of the big man as he shouldered a massive barrel of the finest French brandy onto the small boat drawn up beside the larger hulk of The Bold Bessie. An Earl he may be, but he got his hands just as dirty as the rest of the men.

"I liked it fine, M'Lord," Mousy replied with a grin, reaching up to take the barrel from him. "S'pecially as it kept me out o' harm's way for a day or two."

"You can't hide from her forever," Alex said, not bothering to hide his grin. "She's going to want you to ask her on your return."

Mousy went quiet and looked a little queasy. "Aye, well. Maybe I'll jus' lie low for a day or two. 'Till it blows over. "

Alex chuckled. His sister in law's maid, Annie, had set her eyes firmly on Mousy and had made no secret of the fact she wanted them to get married. She was a formidable woman and Alex very much doubted the likelihood of the situation *blowing over*. She expected Mousy to return with a ring and a question for her and heaven help the poor blighter if he didn't.

"Right, thisun' is full, 'ow much left?"

Alex turned to regard the remaining haul. Boxes of tea and bolts of the finest French silk, all wrapped in oil cloth to protect them from the elements and the salt spray, and over a dozen or more half anker tubs of brandy remained. Alex could see the beach in the moonlight, a hive of activity with maybe two hundred tubmen running back and forth with barrels on a harness over their shoulders, loading the ponies and getting the shore cleared as fast as they may. The crew of his brother's old ship The Wicked Wench had switched from pirates to smugglers like the proverbial ducks to water and the extra hands made light work of the offloading. Mousy had stood as spotsman, guiding the ship to its location from a signal offshore to one of various landing points. The more hard-headed and ruthless volunteered as batmen and patrolled the cliffs, eyes on alert for the Revenue.

"One more and we're done."

"Righty' ho." Mousy nodded and then looked up, frowning. "Wha's ..."

He didn't have time to finish the question as the boom of canon fire exploded overhead and shouts bellowed from all round the beach as the men saw the boat approaching.

"Hell and damnation!" Alex cursed, untying the line. "The Revenue are upon us, lads, get moving!"

All hell broke loose as he pushed the small boat with Mousy in away from his ship, The Bold Bessie, with force. "Get back to shore, get everyone safe away," he yelled.

"You'd bes' come n' all, ye Lordship," Mousy exclaimed as Alex shook his head.

"No, I stay with Bessie, get away ... *now!"*

The sails unfurled with a snap as the wind caught the single-masted cutter, pulling them away from shore. In the distance Alex could see the men scurrying back and forth but the Revenue were not on the beach at least. The greater part of the cargo had been unloaded, now all that mattered was getting free. He looked up at the skies, frowning as the moon disappeared. Disappearing in the dark was not a bad thing with Water Guard sticking to his arse like a burr, but the approaching storm would do nobody any good. He prayed that they'd ride it out.

"What now?" called his man from the helm and then threw himself to the deck as cannon shot screamed overhead.

Alex flinched as the cannon overshot and hit the waves on his far side, dousing him with icy water. "Back to Roscoff," he yelled, his face grim as thunder cracked overhead. "And pray we make it."

***

Céleste reached down and grabbed another piece of driftwood, barely feeling the smooth, worn surface between her numb fingers. *Merde* but it was cold. Mimi wandered behind her, humming a little tune that had begun to irritate her over an hour ago. Barely more than three notes, he repeated it over and over. His voice was surprisingly childlike, considering his bulk and the ugly, craggy face. But Mimi was a gentle giant. His mind was gone, lost somewhere on a battlefield thanks to a stray bullet that almost took his life. Instead it let him live and simply took all the meanness and pessimism that seemed to thrive in all other men, and left him sweet but stupid. He had become her shadow, her protector, and she was thankful for that. He had saved her more than once now, and she would happily endure the irritation of his annoying little habits and endless silly songs in gratitude for that.

She straightened as Mimi grunted and gestured further down the beach. Céleste looked up, blinking as the frigid wind made her eyes water.

"I don't know?" she replied, looking at the large dark shapes laid out on the shingle. They walked a little closer until the image arranged itself into shapes her mind could recognise. *"Mon Dieu!* They are men," she cried and moved to run towards them. Mimi stopped, dropping his clutch of drift wood and it clattered to the ground. His large hand grasped her arm and he shook his head, his eyes fierce.

"Let me go!" she said, her voice firm. "I won't let men die if I can help them." She had seen enough death in her short life. Death from war, from violence, from poverty, from filth, illness, starvation and old age. No matter how many times she saw it, it was ugly and to be fought at all costs. She shook her arm from his grasp and ran to them. Turning the first, her heart grew heavy. Certainly dead, drowned last night, and by the stillness of the three others they were all beyond saving. She looked around and saw other shapes among the corpses. Barrels and boxes wrapped in oil cloth. A wreck. They must have run afoul of the storm last night, the poor bastards. Smugglers most likely, the English were always here, stocking their boats with brandy and gin, tea and silk and lace. All of it a fraction of the price without the heavy taxes the English Prince Regent levied. Well it would do them no good now but ... It was an ill wind.

"Mimi, see all the boxes and barrels?"

Mimi nodded, his slow eyes scanning the beach.

"They're ours now, our secret. We must get them hidden as fast as we may. Can you do that? Can you be clever and fast, *mon brave?"*

Mimi beamed at her and nodded.

"Alors, off you go then."

With a heavy but practical heart, Céleste began to search each of the bodies in turn, checking pockets for money or gold. She left anything personal but took what she could that might keep the cold out and her belly full for a little longer. They'd be robbed soon enough of boots and anything else when the scavengers found them. She'd been lucky to get here first.

She was methodical, checking each body in turn with quick fingers. The farthest away was a fair distance up the beach and she ran, her feet slipping on the shale, aware that they could be discovered at any time and their plunder taken from them. She turned and noted with satisfaction that Mimi had done well clearing the beach and disguising their haul under the hull of a ruined boat. It would do for now. They'd have to come back when it was dark and find a better hiding place until it could be sold.

Turning her attention to the last body she struggled to turn him over. He'd been a huge man. Heavy broad shoulders and long, long legs, he would have towered over her. She gasped as he finally rolled onto his back and looked in sorrow at the still face. My, he'd been a handsome one, she'd bet he'd been a scoundrel with the women in life with a face like that. Carefully she pushed the thick dark hair from his face and leapt back with a squeal as he murmured and his eyelids flickered.

"Mon Dieu," she whispered. "You do have the luck of the devil, smuggler." She looked up to see Mimi walking back towards her and gestured for him to hurry. "He's alive!" she called. "Quick, we must get him indoors and out of the cold before he freezes to death."

This was easier said than done. Big as he was, Mimi struggled with the dead weight, dragging him by increments, and it was a blessing when the man came round, though he seemed not to know what had happened.

"Bessie?" he mumbled as Céleste patted his hand. *"Non,* not Bessie," she said with care, her English was excellent, or so she'd been told, but she hadn't practised it since her mother died. "I am Céleste, and you are very 'eavy. Please, you must help us and walk."

The man did his best to oblige and leaned on Mimi, putting one foot in front of the other with effort until they reached the door of Madame Maxime's. At least the whores would all be abed at this early hour of the morning. They might just make it up to the attic if they took care. She turned to the man and his eyes flickered open, trying to focus on her. Flinty grey, they spoke of a determined soul and for that she was glad. He was half drowned and frozen, his teeth chattering fiercely now. He'd have a fight to recover his strength.

"You must be quiet. *Silence,"* she whispered, putting her finger to her lips.

He nodded his understanding and they began the arduous journey up the stairs to the cramped attic where she slept.

Mimi had just pushed him through the door to her room when Madame Maxime herself stuck her head out of the door on the landing below.

"What the devil are you doing, you stupid girl? Some of us have been working all night. Have you lit the fires?"

"Oui, Madame, I have. I'm sorry to have disturbed you. I tripped on the stair."

The door slammed shut without another word and Céleste breathed a sigh of relief. Up all night working, *bah!,* she thought to herself, scowling. The other girls had been working perhaps, for work it indeed seemed to be with some of the disgusting characters that passed through Maxime's door. But the Madame herself would simply *arrange* and swallow enough brandy to keep her sour temper sweetened for the benefit of her paying customers.

Céleste scurried up the narrow, curving stairway to her attic room, where Mimi had laid the smuggler down on her pallet bed. Everything seemed even more cramped than usual with the two big men taking up all the available space, and she squeezed past Mimi and ducked the rafters as she moved around to the thin, straw-filled *palliasse* that served as her bed.

"We must get these wet clothes off him," she said, reaching forward to get started and yelping as Mimi smacked her hand away. *"Merde!"* she exclaimed, rubbing her stinging knuckles, and then began to laugh at the mutinous look on Mimi's face. "Oh, Mimi."

She giggled. "I've lived in a brothel for the last six months. I promise he has nothing I haven't seen before."

Though she began to rethink that particular statement once Mimi relented and they began to peel away his sodden clothes. She had seen plenty of men, and women, in various states of undress, and a bewildering array of positions, some that seemed undignified. It was hard to miss such sights in a house like this one, no matter how hard she'd tried, to begin with at least. By now she believed she was unshockable; there was nothing left in the world that could possibly surprise her. And yet her curiosity was peeked as the layers were stripped away to reveal a hard, muscular body, quite unlike those she'd seen up to this point.

His large frame on the mattress shivered, his skin puckered with goose-flesh and she reached for the dry scrap of coarse linen that served her as a towel.

"Alors, you go, Mimi," she said, rubbing the linen hard over the man's heavy arm, both to dry him and to warm him. "You need to fetch the bread from the *boulangerie* and get some water on to boil. If they don't get their breakfast there'll be hell to pay. You must cover for me."

Mimi glowered at the unconscious figure and Céleste huffed. "Oh be reasonable, he's in no position to do me any harm, now is he?"

Mimi left, though clearly unhappy about it, and Céleste returned to the job at hand, relieved to be able to look her fill without an audience. She rubbed dry one muscular arm before moving onto this chest. His skin was smooth but marked in places with scars that spoke of a violent life. One was perhaps a bullet wound, high on his left shoulder. She paused for a moment to place her hand flat on his chest, feeling the reassuring thud of his heart, strong and steady under the heavy muscle and coarse hair on his chest. Forcing her attention back to the job at hand she moved to his feet and dried them, rubbing them with vigour to get the blood moving and carrying on up his legs. She ground to halt as she came upon the sodden under drawers which clung to his massive frame. They would have to come off. With difficulty and much cursing, she finally managed to wrestle the damned things off and then swallowed as she turned back and looked at the naked man, sprawled on her bed.

"Mon Dieu," she whispered. He was perfection in masculine form and she couldn't help but take a moment to admire him, from this thick dark hair, square jaw, full mouth and the slight cleft in his chin. Her gaze drifted lower. She took in the impressive width of chest and shoulders, the sculpted belly and the intriguing trail of dark hair that led to his manhood. This she lingered on with interest, for she had been truthful in her words to Mimi, but she had never had the opportunity to see a man in repose, and so close. She bit her lip considering the things she had seen with the whores, if he was this size before he was roused ...

He shivered again and she scolded herself forcefully, the poor devil would die of cold while she sat there staring at him like a fool. Chastened, she covered him as best she could with her only blanket and piled every scrap of clothing she possessed on top of that. Then she lit the tiny stove with what remained of her driftwood. Maxime allowed her the room and a meagre supply of food in return for working her fingers to the bone from dawn till late at night. But she had to provide her own fuel, and so collecting driftwood from the beach was always an early morning chore if she didn't want to shiver all night.

She coughed as the tiny space filled with smoke until the fire caught and the little chimney drew. With one last look at the handsome smuggler she sent a prayer to whatever cruel God seemed to look down on her, and begged that he let the man live. She would work twice as hard, she would be very, very good, if only he would live.

Chapter 2

"Wherein angels appear to those close to the other side."

Céleste grimaced at the shrill giggle that pierced her brain as she dragged her tired body up the stairs. The girls were earning their keep tonight and no mistake.

She held a candle aloft in one hand, lighting the pitch dark stairs to her room, and a jug of water in the other. It was close to midnight now and Maxime had sent her running in circles since mid-morning, when she'd deigned to appear and start ordering her about. Now though, the clients were busy with the whores. Maxime was drunk and happy and had sent her off to bed with a regal wave of her hand that had made Céleste grit her teeth and curse. She had only been able to snatch a moment to check on her smuggler and that had been hours ago. He'd been sleeping still, though his breathing was increasingly uneven and she was afraid he was starting a fever. She had sent Mimi to fetch wood and to check the fire, and so her tiny attic space was a little warmer than the usual freezing temperatures she was used to finding at bedtime as she opened the door. She sat down beside him with a groan and eased off her boots. Wriggling her sore toes, two of them visible through holes in her worn stockings, she sighed at the pleasure in taking the weight off her aching feet. Reaching for the candle, she held it up, close to the man's face.

His breathing was too fast, and even in the candlelight she could see his skin was flushed with fever.

"Don't die," she whispered. "Please don't die." She laid her hand on his forehead, feeling the skin blazing hot beneath her cool palm. He sighed and his head turned towards her. "You must drink something," she told him and poured a little water from the jug into a small wooden cup she kept beside her bed.

With difficulty she managed to lift his head a little with one arm cradled behind him, and held the cup to his parched lips. "Here, drink," she said, keeping her voice soft. "You must."

She tilted the cup, and though some spilled he managed to swallow a little. His eyes flickered open and for a moment she saw him look at her, uncomprehending, before his eyes closed again and the fever took him away.

She blew out the candle and lay down beside him, grateful at least for the heat he brought, and sank into an exhausted sleep.

She awoke a little later with a start to hear the man beside her muttering and thrashing in his sleep. She moved away just in time before his heavy arm struck out and landed hard on the narrow strip of mattress she'd been sleeping on.

"Shhhh," she said, trying to soothe him by laying a hand on his forehead but finding herself increasingly alarmed by the raging fever that burned under his skin. *"Oh, non, non."* She watched him with growing alarm. He was sick to the bone but she could not afford a doctor, even if she could bring one up here without Maxime seeing. He shouted out, incomprehensible words but loud enough to cause alarm in a quiet house. Thankfully the night was still young for the customers downstairs and his shouts would be lost in the melee of all the other men's as they took their pleasures. Later though, once the house was quiet and the customers departed, he could bring people running to see what was amiss.

Céleste chewed at her lip. What on earth could she do? She was no doctor, she didn't know how to care for a sick man except ... She knew he needed to drink fresh water, get lots of rest and ride out this fever. Laudanum. That was what he needed. The drug would calm him, help him rest and ease any pain he had, and keep him quiet too.

There was Laudanum in the house, that was for sure. Maxime used it to control some of the less docile girls. Céleste had seen it happen. Those that gave her trouble, she would slip a drop or two into their coffee every day without them knowing, until they depended on it and then Maxime revealed what she'd done. Then she would hand it over, for a price, if they did what she told them to.

Céleste was very careful indeed to only eat food she had prepared herself and drink water straight from the well.

The drug was kept in a locked cupboard, however, in Maxime's office, and she kept the key on a little chain at her waist.

Céleste cursed her rotten luck and got to her feet, at least she'd been too tired to get undressed and she didn't bother putting her boots on. She'd be quieter in her stockings.

Praying that Maxime would be drunk enough that she'd passed out, she crept down the stairs. Passing door after door, she heard all manner of lewd noises, grunts and shouts and squeals, none of which caused her to bat an eyelid. That first flush of embarrassment had long since left her, and sex was something she understood to be a commodity. It could be power, it could be used to get your own way, put food on the table and it could lead women and men to disaster and ruin. But even now, she held to the hope that there might be more to it than that. At first she had thought everything about it disgusting and vile. Until Annise, one of the sweeter girls, had sat her down and explained how everything worked, and that there was pleasure to be found in it, if you were with a man that pleased you, and knew what he was about. For a moment she paused on the stairs and wondered if the man in her bed knew what he was about. With a small smile twitching at her lips, she quickly decided she'd bet everything she owned that he did.

She carried on, feeling the worn drugget coarse beneath her stockinged feet, and then paused by the half-open door to the salon.

There were voices and laughter and the scent of opium drifting on the fog of smoke that clouded the air. She risked a peek around the door to see Belle, straddling an older man with a bushy moustache who was wearing an expression of intense concentration. Belle bobbed up and down, riding him hard, her expression bored, simply wanting to get the job done and get to her bed. Belle had a bad temper and a sharp tongue and didn't like Céleste. So it was with a prayer on her lips that she darted past the open door and on towards Madame Maxime's study.

She opened the door carefully, only daring to look around once it was open enough for her to slip though. Well maybe God was kind tonight, for there was Maxime with her head in her arms, asleep over her desk. Her painted face stood out, her lips and cheeks a garish red, harsh and lined beneath the lamplight, and snoring loud enough to wake the dead.

Taking no chances, however, Céleste tiptoed over and unhooked the key from the chain with trembling fingers. Hardly daring to breathe, she unlocked the cupboard and took down the big brown bottle of Laudanum. She took it to the desk and picked up a small glass from Maxime's table. There were a dozen empty ones so she hoped one wouldn't be missed. She poured out enough of the bitter, reddish brown liquid to give her smuggler a dose every few hours for a couple of days, and pushed the cork back in the bottle. Maxime snored on, oblivious as Céleste put the key back on the chain and padded back out of the study. Going on the sound coming from salon, Belle had finally reached her goal as the man was making enough noise to rattle the windows as he reached his climax. Hopeful that this meant Belle was well occupied, she ran past the open door and up the stairs as fast as she could go.

By the time she reached the safety of her own room her heart was thundering. *Mon Dieu*, what had she done? If Maxime noticed the Laudanum was gone there would be hell to pay.

Well it was too late now, and judging by the restless movements coming from the bed, it was just as well. With care not to give him too much, she tipped the glass and encouraged her charge to sip a little of the medicine. He grimaced and turned his head away, but she murmured encouraging words and he did as he was bid, finally subsiding into a deep sleep. Relieved and exhausted, Céleste hid the cup of medicine behind a broken roof tile, high on a rafter, and cuddled up beside him, to join her smuggler in sleeping like the dead.

***

Alex cracked open an eye. His vision was blurry and he was on fire, the pain skewering his fogged brain. It was so fierce that he wanted to reach up and remove his own head, but his arms were too heavy, he couldn't move an inch. He must have been out on one hell of a bender, even by his standards - and he'd been plagued by the strangest dreams.

He closed the eye again and tried to remember what he'd been up to, but his brain was murky and slow. There was a scent in the air which reminded him of something that he couldn't put his finger on and too exhausted to try, he drifted back to sleep.

He woke again with a start. "Bessie!" His heart was thudding and his mind tried to grasp at whatever it was that had alarmed him so, but it slipped from his thoughts too quick for him to snatch at. And then he knew he was either dreaming or dead as the most exquisite pair of blue eyes drifted into view.

"Bessie is not 'ere," she said, her voice soft and the words heavy with the most seductive French accent he had ever heard. "But I am. My name is Céleste, and I will take care of you. *Ne vous inquiétez."*

He smiled and tried to hold onto the vision but his eyes were closing, too heavy to let him look any more. "I'm not worried," he murmured. "I like you more than Bessie."

What seemed like a moment later he was shaken awake and he blinked, even the dim light searing his eyes. His head pounded like he'd been hit with a rock and he was so bloody hot.

"Wake up," said a sweet but insistent voice by his ear.

He groaned; he must have dozed off with one of his mistresses, though he was damned if he could remember which. "Not now, darling," he mumbled. "I will see to you later."

There was a not unexpected huff of annoyance and then a low string of obscene French which was more surprising. None of his light o' loves spoke French, not with a fluency and vocabulary that would have made even his crew blush to their toes.

"Non, you must drink this, quickly before I go to work. I am already late."

Forcing his eyes open again he managed to focus his hazy sight, and he caught his breath. An angel. He scowled and told himself that was beyond foolish, if he was dead he wouldn't feel so bloody awful, and he didn't think an angel would swear like a navvy. And yet the face in front of him was the most perfect he had ever seen. The widest blue eyes, a straight nose and a perfectly kissable pink mouth. There was the faintest scattering of freckles over the sweet little nose which he was certain she must despise but struck him as being quite adorable.

"Oh do stop looking at me like zhis," she said, the perfect mouth pursing into the most delectable pout. "You must drink some water. You have a very bad fever, must drink lots, *oui?"*

"Whatever you say, angel." He didn't have the faintest idea who she was or where she'd come from but his mind seemed too addled to care.

Obediently he tipped his head forward with a little help. It seemed a difficult thing to do for some reason, and he sipped at the water she gave him. It tasted sweet and he drank it like nectar, only now realising how parched his throat was.

"And now, you take this, *oui?* It will help you sleep."

He frowned as she tipped another glass towards him and he recognised the taste of Laudanum. The quack had dosed him with it when he'd been shot, or was it when he'd been injured at Trafalgar ... memories of war and ships and drowning men all merged together until he grasped one that stuck. "Bessie!" he gasped, remembering the cutter, the Revenue men and the storm that had tossed them like a child's toy and thrown them against the rocks.

"Bessie is not here, *mon brave,"* whispered the sweet voice. "But I will take care of you."

Chapter 3

"Wherein our slightly wicked hero attempts to deny temptation and suffers the headache."

Céleste opened the door to her room with relief born of exhaustion, both physical and mental. She had been sure Madame Maxime would notice the missing Laudanum and had hardly dared breathe when she doled out the girl's measures. But she had gone about her business without any remark out of the ordinary and sent Céleste scurrying in circles as normal.

Now the usual sounds of merriment and debauchery filled the air and Céleste shut the door behind her with a sigh. Holding the candle high, she made her way to the bed and stopped in her track with surprise to see her smuggler awake and watching her, curiosity in his eyes.

"You are awake," she said, feeling her heart pick up a little. A sleeping man in her bed was one thing, a conscious one quite another.

"I am," he said, his voice a little rough. "At least, I think I am, everything is a little ... confused."

She smiled and sat down beside him. "It is the drug I gave you."

He nodded. "Laudanum."

"Oui, you were sick, very 'ot." She bit her lip as he smiled at her pronunciation. "*H*ot," she said again, struggling with the 'h' sound.

"Your English is excellent," he said, the curiosity in his eyes deepening.

"Thank you," she said, finding herself far too pleased by the compliment.

"Where am I?" he asked, a frown creasing his brow as he took in the mean little room and its squalid surroundings. She could hear a rat scurrying over the rafters and felt suddenly ashamed. Smuggler he may be, but his clothes had been good quality. He was obviously good at what he did. It suddenly dawned on her that he was quite naked beneath the thin blanket and he must realise she had undressed him. Her cheeks flushed and she looked away from him, glad of the dim candlelight to hide her embarrassment.

"Roscoff," she replied, in answer to his question. "I think your ship must have gone down in the storm. I found you on the beach, close to the 'arbour."

Looking up, she found him gazing at her. "You rescued me?" he asked, smiling.

She shrugged. "Mimi, helped," she said and watched the frown return.

"Your ... husband?"

She laughed at that and shook her head. *"Non,* I am not married. Mimi works 'ere, so do I."

"Where is here?" he asked, laying his head back and closing his eyes. The frown deepened and she knew his head was hurting as he lifted one arm and tried to rub his head. She leaned forward and pushed his hand away, replacing it with both of hers. She rubbed his temples with tender care and he sighed.

"Oh, that's nice," he murmured.

She smiled, though he couldn't see it. "I used to do this for my, *maman,"* she said.

"Is this her house?" he asked, though his voice was growing heavy.

"Non, she died, a long while ago, papa too, and Marie." She sighed, quite unable to keep the sorrow from her voice. She didn't allow herself to think on it, but just saying their names brought it all to the surface with painful force. "It is just me now," she added.

He opened his eyes for just a moment and she thought there was pity there, but then his eyes drooped and he drifted into sleep once more.

She watched him for a moment, reaching up to push his hair from his forehead and he sighed, moving towards her touch. Smiling she leaned down and pressed a small kiss to his temple.

"Sleep well, mon contrebandier."

Turning, she blew out the candle and moved close to him, welcoming both his warmth and the reassuring bulk of him at her side. She was so tired of being afraid, of always having to be brave. It was nice to think there was someone else with her, even if it was only for a day or two.

***

Alex awoke with a raging thirst and reached for his glass of water to find, not only that it wasn't beside his bed as usual, but it wasn't his bed. It wasn't so unusual to wake up in a strange bed but the surroundings ... he looked about at the cramped and dingy space and frowned. What the devil? As his faculties began to struggle through the fog in his head he also realised he was not alone. Again this was not terribly unusual, and he looked down to discover the most delectable bed warmer he had ever seen as his bruised mind struggled to recover the details of last night. The woman had coiled around him, her head on his chest, her hair spilled out around her. It was a light brown, shot through with gold and blonde highlights that glimmered even in the dull light of the room. Her slight, though curvaceous body was pressed firmly against his and he smiled as she sighed in her sleep and snuggled in closer.

Reaching out a hand to touch the guinea gold tresses, he found it silky soft and wondered why on earth he couldn't remember who she was or more to the point - *where* he was? Roscoff! The information burned his mind and his head ached fiercely but the more he tried to remember the details, the further the information seemed to slip from him. Laudanum, he remembered that. The girl had drugged him, so that explained the fog in his memory and ... oh God, *Bessie,* the ship had gone down ... but the girl ...? Perhaps if he could see her face ... Shifting slightly, he tilted his head so that he could look at her. For a moment he was simply in awe of the beauty of the girl, and then it filtered through his brain that she was extremely young. Good Lord, she wasn't much more than a child he realised with a rush of guilt. Seventeen at most, she was probably half his age. He felt at once very old and very wicked. My God, what had he done?

He moved away from her, as far as was possible on the small mattress with a wall on one side and the girl on the other. But the movement disturbed her and she sighed, stretched and yawned. Despite himself he watched her, smiling at the luxurious nature of the movement, like a contented cat. She blinked, blue eyes still full of dreams as a slow smile curved over that perfect mouth.

"Good morning," he said, for the first time in his life feeling at a disadvantage on awaking with a stranger.

"Mmmm, *oui,"* she said, on a sigh, as she moved closer to him. "It *is* a good morning, I like waking up with you 'ere. You are so warm. It is so long since I have been warm." She snuggled back against him and he moved in alarm, trying to sit up to get away from her, but his head began to swim and he groaned. "What are you doing?" she scolded him. "You must not move, you are too weak, silly man." She tutted and cursed a little more in French, words that a young lady should never have heard let alone dared utter. But she was sweet nonetheless as she fussed about him, smoothing his head with her cool hand.

Alex closed his eyes and gritted his teeth as she pressed her warm body against him. My God, he'd been saved by a mythical creature, half angel, half ... foul-mouthed temptress - and he was going to hell for sure.

He jolted as the cool hand left his head and smoothed over him, trailing her fingers through the hair on his chest. "You are very ... big," she said sounding thoughtful, and his eyes snapped open in alarm, though there seemed only curiosity in her expression. "I have never seen a man as big as you." He blinked, wondering if she was for real or deliberately stroking his ego, whichever, it was working. He shifted, suddenly uncomfortable as his body began to wake and make demands that he couldn't possibly act on. His eyes drifted down to the small hand resting over his heart and she frowned up at him. "I thought for a moment you seemed a little better, but ... suddenly you are looking very hot again," she said, her voice full of concern.

Oh God.

"Could I have some water please?" he asked, with just a touch of desperation.

"Of course."

She got up from the bed and crossed the room to pour him some water from the jug. To his chagrin he looked up to find she was only dressed in a thin shift that barely covered her behind, and then she leaned forward ... He closed his eyes and prayed - for forgiveness, for help ... for the strength to survive this ... this *ordeal,* for surely God was testing him to see just how wicked he'd become.

He opened his eyes as the little minx sat down beside him again and held the cup to his lips. With a frown he tried to fix his mind on important matters, and as far away from the warm body curled into his side as he possibly could. He sipped the water with some relief, hoping it would clear his mind.

"My men," he asked, as she took away the cup. Suddenly it all came back to him, the Revenue men, the storm . "What ..." He looked around at her to see her eyes filled with sorrow.

"I am so sorry," she said. "There were *trois."* She held up three fingers and he closed his eyes with anguish in his heart. Three good men dead. There should have been more of them to crew Bessie, but the men were all on the beach and there was no time ...

"Je suis vraiment désolée."

He looked up to see her eyes shining with pity and she stroked his hair.

"Sleep now, *mon brave*, sleep."

And suddenly he was too tired to think any more, and her touch was soothing, her nearness a comfort ... And so he slept.

***

When he awoke again it was dark. At first he was disorientated again by the strangeness of his surroundings, but gradually his memories resolved themselves into some kind of order. Bessie was sunk, three of his men dead, and he was washed ashore at Roscoff. He had no money nor proof of his identity as all was carefully left at home in case the Revenue got him. He was also in the care of a woman young enough to be his daughter and beautiful enough to tempt a saint, and he had long since thrown in his lot with a rather darker crowd to claim any kinship with that pure ideal. He smiled as he remembered the scolding she'd given him and then found himself frowning as his attention was taken by sounds of revelry, and once again that familiar scent on the air. Opium, he realised, now his wits were his own, and the sounds were most certainly familiar too. Damn it all. He was in a brothel.

His heart sank to his boots as he recalled the girl's words to him. Mimi worked here, as did she. He felt suddenly sick. That a beautiful child with such vibrancy and spirit should be condemned to a life like this. Though it certainly explained the familiar way she curled up in bed with him.

Alex felt an ache over his heart at the idea of her prospects. Disease and despair, unless she got very lucky and snared a rich man's interest, which seemed unlikely going on the seedy nature of his surroundings. Although he'd never had any illusions about his own character, he tended to be selfish in his own affairs, his own pleasures being his foremost concern, he was a compassionate man. He knew he had been blessed in many ways, and his wealth and status afforded him a way of life few could aspire too.

Though he worked quietly, so that few knew of his actions, he'd discovered a philanthropic side to his character, rather at odds with the cruel and aloof character he was believed by his contemporaries who he had little patience for. The thought of leaving the girl to her fate was something he could not countenance, especially after she'd saved him from his own fate. He couldn't let that happen to her. He would save her, he decided, refusing to consider the difficulties involved in this particular scheme. It would be a salve for his conscience, though he had at least absolved himself of having taken advantage of her. He may have every man's ego about the force of his own stamina and prowess, but it was clear he'd been unconscious and off his head with fever until this last morning.

But at least if he got her away from here he could repay her for saving his life, and the trouble she must have had to hide him here. For he realised he must be hidden. It was unlikely any Madame would allow one of her girls to keep a strange man in her rooms. Though now he came to think on it, he came to wonder what the damn woman was about. A beauty like Céleste came along once in a blue moon, any Madame worth her salt would make the most of her, keeping her in the best rooms and dressing her in the finest possible attire to appeal to the wealthiest clients she could attract. But here the child was, dressed in rags and sleeping with rats.

The growing urge to throttle the woman and to give any man who had taken his pleasure with Céleste a slow and painful death kept his mind fully occupied until finally the door to the attic creaked open.

A female figure was just visible in the candle light she carried and he watched as Céleste took off her boots at the door. He heard her heavy sigh of relief before she set the boots down and padded silently over to him.

"Alors, you are awake, mon chou."

He winced a little at the familiar way she spoke to him, like a lover, but was more concerned by the obvious exhaustion in her voice and her eyes. But she smiled at him and bade him sit up and accept a plate bearing bread and cheese, and it was only at that moment he realised how dreadfully hungry he was. His stomach gave a loud growl of protest and she laughed, the sound soft against the raucous noises from downstairs. She gestured for him to eat and finding he wanted to please her apart from anything, he did as he was told. She took the plate from him once he was finished and set it aside.

"You're tired," he said, watching her and finding himself anxious about the dark circles beneath those incredible eyes.

She gave a slight huff of laughter before she began to undress. *"Oui*, I am tired. I am always tired. I dream about soft feather beds that I can lie in for days on end and simply ... sleep." She sighed again and once more he felt an uncomfortable ache in his chest. He was curious to know more about her but unwilling to tax her with questions when she was so exhausted. Yet she was obviously well educated, her grasp of English said that much, and she didn't speak like a peasant. In fact she put him very much in mind of an older lady he knew in England. A French Marquise, she had fled during *le terroir* when the nobility were losing their heads daily to Madame la Guillotine and had a haughty turn of phrase and a manner of speaking that was not unlike Céleste; if you ignored the cursing and swearing that was. He turned to look at her, to ask where she was born and found she was once more wearing nothing but the shift, and he averted his eyes.

"Mon Dieu, the old crow has had me at work since dawn," she said, stretching and laying down beside him with a groan. "My back is killing me."

"You ... have been working since dawn?" he asked in horror, trying hard not to stare at the mouth-watering figure, only too visible beneath the threadbare chemise.

"Oui," she mumbled, smothering a yawn. "With barely ten minutes to eat my lunch before she was shouting at me to get back at it." She pressed her body closer to him, shivering. Alex swallowed and shifted as far away as he could manage, only to find she moved closer, curling into him.

He gritted his teeth. "Oh did she?" he growled. Damn the evil bitch, that was it! He would have to get them clear of this hell hole first thing in the morning. The fact that he was barely strong enough to sit upright, let alone find a way for them to leave with no money, was something he ignored as immaterial. By the morning he would be fit enough. He'd have to be.

Despite telling himself he would be better off not knowing, he found himself asking about her work.

"The ... people here. Do they treat you well?"

She snorted in amusement and inveigled herself under his arm like a cat seeking a caress, resting her head on his shoulder. He found himself unable to refuse and tried to keep his response entirely fatherly by letting his hand rest on her shoulder, rather than the inviting curve of her waist.

"Madame Maxime is *une ivrogne,"* she cursed. "Though at least if she is drunk she's less of a bitch. Some of the other girls are OK, but Belle is spiteful, especially if *Le Baron de Merde* is visiting.

"The Baron of ...?"

She giggled and shook her head, the soft tresses tickling his chest in a disturbing manner.

"Really 'e is the Baron de Merdorph, but I call him the shit Baron," she said and he could sense that she was smiling.

He cleared his throat. "Yes, I understood that much. May I enquire what this man has done to you to deserve such a name?" He found his fists were clenched and tried hard to make himself relax but he had the desperate need to strike someone.

"To me?" she asked in surprise. "Oh, nothing to me. I am not worth his attention, but he treat all the girls like dirt. But nobles they are always like this." She gave a dismissive wave of her hand. "They believe they are above the rest of us scrabbling in the dirt but in the end ... we are all the same." She gave a heavy sigh and he heard a plaintive note in it which made the ache in his chest worsen. He couldn't understand what kind of fool this man could be to not notice Céleste, and what kind of Madame wouldn't be throwing the girl in his face. But he decided that he would keep his own title to himself until he had got the girl to a safe place, in case she came to believe he had nefarious motives. He found himself quite surprised by the fact that he didn't, but there it was. He would do the right thing by this girl. He would find her a good home, somewhere she could be safe and happy and have a future.

He listened as her breathing deepened and, content that she was asleep, he moved her over to the side of the mattress, before turning his back on her and doing the same.

Chapter 4

"Wherein evil stalks our heroine and events come to a head."

To his chagrin Alex found the girl had gone when he woke, though she had left him a plate of food and a chamber pot. He grimaced, both at the thought he had been sleeping while the girl was earning her keep and likely giving much of it to keep him fed, and by the idea that she was skivvying for him. He ate everything she had left, aware that he needed to regain his strength as soon as he was able, and then made an attempt at getting to his feet.

At first the room span and he was obliged to cling to the rafters to keep his feet, but little by little he steadied, though he felt weak as a kitten. Nevertheless, they had to get out of here. He looked around the cramped space and came upon his first problem. He was naked as the day he was born and the little wretch had taken his clothes. That problem, however, seemed less insurmountable than the idea of standing for a moment longer, and so it was with self disgust, frustration and a sigh of relief that he laid back down on the thin *palliasse*.

He slept the rest of the morning until he was awoken with a start by heavy footsteps. A large and disreputable figure ducked under the lintel and strode into the room, and Alex reached for a pistol that wasn't there. With alarm he looked the man over and gauged his chances. Alex was likely taller, though this fellow was massive across the chest and shoulders, with hands like mallets. In normal circumstances Alex would have given himself at least even odds but as he could hardly stand ...

The danger of the situation dissipated as Alex noticed the man carried a bowl of food, some kind of stew from the delicious scent, and it made his stomach growl. The big man grunted at him, thrust the bowl in his face - though from his expression he looked as though he'd rather shove it down his throat, bowl and all - and then ducked to pick up the chamber pot.

"Vous êtes, Mimi?" Alex asked, assuming this was the man Céleste had spoken of and received a nod of agreement and another grunt. He found he was relieved that the man was both older than he, ugly as sin and apparently none too bright, and decided not to dwell on his reasons for that. *"Merci d'avoir aidé Céleste à me cacher ici,"* he added, figuring he should thank the man for his help in case it was needed again. Once more he was answered with a grunt as Mimi headed back to the door. With a touch of anxiety he asked where Céleste was. Usually she tried to come and see him at lunchtime. Mimi just shrugged his massive shoulders and muttered something that sounded a little like *travail* as he shut the door and the heavy footsteps descended the stairs.

So Céleste was working. Cursing, Alex forced himself to his feet and made himself walk back and forth across the room. He had to get his strength back. They had to get out of here. Right now that poor girl ... Nausea swirled in his stomach as he considered just what she was doing and he allowed his shaking legs to carry him back to the bed. With his head in his hands he glanced at the bowl of stew and knew it would choke him, as the manner in which it had been paid for made his heart ache and his temper rage. But if he wanted to get them out of here he needed to eat and so he forced it down instead of flinging it across the room in a fury as he was more than tempted to do.

***

Céleste slammed the heavy pot of stew down on the kitchen table, ignoring the raised eyebrows from the girls. Madame Maxime had been redoubling her effort to make Céleste see sense. Didn't she understand how much easier her life would be if she earned her money like the other girls, Maxime had said, her voice all soft and wheedling. She had slung an arm over Céleste's shoulder and hugged her, in a parody of motherly affection that had sorely tempted Céleste to scratch the bitch's eyes out. If Céleste would just do as Madame wanted she would receive only the wealthiest clients, she would have a room of her own with a soft feather bed, fine clothes, wine and plenty to eat, and for all that she'd only have to work for a few hours a night; unless the clients paid enough to engage her for longer, in which case Céleste would earn a pretty penny too.

Madame described her possible life with colour and excitement, as though she was offering the girl a chance at something wonderful, if she would only stop being so stubborn about a silly thing like her honour. After all, what good was that likely to do a girl like her, it's not like anyone would marry her! Maxime had laughed as she'd said it and Céleste had imagined her *contrebandier* and a life where they were married, with a little cottage by the sea ... Her heart clenched as she realised Maxime was likely right. No matter what the papers Marie had given her said, as far as the world was concerned Céleste was nobody, and no one wanted her for anything other than her pretty face and ... well she knew damn well what they wanted her for. It had taken everything she had not to spit in the vile woman's face, but she had politely declined Madame Maxime's kind offer, and ever since the bitch had gone out of her way to show her just how hard life could be.

Her work load had almost doubled and Maxime had even refused to give her lunch in punishment for dropping a pitcher of milk while she was clearing up the breakfast things. The pitcher had been less than half full and Céleste was dead on her feet and famished but that was exactly what Maxime wanted. Well, Céleste thought, she wouldn't let the old crow break her. She kept in mind the end of the day when she would finally be able to see her smuggler. She liked to talk to him. His deep English voice was soothing, his large presence beside her comforting and the fact she had missed visiting him at lunchtime only made her hate Maxime all the more. She'd stolen a large bowl of stew for him and persuaded Mimi to take it up. She knew it was a risk but a man like that couldn't regain his strength on bread and cheese. Though she knew too, once he was strong enough, he would leave, and she would be left here, alone.

She blinked away tears and returned her attention to polishing the silver. It was a job she hated but at least she could sit down and do it. Besides there was no use crying over spilt milk, she thought with a grim smile. She knew that only too well.

She was lost in thought as a familiar and hated voice filtered into the kitchen and she caught her breath. Leaving her work she gathered her skirts and tiptoed to the doorway to listen. Monsieur Pelletier was talking in low tones to Madame Maxime and Céleste held her breath, straining to catch their conversation. She detested the man who always tried to grope her if she was anywhere close to him, and there was a disgusting avaricious look in his eyes when he watched her, which he always seemed to be doing. The other girls said he was cruel, but as a wealthy merchant he paid enough to do as he pleased and none of them dared complain. Clara, who was the only girl who had made an effort to befriend Céleste, had warned her to hide herself when Pelletier was around. She said he was always asking questions about Céleste and Clara had been struck for refusing to answer. She said he'd wanted to know if she was truly a virgin, or if Madame Maxime was hiding the fact she was working from him.

Now Céleste stood with her heart beating too hard and too fast as the conversation between Maxime and Pelletier became clear. Maxime was selling her to him, she was selling her virginity, and for such a price! Céleste covered her mouth with her hand to stop herself from crying out. The idea of that disgusting creature rutting away at her made her want to vomit but she forced herself to listen.

"You will dose her with laudanum, just enough to keep her docile. I do not want her asleep you understand," Pelletier was saying, his voice cool and clinical, as though he was arranging the details of a dinner rather than the serving up of an abducted girl for his own pleasure.

"Oui, Monsieur Pelletier," the bitch Maxime replied with a reassuring tone. "I understand just what you require. The girl will be bathed and dressed in the finest gown we have and will be ready for you in every way. You need not worry."

"Non, I need not!" Pelletier sneered. "For if I find you have played me false, Madame, I promise you will regret it."

Maxime gave an audible gasp, clearly taking the threat with the seriousness it deserved. . Pelletier was not a man to be crossed, certainly not at the price Maxime was demanding.

"You will bring her to me tomorrow night at eight sharp. Do we have an agreement?"

Céleste didn't wait to hear more. She ran out into the garden and out along the street until she reached the beach where she'd found Alex. She retched and retched, though her empty stomach had nothing to give. Oh, *mon Dieu,* she had to get away, she had to get out of here or she would be lost in Maxime's world for good. With panic holding her heart in a vice she ran back to the house to find Mimi.

She found him round the back near the stables, chopping wood for the fire, but he looked up in alarm as she ran towards him.

"Mimi, you said a man offered a sum for the brandy; tell him we accept and get the goods to him tonight."

Mimi shook his head, and she stilled him by laying her hand on his arm.

"I know it's not enough, *mon brave,* it's not nearly enough. But I have to leave. Maxime intends to sell me to Pelletier!" She was heartened at least by the fury in Mimi's eyes and he slammed the axe down into the trunk in front of him, shattering it into pieces.

"I know," she said, pulling the big man into a hug. "I know you would kill him and then what? You will hang and I will be no better off. I have to go, far from here." She hugged him tighter as Mimi made a sound of distress. "And I will miss you too, but I will not become a whore, especially not for that ... *con!"* She looked up at him and already knew what the answer to her question would be. "You could come too, if you wanted?"

Mimi clutched at his head and began to move back from her embrace, making a soft keening sound that tore at her heart. *"Non, non*, it's alright, it's fine, you stay, *mon brave,* you stay. I will be fine. Don't you worry."

She stayed until he had calmed himself and returned to chopping wood before she went back to the kitchens. Poor Mimi. He was terrified of change, terrified of anything that was different from the usual routine of his day. He would never survive anywhere else. At least at Maxime's he had a roof over his head and enough to eat, and the girls were kind enough to him. He would be fine. But she needed to run, as far and as fast from Pelletier as she could. Her thoughts drifted back to the man in her bed and she prayed that ... maybe she would have a companion for her journey if she could only persuade him to take her. But then she remembered just how weak he still was. He had almost died. She couldn't force him to leave, not yet, but she knew she couldn't leave him alone either, not for any price.

Chapter 5

"Wherein deals are struck, temptation beckons the devil and threatens good intentions."

By the time Céleste finally made it back to her room Alex was beside himself. Angry with himself at his own impotence to change the situation she was in, it was beyond frustrating. In normal circumstances he could sweep in with his money and his title, and failing that he would use a willingness for brute force and be assured of getting his own way. It had always worked in the past. But now with no proof of whom he was, not a sous to his name, and not even his own strength to rely on, he felt helpless. It was not a feeling he enjoyed. And yet when he saw Céleste enter the room, with her head bowed and her tread one of sheer exhaustion, he knew he was all that stood between her and utter ruin. He wouldn't fail her.

To his horror she didn't speak but just sank to her knees beside the bed, threw herself against his chest and began to sob. For a moment he was too shocked to move or speak. Weeping women were something he usually avoided at all costs and yet he knew instinctively that Céleste wasn't the kind to indulge in tears just because she was thwarted or to try and get her own way. No in those circumstances she'd probably shout and throw things from what he'd seen of her character so far. Which meant someone had hurt her.

"What is it, *ma mie?"* he asked, making a concerted effort to keep his voice soft though he could feel a now familiar rage building in his chest. "Has someone hurt you?"

"Non," she said, shaking her head and looking up at him with those wide blue eyes full of tears. "Not yet, but they are going to."

"What?" He sat up and held her by the shoulders. "Who, Céleste, who wants to hurt you?"

She blinked and he felt his heart squeeze as a tear rolled down her face. "Do you ..." she began, a small frown creasing her forehead. "Do you think I am ... *jolie?"*

Alex felt himself frown in reply, perplexed at the change in subject. "What? Of course I think you're pretty, beautiful in fact, but why the devil are ..."

His words were stopped in their tracks as she moved forward and pressed her lips against his. For just a second his brain stalled as her sweet, soft mouth sought his. He could feel the heat of her body through her threadbare dress and her heart thundering in her chest. With resolution he grasped her by the arms and pushed her gently but firmly away from him.

"Oh, but *s'il te plaît*, you said I am beautiful, *oui?"* she demanded, and Alex was thrown by the desperation in her eyes. "Then you would like to lie with me?"

"What?" Alex exclaimed in alarm.

The desperation in her expression seemed to grow and she put a hand to her hair in frustration. "Fuck!" she said suddenly, as though this was an answer of some kind.

Alex was momentarily speechless. "I beg your pardon?" he asked with caution.

"Fuck, this is the word, *oui?* You want to fuck me?"

He opened his mouth and closed it again. He knew he was on dangerous ground but he was damned if he knew how he'd got there.

"Please," she said, reaching forward and taking his hand. "Please will you ... do it ... to me?" She pressed his hand to her breast and Alex snatched it away, making her gasp in shock.

"No!" he said, with rather more force that he'd intended.

"You ... you do not ... want me?" Her lip trembled a little and he swallowed a curse. There she sat, looking like a broken angel with her beauty and those big sad eyes and everything in him ached to take her in his arms and show her the difference between a man who would fuck her and one who would make love to her. But he had sworn he would do better than that, he had sworn he would protect her from the world, even from himself.

"Céleste," he said, making sure his voice was soft and as gentle as he could make it. "Céleste, any man would want you, you are ... you are incredibly beautiful, more than I think you realise. But ... but you are perhaps half my age and ... and you deserve better than this. You deserve more than you have here, and I want to help you. We will leave here, you and I. We will leave here and I will take care of you. I will find you a place to live, where you will be safe. You will never have to ... to take another man to your bed, I swear it."

He smiled at her and watched the emotions as they played over her face, from relief, to gratitude to ... sheer fury. What the ...

"Merde!" she cursed, reaching out with one small fist and striking him. "You think I am a whore? You think I am one of those girls down there who spread her legs for any who will pay? You think this? *Va te faire foutre!"* She launched herself at him and Alex grabbed at her wrists before she could do any damage. But she struggled and cursed and so he flipped her onto her back, using his weight to pin her down and keep her still until she calmed ... a little at least. She was glaring at him with utter rage in her eyes and he realised with a wash of guilt that he had underestimated her. Though she *was* in a whore house and she *had* said she worked there so ...

"Céleste, forgive me. I ... I just assumed. You said you worked here!" he exclaimed, unable to keep the accusation from his voice.

"In the kitchens!" she spat back, and then looked away from him as tears began to gather all over again, which was far worse than any amount of anger she threw at him.

"Céleste, truly, I am so sorry but ... but most women do not sleep next to men they don't know and ..."

She looked back at him, apparently puzzled. "I am not sleeping with men I don't know," she objected. "I know you. I save your life!" she added putting her chin up. "We are friends, *au moins*, I thought we were," she added with a pout.

Alex smiled and nodded. "Yes, yes of course we are friends, but Céleste, you don't even know my name and yet you get into bed with me like ... like we are lovers."

"Your name?" she repeated and rolled her eyes. *"Bah!* Who cares for the name, I know you. You are a good man, a kind man. I trust you." She shrugged and with the movement Alex became forcefully aware of the position he was in, of her soft, and apparently willing, body beneath him. "I like you in my bed, I like to sleep beside you. You ... you make me feel safe and ... and warm and I like you, very much."

Sensing danger once more Alex made to move but she stopped him by hooking an arm around his neck and wrapping her legs around his.

"Wouldn't you like to ..."

"Don't!" Alex said before she could say it again. "Don't say that word, it ... it is not appropriate."

"It isn't?" she asked, eyebrows raised. "But it means ..."

"I am perfectly aware of the meaning of the word," Alex snapped, with growing exasperation as he unhooked one arm to find it replaced by the other. "And a young lady ought never to let it pass her lips. A young *unmarried* lady ought not to even know it!"

"Pffft," she said, rolling her eyes at him. "Then you prefer your young ladies to be stupid, *non?"*

"Non! Oh good Lord."

She sighed and moved against him in a way that made his breath catch, something she noted with a smile. "So ... what should I say if I want you to ...?" she whispered, repeating the movement of her hips to rub against his all too obvious erection. There was only a thin blanket covering his nakedness and he knew damn well she could feel his arousal.

With rather more force than he wanted to employ he removed her hold on him and fled to the far end of the pallet, holding the blanket around him for modesty.

Alex took a deep breath.

"I am not going to ... to make love to you," he said, as much for his own benefit as for hers. Perhaps if he said it loud enough his cock would listen up and behave itself. Seeing the disappointment in her eyes didn't help, though he'd admit his ego enjoyed it.

She shrugged and all of the fight seemed to go out of her. "Then Madame Maxime will send me to Pelletier and I will be the whore you thought I was after all."

"What?" Alex demanded. "What are you talking about?"

But Céleste turned her back on him and faced the wall, wrapping her arms around herself and shivering. "It does not matter now, *mon brave."*

Alex suddenly realised how damned cold it was and he shivered himself.

"Where are my clothes, Céleste?" he demanded. If only he could get dressed he would feel in more control of himself and this ... this ridiculous situation.

"Mimi, 'as them," she said, her voice quiet. "They needed mending and I didn't want Maxime to see. I will give you back your things tomorrow."

He sighed and lay back down beside her, pulling her into his arms but keeping her facing away from him. He felt her shiver and wriggle closer, and he gritted his teeth as her shapely behind fitted itself perfectly into his lap.

"Now then," he said, trying to focus his mind on anything but the inviting body next to him. "Explain to me what is going on. Why were you crying, why did you try to seduce me, who the devil is Pelletier and why would Madame Maxime sell you?"

He heard her sniff and waited until she was ready to talk to him.

"Madame Maxime wants me to work for 'er, like the other girls, you see?"

"Yes," Alex said, his voice grim. "I do see."

"She 'as been making my life, my work, 'arder and 'arder, to try and make me do as she want. And now, today I 'ear her talk with Monsieur Pelletier, tomorrow night she is to drug me and make me ... *ready* for this man, Pelletier, for he 'as paid a lot of monies to take my ..."

She stopped and began to sob and Alex pulled her close. Any desires he may have had fled in the face of such a story. *Pelletier*, he turned the name over in his mind and swore to remember it. He would be sure to make the acquaintance of this man as soon as Céleste was safe and far from his grasp. She turned in his arms and he held her close, stroking her hair and talking to her quietly until she stopped crying.

"So that is why you wanted me?" he asked with a rueful smile hiding his own hurt pride. "So that you were no longer a virgin."

She was quiet for a moment and then she looked up, with an expression that stopped his heart. "Not just for that," she whispered.

He pulled her down so that her head was pressed back against his shoulder and reminded himself of everything the girl was up against until he could think of anything past his own desires. She had been fighting for survival in a cruel and callous world where even her own beauty could be used against her. He would not add to it by taking advantage of her innocence. With ruthless control he squashed any feelings he may have and reminded himself of his promise to her. She was clearly in need of a protector, a father figure, and he could only thank God that she had fallen into his hands. He wouldn't let her down.

"Well, I am more flattered than you can imagine," he said, stroking her hair. "But it is not necessary, as I said before, we will leave here and I will take care of you."

"But you are not strong enough to leave yet," she protested. "I had 'oped you would take me when you leave 'ere, but Pelletier expects me tomorrow night. It will be too late."

Alex frowned and shook his head. "Then we will leave first thing in the morning."

"But you are still sick."

He waved away that argument. "Of more concern is my current lack of funds."

"I 'ave a little money," she said. To his surprise she sat up and chewed her lip, looking guilty. "I must ... confess."

"Oh?" he asked, wondering what the little devil had been up to now.

She nodded and began to wring her hands together.

"Promise ... don't be angry."

He frowned at her. What on earth had she done? "I promise," he said, if a trifle cautiously.

"When I found you, there was also many ..." she frowned, apparently searching for the relevant word and coming up empty. *"Barrique?"*

"Ah," he said as he began to understand. "Barrels."

"Oui." She nodded. "Barrels of Cognac and boxes of tea and ..." She swallowed and looked at him with big anxious eyes. "I sold them."

He stifled a laugh of surprise. "You did?"

"Oui." She nodded and bit her lip once again.

"How much for how many barrels?"

She mumbled an answer which made his heart sink. It was a fraction of its worth in England and far less than he'd paid for it, but then with no connections and for a quick sale, she really hadn't done badly. He sighed and smiled at her.

"Well done, Céleste. That is at least enough to get us most of the way to Bordeaux if we are careful."

"Bordeaux?" she repeated in surprise. "Why Bordeaux?"

"Because," he replied with a smile. "I would prefer to lie low and avoid home for a while in case the Revenue are asking questions, and that is where my brother is."

"Oh," she said with a nod of understanding and then shivered, rubbing her hands up and down her arms. "Please let me under that blanket now, I am very cold."

Alex frowned and she tutted at him impatiently.

"Oh, for heaven's sake. I 'ave lived in a *bordello* for the past six month, I 'ave seen much ... and I 'ave certainly seen everything that you 'ave," she added with a smirk.

Alex scowled at her and tried to consign that information to the far reaches of his mind where it wouldn't trouble him; though he had no faith in the possibility of it staying there. He could hardly allow the girl to freeze, however, and so it was with a triumphant grin that Céleste snuggled up to him and he knew he was in for a night of utter torment.

He thought she was already sleeping when a whispered question reached his ears.

"What *is* your name?"

"Alexander," he replied, amused at her drowsy words. "My friends call me Alex."

"Alexandre," she repeated in the French manner, making him smile. "I like this name very much. It is strong, like you. Goodnight, Alex."

"Goodnight, Céleste."

Chapter 6

"Wherein journeys are undertaken, and our heroine puts le chat among the pigeons."

Alex listened to her gentle breathing as Céleste settled into sleep. Thoughts of some faceless bastard called Pelletier swirled in his head. He wished once again he had access to all that was usually at his fingertips, though he'd settle for a pistol or a sword. He promised himself the pleasure of seeking out Monsieur Pelletier and taking vengeance on behalf of a young woman who could not defend herself against such wickedness. He satisfied his anger for some time in devising a fitting punishment for such a vile creature. But once he had put an end to Pelletier in many and varied fashions he was still wide awake, and though he knew he must sleep to be able to face the days ahead he found himself unsurprisingly restless. No matter the promises he had made to himself, and to Céleste, the reality of a beautiful female curled around his naked body was impossible to ignore, and so it was with the ache of frustration and bleary resignation that he saw the first lightening of the sky and shook Céleste awake.

She sighed and blinked up at him, still half asleep, and he tried to ignore the strange feeling that bloomed in his chest as he watched her. He only knew that she had put her trust in him, and he would do everything he could to be worthy of that trust.

The quiet seemed too fragile as Céleste moved about the room, as though the ears of the inhabitants of the house were straining for sounds of their departure, which was clearly foolish. But Alex was only too pleased once Céleste had disappeared downstairs and Mimi appeared a short while later, bearing his clothes, the luxury of hot water to wash with and their share of the money for selling the goods.

Alex washed and dressed as fast as he could, spared a moment to regret the fact he couldn't shave, and then followed Mimi back down the stairs, carrying his boots to make as little sound as he could.

They arrived in the kitchen to discover Céleste cramming as much food as she could into a small sack.

"Mimi always takes the cart into town on Fridays for the market," she explained, her voice low and urgent in the dim surroundings of the dingy room. "So 'e will take us there and we will find a carriage."

Alex nodded and followed them outside into the frigid morning air. The house was clearly on the edge of town, close to the sea and with the salt tang of decaying seaweed thick around them as the gulls cried overhead, unheeding of their desire for quiet. Alex watched their breath cloud around their faces as they made their way to the cart and felt his lungs ache as the cold seared inside his chest. A pony stood in the harness of the cart, eyeing them with a resigned air and a huff as they approached. Mimi made a fuss of the animal and slipped him a carrot and the crunching sound seemed to echo around the streets.

Alex helped Céleste onto the seat before joining her and she slipped her arm into his, leaning into him and looking up with anxiety bright in her eyes. *"Mon Dieu,* 'e makes enough noise to wake every neighbour for miles," she hissed, glaring at the pony in horror.

He chuckled and gave her hand a reassuring pat. "I promise you we are not going to be given away by a carrot. You are just on edge, all will be well, don't worry."

To his surprise she seemed reassured by his words and once more he felt the responsibility of everything he had taken on. He had been responsible for many people in his life, both in his work and family. It was the duty of an earl to see to the welfare of all those who lived and worked on and around his estate, but he had never before felt the weight of that responsibility as he did with Céleste. She leaned her head on his shoulder and he was very aware of the preciousness of her trust. He must get word to his brother as soon as he may, so that he could send more funds and a carriage to meet them.

The sooner he could find her a safe place to live, somewhere she could be happy and find a life for herself, a place in society, the better for both of them. He wasn't blind to the look in her eyes or the fact that she admired him, and as much as he was beginning to appreciate that look it would do neither of them any good. No, the sooner they parted ways the better. She would find herself a suitable husband, a nice young man who would be kind to her and provide for her and any family that came along. For some inexplicable reason he was suddenly gripped by melancholy and was moved to reach out and touch her hair, whether to reassure himself or her he wasn't sure. Céleste leaned into the touch though she was sleeping now, her head heavy against him and Alex looked up to see Mimi watching him with approval.

"I'll take care of her, I promise," Alex said to him in French. Mimi nodded and turned his attention back to the road.

There were many carts moving now, loaded with onions, cauliflowers and potatoes and many more with fish and shellfish as the smell began to indicate the closer they got to the market.

The stage coach, or *Diligence,* was already being loaded by the time they arrived. Alex roused Céleste and left her to say her goodbyes to Mimi as he paid for their travel. He eyed the large coach with the trepidation of a nobleman glad to have never before had to suffer the inequity of public transport, and worse than that, *foreign* public transport. However there was nothing to be done about it so they would simply have to make the best of it.

The best of it was far worse than he feared. Céleste was teary eyed and fragile after waving goodbye to Mimi and he was glad he had spent a little more of their meagre funds than he perhaps should have to secure a place on the more spacious interior of the carriage. The roof was already crammed with people and a pile of luggage half as high again as the carriage itself. Everything was lashed on with rope and chains. In fact with the postilions and conductor, he counted seventeen passengers including themselves, and stifled a groan of disgust.

Their names for now were *Monsieur et Madame Smith,* and he handed her into the carriage. To his further dismay it was apparent the corner spaces had already been taken and he was obliged to seat himself and Céleste between two strangers.

To his side was an attractive lady in her thirties, who was perhaps rather over-made up and perfumed, though it was welcome enough to disguise the odours of some of the other travellers which was perhaps her intent. On Céleste's side was an older lady with a kindly face who promptly settled herself to sleep and whose soft snores were thankfully soon to be drowned out by the noise of the carriage. Opposite them were four more passengers. A small, fussy looking single man who bore the look of a lawyer or physician, a middle-aged couple and to Alex's intense disquiet, a priest who regarded him with a look of deep disapproval. Alex reminded himself that his intentions towards Céleste were entirely honourable and met the priest's cold stare with one of equal merit until the man looked away. Céleste, however, was still sniffing and wiping away tears and very soon it wasn't just the priest who was looking at him askance. Alex glared at everyone in turn, daring them to make a comment, and then closed his eyes and ignored everyone with impunity.

The carriage was quiet, or at least as quiet as it could be over the noise of the carriage itself as it travelled at a remarkable clip considering the state of the roads, while everyone dozed or made themselves as comfortable as they may. It wasn't an easy task as the carriage lurched and often threw the passengers together in rather closer contact than they may have liked. The attractive woman beside him, a widow by the name of Madame Durand as she had introduced herself, seemed to almost end in his lap, or with her generous charms pressed firmly against him at fairly regular intervals, much to his annoyance, the priest's disgust, and earning herself a furious scowl from Céleste. However as the darkened skies of the dawn brightened into a rather dismal, if dry, day the tedium of the journey began to take its toll on some who began to converse with one another. Alex kept his eyes resolutely shut and wished he'd had the forethought to school Céleste on what she should or should not say about who they were and where they were going, and could only pray that the girl kept her own counsel. His prayers, however, appeared to have fallen on deaf ears and he was forced to open his eyes in alarm as she fell into conversation with the older lady beside her.

At first the conversation had appeared innocuous enough. Madame Audet was also recently widowed and going to live with her eldest daughter in Gascony. There was time spent in listening to Madame Audet wax lyrical about the many and splendid accommodations to be found at her daughter's, who had apparently been blessed with fortuitous marriage, and then she asked about Céleste. Alex could almost see the naughty smile on her lips as the girl spoke and wondered if she knew what she had let him in for, when she explained to all the assembled company that she was just that week married, and yes, this was her husband.

On reflection he wished he'd just kept his eyes shut and feigned sleep for the rest of the day, but as it was he was subjected to speculative gazes, many of whom he was in no doubt, quite rightly questioned the validity of such a marriage. Especially as his *wife* was not in possession of a ring. It had no doubt also been noted that they carried no luggage further than Céleste's bag, which was stuffed with her meagre belongings and what food she'd stolen from the whorehouse.

Madame Audet cast him a look of her own which he couldn't quite read, but heard her say to Céleste that her husband was very handsome. At which point Céleste, the little wretch, sighed and laughed and agreed with her with enthusiasm. She then leaned into him and entwined their fingers together, looking up at him with such a look of adoration that he didn't know whether to spank her or kiss her. As it was he gritted his teeth and endured an interminable journey, broken only by brief stops to change horses, until they arrived at the inn for the night.

Of course, as Céleste had well known, the announcement of their recent betrothal meant that Alex would have to book just one room. Whilst this was indeed a good thing for the budgeting of their slender purse, it was a tremendously bad thing for his nerves.

Once they were alone he took her to task before they went down to dinner, before she could spread any more stories that would have his fellow travellers condemning him as a black-hearted fiend and stealer of innocence.

"That was an abominable thing to do to me," he said, the moment the door had closed behind them.

Céleste snorted and threw herself down on the bed, bouncing on the mattress in a gleeful manner, and looking thoroughly unrepentant. "Oh, and so?" she demanded. "They were already looking at us, so ... I jus' let them have their story. Now they believe we are perhaps married, perhaps not ... let them consider. Better thoughts like this, not of runaway maids and smugglers, *eh bien?"*

Alex snorted and shook his head. "You'll be the death of me yet, Céleste."

"Mais non!" she objected, laying across the bed with a sigh of deep content. "I saved you. I will not let you die now. *Non*, never. I will protect you as you protect me."

He turned to look at her spread over the bed. Her hair was tousled, arms and legs akimbo and yet it wasn't just desire that rose in his chest, though that was undoubtedly there, but he was touched by her words. She smiled up at him, as if she knew every thought that travelled through his mind. "We will save each other, *mon contrebandier,"* she whispered.

Alex turned away from the look in her eyes, reminding himself of the promises he'd made. He walked to the door, pausing before he opened it. "I'll go down and give you some time to rest. I will see you for dinner, *ma mie."*

As he closed the door he berated himself for the endearment. He shouldn't encourage the girl, but the term had fallen from his lips without him really having thought about it. And so it was he took himself off for a walk, despite the bitterness of the evening air and the uninspiring place they appeared to have stopped in. Anything to keep his mind from the beguiling creature who was beginning to occupy far too many of his thoughts.

Chapter 7

"Wherein battles are waged and a winner declared ... but the war continues."

Céleste stretched out on the mattress and sighed with content. She had done it, she had really done it. She had run away from Madame Maxime's with Alex! And he was so funny, her *contrebandier,* so concerned for her reputation and her morals and ... *bah!* She remembered the feel of his big, hard body against hers as she had fallen asleep last night. It had felt so good, to lie with his strong arms around her, it made her wonder what else would feel good, what it would be like to do some of the things she had seen at the brothel, with a man like Alex. She felt her body heat as she imagined those big hands travelling over her skin, as she thought about his mouth upon her, the weight of him lying on her. Her breathing picked up and she felt desire coil in her belly, liquid and hot, making her skin ache with the need for him to touch her. Yet she felt sure he had appointed himself her guardian or some such nonsense. He seemed to want to save her, which was all well and good and she was all in favour of it, as long as it didn't mean saving her from him. She pouted with frustration and she realised this was likely exactly what he did mean. Well she would just have to make him realise that virgin she may be, but she was very far from innocent, so really, what was the point in trying to pretend she was?

With this thought in mind she tidied herself as best she could, scowling in the mirror at the state of her dress. She wondered what it would be like to be well dressed, like the woman who'd sat beside

Alex in the carriage. She had disliked the woman on sight, and liked even less the covetous looks she had cast his way and kept pawing at him. Thankfully Alex had been ignoring everybody and so hadn't seemed to notice. She hoped he would continue not to notice because she felt ill-equipped to fight for his attention dressed as she was. With a heavy sigh she turned away from the mirror and closed the door to their room before hurrying down the stairs. The enticing smell of food wafted around the building and Céleste found she was almost beside herself with excitement at the idea of eating a meal that not only had she not prepared, but that would be served to her, and she wouldn't have to clear up afterwards. It was almost beyond belief.

To her relief she found Alex waiting for her at the bottom of the stairs and then blushed as she remembered everything she had been thinking about in the bedroom. A vivid recollection of her daydream flashed in front of her and she bit her lip, quite unable to meet his eyes.

"Are you quite well?" he asked as she reached the bottom of the stairs.

She nodded, as he placed her hand firmly on his arm and her blush increased as she considered those hands again. He paused, forcing her to look up and meet his eyes and finding his expression one of curiosity and no little amusement. She had the most awful feeling he knew exactly why she was blushing. "Are you quite sure, *ma mie?"*

"Oui," she muttered, finding her eyes falling to his lips and then cursing herself as she had to look away again.

Thankfully he didn't question her any further but led her through to dinner, where most of the other guests were already assembled. To her and - she had no doubt - Alex's relief, they were left alone and she savoured both the meal and the wine with quiet delight. It was a plain and rather run-down little inn, and the fare simple but tasty. A vegetable soup and rabbit stew with cabbage was followed with a generous slice of Camembert and fruit. She ate every scrap put in front of her with relish and even enjoyed the look of amused indulgence Alex seemed to regard her with.

"Well, I am sorry, Alex," she said, folding her napkin with care and placing it back on the table. "But you will 'ave to carry me upstairs. I am too full."

"Well for my part I am relieved to find it is possible," Alex replied, the corner of his mouth twitching slightly. "I was about to send to the kitchens and instruct them to kill a pig to sate you."

She stuck her tongue out at him, which was entirely childish but made him laugh, and a smile bloomed on her own face. She liked to hear him laugh.

"Well then perhaps you should go up," he said, twisting the stem of his wineglass back and forth in his long fingers. "I will be along presently."

"Oh?" she replied, quite unable to keep the disappointment from her voice. "Why not now?" She looked around the room to where Madame Durand was talking in low tones to the proprietor and hoped she wasn't his objective. She looked back at him but Alex merely shrugged, avoiding her eyes.

"I thought I might take a walk."

"But you already took a walk," she objected, feeling her temper rise. "You said so!"

"Céleste, lower your voice," he growled, looking uncomfortable. "I have been cooped up in that damn carriage all day and I need to stretch my legs, that is all."

"Hmph," was all the reply she would give that comment, before she got to her feet. She paused and leaned down to whisper in his ear, "Coward." Before leaving him alone at the table.

Not one to be thwarted, however, Céleste took a considerable time getting herself ready for bed, enjoying the luxury of having a room with a real bed in it, though she noted that there was dust underneath it and that the sheets were poorly aired. Madame

Maxime would have never have stood for it. So she turned down the covers and built up the fire, making sure she was very much awake when Alex finally opened the door.

He sighed, scowling as he regarded her sitting up in bed with just her shift on. She had taken care to make sure that the drawstring around her neck was too loose and fell down to reveal a bare shoulder and the swell of one pert breast.

"Why on earth aren't you asleep?" he demanded.

Determined not to be cowed by his annoyance she just shrugged. "Because I wanted to see you before I go to sleep."

"There is really no need, Céleste, we will be in each other's company all day tomorrow," he said, and she noted that he sounded weary now and he looked drawn, his face ashen.

Tutting, she threw back the covers and crossed the room to help him unbutton his coat.

Smacking his hands out of the way she scolded him in French. "Now look what all this walking 'as done," she added, scowling at him. "You 'ave tired yourself out."

"Céleste, I am not in short trousers," the stupid man objected though he was barely able to stand without swaying.

"Non," she agreed. "Lucky for you, for I should spank you!" She cursed him under her breath as she removed his jacket and then got to her knees to pull off his boots. Idiotic creature, he had almost drowned and then only just recovered from being frozen half to death, and so he must go tramping about the countryside in the icy cold and damp. She carried on her litany of objections and curses against him until she reached his trousers, at which point he called a halt.

"Thank you, that will be all," he said, with a cool and dismissive manner, like he was addressing a servant or something. She gritted her teeth and then felt her temper rise further as he took a pillow from the bed and put it on the chair.

"What are you doing?" she demanded, picking the pillow up and flinging it back on the bed with some force.

With resignation, Alex picked it up again and put it back on the chair. "I will sleep here tonight. You may have the bed."

She narrowed her eyes at him. "Oh, may I?" she repeated, mocking his accent.

Céleste watched as he sighed and prepared himself for the coming battle. She folded her arms. "'Have you listen' to nothing I have said? You nearly died; you are not yet well. I will not 'ave you sitting all night in a draughty chair, *non!"* She stamped her bare foot on the bare boards and dared him to contradict her.

"Good Lord, Céleste, you are not speaking with your maiden aunt you know," he replied sounding really quite angry now. "I am not an invalid!"

"Non, is true," she agreed, nodding at him. "Because I take good care of you!" she yelled, smacking his arm with the back of her hand. "Ozerwise you are dead now!" she yelled, her accent becoming stronger as her fury grew. "So now you must do as I say and sleep in the bed."

"Will you keep your voice down," he hissed at her, and then she realised she had him.

"Non," she said, smiling sweetly at him. "And I will continue *not* to keep my voice down in a moment when I begin to make sounds like those I 'eard at Madame Maxime's, *hein?"* She had to fight a giggle at the utter fury on his face, but instead collapsed back on the bed with a low moan, stroking her hands over her own curves in a suggestive manner and saying, loud and breathless, "Oh, Alex, oh *oui, oui,* like this, *oui, oui,* oh 'arder ... mmm, oh please fu--"

"Stop!"

Though she actually had no choice in the matter as a large hand covered her mouth. He was staring down at her, his eyes dark and wild.

"Very well, you little hell cat, you win," he said, his voice one of restrained rage, but Céleste didn't care a button. She *had* won.

She watched with satisfaction as he carefully folded his trousers before he flung back the covers with a sharp angry movement. She didn't dare suggest he remove his shirt too, which was a pity, but the look in his eyes suggested it wouldn't be a good idea.

He pounded the pillow with his fist, turned his back on her and blew out the light without another word.

Céleste sighed. Well, at least he was in the same bed.

***

Alex laid in the dark, torn between amusement, a raging desire that was driving him insane and white hot anger. What manner of crafty, doe-eyed, fury had he taken on? When she had had laid back on the bed and started writhing and saying his name with that ... that low breathy voice, my God, he had been so close to losing control. And now, once again, he found himself sleepless and on edge. If he thought the girl would sleep soundly he would take matters into his own hand and ease the ache that was keeping him from sleep and making him thoroughly bad-tempered. As it was he didn't dare.

He wondered what his brother Lawrence would say if he knew, and then grimaced. He knew exactly what he'd say; he'd laugh himself stupid.

And so it was in this spirit Alex spent the night, alternately staring at the ceiling and devising plans for how he might rid himself of his beautiful temptress at the earliest opportunity. He heard the comings and goings of the night staff and the ostlers, changing horses for carriages that rumbled in and out of the place at regular intervals, and finally fell asleep from sheer exhaustion as the sky began to show the first signs of dawn.

He awoke with a start as a horn blasted, announcing the arrival of a carriage in need of a quick change of horses, and discovered Céleste coiled around him in such a manner that his breath caught. He was rock hard and she was laying half across him, her bare leg between his, and her hip pressing into him in a manner that was both delicious and torturous. He held his breath, hardly daring to move when a sharp rap on the door made them both jump and someone announced breakfast would be served in ten minutes and the carriage would leave in twenty.

He froze as Céleste rubbed her eyes and watched with alarm as she became as aware as he of their position. He hoped he didn't frighten her - though it was none of his doing - but she was after all a virgin, for all of her bold words. She didn't move and just rested her head back on his chest. With an inward sigh of relief he went to open his mouth to say they must hurry, when her hand slid down, over his stomach and beneath his drawers to tangle in the coarse hair just below and then caressed his aching member.

The words died on his lips and the pleasure was so intense as her hand slid down and back up again, that it took every shred of willpower he possessed to reach down and grasp her wrist rather than tumble her onto her back and spread her legs.

"No, Céleste," he said, the words barely comprehensible as he bit back a groan.

"Your skin is so soft," she replied, with wonder in her eyes, quite ignoring his protest. "Like silk," she added and he sucked in a breath as her thumb slid over the little slit at the head and smoothed over the moisture already gathered there.

He muttered a heartfelt curse and pulled her hand away, throwing her onto her back and himself out of the covers before he lost his last grip on sanity.

"You will not!" he raged and then ran out of words. He snatched up his trousers, feeling that perhaps he could regain some semblance of control if he were only dressed. "Tonight you will have a room of your own," he said, his tone cold. "And I care not what any of them make of that. You ... you ..." For possibly the first time in his life he was quite at a loss for words and the fact that she was staring at him, looking tousled and sleepy and totally perplexed by his sudden outburst did not help. In lieu of any words that might have helped him explain, he decided retreat was the only option and exited the bedroom, slamming the door behind him with some force.

Chapter 8

"Wherein you should have a care what you wish for."

Alex refused to look at or speak to Céleste for the rest of the day and the journey dragged on and on. It was quite clear to everyone in the carriage that he was in a foul mood, and all avoided his eye and were careful not to speak to him. This of course roused sympathy in every bosom towards Céleste and the group fussed over her, with enquiries into her well being coming so frequently that Alex was close to shouting for the carriage to stop so he could get out and leave them all to it.

The fact that Céleste was in fact looking rather pale and hadn't spoken a word all morning didn't help matters. It was clear they had rowed. He wondered with a grim smile what the passengers would think if they knew why. Because he'd lay his fortune on their ideas being quite the opposite of the truth.

Alex laid his head back and closed his eyes. His head was pounding and despite the rain that had been lashing at the windows for the past hour the carriage was unbelievably hot and stuffy. He thanked God that they were almost at their destination for he felt bloody awful.

"Alex?"

He was surprised to hear Céleste's voice. She hadn't addressed him directly all day, in fact come to think of it she hadn't spoken at all except to reply to the idiotic questions demanded of her. Opening his eyes he saw concern in her eyes and flinched when her cool hand reached out to touch his forehead.

"Alex, you are not well."

He opened his mouth to contradict her but his throat was sore and damned if he didn't feel like the blasted Diligence had rolled right over him. To his horror and disgust the smartly dressed man opposite was, as he had guessed, a physician. Happily he still had enough wit about him to refuse to be mauled in a public carriage but once they had arrived at the next staging post, neither the doctor nor Céleste would be thwarted. He was forced to submit to the good doctor's attentions the moment they were shown to their room at the inn which he allowed with little grace. Alex looked around yet another shabby chamber with just one chair, a bed, a fireplace and a washstand. He lowered himself into the chair and eyed the greying linen on the bed with a grimace. This was not the way he liked to be accommodated and he longed for the crisp white sheets of his own bed.

"Has he been ill recently?"

Obviously deciding that since he had caught a slight chill, it had addled Alex's brain, the doctor addressed his question to Céleste. Alex opened his mouth to override her, afraid she would say too much, but once again found he had underestimated his young ward as she spoke in nicely accented French. Though the tones of a proper lady only made it look more like he, the rum looking character, had run off with some good family's innocent daughter in tow.

"Oui," she said. "He had a very bad accident and fell from his horse, into the river. The fall was itself not bad but he almost drowned and we didn't find him for hours. He was very sick."

Céleste caught his eye and he raised his eyebrow at her, amused as she looked away and studied her toes.

"Mon Dieu!" exclaimed the doctor. "And when was this?"

"Last week, *monsieur."*

"Last *week?"* the bewildered physician replied in shock. *"Mais*, of course he is sick! It is incredible he is up at all? *Monsieur* you must have the constitution of an ox," he said to Alex with a tut and a shake of his head. He then cast a thoughtful look at Céleste and cleared his throat. "Ahhh ..." he began, looking a little awkward. "May I enquire as to whether *Monsieur* has been sleeping well?"

Alex stifled a bark of laughter at the flush of colour that rose on Céleste's cheeks.

"No, not much if I'm honest," he replied, holding her gaze with amusement.

The doctor cleared his throat with clear disapproval. "Well I suspect exhaustion. I will give you something to help you sleep, and suggest that you do *sleep,"* he added. "I will instruct the inn to bring up some soup for you before you retire and to put a cot in the room for your ... *wife,* to sleep on without disturbing you." The word *wife*, he noted, was spoken with no little disbelief, and if he'd had more energy the man would have suffered the sharp side of his tongue for it, despite the fact he was entirely in the right.

As it was Alex watched as the man poured out a draft of something into a small glass and set it beside the bed.

"Merci, monsieur," he replied, hoping the snooty bastard wouldn't charge them too much. At least he would get a night's sleep without Céleste to torment him.

"You are welcome," replied the doctor, who then bent to speak. "Though I cannot help feel that you have brought this on yourself." He righted himself, staring pointedly at Céleste who blushed with fury as his words had been perfectly audible to her.

"What are you suggesting, *monsieur?"* she demanded, as the doctor took a hasty step backwards in the light of her expression. "Do you think this man has taken advantage of me, is that it?" She advanced on the doctor who opened and closed his mouth as the vision, who had indeed looked like a lost and frightened miss just moments ago, turned once more into the fiery little hell cat Alex well knew she was capable of becoming. As her anger grew her French became more rapid and Alex decided he would really have to polish his up if he was going to keep track of what was said.. "This man is my husband and he is a fine and honourable man, you have no idea *how* honourable!" she added, and Alex felt his conscience prick at the slight catch in her voice. "How dare you imply such a thing! I demand that you apologise to him."

The doctor blinked and turned to Alex. "I apologise if I caused any offence, *monsieur*. Please do not worry about the bill. I wish you a speedy recovery."

"Apology accepted," Alex replied and watched in amusement as his small Fury ushered the poor man out the door, practically slamming it after him. She continued to mutter to herself, a low, angry litany of incomprehensible French, liberally spiced with an inventive stream of swear words as she turned down the bed, and built up the fire. By the time she knelt down in front of him to help him remove his boots her temper seemed to have fled and he was surprised when she took hold of his hand and pressed it to her flushed cheek.

"Forgive me," she blurted out suddenly and he was alarmed to look down and see such anguish in her eyes.

"What on earth for?" he demanded.

"This is all my fault," she said. "If I hadn't made you so angry ... please, Alex, please forgive me. Don't leave me 'ere by myself. I promise I will be good and I won't tease you any more."

"What the devil gave you that foolish notion?" he asked her but she had put her head in her hands and refused to look at him.

"Céleste, come now." He leaned forward and put his hand under her chin until she looked up at him. "I am just a bit under the weather. You see, you were quite right to scold me for walking about so long last night. I didn't feel well then."

"Oui." She nodded, her big blue eyes full of guilt. "And if you were not scared to come to bed you wouldn't have done it, *hein?"*

She shook her head and it made his heart ache to see her look so unhappy. "I promise to be good, Alex. I won't ... I won't ..." She shrugged looking utterly miserable and Alex smiled. "I am quite alright, *ma mie,* nothing that a good night's sleep won't cure, and you have my word of honour." He took both of her hands in his and looked her in the eyes so she knew he meant it. "I will never abandon you. You are safe, as I promised, you need never fear that." She sniffed and nodded, trying to smile at him, though it didn't reach her eyes. "And we will be friends, you and I."

He watched as she nodded again. "Friends," she repeated, her voice dull. *"Oui,* Alex, we will be friends."

She got up and answered a knock at the door and accepted a tray with a bowl of thick soup and some baguette. He ate, watching her with sorrow. She wouldn't go down and eat alone, saying that she had eaten too much yesterday and wasn't hungry, and refused to share any of his. Once the small pallet was installed for her to sleep on she watched him take the medicine the doctor had ordered and then she lay down by herself.

Alex looked across the room at the slight figure curled under the blanket and sighed. He had never before missed the days of his youth. Until the past week he had always been fit and strong, he knew he still attracted women with no problem at all, and though he was not a vain man, he also knew he was handsome and well made. Yet although he was hardly in his dotage, when put beside her youth he felt old, and somchow to blame for the girl's unhappiness. But he couldn't allow her to believe there could ever be more than friendship between them. Indeed she ought to regard him as a father figure. He knew it was likely that once this adventure was behind them and she was settled into a new life, that would be how she came to regard him. These days would be forgotten or recalled with embarrassment and shame, and he would be relegated to the status of kindly guardian. God help him but the idea made his heart hurt and he wondered how he would bear it.

***

When Alex woke the next morning, Céleste had already left the room. He washed and dressed, finding to his relief that he did feel much better than he had. Not his old self perhaps, he thought, and then grimaced, *old.* God damn it.

He made his way downstairs to find she had already eaten, and ate his own meal with haste, anxious to see how she was this morning. Striding outside into a bright and sunny morning, he passed the ostlers holding the many horses that drew the weighty Diligence, urging them into their harnesses as they stamped and tossed their heads. The fields around the inn were thick with frost and a low mist crept over the fields, giving the land an ethereal quality in the winter sunshine as the frozen grass glittered, crunching under his boots. He found Céleste leaning over a fenced paddock, talking to a fat pony who was submitting to her caresses with a look of appreciative bliss.

She turned as she heard his footsteps approaching and Alex found himself disturbed by the quietness of her greeting. In a very short time he had become accustomed to the way her eyes lit up when she saw him. It had gladdened his heart and yes, it had stroked his ego. And damn if he didn't miss it.

"Are you ready to leave?" he asked, knowing she was as he had seen her bag packed, but at a loss for anything else to say.

"Oui, Alex," she said, and turned away from the pony, taking his proffered arm as he led her back to the carriage.

***

Three more days and nights passed. They still shared a bed, for their finances were dwindling, but they slept with their backs to each other and Céleste kept her word. She no longer flirted with him, or leaned into him, searching for a caress or a hug. Her eyes remained downcast and she smiled less. She never laughed.

It was for the best, he told himself. She was sweet on him in the manner of young girls, it was merely an infatuation. It would pass soon enough and when it did he would have to be relieved he had navigated it without making a bloody fool of himself. For while she would forget him with the callous ease of a youthful heart, if he allowed himself to care ... He simply couldn't risk it.

But she never spoke now unless spoken to and he missed her conversation, even missed her scoldings, and he hated to see the brightness gone from her eyes.

It wasn't until they arrived at the posting-house that night that she spoke to him at all.

"Where are we, Alex?" she asked, looking at the landscape around the inn with curiosity.

"We're in Morbihan," he replied, simply relieved to have been addressed at all, but wondering why she asked.

She drew in a breath and he felt his heart lift as she turned to smile at him, a true, genuine smile that made his own breath catch in response.

"This is where my family comes from," she exclaimed and he looked at her in surprise. It had never occurred to him that she hadn't been born and raised in Roscoff. She was looking around with excitement and ran to one of the ostlers who was busy unhitching the tired horses.

"Monsieur, excuse me but are we close to Allaire?"

"Oui, mademoiselle," the man replied without looking up. "It is perhaps an hour's walk that way," he added, throwing an arm out and pointing at a road leading off at an angle to the inn.

"Oh," she said with a sigh that illustrated all too clearly her disappointment. "I would so liked to have seen it."

Alex smiled, it was too wonderful to see her happy again, if somewhat wistful. "Well, it is too late tonight, *ma mie*. It will be full dark shortly, but perhaps tomorrow?" She looked up at him in astonishment.

"Mais, we won't 'ave time before the carriage leaves."

Alex shrugged, knowing he was being foolish, they really couldn't afford the extra expense but ... "There will be another carriage ... if it means that much to you?"

"Oh!" For a moment she forgot herself and ran to him, hugging him tightly and kissing his cheek, apparently before remembering that she had promised not to behave in such a way. She blushed and her eyes cast down. "Forgive me, Alex, I forgot. But I do thank you, very much. It does mean a lot to me."

She turned and walked away from him and he cursed his own stupidity. She was behaving just as she should, as he would hope she would, and yet he missed the sudden hugs and the way she would wheedle her hand into his, as if he might not notice. Good God but he was a fool.

Chapter 9

"Wherein a curtain is drawn back to reveal the past, a tragic story and a lonely Comtesse come to light."

"You have never told me anything of your family," Alex remarked as they walked the lane that led to Allaire, early the next morning. The fields were heavy with dew though at least no frost, and they skirted the puddles that filled the scarred and overgrown path.

Céleste looked up at him, and quickly away again. He felt there had been something worrying her today. She was clearly excited to see where her mother had been born, but he sensed there was more to it than that. She was nervous; he could see the anxiety in her eyes and tension in her posture. He stopped in his tracks, forcing her to turn and look at him.

"Won't you tell me what's wrong, *ma mie?"*

She shook her head and smiled at him, though the smile didn't reach her eyes. "There is nothing wrong."

"Don't you trust me anymore?" he asked, foolishly quite unable to keep the sadness from his voice.

She frowned at him and put her hand on his arm. "Of course I trust you, Alex! As if I would not? You are the only person I trust in the 'ole world, surely you know this?"

He smiled and nodded, but couldn't help but observe he was the only friend she had in the world too.

They carried on walking, passing small stone cottages on occasion and a farm off in the distance with cows lowing on the horizon, but no one was in sight and Céleste didn't seem inclined to stop, so he assumed she was walking with some particular destination in mind. They carried on for another half an hour until a large and beautiful building came into view. It was in obvious disrepair, no doubt a victim of the Revolution, or the war that had followed it. It was a Château, built in the style of a grand Manoir with a courtyard and a chapel, and surrounded by an enclosure wall.

"A beautiful place," Alex remarked, meaning it. It was an idyllic setting and the building itself had great charm, full of the romance of days gone by. He looked around to see Céleste's eyes full of tears.

"Ma mie? What is it *mignonne?"* he asked in alarm. Despite all of his best intentions he reached out and took her hand, squeezing it gently. "Céleste, won't you tell me what's wrong?" He looked around at the Château and finally understood. "Is this where your mother was born?"

She nodded, apparently too emotional to speak and Alex imagined that perhaps her mother had been in service here, but then the Revolution had come and thrown everyone's lives into disarray.

"They 'ad to run, during *la terreur.* They never saw this place again."

"I'm so sorry," he said, reaching out and caressing her cheek with his hand before he could consider his actions. She closed her eyes, leaning into his touch, and then seemed to remember that this was no longer allowed, and moved away from him.

"Do you think we could go inside?" she asked staring up at the building with such longing that it tugged at his heart.

He looked back at the Château with its broken windows and air of decay. It was obviously abandoned and there was no one here so ...

"Why not," he replied, smiling, and keeping her hand clasped in his he drew her behind him, seeking an entrance. They circled the building and Alex found where part of the high wall had been destroyed, leaving a pile of rubble and a large hole. He helped Céleste pick her way over until she stumbled and then swept her up, and if he enjoyed the feel of her in his arms he did not allow himself to linger, or to pull her closer when he set her on her feet again.

As he watched her run from empty room to empty room he was glad he'd prolonged their journey, and damn the expense. He would carry her the rest of the way home if necessary. It was worth it to see the delight in her eyes at discovering the place her parents had called home. They made their way up the staircase with care, alert for rotten timbers, but it all seemed sound enough and they reached the next floor without mishap. Suddenly Céleste fell silent once more and he felt the change come over her as she walked into a large, bright room. The sun was shining in and he could imagine how it must have once looked, decked out in all its finery.

"This was my mother's room," she whispered. Alex frowned and looked around. This was clearly the grandest bedroom, but he said nothing. So what if it was or not, if it comforted her to feel she had seen her mother's room, then all the better. "See, she said you could see the lake and over the courtyard. *Oh, oui*, and look, that is where the fountain was and ..." She stopped and turned to him grinning. *"Maman* said she carved hers and *papa's* initials together, the first time he kissed her!" She flew across the room to an oak door that clearly led into some kind of wardrobe and opened it, running her hands over the old wood and falling to her knees to search the very bottom, until she cried out in delight. *"Voila!"*

Alex crossed the room to look at the initials carved deep into the wood and frowned as he put the pieces together, and with his heart pounding he asked Céleste. "What was your mother's name, *mignonne?"*

She looked up at him and he could see trepidation in her eyes, and then she raised her chin, looking almost defiant as she spoke.

"She was Louise-Marie de Lavelle." She waited, silent and he felt she was waiting for him to laugh or tell her she must be mistaken, but he reached his hand down and raised her up again.

"And so," he prompted. "You are ..."

"Célestine de Lavelle," she whispered. *"La Comtesse de Valrey."*

For a moment he stared at her in astonishment, surely she was daydreaming? But then he began to piece together everything that had seemed so very unusual about a girl who'd been born in the gutter. Suddenly her educated mind, her grasp of English, her vocabulary and the pretty accent all made sense. He bowed to her and raised her hand to his lips with great solemnity. *"Enchanté, Comtesse,* it is an honour to make your acquaintance."

He looked down at her and found her eyes shining. "You believe me?" she said, her voice quiet and tremulous. "You don't think I make it up?"

Alex shook his head. "You would never do such a thing. You are too honest for your own good."

"Only with you," she whispered, blushing a little and he chuckled in response, unaccountably pleased.

"Perhaps that is just as well," he replied. "Then," he added, looking around at the lovely old Château. "This is your home." It seemed fitting somehow, the place had suffered and lost much in the course of war and conflict, but it had lost none of its beauty.

She shrugged and walked away from him. "No, it was never mine, I 'ave never even seen it before today, though I 'ad imagined. *Maman* would often talk of it," she said, sounding wistful. "But I am just Céleste not Célestine, born in a slum in Roscoff not a Château in Allaire, and working in a whore house." She shrugged, such a hopeless gesture that he wanted to change the past for her, as well as the future. "It is all gone now, and there is no point in wishing it was otherwise." She turned and looked at him with such longing in his eyes that it took everything he had not to cross the room and take her in his arms. "I 'av wished for many things in my life but ..." She turned away and her words were barely audible. "They never come to me."

Alex knew she was speaking of him, and his heart both soared and ached. It was foolish and impossible and something she would realise she was better off without in time; but the title, her home, everything she had lost ... that he could do something about. That he could change.

"It is your birthright, Céleste, if you are truly the Comtesse, then this belongs to you." He walked a little closer to her. "Tell me, do you have any evidence, anything that would validate your claim."

She nodded. "There are papers, Marie gave me before she died. She said they prove who I am."

He smiled and reached out, taking her hands in his. "Then I promise you, I will return this place to you. It may take a little while mind ..." he added, looking away and frowning as he considered everything involved in such a task. He turned back to find her watching him.

"I don't need a Château, Alex," she said, her voice soft.

He sighed, and shook his head not pretending to misunderstand her meaning, the soft look in her eyes was only too easy to read. "I am too old for you, *ma mie.* Too old and far too wicked," he said in a joking tone and tried to laugh but found he couldn't. "I want you to have everything, *mignonne*. You have had such a hard life. I want only that the rest of it be everything you deserve."

She moved closer to him and reached out, the gesture hesitant and unsure as she placed her hand over his heart. "But I only want you," she said, her voice small and pitiful.

He smiled though his heart felt pulled tight, as though it were held in an iron clamp. "That is because I am all you have right now," he said, his voice firm, as much to repeat the sense of it to himself as to her. "But once you take your rightful place in the world you will be surrounded by handsome young men, all desperately in love with you and throwing themselves at your feet. And then you will be relieved you didn't tie yourself to a dull old man before you had even set a foot outside the door of your experience."

"You are not old," she protested in annoyance, and he smiled for real, pleased at any rate, that she did not find him so.

"And how old are you, Céleste?" he asked, almost hating to hear the answer.

She frowned as if working it out. "I will be eighteen in ... three weeks."

"Ah, well that we must celebrate," he said, forcing another smile. "But I am thirty six, exactly twice your age, nearly twenty years your senior! Think how decrepit I will appear to you in another ten when you are still a mere twenty eight." He made light of it, though his chest felt tight with the effort, but she just snorted and shook her head.

"Bah!" she replied dropping her hand from where it rested against his chest. "I give this for your young men," she said snapping her fingers. "And I know you will not be decrepit," she said, casting an appreciative eye over him that made his blood heat beneath his skin. "You will still be strong and fit and ..." She sighed and shook her head, turning away from him. "Oh, Alex. If I thought you wanted me I would fight for you. But I don't want to make you angry again."

Alex closed his eyes and was glad she was turned away from him, for if she had looked at that moment she would have seen all too clearly how much he wanted her.

"I was never angry, *mignonne*, but it isn't right, and I won't let you make such a mistake. Besides, you are *la Comtesse de Valrey,* and far above my humble ambitions."

She snorted in disgust. *"Non,* I am only Céleste, it is just a name and one that has never been mine. I do not care for it, only that I promised Marie I should get it back one day."

"And so you shall," he said, smiling at her. "Tell me about Marie," he asked, desperate to move the conversation onto safer ground before his resolution crumbled.

"Marie was my mother's maid," she said, looking out at the enchanting vista of soft rolling hills, of fields and verdant woodland beyond the window. Smoothing her hand over the rough stone of the grand window surround she imagined her mother standing on the exact same spot as she spoke. "She ran away with my parents. They were given word that the authorities were coming for them and so they ran. Papa joined the army under a false name and so they 'id from *Madame la Guillotine*. For a while I think things were not so bad, but then when I was eight Papa was killed and Maman tried to go on but ..." She shrugged, though there were no tears, just the harsh facts of her life that she had become accustomed to. "Poor, Maman," she said. "She was born to be beautiful and 'ave lovely things and be adored. The new world was too ugly for 'er, and when Papa went ... she did not want to stay with all the ugly things, and so she killed 'erself. After that it was just me and Marie."

"Oh God, Céleste," he whispered, appalled that things had been so much worse than he'd feared. He didn't know what to say and was too afraid if he made a move towards her he would take her in his arms and all his good intentions would have been for nothing. But Céleste just shrugged again, as if it was of little consequence.

"It is 'ow things are."

"Your father," he asked with trepidation, though he knew what she would say. "How did he die?"

"In the war, shot in some battle with the English, I do not know where."

"Céleste," he said, feeling helpless. "I am so sorry, my God it's a wonder you don't hate me."

"Why?" She looked up at him in surprise. "You did not kill him, Alex."

"No," he said, his voice cautious. He didn't want to spell it out, but he wouldn't lie to her either. "But I've fought in the wars against your country."

She gave him a sad smile and nodded. "And so did millions of others. You did not kill Papa, and 'e did not kill the men who stood beside you. Emperors and Kings and Generals, these people make wars and put weapons in people's 'ands. You defended your country as my father defended *La France,* and that is all."

He felt humbled by this view, by her acceptance of his country's part in the conflict that had caused her such pain, and could find no words to express how he felt. He knew all too well if he told her what was in his heart he would say too much, and so he said nothing.

Chapter 10

"Wherein dreams and fantasies bring both pleasure and pain in equal measure."

Céleste made her way back down the grand staircase, imagining her mother sweeping down in some gorgeous dress, swathed in jewels with her father waiting for her. He would have looked handsome and fine, looking at Maman with adoration, as he always had. Right up until the last time he said goodbye to them. She wondered what life would have been like if she had been born here. Would it really be as idyllic as it seemed in her mind? Of course not, it was just a silly day dream, she knew that. Life was hard, life pushed and pulled you this way and that, and took everything away, if you didn't hold on as tight as you could.

She cast a glance back at Alex and caught her breath. He was striding down the stairs and looked so much more like a nobleman than she ever would a Comtesse. She smiled, believing she could imagine him as a brave Knight from the old tales of chivalry and battles. He was so tall and broad, with that thick black hair and those cool grey eyes that could be so hard and intimidating to those he disliked, but he never looked at her like that. When he looked at her his harsh features softened, that mouth that looked as though it could be cruel would curve into a smile that seemed to be for her alone, and she would feel her insides melt and her skin ache with longing.

She had thought that he smiled that way for her because he desired her as much as she did him, but she could see now she'd been wrong. He thought of her as a silly child, someone to be spoiled and petted and kept safe. His reaction to her clumsy advances the other morning had illustrated that clearly enough. He had been so angry with her. She never wanted to see him angry with her like that again. The whole day she had been terrified, convinced that he would leave in the night and she would wake to find him gone. She would never risk that again. Better to love him from afar than never to see him again.

They walked out into a grand hall and she remembered her Maman's tales of the extravagant balls that had been held, of the dancing and laughter, the beautiful dresses, wine and food ... It all seemed so improbable, so far from her own experiences it may as well have been a fairy tale.

"May I?"

She turned with a frown to see Alex smiling before executing a very elegant bow and holding out his hand to her.

"I don't understand?" she replied, perplexed.

"Well," he said. "This is a ballroom isn't it? We should dance, it is only fitting."

She laughed, surprised by his fanciful idea, it seemed so out of character. "But there is no music."

He shrugged and took her hand, apparently allowing no protests.

"It matters not."

But she had one problem that would matter. "Alex, I--I don't know how," she replied, blushing and feeling foolish.

"Well then," he said, with a matter of fact tone that put her at ease once more. "It is about time someone taught you. So you take my hand, and we stand side by side, like so, and then we take two steps forward and raise up on your toes. And then two steps back again, and up on your toes." She watched him and copied his moves. "And now take my hand, and turn, like so ... and ..."

She watched him in fascination, moving in the manner he indicated, and savouring every touch of his hand against hers, and most especially the slide of his hand around her waist. At times they stepped towards each other, so close she could almost kiss him and then he would step back again or move past her, leaving her breathless. He moved with such grace and she felt bewildered by him.

How had her smuggler learned to move like this? What kind of life did he lead? She was desperate to ask but didn't want to break the spell that seemed cast between them as the steps became familiar and she moved naturally, without his instruction. He beamed at her, apparently delighted at her accomplishment and she basked in his approval, so happy to have pleased him after the tension of the past few days. But all too soon it was over and he seemed to remember himself and the rather more distant and formal air he now adopted seemed to settle over him like a cloak, casting her outside in the cold again and taking the warmth of his smile from her.

"You must be hungry," he observed, holding out his arm to her. "We should be getting back."

She nodded and allowed him to place her hand on his arm and followed him out. He paused in the doorway to allow her a last fond look around and she looked up at him, hoping he could see the gratitude in her eyes. *"Mille mercis,* Alex, for bringing me 'ere, I will never forget it."

"You will be back again, *ma mie,* soon enough," he said.

She smiled and nodded, not because she believed it, it seemed far too unlikely, but because she wanted to please him, because he wanted it for her. She didn't care so much for the house. Yes, it was extravagant and beautiful and she loved it, but it had been built and used by a wealthy family and she had nothing, and she likely never would.

No matter Alex's thoughts on the matter, the idea of finding a life for herself and a man who would love her and make her feel in some small way of value for something other than her face. It was far beyond anything she would believe real life could deliver to her. And yet when Alex looked at her, when he spoke with her and asked her opinion she felt she really existed, that what she said had a value, that she mattered for something more than lust or fleeting passion. Alex made her see the world differently and believe perhaps that there was something better for her, but even he could not make her trust in fate or fortune, for he would deny her everything she truly desired. For she knew now, with no doubt in her mind, that she loved him, and that she always would.

They stepped back outside and it was almost warm in the sunshine after the chill of the old stone building.

"I sent a message to my brother this morning, instructing him to send a carriage and money. Hopefully it should be with us in a week if there are no mishaps," he said, smiling down at her. "So we can come back here again, if you would like?"

She paused, unsure of what to say. In truth, although she was so glad to have seen it, the old house made her melancholy. But if it meant time spent alone with Alex, perhaps dancing with him again ... "I would like that, very much."

He nodded and they were silent for a while as they retraced their steps to the inn.

"I thought, while we were here, that perhaps I would make some discreet enquiries, see if perhaps any of your family still live?"

She gasped and shook her head in horror. *"Non!"* she said, as fear slithered down her spine. *"Non,* please, you must not!"

He frowned at her sudden outburst. "But why, Céleste? Don't you want to know your family?"

She shook her head, feeling tears prick at her eyes. "And why would they want to know some girl who was born in the filth and lived there all 'er life? *Non,* Alex, they will sneer at me, and ... I ... *non,"* she said again, feeling quite terrified by the judgement of people who might share the same bloodline, but had no understanding of what her life had been.

"Céleste," he said, looking truly shocked and taking her hands. "I don't mean to present you to them this week. It will only happen if you want it to, when you are ready. But let me assure you I would never, *never* let anyone belittle you or make you unhappy. They will have no knowledge of your background save what we decide to tell them, and I assure you I will deal severely with any that make you feel in any way unwelcome. And believe me, they will certainly never sneer at you."

There was such force in his voice, such surety, that she couldn't doubt him, though how a man who was a smuggler could possibly deal with the nobility was beyond her. But he believed it and she believed him, and so she sighed and nodded. "As you wish then, Alex. I trust you."

***

The week passed all too quickly for Céleste. She had the feeling that things would change when they got to Alex's brother's house. And so she savoured every moment of her time with Alex. They went to the house every day and Alex insisted she make plans for how the place would look when she had renovated it. Which was beyond foolish of course.

Even if he managed to reclaim her title and property, the money would be long gone, she had no doubt. But it seemed to please him to hear how she would have the place if she had her way, and so she indulged him. She remembered all the details that her mother had told her and created some more, as though she was inventing a fantasy world. Indeed the more she invented and he listened - apparently with all seriousness - to her plans she could almost believe she would be able to step into the rooms just as she had described them to him.

She knew too that he had begun to ask around, enquiring what had happened to the family, where had they gone, were any still alive ... He never told her the results of his investigations, assuming, quite rightly, that the knowledge would make her anxious. And so she let him do as he might, but had no expectation that anything would come of it. Theirs had not been an extensive family, that much she knew. Maman was an only child and Papa had two brothers, but one had certainly died on the Guillotine and the other papa had believed dead.

At night they would eat together and talk of many things. Alex, she discovered was well read and she listened with fascination both to stories he had enjoyed and to tales of his own life and places he had seen. He had joined the English navy at a very young age and had seen much of the world, until he had been injured at the battle of Trafalgar, a severe blow to the head that had left him unconscious for many days. Then he had been sent home to recover. And home was in Cornwall, a wild and beautiful place as he described it, and somewhere she longed to see. Not only because it was a place he so clearly loved but because his description of the rugged coastline and the pretty villages that sat huddled in the shelter of the cliffs fired her imagination.

He told her of the men he worked with and their adventures on the sea, forever evading the Revenue and bringing silk and lace, tea and brandy and tobacco into the country, and supplying people far and wide with luxuries they would never have afforded without the free trading gentlemen. She realised as he talked that he didn't speak of a small venture but something large and well organised with many people involved and vast quantities of trade. It explained the quality of his clothes and his manner of speaking and dealing with those around him, as though he expected immediate obedience and would accept nothing less. She had noted that even though he looked a little shabby and down at heel, people would jump to do his bidding simply because he had no doubt that they would.

With every story she pieced together a fuller picture of the man in front of her. A loyal friend with a good heart, but no fool, and ruthless to those who crossed him or he had no patience with. He certainly didn't suffer fools and she suspected he was not a man who was crossed often. There was sometimes a look of steel behind those grey eyes that made her think he could be an enemy most would heartily wish to avoid gaining.

When it was finally time to retire, they would bid each other a good night and slip under the covers, turning their backs on one another; chaste as nuns.

By the end of the week Céleste thought she might run mad with his proximity, when she could never touch him. He was so very close, she could feel the heat of his body across the short distance that separated them. She need only stretch out an arm and she could run her hand across those powerful shoulders and *Dieu* but she longed to, but she didn't dare. And yet it was a sweet kind of torment, and one she dreaded ending. For he would not allow them to continue in this manner when they reached his brother's house. That was only too clear. She would be given her own room without a doubt and she would never again be allowed to get this close to him.

She closed her eyes and allowed herself to imagine for a moment the way it might feel if he turned and took her in his arms. The warmth of his skin sliding over hers, the weight of that strong body on hers. She imagined his skin, hot against her own, the feel of his chest against her naked breasts, the weight of him between her thighs. Her breathing quickened at the idea and she froze, listening out for any sound from the other side of the bed, but all was still. He must be sleeping.

With care not to move too much and disturb him she slipped one hand between her legs and sought to soothe the ache that had begun to throb like a heartbeat. She remembered the feel of him in her hand, the thick weight of his erection and the satin soft skin. What would it feel like if he made love to her? She imagined it, imagined how the hollow ache that clamoured to be filled would be sated by his body, his hands over her skin, his mouth on hers ... It took little time for her to find release, and despite her best efforts to keep silent a slight cry of pleasure escaped her and she gasped, fighting for breath as the tremors racked her. She tried to calm herself quickly, to return her breathing to normal and prayed Alex would not wake. It would be mortifying if he knew what she'd been doing. But the bed was still and she relaxed once more. At least she could sleep now, but like a starving man given bread to eat while a lavish banquet was right under his nose, it had taken away the pain of emptiness for the moment, but the longing for more still remained.

***

He had heard the moment her breathing changed. Unable to sleep himself he knew she was awake but had tried to keep his breathing deep and even, so she believed he slept. But now he cursed himself for that, for if she'd thought him awake she would not have devised such a delicious form of torture for him. The soft sounds she made as she pleasured herself were unendurable, all the more so for knowing she thought of him. It was his body she craved, his touch. He wondered if it was possible to die from desire, if perhaps his heart would give out under the strain of denial? It would be a kindness, he thought in desperation. Anything to escape this delicious torture.

He need only turn and take her in his arms and he could release himself from this exquisite hell and show her exactly what it was she needed, what it was she was dreaming of. He had never been so hard in all his life, his balls pulled taut and aching with the need for release. And when she came, that soft, muffled cry, the tremors that rocked the mattress ... how he hadn't come himself he would never know. And now he heard her breathing deepen as she finally fell asleep, and the unfulfilled pain of desire in his body was only matched by the ache in his heart.

Chapter 11

"Wherein a heroic smuggler may lose a little of his shine."

It was with trepidation that Céleste saw the glossy black carriage draw up outside the inn. Alex jumped to his feet in an instant, dashing outside to greet the driver and get news, for apparently this was his brother's carriage. She looked over four perfectly matched chestnut horses, tack jingling as their heads tossed with an imperious air, as though they knew their own worth and the fact that they were far superior to the shabbiness of their current surroundings. In fact combined with the quality of both the carriage, and the pristine livery of the postilion and the driver, it was clear that Alex's brother must be incredibly wealthy.

Céleste tried to keep her hands clasped in her lap but the fingers twisted together try as she might to keep them still. What would a man like that think of Alex turning up with some waif in tow and improbable stories of an impoverished countess? Would he demand Alex turn her out? Would Alex consider such a thing? Of course not, she scolded herself. Alex would never go back on his word to her, she knew that, she trusted him; but she feared being the cause of any animosity between him and his brother. She had caused him enough trouble already.

Alex strode back into the inn and smiled at her.

"Well then, our bill is paid in full and I finally have some finances to provide for us," he said, with obvious relief. She nodded, trying to smile, but aware that their nights together had ended sooner than she had considered. Of course he had his brother's money to fund them now. He would obviously pay for another room. She had been stupid not to consider that. She allowed him to hand her into the carriage and settled herself in place. Glancing back at the inn she felt a wave of sorrow. Things would change now and perhaps in some ways for the better. Alex need not worry about the money stretching far enough, and she was sure that his brother's house would be comfortable and more luxurious than anything she had ever known, and yet she would gladly turn her back on all of that if she could keep Alex close to her. But their intimacy would be frowned upon in front of his family and she would do nothing to embarrass him. So from now on she would have to be careful how she acted unless they were alone together, for fear of betraying him in some way.

The remaining journey to his brother's home passed with increasing tension. As she had expected the change in circumstances, the separate rooms, it all served to bring a formality between them, a distance that seemed to grow the closer they came to their destination. For her part Céleste bore it as best she could. She tried to take pleasure in her surroundings but the increase in quality of the accommodations made her feel ever more out of place and more than once she heard the staff at the coaching inns whispering about them.

Her tatty bonnet, old clothes and boots that had almost worn through seemed shabbier than ever with each stop, as smart ladies and gentlemen cast considering glances her way and talked behind their hands. She told herself she didn't care. Let them think what they liked. But it hurt to consider that perhaps Alex was beginning to feel ashamed of her. Not that he ever betrayed it, he was far too much the gentleman to do that, and in fact he demanded respect for her. Though she wished he wouldn't as it only made her feel worse, as though she was trying to put on airs she had no right to own.

And now they would soon be at Longueville, which was apparently the name of his brother's home. Alex had been pointing out places to her as they had begun to travel through a landscape he seemed to know well, and she was surprised to discover he had spent a lot of time here as a boy. But despite his enthusiasm, and his obvious desire for her to be pleased, she felt her heart sink further and depression settle over her like a cold shroud. For she was sure now that his brother would not want Alex to keep Céleste around; it would inevitably cause talk and scandal. Not that Céleste cared a button what people said of her, but for families like this it would matter. They wouldn't stand the whispers and murmured slights like those she had caused on the journey here. And so she would be sent away, somewhere she could not cause any embarrassment, and she would likely never see Alex again.

***

Alex watched Céleste pull ever farther away from him and wondered what on earth he was supposed to do. She was clearly terrified at the thought of meeting his brother and had posed several pointed questions as to the fact of how wealthy his family was. That he had yet to tell her that he was by far wealthier than his brother gnawed at his conscience, not to mention that she had no idea he was an *earl*. Whenever he tried to tell her who he really was, he remembered her scathing words about the *Baron de Merde* and her general assessment of the nobility as a whole. He didn't want her to consider him in the same light, to believe that he thought and behaved as they did, no matter if perhaps there was truth in it.

He'd tried hard to convince himself that it would be better for all concerned if she did think of him like that. If she felt distance from him so much the better, it would make their parting much easier all round, for part they must. He should tell her who he was, settle enough money on her to make sure she was well provided for and send her off to live with some far off branch of his family. She would be angry at him for lying to her, disappointed that he was not the man she had come to believe he was, because for some strange reason she found the idea of him as a smuggler desperately romantic.

It was the right thing to do, to pull the shades from her eyes and make her see the truth, and yet ... and yet ... He couldn't do it.

Despite the fact that she would know in any case within moments of setting foot at Longueville, despite the fact that it was for the best, despite all of his promises and good intentions, he couldn't bear the idea of losing the adoration that shone in her eyes when she looked at him. It was selfish and cruel and cowardly, but there it was, and he didn't know what to do.

The letter he had sent his brother had been brief and only alluded vaguely to the truth of what had happened. He couldn't risk setting everything out in case the letter fell into the wrong hands. So Lawrence only knew that Alex had suffered some difficulty on his travels and had been taken unwell. In any case Lawrence would well know what kind of difficulties had likely beset him, being well acquainted with the Revenue himself. He had also written of stumbling upon a young lady of good character in unfortunate circumstances, and for some reason he had been unable to convincingly write an explanation as to *why* he had taken it into his head to become the girl's guardian. *But it was the right thing to do,* which he felt certain was going to become his mantra in the near future. He could only imagine what kind of ideas where flitting through his brother's mind and could only hope the fool didn't dare voice them, for he would likely strike him.

Inevitably the carriage drew up outside Longueville and he saw Céleste's eyes grow round with surprise. For where the Château that had belonged to her family was a beautiful ruin, Longueville was fine and polished and spoke of wealth and ease. From the shock in her eyes he could only be thankful that he was breaking her in gently, for if he had taken her straight to his own home at Tregothnan, she would have been shocked indeed.

"It is ... *magnifique*, Alex," she breathed, and he saw the effort she made to try and smile at him though her terrible fear was obvious.

Though he should know better he leaned forward and took her hand in his, squeezing it gently.

"Do not be afraid, *ma mie,"* he said, hoping she would continue to trust him, when she was about to discover so much of what he said was a lie. "There is nothing and no one here to hurt you."

She hesitated and he could see the anxiety in her eyes. "B-but your brother ..." she began, but was cut off by a familiar voice yelling at him from outside the carriage.

"Alex?" He looked out to see Lawrence striding towards them and gave her what he hoped was a reassuring smile before getting out and greeting his brother.

"Lawrence," he replied, smiling at his brother whose jaw hit the floor at the sight of him. Of course he had decided not to send for his own belongings, aware that his normal clothing would have given them away on their journey. However he had forgotten quite how disreputable he must look, though the raised eyebrows from some of the inns they stayed at should have alerted him. Now, however, his appearance was quite obviously shocking as reflected in the gaze of his younger brother.

"Good God," Lawrence exclaimed, shaking his hand and looking him over in astonishment. "What in the blue blazes happened to you? You look like one of my crew."

Alex snorted and shook his head. "It is rather a long story, but I will regale you with it later." He turned back to the carriage to see Céleste regarding Lawrence with a frown. He gave her a hand down and saw his brother's eyes widen further as he set sights on Céleste. For even dressed in the shabby garments which comprised everything she owned in the world, it was clear she was a diamond clad in rags. He felt a pride in presenting her that he had no right to own and Lawrence gaped, quite clearly lost for words.

"Lawrence, this is Célestine de Lavelle, *La Comtesse de Valrey.* Céleste, may I introduce my brother, Mr. Lawrence Sinclair."

To his relief Lawrence never questioned the introduction; he didn't even blink, but bowed with great deference and kissed her hand.

"I am honoured to make your acquaintance, Comtesse," he said with a welcoming smile, and Alex felt a swell of gratitude and affection for his brother, for accepting Céleste so immediately and without question.

"The 'onour is mine, *monsieur,"* Céleste replied, though her gaze turned from him to Alex, and he could see the many questions in her eyes.

"Please, we have no formality here at Longueville and I think perhaps circumstances will allow that I ask you to call me Lawrence," his brother said.

"And then you must call me Céleste."

"With pleasure," Lawrence said, beaming at her and Alex was relieved that his brother could always be relied upon to break the ice in awkward social situations. "I hope you will forgive us," Lawrence added. "But my wife will be with us in just a moment, she was feeling a little under the weather this afternoon and ... went for a lie down."

Alex caught his brother's eyes and raised an eyebrow and Lawrence smirked a little, but Céleste was apparently too lost in thought to notice. She turned to Alex.

"Lawrence is your brother?" she clarified, clearly puzzled.

He nodded, knowing that that she would have assumed his rich brother was older, that the family wealth had been passed to him leaving Alex to make his own way, but now ...

"Yes, though I'm sure he'd rather disown me," Lawrence remarked with his usual cheer and forthright attitude. "As I'm afraid I am a terrible burden and no end of trouble to the fourth Earl of Falmouth."

Alex stiffened and he glanced back at Céleste who looked like she might do something terribly out of character and swoon, but all the colour had left her cheeks and she was staring at Alex in horror.

"C'est vrai? You ... you are ..."

"Oh dear," Lawrence said, looking aghast. "I've put my foot in something haven't I?"

Alex sighed. "Yes, Lawrence, but it is entirely my fault I assure you. Perhaps ..."

Lawrence didn't need another word and held out his hands. "I'll leave you to it, please come in as soon as you wish." And with that he beat a hasty retreat.

Alex held his hand out, feeling anxiety crawling down his back at the horror in her expression. "Céleste, will you walk with me please?"

She was just staring at him, apparently too shocked to reply, so he took her hand and laid it carefully on his arm before leading her into the garden. They walked for a few minutes until he reached a bench in a secluded corner where they could speak without fear of interruption. "Are you angry with me, *mignonne?"* he asked, hardly daring to hear the answer.

Those wide blue eyes blinked, looking at him with bewilderment.

"I don't know," she said, sounding so lost that Alex wanted to pull her into his arms and reassure her that she had nothing to fear, but he knew he couldn't do that. "You are really ..."

He nodded. "I am Alexander Sinclair, the Earl of Falmouth."

She nodded and to his horror her eyes filled with tears. "And ... you will send me away now?" she said, the truth of her words apparently a foregone conclusion from the fatalistic tone with which they had been uttered.

"What?" he exclaimed, horrified even though this was exactly what he needed to do, what he had planned to do. "No!" he said, desperate to take the misery from her eyes. "Of course I'm not going to send you away." The words were out before he could stop them, if he had only thought for a moment he would have couched them in such a way that would make her understand she would have to live elsewhere eventually. It wouldn't be seemly, for a young girl to live with an unmarried man. But he had spoken from his heart because he couldn't bear the idea of letting her go. But now the damage was done, her cheeks flushed with pleasure and the sparkle returned to her eyes.

"Oh," she breathed, and the relief was only too clear. "I was so frightened."

Alex felt his chest grow tight. He knew he had not done the girl any good deed, for though she was reassured for the moment, at some point she would have to see the truth. He only hoped he could make her understand. But for now at least she was happy, and he was only too pleased to bask in the glow of her pleasure, for as long as it lasted.

"You are not too angry with me then?" he asked, still wondering if he had lost some of the lustre she had painted him with as her *contrebandier.*

She shrugged, and looked up at him as her lips pursed. "I am a little angry," she said eventually, with a sigh. "I wish that you 'ad told me the truth, but ... I didn't tell you I was a comtesse right away, so ... I understand."

It was Alex's turn to let out a breath he hadn't realised he was holding.

"And after all ..." she added. "You are *also* a *contrebandier*, I think?" Her expression was one of such seriousness that he couldn't help but laugh.

"Yes, *ma mie*, I am also a *contrebandier,* and just as wicked as you supposed."

She smiled at him, delighted and he felt his heart ease as he saw he had been settled once more upon the pedestal she had so obviously placed him on. *"Bon,"* she said. "Well then, it is not so very bad, *hein?"*

***

Lawrence and Henrietta were waiting for them when they entered the parlour and Alex could see Henri was bursting to discover what was going on.

"Henri, you are looking as lovely as ever," he said sincerely, greeting his brother's beautiful wife with genuine pleasure. He liked Henri very much and knew that she would take Céleste under her wing, in fact she looked like she couldn't wait to get her hands on the poor girl. Alex made the introductions and Lawrence raised an eyebrow at him, clearly alluding to the shock of Céleste finding out he was in fact an earl.

Alex smiled. "It's alright, Lawrence, I came clean and explained to Céleste that I am not just a smuggler as she believed. She is rather disappointed I fear, but has been so kind as to forgive me." Lawrence looked utterly bewildered and at a loss for words which was an event of such rarity it was rather amusing, so Alex carried on. "It is not so bad after all, is it, *mignonne?"* The endearment slipped far too easily from his lips and revealed rather more than he had hoped to in front of his family.

Céleste rolled her eyes at him. *"Bah!"* she said

Everyone laughed, but there was a light of speculation in his brother's and Henri's eyes which he did not relish.

Chapter 12

"Wherein loved ones conspire for the best, and the worst of outcomes."

Céleste looked around the room that Henri showed her to with awe.

"Mon Dieu, it is so beautiful, I am afraid to touch anything! The 'ouse is just ... perfect."

"Yes, isn't it?" Henri agreed, beaming at her. I fell in love with it the first time I saw it. We are so grateful to Alex for letting us live here. Oh," she continued, as though Céleste was a dear friend, and not some stranger thrust upon her just hours before. "But wait until you see Tregothnan."

"Tregoznan," Céleste repeated, stumbling over the strange word. "That is Alex's 'ome?"

Henri nodded. "Yes, it's vast, far, far bigger than this and very beautiful." The young woman looked guilty as she saw Céleste's reaction and the way the colour leached from her face and she ran to take her hand, steering her to sit down on the bed. "You really had no idea did you?"

Céleste shook her head. *"Non."*

"I didn't mean to frighten you," Henri said, looking mortified. "And really there is no need. Alex is just the same as you believed him to be I'm sure. He's really not one for formality among his friends and family."

Céleste nodded but knew she didn't look reassured. *"Oui,* but ... I *'ave* nothing." Somehow the words didn't convey what it was she wanted to say. She knew Alex didn't care if she had a fortune or not, but what on earth was he supposed to do with her? They were silent for a while and Céleste looked at her stained grey dress against the beautiful light blue silk, figured weave that Henri wore, the woman's charming and stylish coiffure, the dark blue silk fichu over her shoulders, all of it seemed to cast her into a world very far removed from anything Céleste had ever known.

"Are you very much in love with him?"

Céleste started and looked at Henri in shock.

"Oh, don't worry," Henri soothed, taking her hand and squeezing it. "I won't say anything, and really it's hardly surprising is it? I mean, I may be married but I do have eyes in my head and Alex is hard to ignore."

Céleste let out a little huff of laughter, torn between mortification that she had been so obvious and relief that finally she could speak to someone.

"So then," Henri prompted, her warm smile inviting an intimacy that Céleste was desperate to accept. "You do love him?"

"Oui," she replied, colour flooding her cheeks as she nodded. "But 'e thinks I am just a silly child," she added, looking away before the emotion of the day tripped her up and made her cry. "Alex ... 'e does not want me this way," she said, her voice halting and excruciatingly embarrassed.

She turned in time to see Henri give her a curious look but it was quickly gone.

"Come, you must be exhausted," her new friend said, moving onto more comfortable topics. "I have put some things of mine in here for you that you are welcome to borrow for the moment and tomorrow I will take you shopping for things of your own." Céleste opened her mouth to object that she couldn't possibly go shopping, when Henri reached forward and put a finger to her mouth. "Dear

Céleste, I cannot tell you how happy I am to have you here. I have only my maid for female company and whilst I love her dearly she is ... well you'll meet Annie. Anyway, I am thrilled to have you and I won't have the pleasure of shopping with you stolen from me. And further than that - to put your mind quite at ease - you must understand that Alex is quite disgustingly rich, and if you don't go and spend some of his money for him I assure you he will be quite put out of countenance with both of us."

Céleste laughed and found Henri quite impossible to resist, so she just nodded and meekly accepted a sisterly kiss on the cheek before Henri left her alone to sleep.

***

The next morning, after the undreamt of luxury of beginning the day with a cup of hot chocolate with sweet biscuits whilst still in bed, delivered by a maid who was as solicitous as she was incomprehensible, Céleste found herself in a carriage bound for Bordeaux. She hadn't even caught a glimpse of Alex that morning, much to her frustration. Henri had informed her that he had urgent business to take care of with his notaire but he would see them both later for dinner. For the hundredth time in the space of a few minutes Céleste smoothed her fingers over the material of the pelisse that Henri had leant her. It was a deep, rich, plum velvet and she had never worn anything so fine in all her life.

"Do you like it?" Henri asked with a smile.

"I 'ave never ..." Céleste began, only to feel her throat grow tight and stopped abruptly.

"Oh, poor child," Henri exclaimed and moved to sit beside her, pulling her into an embrace. "I am so sorry, Céleste. I hope you don't mind but Alex explained a little of your circumstances to us last night."

Céleste shrugged. "I don't mind," she said, and then added with a little heat. "But I am not a child."

Henri smiled at her and nodded. "Forgive me, of course you're not. In fact I am only about eighteen months older than you I think."

Céleste looked up at her, wondering at that, Henri appeared to be everything that spoke of good breeding and quiet English sophistication. Once more the picture of elegance, she was dressed in a sea green pelisse with a broad collar and with matching kid gloves and a charming straw hat, also in the same shade and lined with gold satin that made her face glow as though the sun was shining upon it. In fact she seemed to be everything that Céleste was not. She swallowed down a revolting wave of jealousy, scolding herself for being so ungrateful when Henri had been nothing but kind. She tried to return to the conversation and grasped a point of interest. "And Lawrence, 'e is older than you, yes?" she asked.

Henri nodded. "A little, yes, just over eight years I think."

Céleste sighed and then looked up as Henri clasped her hand. "I think part of the problem was your situation and ... well the clothes you see, they made you look so terribly young and fragile, in need of saving. *Do you* see?" she asked, clearly afraid she'd caused offence. "Alex ... well, he doesn't usually *save* women ..." She stopped abruptly and Céleste could easily finish her train of thought. She could too well imagine what Alex usually did. "But don't worry, by the time we've finished with you today he won't know what's hit him." The young woman winked at her in a conspiratorial fashion and Céleste laughed despite her misgivings that she could ever carry off anything like Henri's elegance and assurance. But she was more than happy to give it a go.

***

Alex returned to Longueville later that same day with a lighter heart. He had taken the paperwork Céleste had given him and as he had suspected it was all quite right and proper. The firm of notaires had served his family for many generations and he trusted them to do the right thing and help him to return to Céleste everything that she'd lost, though they had impressed on him that it would not be something that happened quickly, no matter how much he wanted it to.

It was the first day in some time he had spend without her company, however, and he was disturbed to note how acutely he'd missed her. This was something he must overcome. Somehow she had become a part of his life without him even realising it and now ... he tried to dismiss the anticipation he felt as Longueville came into sight. He was just tired and hungry and glad to be home, that was all. He washed and dressed, and if he did it with a little more care than usual, it was only that it was a luxury after so many days with the same clothes and the begging of the loan of a blunt razor from the various inns they'd stayed at. There was no other reason that he lingered in front of the mirror, or changed his waistcoat three times. None at all.

He joined Lawrence for a drink in the study and they both looked up as first Henri and then Céleste walked through the door.

Alex knew that he should say something, that everyone was waiting for him to say something, curse it. But he was damned if there was a single thought that could be heard over the pulse of desire that was ringing in his ears. Good God, he really was damned.

"Revenge is a dish best served ... at body temperature?" his brother whispered to him with undisguised amusement.

"Bastard," Alex replied, sounding terse and extremely unamused and remembering well that he had dealt Lawrence a similar blow. He should perhaps be grateful that the dress was a little more modest than Henri's had been that night. But damn it all, didn't they realise what he was up against? Here he was trying to be a gentleman and they ... they conspire to present the girl to him like the most succulent dish that he had ever seen in his life, and was it any wonder that his mouth watered at the sight of her. With a great effort and strength of will he pulled himself together and crossed the room, taking Céleste's hand and raising it to his lips.

"May I say, how very lovely you look tonight, Comtesse."

He at least managed to keep his tone cool and with all of his usual reserve but nonetheless he was rewarded with a pleased smile and a slight blush of colour that tinged her flawless skin. The dress was stunning in its own right, but on Céleste it became a masterpiece. A gold crape petticoat over ivory satin, ornamented at the feet with a deep border of tull, trimmed with gold lace and bronze-coloured ribband and festooned and decorated with roses it was at once sophisticated and tantalising without being in any way shocking.

The warm gold highlighted the colour in her hair and accentuated her porcelain skin; it also showed off her many other attributes to great advantage. All in all she looked exquisite, and when she was finally able to come out in society, with all of the fanfare that her parents would have wanted for her, she would indeed set the *ton* on their ears.

She would have every man eating out of her hand in no time and, much as it made him grit his teeth with jealousy, it wasn't for him to take that from her. He could obviously offer her *carte-blanche* and keep her under his protection as his Mistress, but something about the notion repulsed him. It was unlike him to suffer so much sensibility over a woman but there it was. So much had been taken from her in her short life; her home, her parents, her title, good God she'd nearly been forced to sell her own body in order to survive and it had only been her own sheer determination and courage that had prevented it. No. Though it made his chest ache he would not take her future too, not before she even knew what it was. He would have to make it clear to her that they could have no future together, no matter what foolish ideas she had in her head. He would have to shatter any romantic dreams she might be harbouring and show her reality, show her the kind of man he really was; and why she'd been so very wrong to put him up on that ridiculous pedestal like some kind of knight-errant. But damn, it was a hard thing to do.

Dinner was a great success, the cook, Mme Bertaud having pulled out all the stops on having discovered there was a comtesse in the house. *Consommé,* clear and light and delicious and then a mouth watering *Saumon avec Sauce Crevette* was followed by *Poulardes a la Perigourdine* with *petits pois a la francaise* and for dessert a *Baba au Rhum* so good that Céleste actually moaned with delight, which was at once quite understandable and enough to make him want to cry himself.

Despite his physical frustrations Alex felt himself relax, lulled by good food, excellent wine, familiar surroundings and the people he liked most in the world. His eyes inevitability strayed back to Céleste, however, no matter how hard he tried to restrain himself. She was in fine form tonight, especially as Lawrence began to tell tales of all the trouble he had got himself into as a lad, and how Alex had always been the one to pull him out of it, often at his own cost.

Lawrence was as always, amusing and easy company and his stories cast his older brother in a rather heroic light which was something Alex had never been able to see. He had always lacked Lawrence's *hail-fellow-well-met* nature and combined with a natural tendency to be taciturn and rather cool with people he didn't know well, he was viewed in a very different light by most everyone else. And yet here was Lawrence speaking of him like he admired him and Céleste gazing at him with such adoration that he felt his throat grow tight. It was all nonsense.

He had caused scandal upon scandal in his personal life, was known to gamble and drink and keep any number of mistresses. Any glory he may have brought down on himself in the course of his naval career was always to be precariously balanced against a litany of complaints against him from other officers who he had in some way offended with his ruthless honesty and hatred of anything that resembled flattery or brown nosing. He had more enemies that he cared to consider and his friends outside of the three people in this room were all smugglers.

Little by little these black marks against his own character seemed to tally up until his mood had sobered considerably.

"Forgive me," he said, casting what he hoped was a benign smile at his brother and the ladies. "I find I am feeling rather tired, would you excuse me?"

He got to his feet, ignoring the puzzled look that Lawrence gave him as he went. Harder to ignore was Céleste who got to her feet also and ran around the table to him.

"Mais, Alex, you are well? You are not feverish?"

To his chagrin she reached up and placed her hand to his cheek and it was all he could do not to turn his face into it and close his eyes, instead he removed her hand as though its touch offended him.

"Quite well, I assure you, please don't make a fuss." The words were rather sharper than he had meant them and he cursed himself for the glimmer of hurt in her eyes. But she dropped her hand and stepped away.

"Of course, Alex, forgive me. *Bonne nuit."*

He felt Henri and Lawrence watching him and said nothing further, but stalked from the room feeling like he had purposely trodden on a kitten.

***

Over the next week Lawrence had cause to observe his older brother and Céleste together and the more he saw, the more troubled he became.

A heartfelt sigh came from beside him, followed by, "What *shall* we do?"

He looked up from the comfort of his bed to see the deliciously rumpled picture of his wife staring down at him.

"Good Lord, woman, you're insatiable. Let me get my breath back at least."

He was rewarded with a half-hearted clip round the ear. "I don't mean *now,"* Henri said, tutting at him. "I mean what are we to do about Alex and Céleste?"

Lawrence snorted. "I really don't know."

"Do you think he knows he's in love with her?" Henri asked, settling herself more comfortably against him and drawing his arm over her shoulder. "I mean you have to admit, you Sinclairs aren't exactly quick on the uptake are you?"

"Well I like that!" Lawrence huffed. "You know damn well I was trying to protect you, and if I know Alex that's exactly what he's doing. After all it was a new experience for me but he's been doing it all his bloody life."

"But protect her from what?" Henri demanded, perplexed. "I mean he's wealthy and titled, she couldn't do much better unless she snared a duke, and I'll admit, looking at her tonight I wouldn't say it was impossible even if she is penniless. But she's so obviously in love with him the poor girl. And I know he keeps going on about how young she is, but I'm not that much older. He would have married me if things had gone differently."

Lawrence scowled, momentarily annoyed to remember his older brother's first claim on his wife, thankfully things had worked out perfectly, for *him*, and Alex had undoubtedly played a large part in that happening.

Lawrence nodded. "I know. But you have to remember the deeply honourable part of his nature. Don't take this the wrong way, darling, but your father begged him to marry you to save you both from ruin."

Henri pursed her lips but said nothing so he carried on. "And you told me yourself what kind of reputation he has back home. He's been tied to everything from murder to adultery, rightly or wrongly, in fact from the things you've said the only thing he's never been accused of is smuggling!"

She sighed and her warm breath tickled over his chest. "So you think it isn't just her age, he believes he's not good enough?"

Lawrence shrugged, reaching over and snuffing one of the candles that had begun to gutter before settling back against the pillows. "I think it's all of those things; he feels he is a black hearted character, and she is all innocence. Then he's nearly twenty years her senior, which admittedly is not that unusual but we've both made observations of the kind of men who usually marry very young girls and they weren't very complimentary on the whole. It's clear he wants to make sure she has everything she has missed out on. He seems to have it in mind to launch her into society in such a way that she'll dazzle everyone."

Henri snorted.

"What?" he asked, frowning.

"Good Lord, Lawrence, she'd dazzle enough if she walked out wearing the clothes she arrived in and you know it. But you're quite wrong if you think any man would dare approach her with Alex glowering at them over her shoulder. Not to mention the scandal if he paid her too much attention when it is discovered his family is sponsoring her. Besides, you only have to see the two of them together, the air practically sizzles between them."

Lawrence groaned and rubbed his eyes.

"Well in that case there is only one thing for it."

"What?" Henri asked, turning to him with a frown.

He sat up, leaning forward and planting a kiss on his wife's lips. "You'll just have to speak to him."

"Me!" Henri exclaimed in alarm, her big brown eyes growing wide with horror. "Why me?"

Shrugging his shoulders, Lawrence pulled her closer. "Because he won't listen to a word I say. I'm fairly sure he still regards me in the same light he did when I was twelve, and nothing I say will make a mark on him. You, however, can speak to him on Céleste's behalf. You know how she feels and what's best for her. Try and make him see he's being an idiot."

"Oh is that all," Henri replied, adjusting the bed covers with an air of slight irritation, especially when she found Lawrence hogging the sheets. "Because if he's not going to do the decent thing and marry her there is only one thing left to do - he has to let her go." Finally satisfied with the blankets, she snuggled into Lawrence with a sorrowful sigh. "For she'll never forget him while he's so close, but you know as well as I do, if he sends her away ... he'll break her heart."

Chapter 13

"Wherein their happy idyll is brought under threat."

Henri spent the next few days in a state of extreme agitation as she tried to find the right moment to approach Alex and speak to him about Céleste. The trouble was the two of them were always together. She had noticed the days often followed the same course. Alex would go and secrete himself in the office, no doubt with the best of intentions of keeping out of Céleste's way. But of course Céleste would find some reason to go and see him, usually because she had finished a book and the room doubled as a library, or because she was reading in English and the meaning of something had apparently eluded her, and only Alex could explain to her satisfaction.

Henri had listened in once, hearing Alex trying hard to shut down every conversation to no avail. Eventually Céleste's easy manner had cajoled some small remark that undid all of his previous good work and then his *mignonne* suggested they get some fresh air. Alex would always agree to accompany her for a walk and most afternoons would take a stroll with her. Henri had suggested various trips out to the girl, thinking that perhaps country life was dull for her and she would like another shopping trip, but Céleste would just laugh and reply that she had more dresses than she'd ever thought possible, and why on earth would she need more? There was really no answer to that and so Henri had let her be.

It had to be said that the girl wasn't the least bit vain, during the day she was quite happy to wear a plain cambric gown and no adornments, not that she needed them. But of an evening, when Céleste was dressed more formally along with Henri, she would look like she could be equally at home in a royal court, and this was when Alex would begin to scowl and fall silent, excusing himself ridiculously early to retire to bed, or work alone in the study until the early hours. Céleste in turn would try and smile and carry on with the evening out of politeness, though it was clear that it was an effort to do so.

She had tried to discuss the matter with her maid, Annie, to get her opinion but her usually garrulous abigail just sucked air in through her teeth and shook her head.

"Disaster lookin' for a place to 'appen that is," she said in her easy cockney accent with a mournful expression and her mouth full of pins as she let the over tight bust line out one of Henri's dresses.

"Whatever do you mean?" Henri asked in alarm. Although Annie and Céleste liked each other well enough the two of them didn't communicate much at all, each finding the other's accent totally incomprehensible.

Annie removed the remaining pins so she could speak and took a deep breath, her pale bosom heaving dramatically. "I mean that 'is lordship is determined to be a martyr to the comtesse's cause and he'll do what's right by 'er, no matter what the consequences be for 'im or for 'er. The fool will go on makin' them both miserable rather than do somethin' 'e thinks is reprehensible and love the chit."

"Well yes," Henri said, laying aside the book she'd supposed to have been reading but hadn't looked at for over an hour. "That's exactly the conclusion Lawrence and I came to last night. But what to do about it, Annie? How do we stop him?"

"Can't," Annie replied, with a shrug and what Henri considered a most unhelpful reply. The woman just huffed as she noted her mistress' look of reproof. "Aint no doin' nuthin' with a fellow like that. Won't listen to sense nor reason. May as well save ye breath, my duck."

Despite this augury of doom, Henri's chance finally came the next day and she decided she'd best grasp it. Alex had disappeared early that morning and not returned until almost noon. When he did, however, he came bearing a wriggling bundle of cloth, which he uncovered and passed to Céleste.

"Oh!" The girl squealed with delight as a tiny, glossy red and white spaniel whined and reached up to lick her face. "Oh, Alex, *il est adorable!"* she said, quite as ecstatic as the puppy appeared to be. "Oh, *oui,* you are 'andsome, *mon brave."*

Alex snorted and shook his head. "And how do you know it's a boy, quite apart from the fact it's clearly besotted by you already?"

"Oh, well 'e is very 'andsome," she said and then bit her lip, considering. "Perhaps I will call 'im *Contrebandier."*

Alex gave her a despairing look and a sharp tut of disapproval, though Henri thought it was all too obvious he was pleased by the remark. "I'd rather you didn't, *mignonne*, we don't need to give anyone any clues. How about Bandit, is that a disreputable enough name to please you?"

"Oh, *oui,* Bandit, I like it very much." She ran to Alex, clutching the puppy under one arm and reaching up on her toes to kiss Alex's cheek. *"Mille mercis,* Alex, you are very good to me."

Alex glowered at her for her familiarity but once she turned away Henri caught sight of a look which was all too revealing before he caught her watching him. He cleared his throat. "You're welcome, but I suspect the little devil has fleas so you'd better go and get him bathed before everyone else is cursing me."

Céleste hurried off to deal with the puppy, leaving Alex alone with Henri. He took off his great coat and handed it to the footman.

"Is Lawrence not at home?" he asked, as Henri followed him into the study.

"No, Alex, he's gone to speak to the neighbours about buying that five acre plot near the woods." Henri closed the door behind her, ignoring Alex's look of surprise and nodding when he offered her a drink.

"What does he want with that?" he asked, frowning and Henri took a breath, steeling herself for an awkward conversation. Alex had always been kind to her, and when required, blunt. It had been embarrassing at the time but she had come to be grateful to him for it. She had now to return the favour, such as it was.

"I'm sure he'll tell you later," she replied, waving her hand and taking the drink from him with relief. She took a large sip and prayed it gave her courage. "I need to speak with you, though," she added with some force, before she could change her mind.

"Oh?" Alex looked every bit as wary as he sounded and sat down, crossing his long legs and regarding her with those cool grey eyes. There was no doubt in her mind that he had a fair idea what she was there for and the temperature in the room seemed to drop several degrees. He really was a dreadfully intimidating man when he put his mind to it and she could just imagine how easily all those rumours got going.

Henri cleared her throat and nodded, determined not to be cowed. "Yes ... about Céleste."

"Oh."

There was no doubting his tone now, it had *this is none of your business* in every nuance. Henri put up her chin and reminded herself that she had faced an angry pirate and his crew by herself. Alex really couldn't be worse. Looking at the stern expression and those dark eyebrows drawn together, she wasn't entirely certain that was true. Nonetheless she cleared her throat and stepped into the fray. "What are your intentions towards the girl, Alex?"

The eyebrows flew up, his whole posture changed from guarded to one of furious indignation. "I beg your pardon?"

Henri flushed, and looked at him in horror. "Oh, no, Alex, I didn't mean that ... that you would take advantage of her, not at all!" she replied, wiping her clammy hands on her skirts by pretending she was smoothing out creases. "Quite the opposite in fact," she added, cursing her husband for persuading her to do this at all.

"Henri," Alex replied with some force, his tone frigid with disapproval. "Either speak your mind or mind your own damn business, but either way, do it quickly. I have no patience for riddles."

"Very well!" Henri glared at him. If he was going to be rude then she wouldn't soften her words either. "Then I want to know if you are going to marry the girl? It is all too clear that she is in love with you, and no matter what you say next, I happen to believe you feel the same way. However Lawrence is of the opinion that you won't marry her, in which case I must demand that you send the girl away as quickly as possible before you do any more damage."

For a moment Alex stared at her with such fury she felt a tremor of real fear, but then his expression changed and he got up, walking away to stare out of the window, and her heart bled for him. For there had been real pain in his eyes, and she realised she had been right. Céleste's heart would not be the only one bruised by their parting. He was silent and now her words seemed harsh and she regretted having said them with such force. "Alex, I-I wish you would marry her. You would have married me and really ... there is barely eighteen months between her and I."

He shook his head and when he spoke his voice was cold and hard. "It is very different, Henri. Although you have not had the easiest life, I can promise you, compared to the hell that girl has lived through you have led a charmed existence. I would have married you because your father was known to be in financial trouble, because of it he could not afford to give you a season. Tucked away in that village at the back end of beyond, you would never have found a suitable match. But you were, I believed, a sensible girl and would be able to make a life for yourself without me in it. I had no intention of being a proper husband to you, further than whatever was my duty to give the family an heir. Once that was established you would have been free to live as you wished, to take a lover as long as you were discreet. But with Céleste ..." He stopped and she waited for him to speak again.

"But with Céleste it is different, because you love her," she said.

"Don't be so utterly foolish," he replied, his grey eyes as cold and haughty as she had ever seen them. "You are not given to romantic flights of fancy, Henri, so I beg you do not give into them now. What interest you can possibly believe I have in the child is beyond me? I'll admit her beauty is a devilish temptation but even I am not sunk quite so low. She has lived with the rats, been forced to steal food at times, and if I hadn't found her when I did ... " He let out a breath, his eyes closed. "She has no idea of what life can be when it is kind to you. I want her to know it, I want her to experience laughter and fun and all the ridiculousness of youth. To cause mischief with her friends and find merriment where ever it pleases her."

Henri nodded totally unconvinced by his words, but understanding finally what it was that held him back, but still ... "Could she not do those things with you, Alex?"

"You jest, I'm sure?" he said with his most quelling tone. He raised one expressive eyebrow and she understood how foolish he would feel, surrounded by a gaggle of giggling girls, and young men he would consider little more than boys.

She sighed and shook her head. "Then, if that is your final decision, you must send her away, Alex. It is cruel to keep her here with you. She will never get over you, never find another, all the time she has you to compare them to, don't you see?"

"I know I have to send her away!" he snapped and then turned his back on her, knowing as well as Henri did that his anger gave him away. "I will thank you not to remind me of my own duties," he added, his cool and disdainful manner returning at once. He sat back down in the chair, looking so weary and care worn that Henri began to wonder if it was really Céleste she should be most concerned for, despite all of his protests. "I haven't found the heart to do it," he admitted. "Foolish as it is the child has placed me on some ridiculous pedestal and I know she'll be terribly hurt when I tell her she must go." He looked up at her, no little demand in his eyes. "I don't suppose ..."

Henri's hand flew to her mouth and she gasped. "Oh, Alex, no! Please don't ask me to tell her."

He smiled and shook his head, looking away from her. "No, that would be cowardly wouldn't it?" he said, his voice quiet now. "Only I don't know how I shall bear to hurt her so." She watched him as he looked up, and found his grey eyes as bleak as a winter sky. "I promised her you see. I didn't mean to, but ..." He laughed, but it was a derisive sound that made Henri feel desperately sorry for him "It seems so terribly difficult to tell her anything she doesn't wish to hear. Not a problem I have ever suffered with before I assure you," he added with a self-deprecating sneer. "But you are quite right of course, I'll make arrangements. I thought perhaps I would send her to the Aunts in Hertfordshire, they'll look after her and being so far away ... Well, she will be a good distance from Tregothnan." Henri got up and went to him, crouching down by the chair and laying her hand on his arm.

"I'm so sorry, Alex, truly, but I do wish you would change your mind and marry hcr. I think you would be happy. I don't think she wants all the glamour and parties and nonsense as much as you believe."

He snatched his hand away, giving her a cold look in return for her familiarity. "You are quite wrong I assure you. You didn't hear her at Allaire," he replied, his eyes harsh, daring her to contradict him. "With all the plans for that old house, the parties she would host ..." He shook his head. "She should marry a young man who wants to be in society as much as she does. They'll be wild and extravagant and the talk of the town, and she'll have long forgotten me I assure you."

"Are you really quite sure about that, Alex?"

He ignored the comment, saying only, "It is her birthday in a few days, I'll tell her after that, once everything is arranged." The words were spoken lightly, as if it was a trifling matter that concerned him not at all, but Henri was far from convinced. She may not know Alex well but Lawrence did and he believed his brother loved the girl. Added to that the many soft looks she had caught when he believed no one was watching, and the little endearments and occasional comment that escaped him ... the gentleman protested too much she feared.

She left him staring at the fire, quite unable to find anything else to say, and feeling like a monster. She had wanted to help, and even knowing everything she had said was true, she felt like she had caused two people she cared about very much, a great deal of distress.

To her relief Lawrence walked through the front door as she left the study and she ran down the corridor and practically threw herself into his arms.

"Henri! Whatever is the matter," he lifted her chin, looking at her with alarm in his eyes.

"Oh, don't ever ask me to interfere again, swear that you won't!"

He sighed and held her close. "Oh dear, you spoke to him. He wasn't angry with you was he?" he demanded. "Because if he was ..."

"No, no he wasn't angry. Well he was, but only at first but .. Oh, Lawrence, he denies it of course but I really think he's in love with her, but he's so stubborn. He wants her to have the world and everything in it."

"Well," he said, stroking her hair. "That's not such a bad thing, is it?"

"Yes," Henri sniffed, feeling miserable for both of them. "Because I don't think she wants it."

***

Alex sat in the study, ignoring the fact that the fire was dying and all the light gone from the skies. The room was growing darker and he couldn't help but feel that was perfectly apt. And then the door burst open and in came Céleste with the puppy yapping at her skirts.

"Oh, look, Alex, look 'ow 'e follows me about, isn't 'e clever? Even though 'e was really very cross about the bath. Weren't you, *ma puce?"* She looked up and frowned as she took in the dying fire. "But why are you sitting all alone in the dark? Are you sad, *mon beau?"* She sat down on the floor at his feet and put her head on his knees. "Why are you so sad?"

He forced himself to smile at her and shook his head. "Don't be foolish, *mignonne.* Of course I'm not sad, I must have fallen asleep. You see how stricken in years I am that I cannot stay awake for a whole day," he tried to joke with her but somehow there was a bitter tone to the remark that he felt she heard. Reaching out she took his hand and put it to her cheek.

"But you are really not sad? You are not unhappy to have me 'ere, with you?" she asked, her voice low and so unsure that it made his chest tight.

He was silent for a moment, wondering how on earth he could reply. How on earth he could explain that when she left, she would take all the light and the joy from his life, and he feared there would be nothing left in it to find pleasure in.

"I am not unhappy to have you here, Céleste. That much I can promise you."

Chapter 14

"Wherein the future looks bleak and the past catches up."

Alex got through the next few days, only by holding to his reserved demeanour as far as he could in Henri and Lawrence's company, and by extracting every ounce of happiness he could find in Céleste. When he was with her he plastered a smile to his face that seemed to reassure her and he spoiled her beyond good sense for her birthday, to a point where she was quite dazed and overwhelmed. Dresses and lace, books and jewellery, and boxes of marzipan candies that were such a delight as she had never seen anything as sweet and frivolous as the miniature fruits.

She had exclaimed in wonder and run about the room insisting everyone share them with her until they protested they would be sick if they ate any more. He knew he would remember for the rest of his days the image of her surrounded by wrapping papers, looking up at him as though he had given her the world on a plate. Well, he hadn't, not yet, but if it was within his power, he would do just that.

Her favourite gift of all was a gold locket which she had insisted he put on her immediately and swore she would never take off. They had all stayed up until the early hours, and he knew that Henri and Lawrence were aware of his decision. He would tell her in the morning, and so this last day was one to not let go, not until the very last moment.

He didn't sleep that night, too aware of what was to come, but it was late by the time he came downstairs, aware that Céleste would probably sleep in after her late night. So it was with some surprise that he found her in the study, waiting for him.

"Enfin!" she said, with a huff, pretending to be cross with him. "I thought you would sleep all day, and look, it is so bright and sunny. Will you walk with me, *s'il te plaït?* I am so full of ... of ..." She laughed and shook her head. "I don't know what, just everything 'as been so wonderful and I feel like I could run for miles or climb a mountain ... or anything at all. Is that very foolish?"

"No, *ma mie,* not foolish. It is what it is to be happy."

She sighed and took his arm, leaning into him. "Oui, *mon beau,* I am very 'appy."

He pulled his arm away from her, his expression fierce. "Don't call me that, Céleste, it is not appropriate."

A puzzled look marred her beautiful face as she looked up at him and tried to take his arm once more. "But why? I am your *mignonne,* why can you not be *mon beau?"*

"Because it isn't the same," he said, his voice sharp as he tugged his arm from her grasp once again. "I speak to you like ... like a niece, someone I am fond of, that's all. There is nothing more to it than that so kindly stop inferring that there is."

She looked up at him, and he waited for her to be angry but she just looked away. *"Oui*, Alex," she said, her eyes cast down. "I am sorry."

He hardened his heart against the need to beg her forgiveness. This had to be done, he was doing it for her after all.

"Come then," he said, allowing his voice a little more warmth. "Let's take that walk shall we?"

They walked rather further than he had intended, but with every moment he promised himself he would broach the subject, he found another to put it off, just a little longer. She looked enchanting in a light green redingote over a pale yellow walking dress and a pretty straw poke bonnet lined with yellow satin completed the ensemble and put Alex in mind of primroses, so sweet and fresh was the result. It was on the tip of his tongue to tell her so but he held the words back with regret. He had no right to offer such compliments and confuse her young heart any further. He had to tell her what her future held.

But it was such a beautiful day, he didn't want to spoil it for her. Perhaps he should tell her tomorrow after all. Because today was too perfect, there was real warmth in the sun and the first tentative signs of spring were all around. Catkins dangled from the branches, fat as caterpillars, and new shoots pierced the soil like tiny green daggers. In the fields the lambs were new and well pleased with themselves and the cranes announced their triumphant return, calling from high in the bright blue, their precise arrow formation pointing the way.

"It is so beautiful 'ere. Is it very different from Tregozhnan?"

Alex smiled, loving the way she spoke the old name, it sounded somehow new and exotic when she said it, as though the dusty old house had some mysterious secret he had yet to discover. "Very, *ma* ... Very different, yes," he said, catching himself. He had to put a stop to that. "Cornwall is not as soft and pretty as here. It is very beautiful, but it is a great and sometimes dangerous beauty I feel. It is a hard place and breeds tough people, but they live fiercely for it."

"You love it very much, don't you?" She looked up at him and he avoided her eyes.

"I suppose. I was born there after all."

She paused, turning to him. "Alex?"

"Yes."

"I wanted to thank you, for everything. Yesterday ... I will never forget it. It was so perfect." He turned away from the gratitude and adoration in her eyes, wondering how he would get through the coming days, weeks, years ... without that warmth to nourish his soul. He had come to know how it felt to have someone depend on him, not just for their security like any number of tenants and dependants, but for comfort and happiness and reassurance and ... the thought of losing that was beyond anything he'd known before.

"You have already thanked me, Céleste, there is really no need to keep on doing so," he said, hating the indifferent tone of his words. He sounded bored and derisive, a tone which any of his contemporaries would find very familiar from him. But to use it with her, to give her such a set down made his soul recoil in agony. "You must know by now I am very wealthy. They were merely trifles. However I am glad they pleased you."

"They did," she said, and now he could hear the hurt and confusion in her voice. "Especially this," she said, trying to smile and holding out the locket to him. "I love it, but you must give me a lock of your hair to keep in it, then ..."

"No!"

He felt her jump in shock at the anger in his voice.

"You must stop this utter foolishness, Céleste. I have tried to tell you gently but now I must make things perfectly clear. You will stop speaking to me as you would a lover. It is disgusting to me to consider one as young as you could ever be anything other than a ward. I am not and never will be anything more than your guardian. I will sponsor your entry into society via my Aunt Seymour as soon as you are ready to come out, but further than that, this ... this intimacy that you have somehow fallen into will cease immediately."

He paused and dared to look at her but she had turned her head and was staring away from him and he could see nothing of her face, hidden as it was by the brim of her bonnet. "I blame myself, I should have put a stop to it earlier. It is entirely my fault for being too lax with you and allowing it, but you must understand that there is not and never will be anything between us. I have no intention of ever marrying but if I did, it would not be to a penniless little chit barely out of the schoolroom!" He stopped again, raging inwardly against the words and praying she would turn on him. Let her be angry, let her hate him as she damned well ought to. She should despise him and he would help her do it. But still she said nothing. He could see the rapid rise and fall of her chest but her face still turned away and he couldn't bring himself to look at her, for if she was crying all of his words would likely be for nothing as he couldn't bear to hurt her so. "Do you understand?" he demanded, his voice appallingly cold and hard.

There was silence for a moment, save for the cheerful bleating of the lambs, but then she nodded. *"Oui,* Alex, I understand."

He breathed a sigh of relief, grateful that she was taking it so well. Perhaps the next part would not be so very much of a surprise now.

"On Monday I will be taking you to England," he said, trying to keep his voice even and firm, and wondering why his chest felt so damned tight. He could barely breathe for the weight that held his lungs in an iron grip. "My aunts will be waiting for us at Tregothnan and they will take you from there to go and live with them. They will prepare you for your first season and when they feel you are ready they will help to launch you into society. They are a formidable pair and know everyone worth knowing." He paused, noticing how still she had grown with foreboding. "I am sure you will be a great success," he added.

The silence was so profound that he had the strangest sensation he could reach out and touch it. Tension radiated from every line of the slim figure beside him and he wished she would say something for he felt compelled to fill the silence. Perhaps he had been too harsh, perhaps he should reassure her.

"My aunts will adore you of course," he said, his voice sounding suddenly too loud and callous, and still she remained facing away from him, silent. "Aunt Seymour is rather terrifying I grant you, but you'll get used to her, and Dotty- that's Aunt Dorothea to you unless she gives you leave, well, the old dear is a little vague to be sure.

But she's sweet and very affectionate. She'll be so thrilled to have you with them."

He stopped, quite at a loss for anything else to say to her and he prayed she would speak as his usually iron resolve began to weaken and crumble to dust like ancient paper.

"You lied to me," she said, her voice clear and distinct despite the quietness of her words. She didn't say anything else for a moment and he searched his brain for anything to justify his actions or prove her wrong, but he had nothing. He had lied. He had known it at the time, but he had so wanted it to be true.

She turned and he almost took a step back when confronted with the rage and anguish in her eyes.

"You promised! You promised me you would never send me away! What 'as it been, ten days perhaps?" she demanded, advancing on him with such fury he wondered if she would strike him. "I did as you asked, Alex, I didn't tease you, I didn't tell you I love you, I tried to be your friend. It isn't like I expected anything from you," she said, her tone had changed from fury to desperation and there was such pain in her eyes. He didn't know if he could bear it.

"I know you don't want me that way, I understand. But can't you let me stay?" She reached out and clutched at his hand and hers were icy cold as she clung to him. "I will be good and quiet, I won't trouble you anymore, I promise. Please, Alex, don't send me away. I will die of loneliness without you."

He swallowed and reminded himself of all the reasons he was doing this, of everything she would lose if she married him and was consigned to a dusty old house in the middle of nowhere, of the scandalous looks she would receive if he took her out in public, the whispers and the gossip she would be subjected to.

"Don't be ridiculous," he said, sneering at her and shaking his head so she knew he despised the melodrama of her words. "You won't die I assure you. You will forget all about me as I will you.

Soon enough your mind will be occupied with other things. You will be surrounded by admirers; you'll fall in love with each in turn I have little doubt, and you will have far too many interesting diversions to fill your days with. In the end you will thank me I assure you, *if* you even give a thought to me at all." He shook his hand free of her grasp. "And do please stop mauling me. It is very vulgar and shows your lack of education."

"I assure you," she repeated, mocking his accent and sneering at him in turn. "I will never thank you for that. If you truly believe I am so shallow as to forget you and fall in and out of love with every man who smiles at me ... Why then you believe I am nothing more than the whore you thought I was after all! I thought you knew me, Alex! I thought you understood, but if you think I want all this ... nonsense ..." She stopped and his heart clenched as the tears finally began.

"Please God, no waterworks!" He forced the words out, sounding disgusted with her even though he wanted to pull her into his arms and hold her, to reassure her that he thought she was everything that was bright and wonderful.

"I would be 'appy to stay 'ere with you, or to go to Tregozhnan," she sobbed. "I don't need anybody else, Alex, I don't want them. *Please* ... just let me stay with you."

His throat had grown unbearably tight and how he didn't just pull her into his arms and promise her he would never let her go was beyond him. But he didn't, he just stood there, unmoving, as though he didn't care and simply replied.

"No."

She turned and began to walk away from him and he strode after her.

"Céleste, come back here," he demanded. "We need to discuss this. Let's go back to the house."

"Non!" she turned on him, and it was clear there would be no discussion of anything. She was beyond any rational conversation.

There was a wild glint in her eyes that he knew would bring them both to disaster if this conversation continued for he couldn't bear to see her hurt any more. "I will not discuss it, for you will not listen. You 'ave made up your mind what I shall do, what is best for me, because I am just a stupid child without a thought in 'er 'ead and my feelings are not real. They do not count and they certainly don't concern you. So *non*, I will not go back to the 'ouse, I would rather return to Roscoff! I do not want to see you or speak with you or be with you, so there, you have accomplished something at least this day. Now leave me alone!"

And with that she picked up her skirts and ran and he didn't dare follow her, for if he did he would do something unforgivably foolish and undo all his good intentions. He hoped she would walk her anger off and return to the house presently. Her temper was familiar to him though he had only seen it on occasion, but it had always been brief and fiery and quickly gone. He could only pray that it would be the same today.

With the sensation of a heavy weight lying on his chest, Alex retraced his steps back to the house and found Henri sitting on a bench in the garden as he returned. He paused and turned to her.

"Perhaps ... if you don't mind ..." He stopped, afraid that his voice gave away too much and took a breath to steady himself. "It might be an idea if you would take a walk, down towards the river. Céleste ..."

Henri got to her feet and put her hand on his arm. "You told her?"

He nodded, unable to say more.

"Oh, Alex, I'm ..."

"Don't!" he snapped, turning away. "For the love of God, please don't." He walked away from her into the house and slammed the door behind him.

***

Céleste walked in a daze, unaware of quite where she was going. Her boots were sodden and heavy with mud and her skirts damp and stained too. She pitied whoever would have the cleaning of them for they would likely never be the same again. She remembered her days of scrubbing and cleaning for the girls at Madame Maxime's and for just a moment she could almost wish she was back there. At least then she'd had nothing to hope for, nothing that she wanted so desperately past the immediate need to eat and have a roof over her head. She scolded herself soundly for that thought. There was ingratitude. Alex had given her everything he could. It wasn't his fault that he didn't love her.

He had promised her a life of ease, of pretty things and parties and friends and never having to wonder where her next meal was coming from, or if she would have to sleep with one eye open as there was no safety to relax enough to find peaceful slumber. He had given her all he could be reasonably expected to and far, far more, but he had taken something from her too. That he had done it without meaning to didn't make it hurt any less. That he belittled her feelings as though they were of no worth because she was young made her furious with him, and yet her anger was short-lived. For some reason it was an emotion she could not sustain towards him. No matter if she wanted to. At that moment she would like very much for him suffer the pain that she felt in her heart, for him to know what it was to love someone you could never have. Perhaps then he wouldn't send her away from him because he would know how very deeply it would hurt her.

Little by little her anger fell away to be replaced by a bone-weary sorrow that seemed to steal her energy, and she wanted nothing better than to sit down in the mud and stay there. But that would be pitiful and weak and she was neither of those things. So she would go back to the house and she would be sent away as he wanted her to be and then ... and then ... She couldn't think any further than that, the misery was too great.

At last familiar roads came into sight and she breathed a sigh of relief for the sky was growing dark. She had been walking for hours and hunger gnawed at her stomach though the idea of actually eating anything made her feel ill. Heavy dark clouds rolled overhead as the great roof tops of the towers at Longueville came into sight in the distance and the first drops of rain began to fall.

The ground was already sodden and mucky and now, as the rain began to fall in earnest, her boots slipped on the thick, churned soil as she made her way across the field to the road that ran to the Château. She gasped as her footing failed her and she almost fell face first into the mud, but a hand came out and grasped her firmly about the arm, hauling her back and keeping her upright. Turning, she opened her mouth to thank whoever had helped her, and felt a wash of pure, cold fear as she looked into the eyes of the man standing beside her.

Chapter 15

"Wherein a hero grows desperate, and our heroine takes matters into her own hands."

For a moment Céleste just stared, too astonished to be quite as frightened as perhaps she should be, though that didn't last long. She yanked her arm free but then realised the futility of that idea as four more men appeared, with looks on their faces that she knew boded ill.

Before she could speak or make any further protestation she was struck with such force that her ears rang and her legs gave out, and she knew nothing further as blessed darkness swallowed her up.

***

"Céleste!" Alex's voice rang through the growing dark and he heard her name repeated as Lawrence and his men took up the cry. When Henri had come back to say there was no sign of her he had set out to look himself, with Lawrence and the men who guarded their property. That had been two hours ago. Her name echoed around the fields of Longueville and he thought he had never felt such a sick and desperate fear as the terror that gripped him now.

He should have followed her, should never have let her out of his sight. What if she had fallen? What if someone had hurt her? She should never have been allowed to walk off by herself. They had been on the estate though and not so very far from the house and he had thought she would just walk off her temper and return when she was calmer. It had never occurred to him ... If anything had happened to her ... He couldn't get past the thought.

Surely if someone had been close to the property one of the men would have seen. Longueville was well-guarded, both Lawrence and he had enemies enough to take security very seriously indeed, but if she had strayed far from the Château... His heart contracted. Please God, please let her be safe.

He had walked to the farthest edges of the Longueville estate on the north side and held the lamp aloft and scanning the horizon but the rain and the wind smacked against him, blinding him momentarily. He was forced to look down, and saw the faintest glimmer of gold in the mud. Hardly daring to breathe he bent and picked Céleste's locket out of the mud, the fine chain quite clearly broken in two. Oh dear God no. He held the lamp and looked around, finding the ground churned up and covered in men's footprints. He turned carefully, not wanting to disturb the trail and found the place where Céleste's tracks stopped. With terror and fury holding his heart in their grasp he followed the footprints to the road where there had clearly been a carriage waiting.

"Lawrence!" he yelled at the top of his lungs. "Lawrence, bring the horses now!"

***

Céleste woke to a familiar jolting motion. Her head was pounding and she could taste blood in her mouth and something was very, very wrong. She opened her eyes and immediately scrambled away, lunging for the carriage door but the man opposite her struck out with his foot and pushed her back into her seat. She stared back at him in terror, suddenly focused on the pistol in his hand.

"I would not do that, *ma chérie*, for then I will have to shoot you and I really would prefer not to make such a mess in the carriage."

Céleste stilled and looked at her abductor. The neat and precise air about him, from his shiny Hessians to the impeccable blue silk waistcoat and the crisp, white cravat. Everything perfect, not a hair out of place, those too soft, too neat, manicured, long-fingered hands, one holding the pistol with such a casual manner, and those cold, cold, reptilian eyes. Céleste's heart was pounding and her own hands trembling so badly she could not keep them still, but she knew what this man wanted, and she doubted he would kill her yet. He hadn't yet got what he wanted, and he'd come a very long way to get it.

He looked her over with approval and moved forward across the carriage. Using the end of the pistol, he tilted her head, this way and that. "Such beauty, and such a pity I had to hit you. I hope you don't make me do it again. I would so hate to see that pretty skin covered in bruises." The barrel of the gun trailed down her neck and back up again, the cold metal barely touching her skin but making her flinch in terror. "I have thought so much about this, Céleste. You see I was very, very, angry to find you gone. I'm afraid I rather took it out on Madame Maxime." He gave her a nasty smile and revulsion shuddered through her. "You should thank me for that; she never was very nice to you was she? Still, the girls can always find another Madame I suppose."

Céleste sucked in a breath, her eyes growing wide. He'd killed Maxime. It was true that Maxime hadn't been kind to her, but she hadn't deserved that. Céleste was suddenly gripped by a pure, cold rage, that this bastard thought he could just do as he wanted with her, with any woman, because he had money and a gun to hide behind. The words were out before she could properly think them through.

"I am flattered, Monsieur Pelletier, that you would go to such trouble to come and find me," she replied, keeping her tone as cut glass and haughty as her mother had taught her to when speaking to someone of an inferior class. "But I am afraid you have had a wasted journey. For what you sought to take from me is no longer available."

Pelletier frowned at her and she laughed in his face.

"I am mistress to the Earl of Falmouth, you fool, no longer the sweet little virgin you had hoped to take for yourself. So you see you cannot have what you thought to steal for I have already given it away, willingly and freely and to a man I love."

His hand struck out with such speed and force that she didn't have time to make a sound, but just sat in stunned silence with her cheek burning.

"You stupid little bitch," he hissed, his face screwed up with fury. He stared at her as though she'd somehow transformed before his eyes. "Well you're right, you are of no value to me now." He looked at her with more disgust than desire now. "More's the pity for you," he added with a sneer. "I would have made things easy for you, but as it is I won't have wasted my time. I'll still take you with me, until such time as I grow bored of you. Then perhaps I will give you to my men and you can amuse them for a while. Maybe if you survive that you can return to your earl, and we'll see if he still wants you then, shall we?"

Céleste swallowed but said nothing. Her mind was reeling and she fought back the blind terror that threatened to overwhelm her. There had to be a way to get free of him. It wouldn't be the first time she'd had to fight off someone bigger and stronger, at the brothel she was used to fending off men who thought she was one of the attractions. One had been particularly insistent and had cornered her alone. But that man hadn't had the cruel glint in his eyes that she could see now, he had simply been drunk, and thankfully slow because of it. Pelletier was neither of those things, and he wasn't alonc.

She thought of Alex and how he would feel when he discovered her gone. Would he believe her ungrateful enough to run away? She realised he might even believe she had run back to Roscoff after everything she'd said. Would he follow her? Or would he decide life was easier without her? No, she wouldn't believe that. He was fond of her at least, like ... like a niece, that much was obvious, or at least it had been.

. No, Alex would follow her but he wouldn't know to look for Pelletier, seeing him there had been such a shock. She'd no idea he had become so obsessed with her. Yes he was often there, watching, but she had never imagined that he would go so far as to search for her, and she doubted it would occur to Alex. She was on her own, and she had to save herself. She sat back and vowed to keep her mouth shut and her eyes open, until such a time as she could get free. She would pretend to be docile and to do as Pelletier asked, maybe then she would find a way to escape him.

"Whatever you are thinking, Mademoiselle, please do not bother. We are going somewhere no one will find you and you cannot escape me."

She nodded and didn't try to stop the tears that fell. Perhaps if there was anything in this bastard that could be moved she could at least make him go a little easier on her.

"I understand, *Monsieur.* I underestimated you. I will do as you please, only ... do not hit me again."

Pelletier laughed, sounding genuinely amused, and he nodded. "Oh yes, you will do as I please and perhaps if you are *very* good, I will not hit you. But I make no promises, Céleste. You have caused me a deal of trouble and expense and I intend to get compensation in whatever way I desire."

***

"Damnation!" Alex wheeled his horse at the cross roads and they looked again at the ground but there were too many tracks here to be certain which one they had been following. "We'll have to split up," he said, wondering how in God's name his voice sounded so calm when he felt like his heart was being ripped from his chest. "Rob, take four men and follow the right fork. Lawrence, Pierre, and the rest of you come with me."

They split up and the horses thundered into the night. Alex prayed that their luck would hold as it was a wonder the horses had kept their footing as the going was treacherous with the ground churning beneath them. The rain continued to hammer down, freezing and stinging as the speed they rode at forced it harder into their eyes and faces. They rode as fast as they dared until another cross roads came into sight. As they looked around in despair, the tracks had disappeared. Alex cursed in fury and frustration and dismounted, searching the roads for any sign that they had overlooked but there were no tracks of a carriage having come this way recently.

"We must have overshot," Lawrence shouted over the noise of the wind and the rain. "There were certainly tracks at the beginning of this road and a carriage can't disappear into thin air."

"Look!" Alex said, hope leaping to life as a tiny glimmer of light flickered briefly in the darkness across the fields. "Did you see that?"

Lawrence shook his head but continued to scan where his brother had indicated. Alex mounted once again and they looked together until Lawrence whispered.

"There! I see it."

It glittered for a moment and disappeared again, like someone holding up a lantern and walking in the dark. Alex didn't wait for Lawrence to follow but urged his horse back down the road, searching for a pathway off the main stretch that they had missed. About half a mile back he found what he was looking for and the carriage tracks heading down the path. He went to turn his horse but Lawrence, riding beside him, reached over and grabbed the reins.

"Wait! Alex, we can't go down there without knowing what we are getting into."

"But Céleste is down there!" he hissed, the need to find her and bring her to safety so fierce it obliterated any other concern. Dear God when he remembered all the terrible things he'd said to her ...

"And if she is she will likely be guarded," Lawrence returned. "Think, man! I know you need her back but we have to do this right. If they hear us coming they'll barricade themselves in the house and pick us off one by one. We'll hide the horses here, approach on foot.

You go around the back and we'll spread out around each side so that no one escapes. Agreed?"

"Very well," Alex, growled, knowing Lawrence was right, but he couldn't wait to get his hands on whoever was responsible for this. Whoever it was would find themselves very, very sorry for this night's work. "Then for God's sake, let's get on with it."

***

Céleste looked around the soulless room with her hopes disappearing all too rapidly. The windows had shutters closed over them which had clearly been nailed shut. Apparently, from what she had been able to gather, this was just a stop for the night. He had intended to return to Roscoff with her, but her little revelation had now scuppered that plan. He didn't want to keep her now she was soiled goods. What that meant, knowing what had happened to Maxime, made her heart beat so fast she felt light-headed with fear.

The room itself was sparse. There was a neatly made bed with pristine white covers and a single wooden chair. The room was clearly designed to serve one purpose, one that she could not think of too closely for her courage would fail her and she would succumb to hysterics. If she let herself panic she would be lost, and she had no intention of being lost. She had not survived this long, alone, in a dangerous world to let a vile creature like Pelletier win.

Yet the windows were inescapable and she could hear a guard outside the door, a big lumbering, stupid-looking fellow who made the floorboards creak in protest every time he moved. Well stupid could be used against him, she thought. Pelletier had disappeared for the moment but she had no doubt that he would be back very soon. This was likely her only chance. Taking a deep breath she moved to the door and tapped on it with quiet hope.

"Monsieur," she whispered. *"Oh, Monsieur,* please may I speak with you for a moment?"

There was a huff of annoyance and a rough voice replied. *"Que veux-tu, chienne."*

She gritted her teeth against the insulting manner he spoke to her and replied as sweetly as she could. "I wonder if I could speak with you, please? But do open the door, I can't do it without seeing your face."

"Do what?" he demanded.

She gave a heavy sigh. "Well, I can't say, it's ... it's embarrassing."

There was silence and she hoped that the fool's curiosity would get the better of him.

She heard the key turn in the lock and the door swung open. She almost flinched as she looked him over. He was huge and coarse, with a large belly that protruded over a well-worn leather belt. He turned and locked the door again behind him, keeping the key in his meaty fist.

"Alors?"

She forced herself to lick her lips and remembered how the girls at Madame Maxime's would play with their clients, getting their interest so they were chosen over the other girls.

"I noticed you right away, *Monsieur,"* she said, keeping her voice soft and her eyes cast down. "The man who took me, Pelletier, I don't like him." She chanced a seductive glance up at him from under her lashes. "He hit me, and he said wicked things, but ... but I think a man like you would treat me kindly. I could be nice to a man like you." She took another breath, forcing the nausea that was swirling in her stomach to stay put and let her do this. Moving closer she ran her hand over the rough fabric of his jacket, noticing with disgust various stains which made bile rise in her throat. "Would you like it ... if I were nice to you?"

To her relief and repulsion the man's eyes lit up and he leered down at her.

"Well then," she said, very aware of the key in his hand. "Why don't you go and get comfy on the bed." She began to unbutton his jacket and pull it from his shoulders but of course he couldn't free his hand when it was clenched about the key. He obligingly put it down on the window sill and she pretended not to notice, making a great show of neatly folding his jacket while he made for the bed.

The moment his back was turned she grabbed hold of the chair, lifted it above her head and brought it down with everything she had. It smashed against him, making him crash to the bed in a shower of broken wood and Céleste cried out as splinters pierced her hands. Ignoring anything else she grabbed the key and ran for the door, her hands shaking so hard that for a moment she didn't think she would be able to turn it. Once open she sprang free, running for the stairs and finding with dismay another of Pelletier's louts running up, obviously drawn by the crash from above.

Not pausing, she did the only thing she could and hurled herself downwards, her weight forcing the man back and the two of them fell heavily. Céleste was at least cushioned from the worst of the fall, though she was badly bruised, but she couldn't stop now. The man beneath her was groaning and clutching at his head which she was pleased to note was bleeding profusely. Running for the front door she found it locked and with no key in sight, and so fighting panic she turned and headed for the back. With every step she expected Pelletier or one of his men to step out from the shadows and she could hear cursing and movement from upstairs as the man she'd flattened with the chair regained his senses. With terror making her heart thunder in her ears she found the back door, but then a voice called from outside and she recognised it to be Pelletier's.

In blind panic she looked around for a place to hide. There was nothing and nowhere. It was a large, empty room with no convenient corners, nothing in fact but a huge fireplace. The fire hadn't been lit and the grate was cold and full of ash, and she realised it might be her only chance. Running over to it, she found it high enough to stand up in with ease. The walls on all sides were built of stone, and she ran her hands over the rough surface, trying to find a grip. Soot showered down over her and she coughed and spluttered, blinking it away, and then she began to climb.

Chapter 16

"Wherein a bloody price is extracted for the past, and paid for the future."

Alex approached the house from the rear, the sky still dark and moody with purple-black clouds. It ought to be lightening by now, but the cloud cover was too deep and thick and the night persisted. At least the bloody rain had stopped and he could see his hand in front of his face, if barely. He was frozen and soaked to the bone but none of it registered, his blood raced in his veins, burning with fury and fear. The desire to tear whoever had taken Céleste from him limb from bloody limb was so great that he wanted nothing better than to smash the door down and damn the consequences.

But Lawrence was right, if they wanted to make sure Céleste was unharmed they needed to know what they were walking into. Pausing as he heard voices, he saw someone enter the house via the back door. The door slammed shut and he quickened his pace. He couldn't bear to think of Céleste shut up in there, of what could be happening to her right now. His heart felt as though it was being crushed and he ran to the back door, readying his pistol and bearing it at his side.

Though of course there was no guarantee she was there at all, they could have followed the wrong tracks; these people could be innocent. The thought taunted him that he might be miles away from where she really was. No. He had learned to rely on his gut feelings during the war, and every instinct screamed that she was here. He listened as shouting began on the inside. Someone was yelling about a girl, *where was she?* He felt his heart lift. He should have known that Céleste wouldn't wait to be rescued.

Trying the door handle he found it locked and then his heart froze as he heard a woman scream. Not pausing to think or consider, further beyond the reach of sanity than he had ever been before, he simply reacted and kicked the door open.

At first glance the dim room was empty, and then he saw a figure looming at the shadowy opening of the fireplace. The scream came again followed by a shower of soot, and another figure tumbled to the ground. In the dust and confusion it was too dangerous to take aim with his weapon, but he saw the glint of a pistol and threw himself to the side as a shot whistled past his head.

Gathering himself to his feet, he trained his eye on the shooter through the soot-filled air. "Leave her!" he yelled, holding the pistol aimed at the man, though Céleste was not yet clear of the shot as the dirty man held her before him.

The two of them froze at his threat and for a moment he saw such joy and relief in Céleste's eyes, but it was short-lived as a voice spoke behind him in French.

"Take her to the carriage," A male voice instructed with authority. Alex turned his head to see a figure behind him, dressed like a gentleman unlike the man holding Céleste, and this one held two pistols. One was aimed at him, the other at Céleste.

"Non!" Céleste screamed, struggling against her captor. *"Non,* leave him alone! I'll be good, *Monsieur,* I'll go with you, but please don't hurt him."

"Ah, your earl, I suppose?" the man said with a sneer of contempt. He turned to Alex. "Put down the gun, my Lord, or I will shoot you both."

Alex didn't move. He didn't think this creature would care for a moment if he shot the man holding Céleste, and he himself would be dead before he could turn around and get a shot at him. But

Lawrence and his men were around the front, if they would only move their bloody arses.

He watched helplessly as the man bore Céleste away, though she didn't make it easy for him, struggling like a wild cat.

Alex lowered his gun and the man grinned at him, a deeply unpleasant expression that Alex was desperate to wipe from his miserable face.

"Drop the pistol, there is a good chap," the man said with heavily accented English as he gestured with one of the guns. Alex gritted his teeth and did as he was asked and the bastard laughed, well pleased with himself as he raised both pistols at Alex. But then the sound of shots outside made the apparent gentleman glance back to the front door, his gun no longer directed at Alex.

Alex didn't hesitate but dove towards him and the two of them hit the ground. The pistols fired and Alex felt a flash of heat, stinging his cheek. The man beneath him cursed and fought, but Alex dealt him a vicious punch that knocked him out cold.

The sounds of a struggle at the front of the house calmed and Lawrence strode into the room as Alex scrambled to his feet and snatched up his gun. "Guard him!" he yelled. "They still have Céleste." He ran from the room in the direction her captor had left and to his relief could still hear his sweet fury laying a terrible curse on the man holding her.

He turned the corner of the house to see the bastard desperately trying to bundle her into the carriage as Céleste kicked and fought with all her might. But the man was many times her weight and strength and with a roar of anger he hit her, throwing her back into the carriage. Alex cried out in rage and fired, the gunshot aiming true and his target flying backwards, dead before he hit the ground. He ran to the carriage, quite certain his heart had stopped in his chest as he looked at the still figure on the carriage floor.

She was covered in soot and blood, but the bruises on her lovely skin were only too visible in the dim glimmer of the morning light.

Alex snatched her up, holding her to him. "Céleste?" he cried out, his hand cradling her beautiful face and hardly daring to breathe as her eyelids fluttered and she came to. "Céleste," he said again his voice shaking with relief that expanded his chest and seemed to allow him to breathe again. He looked down at her in wonder, only too aware of how close he'd been to losing her. For a moment she froze, blinking up at him in a daze before throwing her arms around his neck.

"Alex?" she sobbed. "*Est-ce vraiment toi*?"

"Yes," he replied, holding her to him as tight as he could and thanking God. "Yes, *mignonne,* it is really me." Reluctantly he held her away from him and with growing rage looked over her injuries, evidence of bruises and vile mistreatment. "Who did this to you, Céleste," he growled. "Who is he?"

"Pelletier," she managed, though she trembled so she could hardly say his name.

Alex was utterly still as the name registered in his mind. He should have dealt with the bastard before they'd left. He had known he was a threat to her and instead of facing him they had fled. He could have stopped this, somehow. Guilt merged with fury but he lifted Céleste and sat her down on the seat of the carriage with care. "Stay here," he commanded. "And don't move until I come for you."

"Non!" she cried, leaping to her feet and clinging to his arm. "Alex, I won't stay 'ere alone, where are you going?"

"To kill Pelletier," he said, his tone fierce.

"Oui!" she replied, her eyes flashing in the darkness. "He killed Madame Maxime, Alex, and the things 'e said to me ... the vile, disgusting things 'e said 'e would do," she cried, her voice full of fury. "Yes, I want you to kill 'im, but I want to see, I won't stay 'ere by myself!"

He looked back at her, wondering if he should be appalled, but then he saw the fear in her eyes. She needed to know the bastard would never trouble her again. Besides the likelihood of her not just following him anyway, no matter what he said, was slim indeed. He nodded, stroking her cheek with his fingers and giving her a grim smile. "Stay close then."

They returned to the house to find Lawrence, Pierre and the others had dealt with the remaining three men, though apparently the one at the bottom of the stairs had died before they got there. But one man remained alive.

Alex took Céleste to Lawrence, and then turned to face the man who had done this to her. The man who had planned to do things that had filled the girl's eyes with terror.

Pelletier stilled and there was a horrified understanding in his expression as Alex advanced on him. *"M-Monsieur,* forgive me, there has been some silly misunderstanding. I thought she was just a common whore. I--I paid a great deal for her and ... and ..."

"And so you thought you would come to my home and steal her from me," Alex replied, his desire to vent his fury on this man only too clear. "Despite the fact you knew damn well that she wasn't a whore, because you paid for a virgin. And whore or not, no woman is yours to take, just because you can."

Pelletier glanced behind him and back at Alex with growing desperation as he realised there was nowhere to run. He was sweating profusely and as Alex looked at him he had a sudden and vivid picture in his mind of this filthy creature's hands on Céleste, on his sweet girl. He was filled with a rage the like of which he had never experienced before. He hit Pelletier full in the face, and the man went down in a shower of blood and a high pitched scream of pain, and after that he remembered little more. There was simply his anger and the man under his fists, and then shouts as he was pulled away, fighting against those would stop his desperate need for retribution.

"Alex!" He blinked, knowing the voice was familiar but still struggling, though in some dim part of his mind he began to realise it was his brother who was holding him still, with some help from

Pierre. He was pinned to the wall and vaguely aware of the shock in their eyes. "For the love of God, he's dead!" Lawrence shouted at him, shaking him hard.

Alex nodded, realising that he was supposed to acknowledge that fact.

"Will you be calm now?" Lawrence asked, his voice a little shaky, and as Alex looked down he could understand why. Something pulped and bloody lay on the floor wearing the clothes Pelletier had worn. He looked down at his own hands and found them in much the same state.

"I'm calm," he replied, though he wasn't sure that was entirely true. Lawrence let him go and gestured for his men to clear the room. They hauled the body away and left them alone. "Céleste?" he asked.

"I had her taken outside when ..." Lawrence stopped and Alex nodded.

"Thank you."

Lawrence let out a breath. "You're welcome." He took Alex by the arm and towed him out to the front of the house where there was a water pump. "Now for heaven's sake clean yourself up."

Alex did as he was told, moving automatically and washing Pelletier's blood from his hands.

"Your face too," Lawrence said, his expression grim.

He splashed the freezing water on his face, relishing the clean, cold feel against his skin. "I've shocked you," Alex said, wiping the water from his eyes on his sleeve.

Lawrence made a noise of amusement though there was little humour in it. "I saw a lot of things in the ten years I was a pirate, Alex, and I figured there was nothing left that could shock me but ... but you're my brother damn it and ..."

Alex smiled at him. "I told you some time ago, Lawrence. I am not the man I was," he said. He paused and took a deep breath, wondering how much Céleste had seen, and what she thought of him now. "Now perhaps you can see why I can't marry her. I have done too much, seen too much ... been responsible for far too much. I won't bring such darkness in her life. She's had enough of that. It needs to end here and now. She needs to get away from me, from this life, to start afresh."

Lawrence nodded. "I understand, better than you might think, but it isn't a choice who you love, Alex, we both know this."

"No," he replied, knowing just how true that was. "But she is young enough to heal and start over, and the best thing I can do for her is give her the chance to do that."

"And what about you?" Lawrence asked, the pity only too clear in his eyes. "No matter if you won't admit it, I know you love her. How will you heal?"

Alex shrugged. "I'm past saving, I have been for a long time. But if I can do this for her ... well, at least that is something I can be proud of, and I'm not sure there is truly anything else in my life that I can say that of."

Chapter 17

"Wherein our courageous heroine is safe once more, but faces a lonely future."

It took some time to bury the bodies and obliterate any evidence of what had passed in the house. Alex took a cover from the bed to wrap Céleste in, though it made him sick to do it. But the girl was shivering so hard her teeth chattered and they had a long ride home yet. Lawrence, Pierre and the men took Pelletier's carriage, saying they would abandon it somewhere remote and set the horses free before returning themselves.

Alex held Céleste close to him, seated before him on the horse, as they made their way home. She laid her head on his shoulder and clung to him, staring up at his face as though terrified he would disappear if she closed her eyes.

"Sleep, *mignonne,"* he said, his voice strained. "I won't let anything harm you again. I swear, I won't, and I know only too well I've said that before but ..."

"It wasn't your fault, Alex."

He closed his eyes, shaking his head. "I should have done something, dealt with him before we left, then ..."

"Non!" Her small hand grasped the folds of his jacket and tugged. "You couldn't 'ave known he would do such a thing, and you were sick, you 'ad no weapon to defend yourself. How could you confront 'im, you didn't even have any proof. Do not blame yourself

for that vile creature. How could either of us have known he would follow us? He was insane; you cannot account for the actions of a madman!"

Alex made a bitter sound, quite unable to agree with her. "I think you would forgive me just about anything," he replied, wondering why on earth she would persist in loving a man like him, though perhaps after everything she had witnessed last night that had changed. If he was any kind of man he should hope that it had, hope that she was free of him in all ways ... But selfishly he didn't want it to be true. He looked down at her to find her smiling at him, and with just as much adoration in her eyes as there had always been.

"Oui, Just about anything," she said, before laying her head on his shoulder and closing her eyes.

***

By the time they got home Henri was frantic. And Alex was touched to see her as she fussed around Céleste exclaiming over her and hustling her upstairs to bathe in between bursts of tears and a great deal of hugging. They called their doctor, a kindly, older man who had been with the family for many years. He proclaimed her fit and healthy in body and that the bruises were superficial and would heal quickly. He recommended plentiful sleep and rest, and that she was not to become over excited or agitated, and then gave Alex a cautioning look.

"It may take rather longer for her mind to rccovcr though, my Lord," he said. "Perhaps a change of scenery would be in order, somewhere new and free of bad associations?"

Alex nodded his understanding and thanked the man. His heart was heavy as he considered that Longueville may no longer be a place she could feel safe, but his previous plan to take her to his aunts seemed the best one. She would be safe there with nothing to trouble her, and he would be far away. He fought against the idea that she would be safer by his side, even though the desire to keep her beside him was stronger than ever. But Pelletier was dead and there was no one else from her old life who could hurt her. Yet there were plenty in his. He sighed and poured himself a drink, turning as a quiet knock came on the door.

"Come," he called, looking to see Henri walk in.

"Lawrence is back," she said, the relief in her eyes only too evident. Alex hadn't told her much of what had happened but the sight of them both, filthy and battered and covered in blood, had spoken volumes. "And Céleste is asking for you."

He looked down into his drink, watching the tawny liquid swirl in his glass as he tilted it before downing it one large swallow.

"How is she?" he asked.

"Exhausted, relieved to be back ... immensely proud of you."

He snorted with disgust and shook his head, looking down at his hands. He had washed and changed but his hands showed evidence enough of what he had done. Not that he regretted it, not for a moment, the only pity was the bastard hadn't suffered for longer. But his hands were unclean still, and no matter they would heal, they would always have blood on them, and he knew he could never lay them on Céleste. She deserved so much more than that.

"She said that ... that you killed him with your bare hands, the man that took her."

"Yes," he replied. He looked up and met her eyes but found no condemnation there.

"Good," she said with simple acceptance, and Henri turned and left him alone again.

Alex finished his drink and climbed the stairs, knocking on Céleste's bedroom door. He was only too aware of the impropriety of entering her bedroom alone, but they had shared a bed for many nights and no one here would care, so propriety be damned. In all too short a time she would be gone from his life. He would see her now if she wanted him to come.

He entered the room to find the curtains had been pulled halfway and a soft light filtered into the room. Céleste was sat in bed in a white cotton nightgown with a cashmere shawl around her shoulders. Propped against a mountain of pillows, her puppy, Bandit, sat curled against her side. Her eyes were closed and she looked younger than he had ever seen her, pale and fragile, the dark bruises against her alabaster skin an obscenity. He clenched his fists against the rage and sorrow that bloomed in his heart and wanted to kill Pelletier all over again. He must have made a sound as her eyes flicked open and she smiled with such pleasure that he felt his heart ache. How could she still look at him so? After everything, all the hateful things he'd said and must keep saying if she was to have a chance at happiness. She frowned as she saw the expression on his face and looked down at her hands.

"Are you well, Alex?" she asked, her voice quiet.

Alex gave a bitter laugh. "I think I am supposed to ask you that."

"Bah!" she replied, waving a dismissive hand. "I 'ave been fussed over quite enough, *merci beaucoup."*

He smiled at her then, pleased that she wasn't so very cowed by what had happened, though he felt perhaps she was performing for him, to reassure him. She held out her hand to him and he hesitated but found he couldn't refuse her. So he took it and sat down on the bed beside her. She looked at his bruised hands, her warm fingers tracing his skin with a delicate touch that made his body and heart ache with longing. She lifted his hand to her mouth and began to kiss the knuckles, one by one, her lips so very soft and tender against his bruised flesh.

"Don't," he said, hearing the desperation in his own voice and pulling his hand from her grasp, before he gave in to his own violent desire to make her his own. And how he could even consider such a thing after everything she'd been through, he truly was an utter bastard. "I am truly sorry for what happened to you, Céleste, and as your guardian I bear the responsibility of it, but further than that nothing has changed."

They sat in silence for he didn't know what to say and he couldn't meet her eyes. For when he looked at her, he was filled with the desperate need to protect her, to hold her to him and never let her go.

"You will still send me away then," she whispered. It wasn't a question, there was resignation in her voice and he tried to tell himself he was relieved she wouldn't fight him anymore.

"It's for the best," he said, staring down at his knuckles and seeing them covered in Pelletier's blood all over again.

"Best for who, Alex?"

"For you, dammit!" he snapped and then remembered himself, appalled at the way he'd spoken to her. "Forgive me," he said, his voice hoarse as he got to his feet, turning away from her.

"There is nothing to forgive. I will go away, if that is truly what you want. But don't think it will change anything, for it will not."

He let out a breath, knowing in this at least she was wrong. He would be forgotten, replaced by any number of handsome young men. "It will change everything, which is how it should be," he said, sounding desperately bored. He turned back to her, looking at her as though she meant nothing to him.. "I am no fit husband for you, you foolish creature," he said, his voice disgusted, but then he carried on, knowing it was cruel but feeling there was kindness in the words even though they would hurt him to say them, and her more to hear them. "Surely by now you must know that I am a confirmed bachelor and happy to be so. My lovers are experienced women who neither want nor need anything more from me than I am willing to give. I grow bored easily, Céleste, and a green little girl would hardly afford me amusement for more than a few days. What then would I do with you, pray?" he demanded, a mocking smile on his lips.

Her cheeks flamed and she looked away from him, clearly humiliated by his words.

"I am sorry, *mignonne*," he said, though it sounded very much like he was laughing at her. "I am fond of you, but nothing more than that."

She nodded and when she spoke her voice was tight and he could hear her struggling to keep the tears at bay. "You 'ave made yourself very clear, Alex, so you need not worry. I will go, and I will not trouble you again."

Alex held himself very still, fighting the desperate need to go and take her in his arms and tell her it wasn't true, that every word was a lie and that he would love her until his last breath, but instead he turned and closed the door quietly behind him.

He walked past Henri on the stairs, who took one look at his face and stopped in her tracks as he picked up his pace and strode for the front door. He had to get out, out of this damn house, away from Céleste, before he lost his mind entirely and ruined everything.

***

Henri flattened herself against the wall as Alex came come down the stairs. There was such pain in his eyes that she almost reached out to him but didn't dare to, such was the turmoil she felt coming off of him in waves. Knowing that Céleste must somehow be at the heart of Alex's torture, she ran the rest of the way to her room, to find the girl sobbing her heart out.

Lawrence had told her a little of what had happened with the man that was responsible for taking Céleste, how Alex had lost control of himself and practically torn the man apart. Lawrence had said it was terrifying to watch, like he was possessed, and she wondered what on earth would happen to Alex without Céleste to stop that dark place in his soul from swallowing him up entirely and leading him to destruction.

"Hush, now, it's alright," she crooned, pulling the distraught young woman into her arms. "Don't cry, Céleste, it will be alright."

But Céleste shook her head. *"Non,* it will never be alright, 'e is sending me away and I will never see 'im again."

"Of course you will," Henri said, keeping her voice gentle and reassuring. "My goodness if you think Alex can get away with never visiting his aunts then you greatly underestimate their intimidation value. He and Lawrence, they're both terrified of the old dears, well, not Aunt Dotty of course, she's a sweetheart, but Aunt Seymour ... Oh, you'll see him again."

Céleste sniffed and wiped her eyes. "It does not matter though, even if I see him, he doesn't want me, he could never love me."

"Oh, Céleste," Henri laughed and then put her hand to her mouth to smother her amusement. "He is so obviously in love with you it's painful."

"What?" Céleste blinked at her in astonishment. "Why would you say that? He thinks I am a child, a stupid little girl, not ... not like his sophisticated lovers," she said, her voice trembling with emotion.

Folding her arms and giving Céleste a hard look Henri gave a huff. "He's lying through his teeth."

Céleste opened her mouth and closed it again. It was all too clear she wanted to believe Henri. "B-but 'e said ... just now, 'e stood there and said ..." she countered.

Henri rolled her eyes. "Oh, what he said!" she repeated with a tut of annoyance. "I tell you, these damned Sinclair men are all the same. They think they know what's best for you, what the *honourable* thing to do is," she said in disgust. "As if they know! They're fools, *both* of them, honestly, the trouble I had getting Lawrence to the alter you simply wouldn't believe," she said, feeling really rather cross about it all over again.

"Really?" Céleste asked, obviously disbelieving.

"Really," Henri said with a smile. "But you must listen to me, because I'm afraid to say that I think Alex is far more stubborn than Lawrence ever was."

Céleste sighed and nodded. "He is a very stubborn man, it's true, but ... but ... Oh, Henri, I can't believe it, after everything he just said. How can you be sure?"

"He practically admitted as much to Lawrence," Henri said, feeling guilty for betraying both Alex and Lawrence's confidence but bolstered by the light in Céleste's eyes.

"C'est vrai?" she demanded, clutching at Henri's hands.

"Well of course it's true!" Henri exclaimed with a sniff. "As if I'd make a thing like that up. He's in love with you, I swear it."

"Oh!" Céleste made as if she would leap out of the bed and follow after him in her nightgown.

"Oh, no! Céleste, you must stay put and listen to me. I mean it!" she added, sounding really quite severe as Céleste returned a mutinous expression. "You mustn't let on that you know."

Céleste settled back against the pillows with a huff of annoyance.

"Now then," Henri said, mustering her own thoughts on the matter. "It appears that Alex believes he is too old and too wicked to marry someone as sweet and young and innocent as you."

"Bah!" Céleste exclaimed in disgust.

Henri nodded. "I quite agree, but like I said, the man's a fool." She sighed and made herself more comfortable. "I think you must go away to the aunts and, you know, I think you'll find them quite happy to help you. They've been desperate to see Alex married for years from what I hear and they've thrown every woman they could find in his path to no avail. If they discover he actually cares for you ..." She gave Céleste a mischievous grin. "Oh, yes, I think we can turn this around." But then she sighed and gave Céleste a stern look. "But you must be patient. You must do exactly what the aunt's say.

They will teach you everything, show you how a countess ought to deal with men for one. And you must allow Alex to miss you." She sighed again as Céleste huffed. "Well do you want him or not?"

"Oui," Céleste snapped, clearly aggravated. "Though I am beginning to wonder why!"

Henri patted her hand and nodded. "I know just how you feel I assure you, but the thing is that it is far too late for you to come out this year. There's simply not enough time to prepare and have everything done to the aunt's satisfaction. Believe me I know, I only spent a little time with them before we returned to France but they are sticklers for etiquette." She smiled at the look of horror in Céleste's eyes. "Oh don't worry, I have no doubt you will be magnificent. And when you do come out, older and more sophisticated, and I have no doubt with dukes throwing themselves at your feet, well, just let him walk away from you then." Henri gave her a knowing smile and Céleste smiled in return, though it was a rather sorry effort.

"Well, I 'ope you are right," she said and then gave a heartfelt sigh. "But oh, that is more than a year away! I will die before then."

"Nonsense," Henri replied, shaking her head. "You will pass the time doing all the things you never before had the chance to, you will make friends and find ways to enjoy yourself without Alex and ..." With sudden inspiration Henri suddenly knew exactly how she should deal with Alex. "And you will write to him every week, and tell him everything you are doing!"

She clapped her hands together and grinned at Céleste. "Oh, yes, and don't forget to drop an occasional mention of some handsome beau's name. Nothing obvious, just a repeat of the same gentleman caller having visited once again should do it."

"But what if there isn't an 'andsome gentleman caller?"

Henri gave her a pitying look. "There will be, don't trouble yourself on that score. Oh, and do not ... I repeat *do not* send him love letters telling him how desperately you miss him."

Céleste pouted. "Right at this moment, I think I dislike 'im very much, so perhaps it won't be so hard."

"That's the spirit!" Henri replied, beaming at her and pulling her into a hug. "Don't worry, Céleste, we'll be sisters yet. I'm sure of it."

Chapter 18

"Wherein the sea takes its toll, England's shores are reached, and the future is regarded as a miserable place to be."

Céleste clung to Henri, both of them fighting back tears on the morning she was due to leave Longueville. The departure had been delayed by a week to give her time to recover and the bruises to fade. Indeed there was no physical mark left of her abduction, though she still awoke in the night crying in fear, and her previous dislike of being alone had become rather more of a terror. In that Henri had been a great comfort and had kept her company as much as was required. In fact the two young women did indeed consider themselves to be already sisters, no matter that one idiotic, pig-headed man would insist on making things difficult.

"Promise me you will write to me often," Henri said, sniffing as Céleste nodded and embraced her again.

"Je promets!" she said, wiping away tears. "And you write to me too, for I shall be very lonely."

Henri winked at her and Céleste coloured, realising she was not to say such things in the future. But at this moment, leaving behind everyone she had come to love, it seemed a hard thing to be sent away to live with people she had never met before. Annie embraced her in turn.

"Good luck, Comtesse," Annie said, surreptitiously pressing a small flask of something into her hand. "Keep ye warm on the journey," she whispered, winking at her and ignoring Alex's look of disapproval.

Céleste tucked the little flask into her reticule and looked around one last time at Longueville and all the people who had made her so welcome.

"Goodbye," she said, her voice heavy with sadness, but Henri grabbed hold of her hand and squeezed, looking her in the eyes.

"Au revoir," she replied, her voice firm, and Céleste smiled at her and nodded.

"Au revoir."

Alex handed her into the carriage and then joined her. In one thing she had been successful at least. He had agreed not to hire some old busy body to chaperone her for the return voyage though he had insisted on hiring her an abigail at the very least, who would travel with her puppy, Bandit. After everything that had gone before it seemed utterly ridiculous, and as the ship was Alex's own, it wasn't like she would be about in public. Henri would have accompanied her, but there had been much celebration in the previous days as she had revealed she was expecting their first child.

Lawrence, beaming and proud, had gone on to refuse point blank to allow her to travel at this delicate stage of her pregnancy. Henri had argued but to no avail, his mind was made up. As it was, the man was driving poor Henri insane, worrying and fussing over her until she confided to Céleste that many months of this would drive her to distraction. Céleste had smiled and sympathised, but secretly thought that Henri didn't know how lucky she was, for she would give anything to carry Alex's child and to have him dance attendance on her.

She kept such thoughts to herself though, and as much as she was looking forward to having Alex to herself, she was careful to be quiet and still and not speak unless she was spoken to as she had agreed with Henri. He should be made to see he was making her thoroughly miserable at this stage, just in case his resolve broke and the next year of misery could be forgotten before it began. They both strongly doubted it would work, but it was not hard to appear sad and withdrawn as it was entirely true. She was utterly miserable, and besides, it was so much easier than having to feign happiness.

She'd hardly seen Alex since he had spoken so harshly to her, and the brief periods she had been in his company had given her no indication to suspect that what Henri had said was true. Yet she clutched the knowledge to her heart. Lawrence had said he'd all but spoken the words, that he loved her, and she knew Henri would never say such a thing if it wasn't true. But oh, how she longed for a sign of it, some tiny clue that would shine a light over the coming months without him, when it would be all she had to cling to.

And so the journey to Alex's ship, The Revenge, was undertaken in almost total silence, which wore on Céleste's nerves and made her almost desperate to speak to him. She stole a glance at him on the other side of the carriage and admired the strong line of his profile as he stared with resolution out of the carriage window. His long legs were stretched out as far as the confines of the carriage would allow, and her eyes travelled over the wide expanse of his chest, those massive shoulders and strong muscular arms that had felt so wonderful when she had slept in their embrace. That seemed to be a lifetime ago, however, and the likelihood of it ever happening again seemed even more elusive.

***

Alex kept his gaze fixed on the countryside as it slid past the carriage windows and did everything in his power to ignore the young woman opposite. He could feel her eyes on him, travelling over him like a caress. He gritted his teeth and ignored the insistent voice of his desires that had been tormenting him since the carriage door closed and Longueville disappeared from view. She wanted him. He knew it like he knew he was going straight to hell if he gave into desire. But he need only say the word and she was his for the taking. He could reach over now and pull her into his lap and discover the taste of her.

And by God he wanted to know the taste of her. The idea of it tormented him, the longing to know ... to touch ... to taste. They could pass the time between now and reaching his ship in the most delicious manner imaginable. He closed his eyes and allowed himself, just for a moment, to imagine how she would feel in his arms, just how it would feel to envelope that slender body with his own and find his way beneath the layers of expensive cloth. He imagined loosening that pretty gown and revealing the lovely flesh beneath, his hands travelling over the silken expanse, his lips closing over first one breast, then the other, for both deserved equal attention. He took a moment to wonder if her nipples would be small and pink, the same shade as her mouth, and had to bite back a groan as his body ached with repressed need. *Stop this, stop it now,* he ordered himself. For the love of God he was an experienced man, not some callow youth who couldn't control his own desires.

"Are you quite well, Alex?"

His eyes snapped open and he was forced to confront the source of his discomfort, those impossibly blue eyes staring at him with such concern. He almost laughed. What a damned fool he was.

"Quite well, thank you," he replied, somehow finding his voice unintentionally cold and sharp as frustration made him irritable. He saw the hurt in her eyes and felt an answering pain bloom in his chest. Why? Why by all that was holy had he kept his emotions successfully guarded all these years, his heart locked away in a cold dark place, only to lose it now? It wasn't like he hadn't been pursued before. There had been many beautiful women willing to brave his reputation in the hopes of redeeming him and snaring themselves a wealthy earl. And there had been many married women and young widows only too eager to welcome him into their beds. He had believed himself immune, invulnerable and more than glad to be that way. Love was all well and good for poets and romantic young bucks, not for him. If you loved people, if you cared what happened to them, they had a nasty way of dying and leaving you alone and in pain. He had discovered the truth of that when he'd believed Lawrence had died on that beach and had ruthlessly shut away any possibility of it happening again. If he could feel such pain for his brother, what could a woman do to him?

And then Céleste had saved him in Roscoff, she had caught him in a vulnerable moment and slipped beneath his defences before he had realised the danger he was in. And she had swiftly reminded him of the perils of such tender emotions when Pelletier had taken her from him. Remembered terror swept through him, cold fear prickling over his skin as the thought of her trapped in that house all alone made his fists clench.

No. He would not allow it. He would rid himself of these debilitating emotions. He would hide her away with the aunts until they deemed her ready to make her way in society. Then he would get her married with as much expediency as was allowable to a decent young man who would keep her safe and occupied with a good home and plenty of little brats to hold her attention.

But of course then he was forced to imagine the way in which those brats would be created by that decent young man. Images of Céleste spread open to some nameless husband rolled through his mind, torturous pictures of a male figure with his hands and lips and body covering hers and making her cry with pleasure. Rage and jealousy exploded in his heart, so fierce that he drew in a sharp breath, making Céleste regard him with curiosity, though this time she said nothing.

He closed his eyes and counted to ten, waiting for the ridiculous desire to kill a man that didn't even exist to dissipate. But the feeling burned like acid in his veins, and he knew that there weren't numbers enough in the universe to reach and find his jealousy diminished. With a numb kind of misery he accepted the fact that when she eventually married he would never be able to see her again. For no matter how decent and acceptable the match, Alex would be driven to kill any man who touched her.

***

Céleste glanced up at Alex's massive frame as he guided her onto his ship. Her nerves skittered, making her breathing shallow and her heart thud. She'd never been on a ship before which was terrifying enough in its own way, but something about the man beside her made her uneasy in ways she couldn't name.

Infuriated by his bad temper and the stony silence that continued for the rest of the journey, she had determined to ignore him as he was ignoring her. And so she had stared out of the window and done just that, only to feel his eyes on her like a brand for the rest of the interminable carriage ride.

He showed her to his cabin, explained with as few words possible that he would give it over to her for the voyage and that her abigail would attend her shortly before bowing with stiff formality and leaving her alone.

Céleste stared at the cabin door with growing fury. If he'd left any faster it would have been at a run. Was he truly in such a hurry to be rid of her? She bit back the misery that accompanied that idea and reminded herself of Henri's words. Against his current demeanour they seemed to mock her, the very idea of Alex having any warm feelings towards her seemed increasingly unlikely as his behaviour became ever colder.

But then her stomach was hit by a wave of nausea as the floor pitched under her feet and she sucked in a breath and went to lie on the bed.

To her misery and shame, this was where she remained for the rest of the voyage as sea sickness claimed her and held her captive for the duration.

***

Alex drummed his fingers on the rail as he waited for Céleste to emerge. He knew he had worn the poor maid ragged with constant demands as to her welfare. The stupid creature would simply shrug and say the comtesse was sick and in bed and nothing more. Though what else he expected her to say he didn't know. He did know that he had missed her company far too much. That the these last days with her, days that he had promised himself he would savour, had been stolen from him.

He took a breath, telling himself he was a damned fool for the thousandth time, for all the good it did, and then found himself unable to breathe at all as he caught his first glimpse of her since he had left her in his cabin.

Dressed in a redingote of pale blue satin with her golden hair visible in artful ringlets beneath her bonnet, she looked pale and desperately fragile. Despite his best intentions he found himself at her side in as few strides as was possible, and her small, cold hand in his much larger, warmer one.

"Mignonne, I'm so sorry you've been unwell." The words were out before he could stop them, as though sea sickness was something he could take the blame for.

She looked up at him, a tired smile upon her lips that didn't reach her eyes.

"It's nothing, Alex. I am perfectly well now, though I am in no 'urry to repeat the experience," she admitted, with a rueful expression.

He felt his heart sink a little and then wondered why. It wasn't as if she would ever sail with him again in any case.

"You know, Admiral Lord Nelson was also horribly sea sick," he said to her in an undertone, aware that this was not a suitable subject for discussion with a young lady but then, this was Céleste who cared little for such niceties. "In fact the first time I went to sea myself I spent the entire voyage hanging over the rail, and it was far calmer than our crossing has just been. But I got used to it, eventually. It doesn't trouble me now."

"Eventually?" she repeated, looking appalled.

Alex smiled and nodded his head. "It is something you can conquer, to varying degrees, if you persevere."

She stared up at him and he felt his heart turn. There was a look in her eyes that quite clearly told him that she would persevere, for him, if he would only ask her to.

He looked away and placed her hand firmly on his arm. She endured the short voyage in the gig from his ship to shore with stoic silence but her gratitude at putting her feet on solid ground was only too apparent.

"Come, the aunts will be waiting impatiently for our arrival. They don't like being away from home and they will be eager to take you away with them." He made himself say the words, trying to infuse them with anything other than the impression that his heart was being ripped from his chest.

"So soon?" she whispered, and the misery in her voice was like a knife in his chest as he could only echo the sentiment.

"Yes, of course. They have been waiting at Tregothnan for over a week as it is. You'll love them I assure you, and they you. And don't be cowed by Aunt Seymour. She's terrifying at first glance but once you get to know her she's really not so bad." He listened to himself prattle on until they reached the carriage, desperate to put her at her ease and relieve the unhappiness in her eyes that was making the weight in his chest a heavy burden to bear.

He tried to keep up the inane conversation for the rest of the carriage ride, finding as Céleste grew increasingly withdrawn that words failed him. Defeated, he gave up, but could not tear his eyes away from her face. She looked out of the window, though she didn't seem to see anything that passed behind the glass. Instead her eyes glittered too brightly and he could see the effort it was taking her not to cry.

Looking away he repeated to himself all the reasons why she could not marry him. All the dirt and scandal attached to his own name that had sullied the title and man who bore it. All the things he had done that had darkened his heart and cast a shadow over his soul. He looked down at his hands, big and rough and scarred, and far too bloody to ever lay them on the gentle-hearted creature in front of him. For despite her spitfire temper he knew that she was far too loving and innocent to be wed to an utter bastard like him. No matter that he wanted to with all his heart.

Chapter 19

"Wherein farewells are made and ancient Aunts prove not so foolish as some might imagine."

"This is Tregothnan." Alex watched as Céleste looked up at him and then turned her eyes back to the window as they passed through the impressive gatehouse that led onto the estate.

"It is very beautiful, Alex," she said, her voice wistful. He bit back the desire to voice his thoughts, to tell her he wished she could see it all. He wanted to walk the grounds and see it through her eyes. To walk along the wild cliffs where the wind snatched at you and threatened to pick you up like a stray leaf and tumble you down to the surging white waters that thundered upon the rocks far below.

He longed to show her the house and ask her opinion of it. To see if she approved of the ideas he'd had to modernise the old, cavernous building. Ideas that had been born a decade ago but had never come to anything in the years since he had believed his younger brother dead and himself irrevocably changed. For what was the use?

He'd toyed with the idea once more when he'd believed he would be forced to take a wife to continue the line. But now Lawrence was, miraculously, restored to them and had wasted no time in doing his duty and providing an heir and the pressure was off. He told himself that it was a relief, that it was best all round that he would never have a wife and family to enjoy the benefits of the work he had considered all those years ago. Better to leave it to the next generation. So he would merely continue to keep the place in good order, feeling forever more like a caretaker looking after a museum than a man with a home.

They travelled for another half an hour in silence and then he heard a soft gasp and knew that the great house had come into view. He watched her face, devouring every nuance of her expression and preserving it as something precious. A forbidden memory to be taken out and looked at like a cherished keepsake once she belonged in someone else's life.

She looked back at him, her eyes full of regret and quiet amusement. "You really are an earl then, *mon contrebandier."*

He smiled at her, unable to keep the warmth from his voice on hearing her strange endearment. "You're still disappointed then?"

She stared at him and then looked away as her eyes became over bright. *"Oui,"* she whispered. He swallowed hard and forced his eyes away from her knowing she believed that he might change his mind if he were merely a smuggler and not an earl. Did she truly think that it was his title that kept him from making her his own? Did she truly believe that some disparity in their bloodline would stop him? He wished he could tell her that it wouldn't have mattered to him if she had been simply Céleste, a girl born to poverty without so much as a name to cling to. He would have felt the same sense of dishonouring her at the idea of taking her for himself. He would still have been just as unworthy of her.

Inexorably the carriage swept up the long drive and rocked to a gentle stop outside the massive structure of Tregothnan.

***

Céleste stood in the vast entrance hall of Tregothnan House and was weighed down with the knowledge of just who the man she had fallen in love with truly was. It hadn't been so very hard to accept that he was a nobleman instead of a smuggler as she'd first thought. With his great height and the air of confidence bordering on arrogance that she had found so very reassuring and attractive, it was clear he was a man well used to being obeyed.

Standing beside the beautiful Château at Longueville he hadn't seemed so far removed from the kind of man her father had been- a wealthy and well respected man, but no one of great consequence. But this house and land they had just travelled through made her realise just how far out of her reach he truly was. He was born to stand among the higher echelons of English nobility and she was nothing but a dispossessed countess with not a franc to her name and no one but him willing to vouch for her. She felt terribly small and insignificant and utterly certain that the moment she was out of his sight she would be forgotten. For why would he remember a cheap little French girl he found in a whore house, who had an unerring way of making him lose his temper at every turn? He would go back to his sophisticated lovers, those cool and elegant English women who always knew exactly what to say or do. They would know how to seduce a man like that, though she imagined they would have little need of the knowledge. He would want them in a way he had never wanted her. A lump formed in her throat and it was only Alex's hand at her back that made her move forwards when all she wanted to do was curl into a ball and sob.

She moved on into an elegant drawing room with lavish, if tasteful furnishings. The walls were panelled and the ceiling heavily decorated and embellished with gold leaf. The vast room, painted in pale blue had a thick, rich carpet that Celeste's slippered feet sank into, more luxurious than anything she had ever known. As she approached two older ladies stood to greet them. They both curtsied formally as Alex approached.

"Aunt Seymour, Aunt Dorothea," Alex said with a smile, first approaching a tall and severe-looking woman dressed in dove grey and lavender silk. "How lovely to see you both looking so well."

The lady snorted and rolled her eyes at him.

"Very pretty, Falmouth, I'm sure. Now stand aside and let's get a look at the girl."

Alex's mouth twitched and he led Céleste to stand under the daunting cool grey eyes of his Aunt Seymour.

"Lady Sinclair, Lady Russell may I present to you Célestine de Lavelle, *La Comtesse de Valrey."*

Céleste curtsied and murmured her greeting before glancing back at Alex who gave her a reassuring smile. She jolted as a small gloved hand reached out and squeezed hers.

"Don't look so frightened," said a kindly voice beside her and Céleste blinked into the misty blue eyes of the sweetest face she'd ever encountered. "Lady Russell won't eat you, I promise."

This lady was rather shorter and plumper than Aunt Seymour with thick white hair and a mischievous glint in her eyes. Dressed entirely in pale pink she put Céleste in mind of a slightly faded little doll.

"Hmmph."

The discouraging noise came from Seymour who was looking at Céleste with her lips set in a thin hard line. *Mon Dieu* she hadn't even opened her mouth yet. To her relief Alex came and stood beside her, his large presence giving a feeling of security that she knew was about to be taken from her. The thought made her look up at him and their eyes met. For a moment she believed every word that Henri had told her as those cool grey eyes seemed as full of every expression of regret and misery as her own, but it was all too quickly gone and he gave her a smile which was perfunctory at best.

"Aunt Dorothea has been looking forward to meeting you, Céleste."

"Oh, no, we are to be very dear friends so you must call me Dotty," the old lady said, squeezing her hand again. "Everybody does you know."

"They most certainly do not," Aunt Seymour snapped, making both her and Dotty jump.

"They do," Dotty whispered to her, holding tightly to her hand still.

Céleste tried to smile but her eyes began to fill and she blinked rapidly.

"Well then. Introductions are over and we should be going," Seymour said, her words more of an order than an announcement.

"Non!" Céleste cried out and then flushed, remembering herself as Aunt Seymour raised an eloquent eyebrow. "That is, I mean ... I 'ave just arrived and ... could I not ..."

Aunt Seymour looked at her closely, making Céleste flush a deeper crimson as the old lady's knowing gaze travelled from her to Alex.

"No," she said, her voice rather quieter. "I think we should leave now, before any greater damage is done."

"Damage?" Alex repeated, with a cool tone and Céleste looked up to see him frowning at his aunt.

"Yes, my Lord, *damage,"* Seymour repeated, her all too sharp eyes focused entirely on her nephew, and earl or not, Céleste didn't envy him the scrutiny. "A young, unwed lady spending any time in your company is likely to be ruined simply by association. If you truly want the girl to make an advantageous match you'll stay as far away from her as possible. Bad enough that your name linked to ours will raise eyebrows, even with our chaperonage. Still ..." She looked Céleste over and tutted as though she'd been in some way misinformed of the girl's suitability. "We must make the best of things I suppose."

"Oh, Seymour," Aunt Dotty said with her soft breathy voice. "Why the girl is a diamond, and don't pretend you can't see it as well we can."

Seymour cast Alex another deeply disapproving look and snorted. "Oh I see, it," she replied with a brittle tone. "I see it with perfect clarity I assure you."

Céleste looked back at Alex in confusion who looked in turn like he was about to suffer an apoplexy of some description.

"Aunt Seymour," he said, his tone polite and full of ice. "May I please have a word with you, *alone."* Despite the courtesy of his request it was very obviously a command, but his Aunt just nodded and stepped briskly to the door as though it had been her idea.

"You most certainly can."

Céleste watched as Alex followed Aunt Seymour out of the room.

"Don't worry, my dear," said Dotty, patting her hand with a fond expression. "Alex can handle Seymour." She gave a heavy sigh. "He's certainly had plenty of practise."

***

Alex led his aunt to his study where the old lady eyed him with a steely expression.

"Aunt Seymour you know how much I appreciate your help in this matter," he began, struggling to keep his temper in check. He owed the old lady deference for all that she'd done for him and the family at large, but dammit he would not allow her to disparage Céleste and he knew exactly what she'd been inferring. His aunt, however, snorted with disgust, interrupting him and shaking her head.

"I'm quite disgusted with you, Alex, to think that you would foist one of your light o' loves on us to pass off ..."

"That will be quite enough!"

He allowed himself a moment of satisfaction at having made his aunt jump and actually look a little startled.

"If you are implying that I would have the temerity to bring a woman here to you that I had used in such a way ..." His rage was such that he snapped his mouth shut before he could say something that truly would be unforgivable. He took a breath and turned his back on the outrageous old woman to try and gather his thoughts.

"You mean to tell me that she's an innocent and not some ladybird you've found in the gutter somewhere?" Seymour demanded, the incredulity in her voice quite telling enough.

Alex took a deep breath before he felt himself equal to the task of framing a polite reply. "I am telling you, *unequivocally,* that she is an innocent. I have not laid a hand on her and neither has anyone else." He took a breath and tried to dispel the memory of Céleste curled around his naked body in the filthy attic in Roscoff. That had been another world, another life, and it didn't make her any less innocent in his eyes.

"She's in love with you," Seymour said with her usual amount of tack and an uncanny ability to strike at the heart of whatever problem was presented to her. Alex thanked God, not for the first time, that she was supposed to be on his side.

"She's a foolish young girl," he said, with a wave of his hand, as though it was of little consequence. "She feels I have saved her and I suppose I have attained a rather heroic status in her mind. She'll forget that soon enough when other opportunities are presented to her." He avoided the all too sharp eyes of his Aunt and turned to look out of the window.

"Hmmmm."

"She needs help, Seymour," he said, his voice quiet. "She's lost everyone and everything. When I found her ..." He paused, and had to take a moment before he could continue without putting too much emotion in his voice. "She was fighting for survival, but with such pride and such ... such dignity." He turned to look at his aunt, holding her eyes this time. "She deserves your help and your compassion, like no one I have ever known."

His Aunt regarded him, her cool grey eyes the match of his own. Cut from the same cloth they had both inherited a tendency for remoteness and detachment, a family trait that had led to a reputation for utter ruthlessness that was entirely deserved. But where his ambitions and desires had twisted and led him down darker paths, Lady Seymour Russell was the height of respectability and the scourge of the *ton.* Nothing and no one had escaped her critical gaze until she had retired from the public eye ten years ago, broken-hearted by the apparent death of her beloved nephew. But Lawrence wasn't dead, and now Alex was giving her another reason to return to the world she had loved so dearly.

He stood still under her scrutiny and prayed he did not give away more than the fact that he admired Céleste and would help her if he could. In the end she nodded.

"Very well. I will do all in my power to create a success of her."

"Thank you, Aunt," he replied, releasing a breath he'd been unaware of holding, only too relieved that this hurdle at least had been crossed.

They returned to the drawing room and Alex was further heartened to see Céleste and Aunt Dotty with their heads together. He had known dear Dorothea would be unable to resist Céleste. The old lady was everything that was good and kind, and he knew that she would enjoy mothering Céleste as much as he hoped Céleste would enjoy her attentions.

Alex opened his mouth, intending to tell Céleste that it was time to go, but naturally Aunt Seymour beat him to it.

"Everything is settled then, Dorothea, and if we want to make the Inn before dark we must make haste." She stood over Aunt Dotty who was looking at Céleste with pity in her eyes. Alex watched, wrapped in misery as Seymour imperiously commanded them to their feet and ushered them from the room. Suddenly everything was happening too fast. He had thought there would be a little more time, a minute or two at least in which he could prepare his heart for the moment in which she would leave his life. But even knowing this moment was coming, even having arranged that this moment *would* come, he found he wasn't ready. The word 'perhaps' flew to his lips but died before he could suggest any notion that they stop for tea, spend the night, stay for a few days ... What was the point in prolonging the agony after all?

They paused on the threshold of the house and made their goodbyes. Alex dutifully kissed his aunt's cheeks, submitting to a hug from Dotty whose eyes were teary. The old lady did hate goodbyes so.

And then there was just Céleste.

She couldn't look at him and he could see she was fighting tears.

"Thank you, my Lord," she said, so quiet and formal that he wanted to shake her and tell her to stop. He wasn't 'my lord', not for her, he was her *contrebandier* and any other ridiculous endearment she wanted to label him, he didn't care. Anything but my Lord. "I must thank you for everything that you 'ave done for me."

"Dear me no, we must do something about that dreadful accent," Seymour said with a tut of disapproval.

No! Alex howled inwardly. Don't change her, don't you dare change a single thing. He clenched his fists, knowing he was being ridiculous. This was why he had sought the woman's help in the first place, so she *could* change Céleste, so that she could be shaped and moulded into a woman who was acceptable to the *ton;* into a woman who wouldn't want him any more. His heart was bleeding in his chest. It had to be, for why ever else was he in such pain? That poor unused organ had been ignored for so many cold and lonely years and now it wouldn't shut up. *Tell her, tell her, you fool! Tell her you love her and you'll be nothing without her. Tell her there will be no joy, no light, no possible happiness without her. Get on your damn knees and beg her to stay with you!*

"Goodbye then, Céleste, I know you'll be happy with my aunts. They will take great care of you."

Better care than he could.

She looked up at him and met his eyes and he knew, in that moment, that he was irreparably and irrevocably changed. His heart was, had always been, would always be hers and hers alone and he was destined to die a lonely and bitter old man without her in his life. A single tear tracked down her cheek and he didn't know how he would survive the next moments, and then she threw her arms around his neck, clinging to him and sobbing.

"Au revoir, mon contrebandier," she whispered as her arms clung about him.

He knew the aunts were watching but he couldn't care, for just a moment he wrapped his arms around her and returned her embrace. He turned his face into the soft curls about her face and inhaled her scent, imprinting the memory of honeysuckle and sunlight on his senses as it would be all he had left to him.

She pressed a sweet kiss to his cheek and then let him go, turning and walking away, and getting into the carriage without a backwards glance. His aunts stared at him, he knew they did, but he couldn't find the will to care that he had shocked them as they finally turned and followed Céleste. And he watched with the feeling of a man drowning, as the only hold he had on anything good was borne away from him, on into a world where he had no right to follow.

Turning he walked back into the empty house, his footsteps echoing along the great hall as he made his way to his study and grabbed the first decanter that came to hand. He intended to get very drunk, very fast, and he intended to stay that way for a long, long time.

Chapter 20

"Wherein two months have passed, and a broken heart is in no way mended, but a little lightened."

Dorothea and Seymour stood side by side at the drawing room window and looked down at the charming picture in the garden. Seymour frowned, though, knowing there was a deep and heartfelt sadness beneath the superficial beauty. Céleste was walking with the little spaniel pup barking and chasing around in circles at her feet. Dressed all in yellow muslin with embroidered daisies over the bodice, Céleste looked as though she too was blooming along with the rest of the garden which was a riot of spring bulbs and bright colours. She picked up a ball and threw it for her excitable pup. But her expression was wan and listless, and she had done everything the Aunts had asked of her and had sat, uncomplaining through endless lessons on deportment and the proper behaviour of a young lady. She had also made a great effort to lose her French accent, though that was proving harder to accomplish.

"She's dreadfully lonely," Dorothea said with a sigh.

"Hmmm," Seymour replied, non-committal, her grey eyes intent on the apparently bucolic scene. "Have you heard from Alex?"

Dorothea shook her head, her faded ringlets more white than blonde now dancing around her face. "No, not since you scolded him for trying to interfere."

Seymour tutted and turned away from the window, returning to the plush sofa and gave her attention to the tea things that had been laid out for them. With neat and precise movements that were at odds with her advancing years she followed the ritual with meticulous attention. Admiring the pretty white blue and gold Limoges porcelain tea set which her nephew had sent her, as thanks for her help with Céleste's entrée into polite society, she prepared a cup to her sister's preferred taste and handed it to her.

"I did not scold him," she said, returning to the conversation now the important business of preparing tea had been attended to with due diligence. "I merely pointed out that there was little benefit in sending her to us if he was going to criticise our efforts at every turn."

She glanced up at Dorothea to find she had pursed her lips in a familiar fashion. It meant she disagreed with her sister but was unwilling to speak out.

"What?" Seymour demanded, setting her tea cup down with slightly more of a clatter than she had intended.

Dorothea opened her mouth, clearly hesitant.

"Oh, honestly, Dorothea, I won't eat you!"

Her sister gave her a look that clearly disputed that fact but decided to brave it anyway. "I just happen to agree that her accent is rather charming."

Seymour scowled and Dorothea rushed on. "I mean to say that ... Yes she must learn the correct manner of speech and appropriate subjects of conversation ..."

Snorting, Seymour shook her head in remembered outrage. The girl had shocked them both to their bones when she had accidentally dropped a tea cup the day before and cursed in a manner that rendered them both speechless.

Dorothea blushed. "Yes, well she certainly does need ... polishing."

Seymour gave a dark chuckle that made her sister stare into the tea cup.

"But I agree with Alex. I don't think she should completely lose her accent."

With a sniff of displeasure Seymour picked up her own tea cup once more. "Well, as the child has made little sign of progress so far I doubt either of you will have any cause for complaint on that score."

They sat in silence for a little while, both sipping their tea.

"I had a charming letter from Henri," Dorothea ventured, clearly hoping this was a safer topic of conversation.

"Yes," murmured Seymour, whose own letter had filled her with concern. She had previously made it clear to Henri that she was well aware of her eldest nephew's exploits in the smuggling world, and that she was wholly unconvinced by the story of Lawrence's return to the family. That particular episode she had let go, too delighted by his miraculous return to want to know the sordid details of which she imagined there were plenty. Her sweet sister might be content to look at the world through rose tinted spectacles but she was made of sterner stuff. Seymour's own husband, Lord Russell, God rest him, had been a dashing sort of man, not unlike her nephews. And she had been well aware of many of his more shocking exploits. But Henri's letter to her had made some subtle hints that alluded to something she herself had suspected when they had collected Céleste at Tregothnan. Alex was in love with the girl.

Really it was not the match she would have hoped for him. Charming as the girl was, and for all her ... disadvantages, she did seem to be a lovely creature, but she was a *foreigner*. Not only that, she was *French!* Seymour shuddered inwardly at the idea. No, no, it really was far from what she had hoped for Alex. But then she had paraded a veritable feast of the best of female English society under his nose since the time he reached his majority and the vexing creature hadn't shown the slightest inclination of marrying any of them. Of course now he'd done his reputation such irreparable damage that any well bred girl would blush and stutter and make a cake of themselves if they got within half a ballroom of him; even if their determined mothers forced them to endure the ordeal for the possibility of capturing one of the most eligible bachelors in the Kingdom.

But if, as she herself had suspected and Henri had alluded to, Alex did have feelings for the child ... it might be her last chance to see him properly wed and fulfilling his duty to provide an heir to the Earldom. She gave a heavy sigh. One thing was abundantly clear. Céleste was pining for Alex.

The vivacious and lively girl that Alex had described in his letters was far removed from the forlorn little creature that haunted their comfortable home and garden and only spoke when spoken to. Dorothea was right. The child was lonely and miserable and there at least they could do something. Now the worst of her obvious faults had been ironed out it was time she met some people of her own age, and perhaps that would restore the bloom to her cheeks.

Seymour returned her attention to her sister. "I've asked Aubrey to come and stay."

"Oh!" Dorothea's tea cup clattered down on its saucer, making Seymour wince. "How delightful! Oh, now we shall have some fun, how wonderful to have young people in the house."

Seymour gave her sister an indulgent smile. Dorothea had never married, thanks to an ill-fated love affair. It had been a devastating blow to dear Dotty, but she had never become bitter or jaded, but had loved her extended family through Seymour with every bit of devotion and rather more demonstrative affection than their mother. Aubrey was her youngest grandson, and at the age of twenty two would be a fine companion to Céleste. He was known for his sense of humour and for getting himself in all manner of scrapes and his father had made it clear that he would be happy to be rid of the 'shiftless blighter' for a few weeks.

"When does he arrive?" Dorothea demanded, her faded blue eyes alight with happiness.

"This afternoon," Seymour said with a placid smile. Well whatever happened, her plans were made, and she must see what she could make of them.

***

Céleste looked at the letter in her hand and sighed. Despite Henri's advice to wait at least three months before she wrote to Alex- *make the devil wait, dear* - she had given in last week and penned a short and very proper missive to him. Thanks to the aunts her written English had made great strides and she wasn't so very ashamed to put pen to paper. She could, of course, have written in French but she wanted to show him that she was applying herself diligently to her studies to become a proper English lady. For she had no intention of giving up on Alex. None whatsoever. If a sophisticated and worldly English woman was what he wanted, then that was how she would style herself. Though try as she might her accent seemed to mock her. No matter how many times Seymour schooled her in the correct pronunciation of 'the, this and that' it came out 'zhe, zhis and zhat'. It was very frustrating.

But nonetheless she had wanted Alex to know she was trying hard, and with that in mind had written a short letter. Thanking him for everything he had done for her, extolling the virtues of his aunts and life in Hertfordshire, she had omitted to tell him that she had met no one and had hardly left the house, unwilling for him to know that Aunt Seymour still appeared to be heartily ashamed of her. It was very formal and proper and sounded just as Aunt Seymour had said it should.

In return she had received an even briefer reply. Thanking her for her enquiries, applauding her endeavours and wishing her further success, it had been stark and formal and had reduced her to tears.

With an unladylike curse that would have had the aunts gasping in horror she stuffed the letter away and walked to the front door. The one joy she could find at least in the monotony of life without Alex was the beautiful gardens. She had walked every inch of the extensive grounds and spent as much time out of doors as her studies and the aunts would allow. She paused to call Bandit, but the puppy looked up at her with one weary eye from the sanctuary of his basket and went back to sleep. Even the poor dog could only take so many walks in the fresh air it appeared. With a sigh she buttoned her new yellow silk pelisse, and rammed on her bonnet with a grimace - *"Céleste, a lady never walks without a bonnet!"*

Snatching up an umbrella she turned smartly ... and walked straight into a masculine chest.

"Ooof!"

"Devil take it!"

She looked up ... and up, at the tall and rather dashing figure of young man with hazel eyes who was looking down at her with consternation. He was dressed in what she was now familiar with as being the very height of fashion after many hours poring over fashion plates in *The Ladies' Monthly Museum* and *La Belle Assemblée.* Indeed to her newly trained eyes the intricate folds of his necktie *a la trone d'amour,* set with one small diamond, the cut of coat and pantaloons, a waistcoat that embraced lovingly an athletic form, the single fob that hung to one side of it and a pair of gleaming Hessians to complete the picture, he looked perfectly splendid, a true Corinthian to be sure. And then he spoiled it by opening his mouth.

"Who are you?" he demanded.

Annoyed by his tone, as he had apparently walked in unannounced, she put up her chin. "I might ask you the same question, *monsieur,"* she replied with as much disdain as she could manage from a good foot beneath his notice.

"Good Lord, a frog!" he exclaimed in astonishment. "What the devil is a frog doing here? And with old Boney back and stirring up trouble again!"

"A ... *what* did you just call me?" Céleste replied, wide-eyed with indignation.

For a moment the insolent fellow had the grace to look a little discomforted.

"Ummm, well, you know, a frog, froggy, that's to say ... er French."

"How dare you!" she replied, and hit him over the head with her umbrella, devastating the arrangement of his hair from an artful Brutus to something rather more dishevelled and rakish.

"What the ..." The young man stared at her in appalled shock but she had endured too many weeks of misery, too many weeks of solitude and loneliness and ... anger at being sent away. Her temper had been lit. Advancing on him with a tirade of obscene French she waved her umbrella in a threatening manner.

"N-now, just wait a moment," the young buck stuttered, before deciding retreat was the better part of valour and running into the house with Céleste at his heels.

He ground to a halt in the drawing room, apparently deciding it was too embarrassing to run any further away from a diminutive young lady, even if she was wielding an umbrella. Though Céleste noticed he had the remarkable foresight to keep a chair between them.

"We seem to have got off on the wrong foot ..." he ventured, eyeing her with alarm as she rounded the chair. He backed up, away from her, and promptly pitched over the sofa table as it hit the back of his knees. With a yelp of alarm he landed in a crumpled heap between the table and the sofa. Céleste stared at him, with his shiny Hessians still hanging over the rosewood table, his arms akimbo and a look of bewilderment in his hazel eyes, and she began to laugh.

At first it was a ladylike giggle, in the manner she had been instructed, but the indignation on his face was too much to bear and within moments she was shrieking like a banshee with tears running down her face. A moment later, however, she shrieked for a different reason as her feet were swept from under her and she landed hard on her behind in a flurry of muslin and silk.

With fury she rounded on the perpetrator of this outrage, to find the bright hazel eyes full of mirth. She paused, rage warring with amusement, until the ridiculousness of the situation tickled her too much and she began to giggle again. In moments the two of them were breathless with laughter.

"I say," the young man demanded as he extricated himself from the floor and hauled her to her feet in a rather ungainly manner. "If you don't mind me asking, who are you and what are you doing with the ancient ones?"

Céleste sniffed and tried to regain a little of her forgotten dignity. Holding out her hand she gave a stiff curtsey. "I am Célestine Lavelle, *La Comtesse de Valrey."*

"Well I'll eat my hat," he replied with a lift of one eyebrow. "I'm Aubrey Russell, Seymour's grandson, you see? Anyway, enchanted, I'm sure. But why are you *here?"*

"Because Lady Russell and Lady Sinclair are preparing me for my come out to society," Céleste replied, smoothing down her rumpled skirts with care.

"Hmmm," Aubrey replied, amusement twitching the corners of his mouth. "But who's preparing society?"

Céleste huffed at him in disgust. "You are a very rude boy!"

Aubrey snorted and gave a short bark of laughter. "Boy is it? 'Pon rep, you're going out of your way to set up my bristles aren't you? And as for *rude,* well that's the pot calling the kettle black and no mistake!" He wagged a finger at her. "I don't know a word of frog, save for a few choice phrases I picked up at Eton, but I know that was not the kind of language you've been learning from m'grandmother!"

Céleste's face fell as she realised this frightful boy could cause her all sorts of trouble if he chose to.

"Oh don't look so Friday-faced," he said, waving a hand at her and flopping down on the sofa with a sigh and the air of someone who was at home. "I'm not about to give you away. Lord knows I'm never in her good books, always scolding me for something or other."

"Merci, Monsieur," she said with a grateful sigh. "Lady Russell is finding me rather a trial I fear."

"Oh, call me Aubrey do, seems like we're family near as, and I can imagine she is," he replied, staring at her with interest as she surveyed him in return. He was really a very good looking young man. Hazel eyes and thick hair with a slightly auburn tint that curled over his forehead highlighted a very pleasing countenance. One particular wayward lock fell close his eye as he spoke and she itched to push it back out of his way. Added to a tall, lean frame with broad shoulders and a strong square jaw and rather endearing dimples when he smiled, he was really very pleasant to look at. With a sigh she wished that such charms could ever be appealing to her, when a certain dark-haired, grey-eyed devil was never going to give her a second glance.

"So," he said, recalling her attention to him. "How did you come to be here?"

She shrugged and sat down on the sofa opposite him. "Alex brought me," she said, quite forgetting all of Aunt Seymour's lessons in the society of the frank and open manner of her new guest, and referring to him in far too familiar a fashion.

"Alex?" he replied, frowning. She watched, wondering how on earth he could forget his own cousin, and then his eyes widened. "You mean Falmouth? *He* brought you here?"

"Oui, I mean, yes. Lord Falmouth, 'e brought me."

"Good Lord." He seemed overcome by this information and just sat staring at her for a moment. "Were your family caught up in all the ..." He grimaced and drew a finger across his neck in a rather menacing fashion.

Céleste nodded. "Oui, my uncle was be'eaded, Maman and Papa ran away." She sighed, feeling altogether gloomy now. "Papa died in the war, Maman killed 'erself."

Aubrey's eyes had grown wide and he appeared to settle down and make himself more comfortable. "Well then, don't stop there," he started, waving an impatient hand at her. "Start at the beginning. Where do you come from? What happened to you? How did you meet Falmouth?"

Céleste looked up at him in surprise but his expression was one of rapt attention, and so she settled down, removed her bonnet ... and told him.

Chapter 21

"Wherein letters say more than words on a page."

July 25th

Glebe House. Hertfordshire

Dear Lord Falmouth,

I hope you are in good health and must thank you most kindly for the parcel which arrived safely this morning.

I did very much enjoy the marzipan fruits which reminded me of my birthday and such a happy time with dear Henri and your brother. I will endeavour not to eat them all in one sitting as the Modiste which Aunt Seymour frequents would much enjoy sticking me with pins to illustrate her dismay at any extra inches.

Aunt Seymour and Aunt Dotty were also very pleased with the Champagne and the brandy wine and send their warmest regards.

I was very happy last evening to see so many friends around the dinner table here. Indeed for the first time in my life I truly have friends, which is a very fine thing, and something else I must thank you for with all my heart. Aubrey was there of course, and Lord FitzWalter and his sister, and Viscount Trenchard and his good friend Lord Blakeney, and a host of other names which will no doubt bore you terribly so I shan't mention them. Indeed although I am not officially out it seems Aunt Seymour trusts me to conduct myself with decorum on these happy evenings. Miracles do happen.

In truth the aunts seem to enjoy these lively evenings as much as I do, especially dearest Dorothea who is quite a favourite among all the young people as she is so drole.

Bandit, I regret to inform you, is a perfect little beast however. Last Friday whilst I was away at a picnic with the aunts and Aubrey, he chewed my favourite yellow satin slippers. I was really very put out but then he did sulk so prettily I was obliged to forgive him.

I hope you see that my English is much better now, in fact Aunt Seymour almost told me it wasn't too dreadful, so you see I have made great progress.

Your sincere friend,

Célestine Lavelle

Alex stared down at the letter on his desk and tried to bring to mind the visage of his cousin. A lanky boy who stuttered if Alex so much as looked in his direction was unearthed from a long-forgotten memory and he heaved a sigh of relief. Then he took a moment to consider how many years had passed since he had last seen Aubrey Russell and a tightness began in his chest. It had to be five ... no, seven years. A boy could change a great deal in seven years. Cursing under his breath, Alex refilled his glass and took a healthy swallow, relishing the burn as the fine liquor slid down his throat.

So what if she was spending time with the boy ... *man.* So what if the names on that list were more male than female. He had no doubt his aunts were keeping a close eye on things. Besides Aubrey's father Baron Russell was not a wealthy man. A penniless countess was hardly going to be a match he would welcome.

But what if Céleste loved the boy and he wouldn't or couldn't marry her? The tightness in his chest increased and he rubbed irritably at the spot over his heart.

There wasn't a chance in hell that the wretched boy ... *man,* wasn't in love with her. He'd have to be blind. He felt a wave of jealousy as he imagined the two of them sneaking off at the picnic, perhaps just disappearing out of sight of the aunts for a moment or two to steal a kiss. His throat grew tight and suddenly it was hard to swallow. He knew, at heart, that Céleste wouldn't be interested in a few sweet little kisses.

In the time they'd spent together Alex had been all too aware that she was a creature of fire and passion. She needed to be schooled by a man who knew what he was about, taught just how those passions could be mastered and indulged, and some wet behind the ears boy would never be able to handle her. He swore, a long low string of obscenities that made him feel no better at all. He hoped to God his aunts were keeping a close eye on the girl because if he discovered Aubrey or any other young fool had laid a finger on her, there wouldn't be enough pieces left to bury by the time he'd finished with them.

He took a deep breath and tried to assure himself that it was just his imagination getting the better of him. His imagination had become a trial of the worst kind over the last months. Not just for imaginings like these which were frequent and humiliating, but for heated dreams that visited him at night and left him hard and aching and numb with loneliness. Dreams in which Céleste ran back to him and he succumbed with every expression of his devotion that could be found. Dreams where he taught her what it was she had wanted from him, where he worshipped every inch of her beautiful skin with the fervour of a zealous and devout supplicant.

He forced the tantalising images from his mind before they could take a hold of him and humiliate him further.

At least she had spoken to him with a little less formality this time. The cool tone of her address in some of her previous letters had sunk him in a sea of despondency of which there had appeared no escape.

In the first weeks after she had left for Hertfordshire he had tried to pick up the threads of his life. Visiting his clubs and even paying a call to one of his mistresses. But the clubs seemed to offer him nothing that he wanted, other than the ability to get drunk which he could accomplish quite satisfactorily by himself without leaving home, and he had realised his mistake on visiting the dark eyed-beauty he had ignored for so many weeks before the door had even opened to him. With cool words of regret he had severed relations with both her and every other woman with whom he'd had an understanding, offering generous recompense for the loss of their protector and his change of heart, but no explanation.

And so here he was still, alone in the echoing walls of Tregothnan, with a decanter of brandy, a letter from Céleste, and a pain in his heart that simply wouldn't be ignored.

With care he refolded the letter and put it carefully with the small pile of her other correspondence. He would reply to her when his emotions were less ragged, so God alone knew when that would be.

He glanced up at the clock and decided to go and meet the men of the Flighty Susan. There was to be another run tonight, though things were getting hot along the coast. Now that Napoleon had finally been brought to account once and for all, after the folly of his last gasp and one hundred days of power, the government would be turning its attentions forcefully back in the smugglers' direction. He had been inclined to tell the men to leave it be for a week or two to let things cool off.

The church vault where they stored much of their goods before it found a home was well-stocked. His inventory yesterday had revealed the place filled to the rafters with casks and kegs of brandy and tobacco and enough silk to dress every fashionable miss of the *ton* in any colour of their choosing many times over. But the crew were eager to go and damn it but he was sick of staring at the walls of his empty home and wondering what the hell Céleste was doing, if she ever thought of him at all ... or if he had been resigned to the recesses of her memories as someone to whom she owed a debt of gratitude but nothing more. The pain of that idea made him catch his breath, though it would be everything that he had hoped and planned for her. By God but he was the biggest hypocrite going. Because if everything turned out the way he had professed to hope for her ... it would break his heart.

***

July 30th

Glebe House, Hertfordshire.

Dear Lord Falmouth,

I must thank you most sincerely for your gift. You are all kindness. I have never in my life seen slippers in so many colours. It looked as though a rainbow had tangled itself in the drawing room by the time I had all the pairs laid out side by side. Bandit's eyes were positively alive with the challenge, but I will endeavour to keep them safely out of his questing jaws. Perhaps you should send more marzipan to distract him? Of course now you have set me the daunting task of acquiring a dress in every shade to match the shoes. I hope you are pleased with yourself?

Is it as dreadfully hot in Cornwall as it is here in Hertfordshire? Your aunts are finding it very disagreeable and keep much indoors. Of course Aubrey is wonderful at keeping all of our spirits up, even when the heat makes our tempers a little fraught. Though you cannot imagine that I would ever lose my temper, I hope? I am become far too much the lady to ever do something so indelicate as to use language unbecoming to my station, especially not in French! That would be 'de trop' and far out of character for La Comtesse de Valrey. You see how I have become a very proper English Miss?

Please find enclosed a small drawing of Bandit. I thought you might like to see how the dreadful creature has grown. I am acquiring skills that Aunt Seymour feels necessary to my education. Sadly the pianoforte is far beyond my comprehension and the aunts have admitted defeat, to the relief of all of our nerves. However I do have some small ability with a pencil and brush. I hope you like it.

Your sincere friend,

Célestine Lavelle

August 1st. Tregothnan. Cornwall.

Dear Lady Lavelle,

Please find along with this letter twelve boxes of marzipan. I hope this will keep Bandit from eating my previous gifts, but will not incur the wrath of Aunt Seymour's Modiste and her pins. I have also sent silk in various shades to help you in the arduous task I unwittingly set you of matching dresses to slippers.

Indeed it has been a very hot summer here also, though there is always a refreshing breeze near the coast which is most agreeable. I have also been spending as much time as possible at sea so have escaped much of it.

Please would you forward my esteemed cousin, Mr. Russell, my sincere regards and a wish that he might call upon me in the near future. It has been many years since we last met and I would relish the opportunity to further our acquaintance.

It would appear you may add modesty to your ever-growing list of accomplishments. The drawing of Bandit is perfectly charming. I can see every glimmer of his recalcitrant nature in the expression you have captured. Your rendering of his character shows a sharp eye and considerable skill. I hope it will please to you know that I have had it framed and placed in my study.

With sincere regard, your friend and guardian,

Falmouth.

***

Céleste looked up to see Aubrey staring at her with undisguised horror.

"The devil I will!" he retorted.

She blinked at him, perplexed by his manner. "But why? Alex 'as asked you to go and visit 'im. Why would you not go?"

He sat with his back against the ancient apple tree and bit into a small green fruit, grimacing as it was too early yet and the apples were far from ripe. "Because if there was one man who has always been able to put the fear of God in me, it's Falmouth," he replied, tossing the apple out into the garden and setting Bandit chasing off after it.

"Alex?" Céleste replied, laughing at him and waving a delicate, hand-painted fan to create something resembling a cool breeze. "Alex isn't the slightest bit frightening."

Aubrey gaped at her, his eyes narrowing. "Are you sure we're talking about the same fellow? A big hulking brute with a sneer, a superior attitude, and eyes that can freeze your soul with one glance?"

"Bah!" Céleste exclaimed with a dismissive wave of her fan. "Of course 'e looks this way, 'e is an earl, but you must ignore that. It means nothing."

"Easy to say when you're female and are purported to look like Botticelli's Venus," Aubrey grumbled. "You'd have the devil himself on his knees, so it's no surprise you have Falmouth wrapped around your finger." He gave her a stern look. "And you're not supposed to say, *bah!* Your accent is as bad as ever when you talk to me."

She glared at him, not sure which remark to respond to first. *"Bah!* I will say, *bah* and zhis and zhat and speak 'owever I wish as it is only you, Aubrey, and you don't count."

"Well I like that!" Aubrey replied, with a look of reproach.

"And who says I look like this Venus? 'Ow dare they! The woman is naked," she hissed at him in outrage.

"Blakeney made the observation, though Trenchard was quick enough to agree with him," he said, scowling.

Céleste huffed and then looked at Aubrey with growing interest. "Is that why Lord Blakeney had a black eye when 'e was 'ere last?"

Aubrey flushed and looked uncomfortable. "Well dash it all, a fellow can't allow chaps to go likening his grandmother's guest to a ... a ... well he can't that's all."

Céleste beamed at him and leaned over, giving him a kiss on the cheek.

"Thank you, Aubrey, you are *très galant."*

"You're welcome," Aubrey replied, nodding.

"But why did you not give Viscount Trenchard a black eye also?" she asked with a little moue of displeasure.

Aubrey tutted. "Because it dashed well hurt," he replied, presenting his bruised knuckles for her inspection. She gave him an indulgent smile, the kind she might have reserved for a beloved younger brother. For that was really how she saw him. For all that he was three years her senior, his life had been far more sheltered than hers, and she often felt that she needed to protect him from realities of life that he seemed completely oblivious to. She gave his knuckles a gentle pat in thanks for his gallantry but then remembered a darker night, and a darker man. She remembered taking Alex's large, scarred hand to her mouth and kissing each knuckle in turn until he snatched it away from her. She gave a heavy sigh as longing threatened to overwhelm her. It had been six long and lonely months since she had last seen him and every day she felt she was further away from ever making him hers.

"You're very wrong in any case, Aubrey," she said, looking out across the orchard and the dappled shadows that sheltered them from the worst of the scorching sun. "Alex is only being kind. He doesn't care about me." She couldn't seem to help the pitiful sound of her words but regretted them as she glanced up to see Aubrey giving her a very odd look.

"Fellows don't go about giving ladies dozens of pairs of shoes if they don't care about them," he said with a reproving tone that was quite out of character. "Nor sweetmeats, and acres of silk! You do know that it was wholly inappropriate?"

"Why?" she demanded, cross on Alex's behalf, even though her heart had lifted at his words.

"Because you don't go giving unmarried ladies gifts of personal items, that's why!" he said, sounding really quite cross, though at her or at Alex she wasn't quite sure.

Céleste frowned. "But Aunt Seymour allowed it."

"Yes." Aubrey scowled and began to pull up tufts of dry grass in a distracted manner. "And that's dashed odd as well." He looked up at her and she saw intelligence glimmering in the warm hazel eyes. For all that Aubrey played up to his carefree, devil may care image, she knew that at heart he was a serious and loyal friend to her. "You're in love with him aren't you?" he said.

She felt a flush spread from her cheeks, down across her neck and picked up her fan, hiding behind it and waving it with quick, anxious waves of her wrist. "Aubrey! What ever do you mean?

Don't be so foolish ... I ... I ..." She huffed and snapped the fan shut. "Oh dear, is it still so obvious?"

Aubrey snorted. "Rather."

"Oh, Aubrey," she wailed. I'm so un'appy. I miss 'im dreadfully. You see 'e isn't at all the dreadfully cold man you think 'e is. Well, not to me at least."

She looked over at Aubrey who was regarding her with a mixture of appalled curiosity and pity. "Does he love you then?"

Céleste sighed and wished that was a question she could answer with any kind of certainty. "I was led to believe, by someone close to 'im that ... that he does, yes, but ..." She threw up her hands in frustration. "But 'e 'as left me alone for six month, and I think perhaps 'e will forget me."

Aubrey raised an enquiring eyebrow. "By sending you dozens of boxes of marzipan fruits, three dozen pairs of silk slippers and framing the drawing you sent him and putting it somewhere he can see it every day? Oh yes," he replied with a shrewd glint in his eyes. "Those are the actions of a man who's totally indifferent to you."

Céleste blinked at him and sat up on her knees, hardly daring to hope. "You ... you think perhaps 'e ... 'e is in love with me?"

Aubrey laughed and shook his head. "I don't see why he shouldn't be. It seems to be an affliction suffered by any other male who gets within a mile of you."

Céleste huffed and shook her head. "Oh, yes but they are just silly young men, they are of no importance."

"Ooof!" he said, striking his hand over his heart. "If I repeated those words there would be hearts breaking from here to London. God help the male of the species when you make your come out, that's all I'll say, you heartless creature."

"Oh, Aubrey, don't tease me so, you are really very provoking today." She picked up her fan again and began to wave it in an irritable manner.

"Well then, so you're after an earl are you?" he said, clearly determined to tease her some more. She glared at him through narrowed eyes.

"If you are implying I love 'im for 'is fortune or title I will strike you," she scolded, wielding the fan at him with an air of menace.

Aubrey held out his hands in the manner of someone who knew well she wasn't jesting. "I wouldn't dare! Besides I know you better than that." He lay back down on the picnic blanket with a sigh, squinting up into the sunlight. "But what are you going to do about it? I mean if he was going to offer for you he would have done it by now wouldn't he?"

She gave him a very dark look as he echoed her own fears back at her. *"Non,* because 'e thinks I am too young and innocent."

Aubrey choked and was obliged to sit up again, gasping for breath. "Sorry," he said, waving a hand as she moved to pound him on the back. "Sorry, I didn't mean to," he replied, looking rueful as she glared at him. "I mean I know you are but ..."

He shrugged and she knew he was remembering the stories she'd told him about her life, especially her time working at Madame Maxime's. He had been at turns outraged, amused, thoroughly scandalised and full of admiration for her. He had also made her promise, on pain of death, to never, *ever* repeat the story to another living soul as long as she lived.

"Oui," she said with a shrug. "You are quite right. I am far from the sweet little innocent I should be, and yet he insists on believing that I am." She gave another hopeless sigh and started with surprise as he covered her hand with his own.

"No, Céleste, Falmouth has the right of it. Despite everything, you are both sweet and remarkably innocent in many ways," he said, his voice soft. "Any fool can see that."

She smiled at him and squeezed his hand. "Oh, Aubrey, why can't I fall in love with you, it would be so much more convenient."

Aubrey snatched his hand back and affected a look of utter horror. "Good Lord, what an appalling notion, I forbid you to ever repeat it again."

Céleste laughed, knowing and secretly thankful for the fact that he looked on her with nothing more than sisterly affection. For she was discovering that having gentlemen declaring their undying love for you and spouting sonnets at every turn was really very wearying.

Chapter 22

"Wherein recklessness brings misery and hope."

"Mousy!" Lawrence regarded his former quartermaster with sincere pleasure as the big man stood in the doorway of his study. "Well this is a surprise, come in, come in."

Lawrence ushered the man into the room and frowned as he noticed the man was ill at ease. "Well don't look so terrified, Henri is taking walk around the gardens and I am fairly sure that Annie is attending her so you're safe for the moment."

Mousy snorted and shook his head. "Nah, t'aint that, Capt'n, though I'd as soon not see Annie, t'is true. She ain't best pleased with me at the moment."

Lawrence raised an eyebrow and gestured for Mousy to sit as he took a chair himself. "Well if it isn't Annie that's brought you back to France looking so shifty, what is it?"

"It's 'is lordship, Capt'n," Mousy said, never one to prevaricate.

"Oh?"

"Aye, 'e's been shot."

"What?" Lawrence was up and out of his chair, fear lancing through him as Mousy raised his hands.

"'E's alright, 'e'll live," Mousy said, rubbing the back of his neck with a ham sized fist. "This time," he added with a dark expression.

Lawrence let out a breath as the Mousy's words registered.

"You're sure? It isn't serious?"

Mousy shrugged. "Got 'im in the arm, broke it but the doc reckons it'll mend clean as long as 'e lets it rest."

Lawrence snorted, knowing how likely it was that Alex would be inclined to do anything of the sort. "What did you mean?" he asked, looking at Mousy with concern. "This time?"

He watched as the hulking figure of his ex-quartermaster settled himself more comfortably on the fine chair he had managed to fit on. The elegant rosewood legs looked as though they might shatter under his bulk at any moment.

"Well," Mousy began, his ruddy face serious. "T'aint really my place to say but ..."

"Oh, spit it out, man," Lawrence snapped. "You've clearly got something to say and I trust your judgement in all things, you know that. So let's hear it."

Mousy let out a breath and nodded. "The night 'e was shot. I tol' 'im not to come. Things are getting harder, ye see. The Revenue 'ave got more men, an they're gettin' canny. T'is a great risk now, bringin' in a run. More 'n ever afore. Now for me 'n the lads, 'tis our way of life one way or another. We ain't got option to do nought else. But yer brother ..."

"Is putting himself at risk for no good reason?" Lawrence surmised, with a feeling akin to ice water sliding down his spine.

"Aye, that's about the long n' the short o' it."

Lawrence got up and poured them both a drink, putting the glass in Mousy's hand as he returned to his seat. "Henri has expressed a wish to return to England for the birth," he said, staring down into the tawny liquid with a thoughtful expression. "If we are to go then we must leave in the next few days so it appears I will be able to speak to my idiot brother before he gets himself killed."

He looked up to see a weight fall away from Mousy's huge shoulders. "Thank God," he said, with obvious relief. "I done what I can, Capt'n, but I don't know 'im like I know you, an what with 'im being an earl andall ... I'm always tryin' to watch me tongue."

Lawrence snorted with amusement. "Well then, I must return for no other reason than to see you try your hand at diplomacy."

Mousy grimaced and knocked back his drink in one large swallow. "Laugh it up while ye may, 'is lordship might get a sight more respect, but if ye think I won't tell ye when ye'r being a fat-headed numbskull ye've got another think comin'." Lawrence laughed as Mousy got to his feet and executed a mocking bow. "Capt'n," the big man said with a grave tone.

Reaching out to clasp Mousy's hand he shook it and gave the man a warm smile. "Thank you, Mousy, for coming to tell me."

Mousy shrugged and nodded. "Didn't want the stupid bugger t' get 'is head blowed off fer no good reason."

Lawrence watched Mousy duck out of the corridor and practically run through the gardens before his wife's marriage-hungry maid caught sight of him. With a heavy sigh he wondered what the devil he was supposed to do about his older brother and his escalating recklessness. He was only too aware of what lay at the heart of the problem, but he wasn't sure what the hell he was supposed to do about it.

***

August 25th. Glebe House. Hertfordshire.

Dear Lord Falmouth,

Sir, I am very, very put out with you. I have heard just this morning that you have been injured and your arm is broke! Not only that but that it happened a full three weeks ago and you have mentioned nothing of it to me. I had hoped you considered me your trusted friend; how could you leave me in such ignorance of your pain. I am deeply wounded that you would not confide such a thing to me. I demand that you write to me by return and reassure me as to your well being.

Your sincere friend,

Célestine Lavelle.

August 28th Tregothnan. Cornwall

My dear Lady Lavelle,

Please forgive me if I have caused you any distress. I assure you that it was as far from my intent as is possible to imagine. I am indeed quite well excepting the broken arm, happily not my right, which I am assured will mend with no problem if left to its own devices. I must admit at this point that the injury was entirely the result of my own foolishness and stubborn nature (of which I believe you are well acquainted) and this perhaps is why I strove to keep the matter to myself. I can, in utter truthfulness, assure you that I would never for a moment doubt the sincerity of your friendship, nor I hope would you doubt the value and esteem in which I hold the honour of such a friend.

Your sincere friend and guardian,

Falmouth.

***

"Get off me, you blithering idiot!" Alex roared at the hapless doctor who had been foolish enough as to try and examine his broken arm to see how it was mending.

The good doctor blanched but returned to his dignity in the space of a few moments, having been well acquainted with both his lordship and a variety of his injuries since the earl had been in short trousers and had attended him when he returned from the battle of Trafalgar. Alex scowled at him nonetheless, fed up with being poked and prodded. His arm was bloody painful and a damned nuisance besides. If it wasn't bad enough that he'd had to endure days of being talked at and lectured by both his younger brother and his wife for the past ten days, now he had to put up with this meddlesome physician.

Thank God that the two of them had gone to visit the aunts before Henri's confinement began, which, God help him, was going to be here at Tregothnan. He wondered with a shudder if his vast property was large enough to allow him to miss the event entirely.

"Perhaps I should bleed his lordship," the doctor volunteered, with admirable courage in the circumstances. "Your colour is really a little high for my liking."

"Out!" Alex yelled in fury. "Get out, you damned leech. All I need is a little peace and quiet."

With remarkable forbearance, and after no little pleading by his physician, Alex did at least agree to let the doctor bind his arm again and leave him bottle of laudanum to help with the pain. Once he'd managed to get rid of old fool, Alex retired to his room clutching the laudanum, a bottle of brandy and last two of Céleste's letters to him.

Slamming the door shut with his foot, he walked to the bed and took a moment to light the lamp before he settled down with a glass of brandy and carefully withdrew Céleste's latest missive from its envelope.

Closing his eyes he held it to his nose and inhaled. She had begun wearing perfume sometime in May, and the heady scent now invaded his dreams, tormenting his senses and adding another layer of misery to the dark world he seemed to inhabit. He stared at the bold, looping handwriting and wished he had both the nerve and the selfishness to send the heartfelt letter he had written in reply, instead of burning it as honour demanded. With an aching heart he returned his attention to the letter.

September 2nd

Glebe House. Hertfordshire.

Dearest Alex,

Please forgive me. I know I ought not address you so, nor write anything in such a shockingly familiar fashion but I must. I saw dearest Henri today and my heart was so delighted to see one I have the good fortune to consider as close to me as a sister. Although I was all happiness at her obvious good health and excitement at her condition, I was thrown into the deepest agitation by her words. For she told me just how you were injured, and now I cannot sleep for fear of you coming to further harm. Please, my Lord, if you have the slightest regard for me, your truest friend, please do not put yourself in harm's way in this fashion again. I cannot tell you how you have deprived me of my peace of mind and I beg you to have a care.

Please write to me and assure me that you will heed my words and save me from further anxiety, for I would never recover from the loss of such a friend as you.

Yours ever,

Céleste.

He stared at the words so long they began to blur and a tightness wound itself around his chest. Raising the brandy to his lips he took a large mouthful but found it hard to swallow past the lump in his throat. She still cared for him. No matter that his investigations had returned information that she and his handsome young cousin were inseparable. No matter that there were rumours that every man who set eyes on her was bewitched by her beauty, and the *ton* was abuzz with questions about the mysterious comtesse. No matter that when she finally came out next year she would be hailed as a diamond of the first water and she could have her pick of any eligible man at the snap of her fingers. She still cared for him. He pressed the letter against his heart and closed his eyes, wondering how the hell he was going to manage to stand and watch as every man with a pulse stared at her and plotted to make her his own.

He prayed that she would make her choice swiftly, so the pain would be clean and sharp instead of this lingering wound that festered and ate away at him. At least once she was married there would be no going back, no point in endless regrets and fruitless dreams and wishes. She would have made her choice, and he would have to live with it.

September 5th

Tregothnan. Cornwall.

My dearest Lady Lavelle,

It pains me far more than any physical discomfort to know that I have been the cause of any anguish on your part. Please assure yourself that my life has been led in much the same way for many years now, and I am well capable of looking after myself. The night in question, I was indeed foolish and stubborn and I promise you that I will endeavour to keep myself from such behaviour in the future. I regret to inform you, however, that both foolishness and stubbornness have long been engrained in my nature, as I am sure you are only too aware.

Please, my dearest friend, do not lose sleep on my account. I assure you, I am not worth the trouble.

Yours ever.

Alex.

Chapter 23

"Wherein our heroine comes out to society and sets the ton on its ears."

April 2nd

London 1816

"Non, I won't go!" Céleste cried into her pillow, aware that she was behaving like an ungrateful child but quite beside herself. It was too much, after so long to be given such shattering news.

It had been decreed, by Aunt Seymour, that Céleste would make her spectacular come out at the Duke of Bedfordshire's ball at the Bedford House in Bloomsbury. In fact Parliament had been recalled in February and the season had been in full swing for some time, but Aunt Seymour had withheld her acceptance until a grand enough event was available for Céleste to make her mark, and until curiosity among those of the *ton* had reached fever pitch. Dozens and dozens of elegant invitations had piled up in a seemingly endless supply over the past weeks and Céleste felt dizzy at the amount of them Aunt Seymour had accepted on her behalf.

There had been endless weeks of shopping and preparation, her wardrobe was stuffed with a terrifying array of finery, the cost of which made her feel guilty at the money which was being frittered away for her sake. Now the event was almost upon them she felt sick with nerves and apprehension. Most of all, however, she felt that she had spend the past fourteen months holding her breath, waiting to see Alex again, except now she discovered it would all be for nothing, as he wouldn't be there to see her *grande début.*

She heard Henri speaking in hushed tones to Aunt Seymour who had become really very cross with her. Not that Céleste could blame her, after so many months of preparation and expense, but truly, could no one see her heart was broke. Henri passed a squirming baby Elizabeth, who'd been born the previous October, into the arms of her adoring great Aunt and closed the door behind the two as they retreated from the battle scene. Céleste looked up and sniffed, accepting a lace handkerchief from Henri as she returned to sit on the bed beside her. She sat up and blew her nose once it was clear Seymour had gone with Henri's daughter, and slumped back into the pillows.

"I've made up my mind," she said, looking at Henri and folding her arms.

Henri nodded. "Yes, dear," she said, with a soothing smile as she reached forward and smoothed Céleste's hair from her face. "I know. And I quite understand. If I were you I'd be in hysterics too, I mean he is quite the most vexing man I have ever known, and *I* married Lawrence!" She gave a heavy sigh and shook her head. "Really it's too bad of him. Though honestly, if I were you I'd be of a mind to teach him a lesson."

Céleste sniffed and looked at Henri with narrowed eyes. "Oh?" she asked, well aware that Aunt Seymour had instructed Henri to get her to the ball by any means possible.

"Well yes, dear," Henri replied with a placid smile. "I mean we know the fool is in love with you, and if you stay home he'll imagine you are nice and safe and pining for him, won't he? So if I were in your position, I'd go out there and make sure every man from here to Cornwall was madly in love with me. I think ..." Henri mused, tapping a thoughtful finger to her chin. "That I might be especially drawn towards the rakes and the scoundrels. You know, those wicked types with nothing but ruining a girl on their minds. For I'm sure if he thought you were going to throw yourself away on someone just as wicked as he was ... *Oof!"* Henri steadied herself as Céleste threw her arms around her and kissed her cheek.

"Oh, but, Henri, you are a wicked genius!"

Henri snorted and patted her hair with a serene expression. "Yes, Lawrence has remarked much the same thing," she said with a smirk, turning to look at Céleste. "So you'll go then? Oh, please say you will. I've never been to such a grand affair and chaperoning you with the Aunts is likely to be my only opportunity."

"Oh," Céleste said, suddenly filled with guilt. "You know if you 'ad only said that I would still 'ave gone."

Henri chuckled and patted her hand. "I know that, you silly creature, but I had to tell you of my devious plan in any case so ..." She shrugged and grinned at her. "Come now, no more crying or you will still be all red and puffy tonight and we can't have that can we?"

"Non," Céleste replied with a sigh. "I suppose we can't."

***

Alex looked at the disgusting scandal rag in his hand, a frown of deep displeasure etched upon his face. His butler had all but grimaced in disdain as he'd handed the pile of gossip sheets to him and, frankly, Alex didn't blame him in the least, but he needed to know what was being said of Céleste.

The C de V made her stunning début last night and has been hailed by all as a diamond of the first water. The mysterious young woman, whose history seems shrouded in secrets, was dressed entirely in white silk and universally acknowledged to be ravishing. The D of S was noted to have claimed more than one waltz.

Alex flung the paper down on his desk in fury. The Duke of Sindalton, also known as Sin, was handsome, obscenely wealthy, and a notorious rake. He was also a *duke!* "Bastard!" Alex cursed through gritted teeth. Of course if he'd deigned to go to the damned ball he would have been able to vet all of the men who approached Céleste and chase off any that he deemed unworthy. But no, selfishly he had thought to save himself the pain and had stayed as far away as he might. Though he would have thought better of his Aunt Seymour than to let her dance with that ... that ... *rakehell!*

Well that was an end to it, he thought with a grim smile.

"Fredrick!" he roared, opening the door of his study and striding through it in search of his valet. "Pack my things, I'm going to London."

***

The fact that Alex avoided his own London residence and therefore the company of Céleste and his aunts, preferring to spend a few nights at his club, was not at all significant. A fact he assured himself of repeatedly. He just didn't want to get caught up in all of their fuss, that was all. It wasn't that he needed time to prepare to see Céleste again after over a year of dreaming about her. It was irrelevant that most of this time was spent being fitted for several new jackets, waistcoats and every possible aspect of his attire, for his reappearance into a polite society which he had eschewed for many years. Such concern for his own appearance was something he hadn't indulged in since his twenties.

His motivation for this renewed interest in his wardrobe and fashion was something he refused to dwell on at all and pushed firmly from his mind. Suffice to say that he would be the centre of a great deal of speculation and he had no inclination to be found remiss in any item of his appearance. He had no doubt at all of the reaction he would get, after an absence of so long, or the gossip that would inevitably begin as to his motives. No doubt it would be rumoured he was in the market for a wife and he would be obliged to withstand a number of foolish women casting their lures in his direction, or at least those who had the nerve. Everyone would also, of course, be watching his interactions with Céleste with rabid interest. So his own behaviour would also need to be impeccable.

By the time he had discovered from his Aunt Seymour at which event Céleste would next be present, he found he was ridiculously and unaccountably uptight. Staring at his reflection in the glass he professed himself satisfied with the results. He took a moment to survey himself and wonder what it was that Céleste saw when she looked at him. He tilted his head, verifying that there was indeed, still no scattering of grey in his thick, black hair and then reprimanded himself soundly for bothering. It wasn't him she should be looking at, but a future husband. The whole exercise was in order to see her safely wed to another, and he would do well to keep that idea firmly in mind.

***

Céleste looked up in surprise as she caught sight of Henri, gesticulating madly to her over the crush of the ballroom. Lady Blakeney was a very popular hostess and the great and the good of the *ton* were out in force tonight. She stood on tiptoes and craned her neck, trying to figure out what it was that Henri was trying to say to her.

An electric buzz seemed to shudder through the assembled company, the volume of speech lowering as everyone whispered at once. Céleste frowned, wondering what had caused the sudden undercurrent that seemed to thrill through the crowd, just as Henri's words became clear.

"He's here!"

Céleste sucked in a breath as her heart seemed to vault in her chest before crashing against her ribcage as though it was trying to escape. *Be calm, be calm,* she scolded herself. The past fourteen months of loneliness and longing would all be for naught if he discovered she was still the silly child he had always believed. Now was her chance to show him just how she had changed, and that there was nothing some sophisticated English woman could give him, that she couldn't.

Nonetheless she was powerless against the urge to turn her head and scan the ballroom along with every other person there, as they fought to get a glimpse of the notorious Earl of Falmouth.

Oh. Mon Dieu. Grateful that she had at least managed to keep the exclamation in her head instead of crying out loud, Céleste stared and accepted an all too familiar ache in her heart as she found his familiar and beloved countenance once more.

Tall and powerful, Alex's figure stood out, even among the crush of people. His cool grey gaze surveyed the scene as though it was something undeserving of his attention. She could see now, why everyone seemed so afraid of him. He had the bearing of a King, and the unmistakable aura of danger surrounded him, making the women want to throw themselves at his feet and the men despise him on principle.

Céleste swallowed, finding her mouth dry as he inclined his head to hear better what Lady Blakeney was saying to him. She watched the way the fine black material of his jacket moved, stretched taut across his broad shoulders and showing the flex of the heavy muscle in his arms. He was dressed to perfection, with a stark simplicity in the black coat, white waistcoat and perfect necktie, that made every other man in the room look like they were trying far too desperately hard or were really rather shabby in comparison. Unlike the pale-skinned Dandies, his skin was darkly bronzed, attesting to his love of the sea and much time spent in the sun. For a moment she tormented herself with wondering if his chest was now as tanned as his face and hands and remembered a day, long ago, when she had stripped him of his clothes and allowed herself to gaze on the perfection of his naked form.

To her chagrin he chose that very moment to turn his head in her direction, and it was as though he knew exactly what she had been thinking of as their eyes met. She felt a flush of colour on her cheeks but held his gaze, wondering if she imagined the flare of warmth that ignited in the usually icy grey as he looked upon her. He watched as she spoke a word to the hostess and moved away, cutting through the crush of people like a shark as people wordlessly made way for him.

"Pinch your cheeks," she heard a mother instruct her terrified daughter in an urgent whisper as he moved in their direction. But his eyes never left Céleste, and by the time he was standing in front of her she was terribly afraid that she would say something dreadfully foolish or just throw her arms around his neck and cling to him. The desire to do just that was so strong that she clutched one wrist with her hand, in case her own limbs should betray her.

She curtsied and held out her hand to him, finding it harder than ever to breathe as he raised it to his lips and pressed a kiss to her wrist.

"My Lady," he murmured. "It is wonderful to see you again, and may I say, looking lovelier than ever, though I wonder how such a thing is even possible."

"Thank you, my Lord," she replied, wishing she could think of something witty to say and finding her brain had ceased to function at all. If she wasn't careful she would find herself simply gazing at him like a ninny for the whole evening.

"Falmouth."

His gaze seemed to be reluctant to leave her face but he moved to greet his Aunts and Henri who had fought her way through the crowd to stand with them.

"No Lawrence?" he remarked to his sister-in-law with a grin.

Henri replied with a crooked smile. "No. Apparently he has met Lord Avebury before, *in the past*," she said, conveying a rather deeper meaning. "Apparently it cost his lordship rather more than he had bargained for to put his feet on dry land a few years back," she added, her tone dry with amusement. "And he doubted his lordship would have forgotten the incident so we thought it best he stay home."

Alex chuckled, a deep and wonderful sound that wrapped itself around Céleste's heart and held tight. "And how is my niece?" he asked, enquiring after her and Lawrence's beautiful baby girl.

Henri's face softened and she smiled with pride. "Young Elizabeth is beautiful and healthy and rules the household, and most especially Lawrence. She has him wrapped around her tiny finger."

"I don't doubt it," he replied with a smile. "I look forward to seeing her again."

"I must call you a liar, my Lord," Henri said, laughing. "Though it was very prettily said." She turned to Céleste with a conspiratorial air. "I made Alex hold her when she was just a few days old. The poor man looked positively terrified."

Céleste looked back at Alex, finding his expression rueful and her own heart melting at the idea of his big hands holding a tiny babe.

"I should like to have seen that," she said, her voice soft, her eyes never leaving his.

A slight frown appeared over his eyes but before she could wonder at it, it was gone.

"I hope you will do me the honour of dancing with me tonight?"

The surprise of his invitation left her momentarily bereft of a suitable answer. Henri had said she'd heard it was well known that the earl rarely danced. Stubbornly she had still kept one dance free for him, just in case, even though she'd been besieged by demands the moment she set foot in the ballroom as every available male asserted his claim on her time.

She held her nerve and gave him a placid smile, at least she hoped that was how it appeared when her nerves were leaping under her skin at the idea of dancing with Alex. "I have saved you a waltz, my Lord," she replied, holding up her full dance card for his inspection after she'd pencilled in his name. With satisfaction she saw his face darken as he took in the long list of names, especially when he noted the name before the small gap where she had saved a space for him. The Duke of Sindalton.

"I am honoured you managed to find a space for me," he replied, though she didn't miss the slight edge to his words. She was saved from having to reply to it however as their hostesses' son, Lord Blakeney, arrived to claim the first dance.

Biting back a smile she watched the two men survey each other with obvious dislike, though to her knowledge they had never met. Blakeney was a good looking young man in his mid-twenties with rather lovely pale blue eyes and white blond hair. Standing a good foot shorter than the earl, though blessed with a pleasing build and an air of energetic good humour, he eyed the older man with a wary eye as they were introduced, and lost no time in claiming Céleste's hand and sweeping her onto the floor and away from him.

Chapter 24

"Wherein a lover dances close to the truth and the ladies conspire against him."

"Well, Falmouth, what do you think of our prodigy?" Aunt Seymour demanded of him as they watched the young fool, Blakeney, lead her around the floor.

It took Alex a moment to disengage his jaw which seemed to be locked tight, before he could form an appropriate reply. Wryly he wondered what he should say. That Céleste had stolen his wits and his tongue and that he didn't dare to veer from the dullest of conversation in case he should say something far too telling? That when his searching gaze had finally settled on her it was like he had found the missing part of himself that had been taken from him the day she walked out of his home and his life fourteen long months ago? Either of those comments would be true. Instead he simply replied, "She is a credit to you."

He felt jealousy bloom in his chest as he watched the bastard dancing with Céleste lean his head down and say something that made her smile and blush. He swallowed, wanting to knock every man in the room down for even looking at her and thinking the wicked things that were in their minds. And he had no doubt that every man in the room had been thinking along very similar lines. Her hair shone a deep guinea gold in the candlelight, touched with lighter shades of Champagne and darker, warmer glints that he ached to twine between his fingers.

Her gown was a fine ivory cambric embroidered with gold thread, the floaty material moulding itself to her curves as she moved, and with a bitter taste in his mouth he watched as Blakeney looked down and enjoyed the view his height afforded him of a wide expanse of creamy white flesh at her décolletage. Dear God, how was he going to endure an entire evening without dragging her into some dark corner and doing something unspeakable, or killing every man that dared look at her. And this was only the first dance!

He had yet to endure the spectacle of her dancing with the Duke of Sindalton. He downed the glass of Champagne he had been offered a few moments previously and snatched another from a passing tray, scowling across the dance floor in fury. For the briefest moment his eyes met Céleste's before the dance swept her away in the opposite direction, but he had been sure there had been the gleam of challenge in her eyes.

With effort he recalled himself to his surroundings as his aunt's voice pierced his tangled thoughts.

"You remember my grandson, Aubrey, don't you, Falmouth?"

Alex turned and scowled at the young man who was standing beside him. Almost as tall as himself he was dismayed to find his cousin an extremely handsome young man, with deep brown hair that glinted auburn, and amused hazel eyes.

"Lord Falmouth," the young man replied, bowing respectfully. "A pleasure to see you again."

Alex couldn't seem to remove the scowl of resentment from his face as he gave a curt nod in reply. His cousin looked rather discomfited but stood his ground, squaring his shoulders slightly under the weight of the Earl of Falmouth's black expression.

"I understand I have to thank you for keeping Lady Lavelle entertained these past months?" Alex said, well aware that it didn't sound like he was the least bit grateful but rather like he would enjoy dismembering one of his closest blood relations- with his teeth.

Aubrey coughed and coloured slightly. "I-I have had the honour of spending some time with her, yes, my Lord."

"Hmmm."

Aubrey was spared further scrutiny for a moment as Céleste returned to them. Her cheeks were prettily flushed, her eyes sparkling with glee as she had clearly enjoyed dancing with Blakeney. Lord Blakeney, Alex noted with satisfaction, had left her abruptly the moment she had been returned to the fold.

"Your turn, Aubrey," she said, pulling at his cousin's sleeve in an all too familiar manner. He scowled and was pleased to see his aunt give her a look of reproach too. Instantly Céleste flushed and recalled a slightly more reserved demeanour.

Alex frowned. He didn't want her exuberance dulled, nor her enjoyment, though he hated that it was Aubrey she looked at with such fondness and felt something dark and ugly twist in his chest.

"All right, Jackson, I'm coming," Aubrey replied, laughing at her.

"Jackson?" Alex enquired, earning himself a deeper blush from Céleste and an appalled expression from Aubrey as he realised he would need to explain.

"A-after Gentleman Jackson," he stammered, looking increasingly awkward as Alex's scowl deepened.

"You would liken the comtesse to a boxer?" he demanded, with a haughty lift of one eyebrow.

Aubrey cleared his throat. "W-well, it's just that ... she has the most amazing right hook."

Céleste stared at Aubrey, her eyes wide and furious, quite clearly impressing upon the young man that she would repay him dearly for that comment later.

Alex felt his fists clench. If he found the little bastard had given Céleste just cause to hit him he'd tear the scoundrel limb from limb.

"Why," he bit out, "would she need to hit you?"

Aubrey opened his mouth and closed it again. "I believe the dance is beginning," he said, sounding rather desperate.

"So it is!" Céleste exclaimed and the two of them ran away from him like naughty school children.

Alex turned his furious gaze to his aunt who was looking at them go with affection in her eyes.

"What is the meaning of this?" he demanded, drawing on every reserve of patience to stand and listen to an explanation, assuming a reasonable one could be found, before he followed the young pup onto the floor and ejected him from the ballroom by the scruff of his neck.

"Why, Falmouth," his aunt chuckled. "Don't be so stuffy, they are merely having fun."

Alex blinked at his aunt in astonishment. This was the woman who wouldn't deign to use his own Christian name rather than his title, and she was calling *him* stuffy?

"I don't see what kind of *appropriate* fun could be had that resulted in Céleste feeling the need to hit him?" he barked.

"Keep your voice down," Aunt Seymour said, glaring at him. "Good Lord, the two of them are inseparable and the best of friends one moment and the next they are at each other's throats. How am I supposed to know which particular argument led to her striking him? From what I understand the first time they met she attacked him with her umbrella!" Seymour took a breath, and shook her head with an expression that spoke of a deep fondness. "Thankfully Aubrey seems to be the only one she reserves her appalling behaviour for, and only in the privacy of our own home. In public she is quite the lady," she said with unmistakable pride. "She has quite an entourage of admirers now."

Alex gritted his teeth so hard that a pain shot from his jaw and radiated through his brain but he didn't seem to be able to relax it. He tried harder as his aunt's all too seeing gaze looked him over.

"I would think you'd be pleased, Falmouth. This *is* what you wanted isn't it?" she demanded, but Alex didn't seem to be able to form a reply. He was watching Céleste laughing at something Aubrey said, the two of them circling the room with such obvious accord between them that he felt the dark and ugly sensation in his chest spreading through his blood like a disease.

"She is a great success," his aunt continued. "There will be offers for her in the next week or two, you mark my words."

A dull buzzing sound had begun in his head and his aunt's words seemed to take form and dance inside his brain, cutting at him like scalpels, tearing at the last shreds of his sanity.

"What are you scowling at, Falmouth?" his Aunt demanded. "Anyone would think you were jealous."

He jolted and swung around to look at Seymour who was staring at him, those cool grey eyes so like his own, watching him with a knowing expression.

"If you would excuse me," he said, his tone clipped and icy. He strode away from the ballroom, needing to get some air, needing to get away. Before he lost his damn mind for good.

***

Céleste put her hand on Aubrey's sleeve and allowed him to lead her back to the aunts, and Alex.

"How could you embarrass me like zhat?" she scolded him. "I am beyond vexed with you," she added with a little huff.

"Oh, we're back to *zhat* are we?" he replied with a snort. "I've not heard your accent in weeks. You must be in a foul temper."

"Oui," she said, shaking her head and making her ringlets dance. "I am. 'Ow am I supposed to make 'im fall in love with me, when you go and tell 'im you have named me after a ... a boxer!"

"I shouldn't worry on that score," Aubrey muttered with a dark tone.

"Why?" she demanded, stopping in her tracks, her eyes wide.

Aubrey scowled and ducked his head to hiss in her ear. "Because the fiend was staring at me with murder in his eyes. He clearly wants my blood, and if it's all the same to you, I'd like to keep every drop exactly where it currently resides!"

"Bah!" Céleste replied, with an irritable snap of her fan. "I told you I might require your 'elp to make 'im jealous. Don't tell me you are backing out already? What are you, a man or a mouse?" she glared at him, furious that he would fail her at the first hurdle but Aubrey just returned her furious gaze with his own placid expression.

"Squeak," he replied succinctly, before turning on his heel and leaving her beside Aunt Seymour.

"Oh!" she fumed, biting her cheek to stop herself from stamping her foot in frustration. Well then, if Audrey wouldn't help her she would have to use the slightly more daunting prospect ... of flirting with the Duke of Sindalton.

She cast her gaze out around the ballroom and didn't take long to find him. As tall as Alex and as broad, he was the one other man in the room whose presence demanded her attention. Though where Alex's strength and arrogant demeanour didn't frighten her a bit and in fact made her feel safe, the duke made shivers of unease run over her skin. His reputation was every bit as bad as the earl's and she could easily believe he had earned every word of it.

He was leaning, with a bored and indolent posture, against one of the ivory columns that ran the length of the ballroom, and he looked up, perhaps sensing her interest, and their eyes met. His were dark and full of silent invitation. A slight smile tilted the edges of a sinful mouth and she didn't need to wonder how he'd earned his nickname and it had nothing whatsoever to do with his title. *Sin,* the word seemed to wrap around him, taunting you, daring you ... Céleste took a breath and looked away, casting her eyes over her dance card. Three more dances and she would be in the duke's arms. She wondered if Alex would even notice.

"Where is his lordship," she asked Aunt Seymour who turned her attention away from her sister and Henri.

"I believe he needed to go and cool off," she replied, with something that looked almost like a smirk on her face.

"Oh," Céleste replied, disappointed. "It is most dreadfully *h*ot in here," she said, making Seymour smile and pat her arm in an encouraging manner.

"You are doing beautifully, child," she said with a warm smile. "I am very proud of you."

Céleste looked up at her in surprise. Seymour had never once said anything that even resembled approval in all the months she'd lived with her. Aunt Dotty was full of warmth and smiles and encouraging words, but the most she got from Seymour was a *hmmm,* of more or less approval depending on how badly she'd fared.

"You are?" she asked, quite unable to keep the scepticism from her words.

Seymour, Dotty and Henri all laughed at her obvious surprise, and Seymour linked her arm to Dorothea's, the two sisters putting their heads together.

"We both are," she replied with real affection in her words that made Céleste's throat tight. "And one way or another, we will have the offer for you that you so desperately deserve in the next day or two or I'll eat my hat."

"Which one?" Dotty asked, laughing. "For if you fail in this I shall be so dreadfully unhappy I will insist that it's that bilious green one with the feathers. It looks awful on you and I'm sure it would be revolting to eat."

Seymour sniffed and looked at her sister with disgust. "I like that hat, and I *never* fail," she replied with dignity.

"You have for the past seventeen years," Dorothea muttered, making Henri and Seymour smile unexpectedly though Céleste had lost the train of their conversation.

"Well some things just take a little longer than others," Seymour said, and then reached out and took Céleste's hand. "And the right woman," she added.

"Quite," Henri said, nodding her agreement.

"I don't understand?" Céleste replied, knowing that they were placing their confidence in her but not really understanding why.

"You will," Seymour said, squeezing her fingers tightly. "You will, if only we can bring my idiot nephew up to scratch." She winked and Céleste felt her heart jump.

"Y-you mean, Alex?" she stammered, uncertain that she wasn't still floundering in the dark.

She stared at Henri, wondering if she had betrayed her confidence.

"I never said a word," Henri replied, putting her hand to her heart, as though she had read her mind.

"You *do* still love him don't you?" Dorothea asked her, such anxiety in her eyes that Céleste couldn't reply for a moment.

"I--I," she said, her cheeks blazing with embarrassment.

Seymour laughed at her obvious discomfort. "I knew the day we met, dear. We both did. It was perfectly obvious. What I was slightly less sure of were his feelings for you."

"Oh," Céleste replied, casting her eyes down. Whilst she was more than glad that his aunts didn't disapprove of the match, she didn't want Alex harried into offering for her from some misplaced sense of duty. She wanted him, with a desperation that was beginning to border on obsession, but she wanted him to love her. If he didn't love her she couldn't bear the idea of being with him, knowing he was only doing his duty.

She felt a slender knuckle touch her chin, and looked up to see Aunt Seymour watching her with amusement.

"I think I have put to rest any doubts I may have harboured on that score," she said gently. "The poor man is at his wit's end already and we're barely half way through the evening. It shouldn't take much to tip him over the edge. And," she added, winking at Céleste in the most scandalous fashion. "You have yet to dance with Sindalton."

Céleste gave a little gasp of surprise and the three women began to chuckle.

"Now run along," she said, gesturing to the smiling countenance of Viscount Trenchard who had come to claim his dance, and leaning down to whisper in her ear. "You have a husband to catch."

Chapter 25

"Wherein torments are endured and the stakes raised."

Céleste watched as the duke approached her and hoped she looked outwardly calm because her nerves were doing an intricate dance all of their own. Prickles of unease ran up and down her spine as envious looks were cast her way from every female in the room. She didn't blame them in the slightest.

Standing beside Alex, darkly handsome and exuding a dangerous appeal, her skin ached with desire. And with the infamous, deliciously wicked Sin stalking through the ballroom towards her as though no one else in the room existed, she felt rather like a haunch of venison dangling between two starving tigers. She could feel tension rolling off Alex in waves. There was a muscle ticking at the side of his jaw that was disturbing what remained of her peace of mind, and the leashed violence in his eyes and the rigid set of his shoulders had kept any possible male suitors from spending a moment longer in her company than was absolutely necessary to claim their dance. She had the distinct feeling that more than one of her amorous admirers had found their ardour quickly cooling under the earl's icy gaze, and would have happily not danced with her at all had honour not bound them to come and claim it.

The duke, however, seemed to have no such qualms and met the earl's eyes with an arrogant tilt of his lips. Alex bowed with such an insolent manner that murmurings of shock rippled around the great room as the closest to them noticed. Frankly Céleste was just relieved he'd managed it at all for she had the breathless feeling that she was standing on a precipice as the two powerful men stood close beside her. Any sudden move by either party could result in disaster.

"Falmouth." Sindalton acknowledged the earl with a mocking glint in his eyes and for an alarming moment she had the terrible feeling Alex was going to hit him.

"Your Grace," Alex replied, though somehow the words were infused with menace.

"My dance I think?" the duke said, his tone changing to something low and intimate as his heavy-lidded eyes slid to Céleste's.

She gave a low curtsey, aware of the man's heated gaze settling appreciatively on the revealing neckline of her dress as she dipped down in front of him. He gave her his hand to raise her up and she arched a glance up at him from under her lashes, wondering how she dared give him such a seductive look, but not nearly brave enough to see how Alex was taking it.

The duke placed her fingers on his arm and led her to the dance floor.

"I wonder, are their scorch marks on my back?" he murmured, as he turned her towards him for their dance. "I rather feel there should be."

Céleste suppressed a giggle but couldn't help but smile up at him. "Oh?" she replied, affecting an air of innocence. "Why would that be, your Grace?"

The Duke snorted and held her gaze, giving her ample opportunity to admire his deep brown eyes, so very dark that the brown almost merged with the black. She was intrigued to notice tiny flecks of gold in their depths, like stars in a night sky.

"I have the growing suspicion that the earl doesn't care for me," he replied, keeping his tone and his face grave, though his dark eyes were alight with humour.

"The earl doesn't care for most people," she replied, with equal gravity, though she was struggling to keep a smile from her lips. "So I shouldn't let it trouble you unduly."

"Oh, I'm not troubled in the least," he said, his words far softer now and he pulled her closer to him as the dance brought their bodies almost but not quite flush. He lowered his head so she could still hear his whispered words. "Not by Falmouth at least." His warm breath tickled the side of her neck and the moment seemed very intimate, despite knowing how many people were watching them.

Céleste blushed. She really didn't want to flirt with this man. He was very handsome, clearly extremely charming and his wealth and title were obviously bait enough for any unwed young lady, but he wasn't Alex. Alex, however, was an idiot, and if she was to have any chance of getting him to realise that fact desperate measures were called for.

"Then what does disturb you, your Grace?" she asked, looking up at him once more from under her thick lashes, with what she had been told was a seductive tilt of her head. It seemed to have the desired effect as his eyes darkened further.

"You," he replied. The word shivered over her skin, thrilling and succinct as he turned away from her, the dance forcing them in opposite directions for a moment. When they returned together his hand slid around her waist, pulling her closer to him for a moment, and there was an intensity in his gaze that made her breath catch and her cheeks heat. "I want to call on you," he said. There was no preamble, no pretty words or *may I have the honour.* It was a demand, tinged with urgency.

The dance drew to a close but he stood over her, his hand still at her waist, his eyes fixed on hers. Somehow she found the nerve to raise one eyebrow at him.

"I imagine a duke can do most anything he chooses," she replied blinking up at him in an innocent fashion.

He chuckled, a slow smile bringing warmth to the strong lines of his face.

"I'm going to take that as a yes," he replied, placing her hand back on his sleeve and keeping his own covering her fingers in a lingering caress. "And now we had better brave the lion's den and return you from whence you came ... for now at least."

There was a promise in his words that didn't escape her and she looked at him in surprise, gasping as he winked at her. It was a deliberate gesture, acknowledging his interest in her and sure to have been seen by everyone watching. It implied that there was a level of intimacy in their relationship that would be seized upon and whispered about before she even returned to Alex's side. She could almost hear the words floating on the air and the bets being taken on how long it would be before he offered for her.

She ought to be victorious, she thought ruefully. This was the kind of match her mother would have considered only in her wildest dreams of a future for her daughter. But it only filled her with panic. What if Alex allowed it? What if he didn't change his mind and offer for her himself? Could she accept such a man, knowing she would always love another? With such disturbing thoughts buzzing in her mind she was too distracted to even notice if Alex was in any way affected by her dancing with the only man in the room who could rival him for looks or eligibility.

Her distraction was short-lived, however, as Alex took her hand, his grip almost painful as he set her fingers on his sleeve and almost marched, rather than walked her to the dance floor. Her heart set upon an unsteady series of leaps in her chest as she realised this was his dance.

There was an air about him that made her afraid to look up and meet his eyes but really what was the point in ignoring it. Why should he be angry with her? He wanted her to make a brilliant match. It had been him after all who had joked about having young men throwing themselves at her feet. Surely if that was truly his ambition for her future, a duke would be the height of achievement and everything he could want for her to have. She swallowed, finding her mouth dry and all too aware of the heat of his large hand holding hers as he positioned her for the waltz, and then she looked up.

Her breath caught at the intensity of his gaze on hers and she found herself powerless to look away. There was tension in every line of his body, she could feel the taut muscle beneath her hand where it rested on his heavy shoulder and she wished he would say something. The silence surrounded them, as though it had sliced them apart from everyone else in the room and they existed in another place entirely. There was only Alex, and his eyes on her, eyes that seemed filled with too many emotions for her to decipher, no matter how she tried as she stared in the grey. It was like looking upon a winter sea, ever changing, dangerous with turmoil, threatening to drown her and never let her go if she dared to get too close to the perilous undertow.

She stared back at him, defying the warning she saw there and hoping he could read the thoughts in her mind ... *drown me, hold me down, never let me go.*

***

Alex sat in the carriage on the way home from the ball with his thoughts snarled up in a tangle of emotions. The whole evening had been torture of the most intolerable kind imaginable. Though the worst part of it had undoubtedly been watching her dance with that bastard Sindalton. The duke's dark gaze had left him in no doubt whatsoever of where the scoundrel's thoughts were when he had taken Céleste in his arms for the waltz. The fact that everyone around him insisted on remarking as to what a striking couple the two of them made hadn't helped in the least. But when he had seen the bastard wink at her, practically announcing his interest to everyone in the room, his reaction had been a shock to him.

For a moment he had felt unsteady as a wave of jealousy and rage swept over him, but it hadn't been those emotions that had hurt him the most. Fear. Cold and sickening it had wrapped itself around his heart like the hand of a cruel god, posed to rip it from his chest at the slightest provocation. Because whilst he had told himself he could live with the sacrifice of watching her marry another - a good man, a man who would love her and respect her and never bring her shame by the actions of his past - giving her to one as besmirched as he would kill him. He would never recover. But the pretty blush on Céleste's face and the soft glances she'd cast up at the handsome duke left him in no doubt that she was not immune to the man's charms.

By the time the waltz had finished his emotions were at such a pitch he had practically snatched Céleste's hand and dragged her back to the floor for his own dance. Too desperate to erase the memory of that man from her thoughts and have her think only of him once more, he had taken possession of her hand.

He wondered if she had the slightest idea what she'd done to him? He closed his eyes and remembered the feel of her in his arms, the now familiar scent of her favourite perfume, and the more subtle fragrance that lay beneath it that was uniquely her and her alone. The simple scent of honeysuckle and sunshine that brought back memories of waking and find her in his arms, her golden hair spread over his chest. Oh God, why hadn't he taken her then, when he could? When she had been his and his alone, before the world had seen her and discovered just what a treasure they had almost lost. Before every man in the bloody world had seen her and coveted what was his.

Giving her up to allow her a better life, a chance with a better, more honourable man was one thing. But he was damned if he'd lose her to Sindalton or one of his ilk. He'd heard the rumours over the past days in town. The man was in the market for a wife, and the bastard was wealthy enough to overlook Céleste's lack of a dowry. He wasn't just toying with her, he meant to marry her and make her a duchess.

His throat worked with unwanted emotion as he tried to formulate a plan. He would have to speak to her, warn her as to exactly what kind of man she was dealing with before things went any further. Maybe he could halt this folly before it went any further.

The carriage drew up in front of his London residence in Mayfair and he stepped down, handing down his Aunts and a yawning Henri who looked like she was more than relieved to be back.

Céleste, however, looked just as bright and alive as she had when he'd first seen her this evening, and his breath caught as she put her gloved hand in his and he handed her down. *Get a grip, man,* he cursed himself.

The butler let them in and they handed their coats and gloves to the footman and everyone said a weary goodnight and began to climb the stairs.

"Céleste," he said, stopping her with a touch of his fingertip against her arm. She looked up at him, her wide blue eyes questioning, and it was all he could do not to allow the fingertip to trail down the length of her arm, over her satiny skin. "May I have a word with you before you retire?"

"Of course, my Lord," she replied, smiling at him. She glanced up at Aunt Seymour who gave her small smile and a nod of agreement before continuing on her way to bed.

Céleste stepped away from the stairs and followed him to his study.

"Can I get you a drink? A glass of ratafia perhaps?" he asked.

"No, thank you, my Lord."

"I think perhaps you may call me Alex now?" he said, smiling at her. She seemed far too composed, he thought, remembering how carefree she had used to be in his presence. Though of course he had hoped to cure her of that. How well his aunts had taught her. Now she seemed perfectly indifferent to his proximity. Perversely he felt the need to do something about that. He wanted to see desire flare in her eyes as it had been wont to do when he was close to her.

"As you like, Alex," she replied with a polite smile, watching him as he fixed himself a drink. He saw her gaze on his glass and remembered that she had a fondness for brandy, which of course was quite unsuitable for a young lady. He took a sip from the glass, allowing the fine spirit to slide over his tongue, appreciating the warmth and the subtle flavours of nutmeg and vanilla. He had a sudden, desperate desire to taste it on her tongue and before he could stop himself he offered her his glass.

"Would you like to try?"

She looked up at him, those wide blue eyes watchful. Taking a step forward she didn't reach for the glass as he had expected but simply raised her chin a little. His pulse picked up, a soft thundering under his skin as he moved the glass to her mouth and pressed it softly against her lips. She opened her mouth a little as he tilted the glass and closed her eyes as she took a sip.

Alex swallowed, trying to tamp down the surge of desire as he moved the glass away and her tongue swept out, tasting the lingering traces of brandy on her lips. He was frozen by the desire to reach down and take her mouth for himself, to search out the taste of the brandy on her lips, to spill the rest of the glass over her skin and chase every decadent drop from her flesh with his tongue.

"Mmmm," she said, the sound sultry and decadent in the dark seclusion of his study. "That is very good."

He took a breath and forced himself to take a step back from her, though his eyes couldn't seem to tear themselves away from her mouth.

"Your accent," he said, his voice rather hoarse. "You've lost your accent."

"Yes," she said, smiling at him. "I have."

He frowned, inexplicably bereft.

"Aren't you pleased?" she asked him, with one slight lift of her eyebrow. "That is what you wanted isn't it?"

"No," he replied, aware that he sounded terse and unappreciative of all the hard work she must have put in to rid herself of it. "I told Seymour to leave you be."

She tilted her head, looking at him with a curious expression. "Why? Aunt Seymour said it was ugly."

"It wasn't!" he snapped, running a hand through his hair in irritation.

"You didn't think it was ugly?" she repeated, her voice soft.

"No," he replied, shaking his head and staring at her, wondering if she could see the desperation in his eyes, wondering if she had any idea of the effort it was taking to simply stand still in the same room as her when all he wanted was to take her in his arms. "I thought it was perfectly charming."

"Oh," she gave a sigh and then grinned at him, looking exactly that tantalising mix of innocence and bedevilment that he found so alluring, just as she had all those months before. "Well, zhat is a relief. It is terribly 'ard to keep up, you see?" she winked at him and he gave a bark of laughter.

"Thank God," he murmured.

She took a step closer to him and all his senses were on alert, his flesh prickling with the need for her to touch him. "Don't you want me to change, Alex?" she said, looking up at him from under her lashes. "I thought that was why you sent me away from you? So that I could be a nice English girl, and not bother you anymore?"

"I-I," he began, no longer knowing what it was he wanted further than the desire to claim her, to tumble her to the floor right here, right now, and lose himself in the lush heat of her body.

"You wanted to talk to me though?" she said before he could manage to find a reply that wouldn't make him sound like a raving madman. She turned away from him, apparently blind to his distress and went to lean on his desk.

Her hands were braced behind her, her bottom perched slightly on the edge and she leaned back a little, highlighting the generous swell of her breasts as the pretty gold embroidered material stretched tight. His brain ground to a halt as he noted the faint rise of her nipples beneath the fine cambric and he was struck by the desperate desire to close his mouth over the material and trace the shape of each enticing nub of flesh with his tongue.

"Alex?"

He dragged his eyes from her breasts and turned away, downing the remainder of his drink with one swallow and raking a hand through his hair as he fought to master his ragged thoughts. He had wanted to talk to her? He had. The Duke. Thankfully the memory of the slick bastard taking Céleste in his arms sharpened his wits a little.

"Yes, I wanted to talk to you. To warn you."

"Oh?" she said, and he could hear the amusement in her voice. "That sounds rather ominous. Am I in great danger?"

Yes, he wanted to shout in fury. You're in danger from me, you little fool, if only you knew it. The fact that she had come to this room with him, alone, at night, that his Aunt hadn't batted an eyelid ... Had they forgotten the kind of man he was?

"The Duke of Sindalton is a rake," he said, trying to invest the words with as much force as he could. He needed her to understand what she was dealing with. "Even if he isn't just toying with your affections for his own amusement, which wouldn't be unheard of, even if he were to make you an offer, he'll never be faithful to you. He'll make you a duchess and then go off and have affairs with anyone he pleases, and I doubt he trouble himself to be discreet either. He's got a reputation for whoring and gambling and drinking to excess ..." he paused, well aware he was repeating words that had been levelled at himself many times and took a moment to look up at her, to see if his harsh words had found their mark. To his horror she merely looked entertained by his warning.

"He sounds positively breathtaking, Alex," she said and he was only too aware she was laughing at him.

"Do you think this is a joke?" he growled, finding no humour whatsoever in the situation.

The amusement fell from her eyes and she stood, walking toward him. *"Non,* Alex," she said, her voice quiet. "I do not think it is a joke." She moved slowly, closing the distance between them and reaching up on tiptoe to place a soft kiss on his cheek. He closed his eyes, overwhelmed, desperate for her to move her mouth the scant inch across his skin to his lips. "Goodnight, *mon contrebandier."* She turned away from him and walked to the door, turning just before she reached to open it. "I think perhaps you should know ... I agreed to let the duke call on me."

Alex stood alone in the dark as she closed the door on him, and he knew he had to make a choice.

Chapter 26

"Wherein plots are hatched in many quarters, the past causes tears, and events unfold."

Céleste regarded herself in the looking glass and then glanced over her shoulder at Henri. Sitting on the bed, nursing baby Elizabeth, she looked the picture of contentment and Céleste bit back a surge of jealousy. She truly did love Henri like a sister and would never for a moment begrudge her a moment's happiness. But oh how she envied her. Hers and Lawrence's marriage seemed to be everything that she could only dream of.

Perhaps sensing her train of thought Henri looked up and smiled at her.

"Oh, Céleste, do you have any idea how very lovely you are?" she said sighing.

Céleste snorted in a manner that would have made Aunt Seymour give her a severe scolding.

"For all the good it 'as done me," she replied with a grimace.

"Come now," Henri said with a reproving tone. "You said yourself he was quite clearly out of his mind with jealousy last night, and even Aunt Seymour thinks you have swayed him."

Henri took a moment to disengage her daughter from one breast and transfer her deftly to the other. Despite the fashion for wet nurses, Henri had been adamant that no child of hers was going to be farmed out to be fed by another. Once again Céleste repressed a swell of longing, as she considered what a child of Alex's might look like. She forced the image away before she became maudlin and ruined all the preparations for the night by doing something as foolish as crying.

"How is Aubrey?" she asked. "He didn't call today I think?"

"No," Céleste said, scowling. "He didn't, the coward. But I shall get 'im back for 'is lack of backbone."

Henri giggled and shook her head. "Oh, poor Aubrey. Really you are asking a lot of a man who isn't desperately in love with you to stand up to Alex."

"Bah!" She waved a hand, dismissing that as a reasonable argument. "Aubrey is supposed to be my friend, my brother almost, if 'e will not help me who am I supposed to turn to? I would help 'im if the situation were reversed."

"Yes," Henri replied nodding at her. "I believe you would and damn the consequences."

"Voila!" she replied, smoothing down the soft drapes of her gown. "And that is what a true friend does."

"Well looking as you do tonight, my dear. I really think you need help from no one. In fact I may even be moved to pity Alex. The poor devil doesn't stand a chance with you looking like an angel ready to fall at any moment."

Céleste brightened at her words, turning this way and that in front of the mirror once more. It was a deceptively innocent gown. White Bengali muslin with all over sprigged Broderie Anglaise and a cotton bodice, it looked almost demure at first glance, but the fabric was very fine indeed and the fit was such that it made much of her figure, especially the generous swell of her breasts. Her hair had been artfully arranged and decorated with pearls that shimmered in the gold tresses.

"Oh, I 'ope you are right, because I don't know what to do for the best. Sometimes I think I should just throw myself at 'im?"

Henri gave a dark chuckle and nodded. "Oh I know exactly, I promise you. In fact ..." she said with a sly look in her eyes. "With that in mind I have a gift for you."

"Oh?"

Getting up Henri placed her daughter carefully in the middle of Céleste's bed and cocooned her with pillows so she couldn't roll off in her sleep. "Wait there," she commanded and ran from the room, reappearing moments later with a large flat box. Laying it down on the edge of the bed she gestured for Céleste to open it.

Céleste lifted the lid and gasped, drawing the gossamer-like material from the box she looked at Henri in stunned silence.

"It's a nightdress ..." Henri said helpfully, grinning at her. "Sort of."

Céleste, who had spent a fair amount of her life in a whore house, was utterly scandalised, and more than a little thrilled. "But it's ... it's ..."

"Totally indecent, yes I know," Henri said, smothering a giggle. "But I figured if you didn't have a proposal by the end of the evening ... well ... this might tilt those scales in your direction."

"Tilt them?" Céleste murmured in something close to awe. "I think they would collapse in shock." She looked up at Henri with a considering expression. "This is yours?"

Henri nodded. "Yes. I didn't wear it the night I seduced Lawrence but to be honest the dress I wore wasn't much less revealing. However, if Alex catches a glimpse of you in that ..." She shrugged. "You can't fail."

Céleste hugged the practically transparent garment against her before throwing her arms around Henri. "You are the most wonderful friend."

"Sister," Henri amended. "If you wear that tonight I'm certain of it. I certainly hope so anyway," she said, a little frown of worry etched between her eyebrows. "I mean I really shouldn't encourage you I know, and if it was anyone but Alex ..." She smiled and reached out, taking hold of her hand. "Oh, good luck, my sweet girl. I do hope everything works out as it should."

Céleste nodded and gave her fingers a squeeze. *"Moi aussi,"* she agreed.

***

Alex stood at the bottom of the stairs and waited for the ladies to appear. Aunt Dotty was chaperoning tonight as Seymour had pleaded a headache and had complained that the theatre was far too hot and noisy for her to cope with. Likewise Henri was tired from her evening at the ball and Lawrence had expressed a wish for his wife to stay at home with an expression that Alex understood only too well.

Alex couldn't blame Seymour for her absence however. The Theatre Royal on Drury lane was showing a production of *Betram, or, The Castle of St. Aldobrand* with their celebrated Shakespearean actor Edmund Kean in the title role. The place was bound to be packed to the rafters and as it was unseasonably hot for spring the place would be unbearably stuffy.

Alex was not a particular fan of the theatre at the best of times, but the idea of being in a secluded and dark space with Céleste for hours, and only Aunt Dorothea for safety, was making him uneasy. Poor Dotty was notorious for dozing off within the first half hour of any performance and not stirring until someone gave her a hard shake. As a chaperone she was laughable and he wondered that Seymour hadn't cancelled the evening entirely. If he was any kind of gentleman he would have done it himself. But then he wasn't, that was the whole problem, he reflected as thoughts of being alone with Céleste in the dark, and yet surrounded by hundreds of people, made his blood thrum with decadent ideas.

Those ideas seemed to form before his eyes as the object of his torment appeared at the top of the stairs. He stared up at her, quite unable to tear his eyes away, knowing that he was lost. He couldn't allow her to go and marry a blasted duke, nor his handsome and charming cousin, nor any other man. He couldn't bring himself to care that she deserved better, or at least, not enough to allow it. He was finished with kidding himself that he could live with it. He couldn't. If she took another man he would kill whoever it was, it was inevitable. She would wed him and allow this intolerable torment to end or he would lose his mind. The idea that she might not want him anymore - perhaps preferring to be the duchess to a handsome young duke - slid into his mind and he quashed it in fury. He couldn't accept that, he wouldn't. He would make her want him again. He would find a way.

He held her gaze as she made her way down the stairs, noting the provocative sway of her hips.

"Good evening, Alex," she said as she reached the bottom and looked up at him, the blue eyes glittering and full of mischief that made his breath catch. "You look very 'andsome tonight."

He reached out and took her hand, lifting it to his lips and kissing the inside of her wrist, a soft and tender brush of his mouth that could not be misconstrued as anything but seductive. He looked up to see a slightly startled look in her eyes and that her cheeks were flushed. Smiling with satisfaction, he placed her hand on his arm as Aunt Dorothea began to make her way down the stairs to meet them.

"And you ... look like you'd far rather go to bed than the theatre, *mignonne,"* he said, keeping his voice low and for her ears only.

She glanced up at him, her mouth open with shock and the colour on her cheeks flushing down her neck to her breasts.

"Why, *ma mie,"* he said, his voice heavy with amusement. "I only meant that you were perhaps still fatigued after your late night." He paused and focused his attention solely on her, his lips quirked slightly. "Whatever did you think I meant?" he asked, raising one eyebrow.

She recovered herself with some effort and gave him an arch look. "I suspect I thought exactly what you intended me to think," she said with a haughty sniff. Before removing her hand from his arm and allowing the footman to help her with her pelisse.

The theatre, as expected, was a crush as familiar faces greeted each other before everyone took their seats for the performance. To Alex's dismay, there was one face he did not want to see in the slightest. But as his eyes met the seductive, dark eyes of one of his late paramours, he was left with a dilemma. The infamous widow, Mrs Lydia Morris, was very clearly on a determined path to come and speak with him and knowing the woman as he did, would risk a scandal before being thwarted. He wondered what on earth had possessed him to get involved with her in the first place, and then remembered with a wry grin exactly what the reason had been.

Such decadent temptations seemed crass to him now, however, and he found he was quite at peace with knowing such entertainments were to be a thing of his past. The last thing he wanted now, though, was to give Céleste a reminder of just the kind of man she would be taking on. Both she and Dorothea were safely ensconced speaking to friends of his aunts and the small group of older women that were with them, and so he decided to head trouble off before it could reach him. With a murmured apology he made his excuses and left the ladies alone for a moment to head off impending disaster.

***

Céleste sighed, waving the fan she held to try and create a stir of air in the stifling atmosphere. Looking around she searched for Alex, wondering why he'd disappeared so suddenly. Since the moment she had seen him this evening her hopes had risen exponentially. Something had changed. He had come to some sort of decision, she was sure of it, and it involved her. That he had flirted with her so openly, that he had returned to using the pet names for her that she loved so dearly, all of it bespoke a change in his demeanour. She remembered the charged atmosphere in the study last night, the moment he had held his glass to her lips. When she had deliberately licked her lips to savour the lingering taste of the brandy, the look in his eyes had been searing in intensity. So what did it mean? Had he finally overcome his objections to making her his own?

She turned her head a little more and saw Alex's dark head above the crowd. Craning her neck she tried to catch a glimpse of whoever he was speaking to so intently. There was a fierce expression on his face, and when the crowd shifted slightly so that she could see clearly, she was hardly surprised. The woman standing before him was exquisite. Voluptuous of figure, with thick dark hair and sloe black eyes that promised all sorts of desperate pleasures, she was undoubtedly the most beautiful woman in the room.

Céleste hauled in a breath, finding her lungs were unwilling to comply as her chest was too tight.

"That's his mistress," a smug voice said from beside her. She whirled around in horror to see the beady, birdlike eyes of Lady Bradford looking on the dark beauty with a malicious smile. She'd met the hateful old gossip at the Vauxhall Gardens some weeks ago and Aunt Seymour had warned her to stay clear. Céleste hadn't needed to be told twice, she was obviously a malicious woman and would stop at nothing for a good story, least of all the truth. But somehow she didn't doubt the validity of her words now.

She wasn't so foolish or naive to think that a man like Alex would be celibate for any amount of time. "He's got several of course, but Mrs Morris is his favourite. Apparently he fought with the Marquess of Rockingham for the rights to her." Céleste stared at the woman, but mistaking Céleste's appalled silence for an interest as salacious as her own, she carried on. "Yes, two years ago that was. I don't think he's ever kept a paramour as long as that one. Though you can see why I suppose. And it's not like he'll ever marry now is it? I mean he's apparently more virile than men half his age, they say his stamina is legendary, but even so. He's the wrong side of thirty five to mend his wicked ways now. No the earldom will go to his brother's offspring I imagine."

"Would you excuse me please?" Céleste pushed away from the old crow, sickened by everything she'd heard. Blindly she fought her way through the crowd, not knowing where she was going, only knowing she couldn't stand beside that malicious bitch for a moment longer.

"Well now, where are you off to in such a hurry, my lady?"

She looked up and sucked in a breath of relief when her eyes took in the imposing figure of the Duke of Sindalton.

"I-I," she stammered, trying to compose herself. "I got a little disorientated, your Grace, and it's so dreadfully 'ot in 'ere." She didn't care at that moment that her accent had slipped but from the look in the duke's eyes he didn't seem to mind in the least.

"How perfectly charming you are," he said, his voice soft. "Come, we'll go up the stairs, it's quieter and you'll perhaps be able to see your companions."

"Your Grace is very kind," she murmured, more than relieved to get away from all the people. Her heart was aching as she turned Lady Bradford's word over in her mind. It wouldn't hurt her so much if it wasn't true. She had been foolish not to see it earlier. But she hadn't been wrong in the change in Alex. He wanted her, she knew he did, but ...perhaps he had fought his own desires for so long because he had no desire to ever marry. Perhaps the reason he had never made advances was because all he would offer her if he did was the position of his mistress.

She tried to breathe, deep and even as it occurred to her just what that would mean. Even if she had enough appeal to hold his attention so that he only kept her and none of the others, she would not be welcomed in polite society any longer. She found this was of little consequence. The beautiful clothes and parties and dancing, all of it was lovely, but she would turn her back on it all in a heartbeat for a life with Alex. The idea that she would never have a family though, that she would never hold his child in her arms, that made her heart ache with misery.

"Why now, whatever is it distressing you so?" She blinked back tears and looked up at the duke who reached out and caressed her cheek with a fingertip. "Tell me Falmouth is the cause of your distress, my lady, and I swear I'll call him out."

She gasped, astonished at the violence of his words and shook her head. Yes, it was Alex making her unhappy, but it wasn't his fault, only her own foolish naivety that had brought her to this moment.

"Non," she shook her head and tried to smile at him. "His Lordship is not to blame I assure you."

He looked at her, his dark eyes unreadable. "I will call on you tomorrow afternoon," he said, but before he could say more or she could answer, she felt a large hand press against the small of her back in a possessive and intimate gesture. Looking round she found Alex behind her, staring at the duke with utter loathing and reached out a hand, grasping his arm.

"Oh, Alex. I'm so sorry, I got lost in the crush and his Grace was so kind as to bring me here and see if I could see you." She turned back to the duke and hoped she managed to give him a grateful smile. "Thank you so much, your Grace."

The duke tore his dark gaze away from Alex and raised her hand to his lips, giving her wrist a lingering kiss. "Until tomorrow, my Lady," he said, before turning and walking away.

Alex glared at his retreating figure. "What did he mean, *until tomorrow?"* he demanded.

"He means to call on me," she replied, watching his face as the words hit home.

There was a second of silence in which in expression darkened further. "I thought I told you to stay away from him?" he said, and she almost took a step back at the fury in his eyes. For a moment she stared at him. Would she give herself to this man as his mistress, content to never truly belong to his life, to only ever be one of his pleasures, like a fine wine or a racehorse - a diversion from boredom? Or would she marry, the duke perhaps. She would be wealthy, powerful, and respected. A half life with the only man she ever loved, or more than she had ever dreamed of - with a man who didn't know her, a man she could never have anything more than affection for. With sorrow she knew the answer had been decided many months ago. Better half a heart, than none at all.

"You think he's going to offer for you," he said, and it wasn't a question. She looked up at him, wondering if he was jealous of her as a possession, as a thing he desired for himself, or if there could be more to it than that.

She shrugged, glad that Aunt Seymour wasn't there to see it and scold her. "Yes, I think perhaps he will."

"Would you marry a man you don't love?" he asked and she couldn't have been more surprised if he'd slapped her. His face was a careful blank but she could feel the tension singing through his body as though it was calling to her, begging her to put her hands on his skin and smooth it all away.

"No," she whispered. "I couldn't marry a man I didn't love."

He seemed to release a breath, relieved, and she was suddenly furious with him. She was overwhelmed, jealous of his dark eyed-lover, furious with months spent alone, disappointed at a future she had begun to yearn for and had suddenly been snatched away from her.

"Of course, Aubrey 'as offered too," she said, putting aside her guilt at the barefaced lie and gaining a small measure of satisfaction at the jolt of shock in his eyes. "And 'e is very dear to me. I think perhaps we could be 'appy together."

He stilled, staring at her, and she felt her satisfaction shrivel and die, replaced by remorse as she saw something that looked very much like fear in his eyes.

"Have you accepted him?" he asked, his voice hoarse and barely audible over the noise of the theatre as everyone started to take their seats.

"Non," she whispered.

"Will you?"

She forced herself to hold his gaze, to make him see what she needed from him. "I don't know. I suppose it ... It depends on what other offers I receive, but ... I must make a decision, very soon."

She saw his throat working, saw the need in his eyes to say something and the realisation that this was neither the time nor the place. He turned and guided her to his private box. Aunt Dorothea was chattering to an old friend some distance behind and totally oblivious to the charged atmosphere between them. As they walked they passed the Duke of Sindalton and Céleste shivered as his dark eyes lingered on her, despite a glacial look from Alex as they passed him.

"I don't want to see you alone with that man again, Céleste," he repeated, sliding a possessive arm around her waist as they entered the gloom of his private box. She paused and glared up at him, daring to take a step closer so that for a moment her body brushed against his.

"If you 'adn't left me alone, I wouldn't 'ave been in 'is company," she replied, unable to keep the thread of bitterness from her words.

His expression softened and his arm tightened around her for a moment as he stared at her intently. "You are quite right, *mignonne,"* he whispered. "Forgive me. I swear to you ... it will never happen again."

Chapter 27

"Wherein torments of various kinds are endured."

The theatre was finally still and quiet as the first scene was revealed. The audience took in the gloomy aspect of a monastery at night with a large Gothic window and the atmosphere was one of anticipation as two monks, apparently running in terror, appeared on the stage. As one the audience jumped with shock as a crack of thunder rent the cavernous room and the eerie howling of the wind swept around them.

Céleste was enraptured. Clutching at the deep red velvet seat beneath her, she revelled in the dramatic opulence of her surroundings. She had never before seen a theatre production, and that her first experience should be such a melodrama was more than she could have hoped for. For a moment she tried to put aside her own concerns and worries and focus her attention on the play. But no matter how enthralling the stage and its players, she was only too aware of Alex's proximity.

He sat close beside her, the hard line of his thigh pressed against hers. It was intimate and distracting and she wondered if he knew he was doing it. He had been acting so strangely tonight, flirting with her, furious at her for speaking to Sindalton, and his reaction to Aubrey's offer had been a revelation. Perhaps it had been simply his foolish ideas about her youth and innocence that had held him back before as she'd first believed and he had finally put aside whatever objections he'd had.

Still, she told herself she had no foolish notions about him offering for her now. Yes she had hoped and dreamed it was true, but she wasn't naive or fool enough to believe that dreams came true. She'd seen enough of life to be pragmatic about her choices and she must take what she could get and be grateful. After all, without Alex she'd be a whore by now, one way or another. Being mistress to a man she loved was really not a hardship when put against that perspective, but it didn't stop her heart aching.

She smiled as she heard Aunt Dorothea's soft snores as the dramatic action on stage continued and had no impact whatsoever on her slumber.

"Heaven for its mercy, what a night is!" cried the first monk.

"Oh! Didst thou hear that peal?" added the second as Céleste nearly squealed in alarm as the very theatre seemed to shudder with the violence of the thunder so realistic was the effect.

"The dead must hear it," wailed the first monk as more thunder jolted the audience. Turning to the first monk he grasped his arm. *"Speak! Speak, and let me hear a human voice!"*

Céleste put her hand to her heart as the drama of the scene pulled her in and then jumped once more as the smooth slide of fingers glided over her other hand which rested demurely in her lap. In the darkness of the box she could just make out Alex's larger, rough hand over her smaller white-gloved fingers. He had removed his own gloves and the heat of his skin burned through the fine silk. She swallowed as his fingertips trailed up, over her wrist until they reached the bare skin at the top of her arm. He stroked her with the back of his fingers, a delicate, barely-there caress that made her heart beat wildly, sending her blood rushing through her veins.

As though caught in a dream she kept her eyes on the stage, though she saw nothing of the dramatic events unfolding as he carefully peeled the glove from her, with slow, deliberate movements, drawing each finger free in turn, and taking her hand, drawing it to him. He moved closer, in the darkness of the theatre, holding her hand between both of his. The heat of him, just from that contact, seemed to burn through her so that her skin blazed, prickling with awareness that only increased as his thumb moved in slow, seductive circles over her palm. Her breath caught as he moved closer, dipping his head to hers as though he meant to whisper something to her, except no words were heard. Instead she felt the warmth of his mouth on the junction between her neck and shoulder as his lips pressed against her skin. It was the softest of kisses, which was repeated, over and over, as he lit a trail of fire up her neck.

Céleste was in turmoil, her breathing at once fast and shallow, desperate that she shouldn't draw attention to herself, appalled and intrigued that he would act in such a way in a public place. Surely someone would see? And yet it was dark and the rest of the audience quite intent on the stage as the drama progressed, and she wasn't entirely sure she cared in any case. Alex continued with his delicious torment, nuzzling the delicate skin just below her ear and nipping at her ear. She suppressed a moan of desire and tilted her head a little to allow him to continue.

A low male chuckle of amusement rippled over her skin and Alex seemed more than happy to oblige her. The constant circling of his thumb over her palm was making it hard to keep her composure. She did her best to make it look as though she was watching the play but the only thing in her mind was crawling into Alex's lap and demanding he satisfy the throbbing ache he had created between her legs that was driving her to distraction. He placed the hand he was holding on his thigh and leaned closer still. One hand reached up to clasp the back of her neck, the warm, heavy weight making her shiver. He continued to kiss her neck as his other hand slid over her stomach and rose higher, until it cupped the generous swell of her breast. With a teasing, slow rub of his thumb he caressed her nipple through her gown and Céleste was forced to bite her lip to stop from crying out. She was gripped with a feeling of desperation, a need for release that teetered on the edge of madness as his lips caressed and his fingers tweaked her sensitive flesh.

"Alex," she whispered, not sure if she was angry or grateful, if she was pleading for him to have mercy or to continue his torment. All she could hear was the sultry quality in her own voice, a tone that was echoed as Alex replied to her.

"Isn't this what you wanted, *mignonne?"* he said, the words slightly mocking and harsh with desire. "You have teased and tormented me, invaded my dreams, kept me from sleep, insinuated yourself into my every thought. Wasn't it so that I would touch you like this?" He pinched the delicate flesh he toyed with through the fine fabric of her dress, making her cry out, a soft startled sound, torn between pleasure and pain, and she had to catch herself, suddenly terrified that someone had heard. "Admit it," he demanded. "Tell me you want this."

"Yes," she replied, the word exhaled on a shaky breath. She was trembling now, every breath, every nerve, every taut inch of flesh aware of his touch, desperate for more. "I want this, I want you."

She heard the fierce exhale, felt his hand grip her neck with more force. "Well now you'll pay for those months of torture, now you will understand how I have felt all this time. Aching to be in your presence and unable to touch you when I was. Longing to come to you when you were so far away from me and flirting with other men, smiling for them, making them want you." She heard the thread of anger in his voice, but under that the longing and desire made her heart lift. She turned her head, searching for the bright glint in his eyes, visible even in the secluded darkness that surrounded them. The noise of the theatre, the reactions of the crowd, the voices of the actors and the tremendous roar of the storm that had been created within the walls of the place, all of it seemed far away and insignificant. There was nothing and no one but the two of them.

"Do you think I didn't feel the same way, Alex?" she said in wonder. "Do you 'ave any idea 'ow hard it was to sleep in the same bed with you, knowing you didn't want me."

"Didn't want you?" he repeated, his voice ragged. He pressed his face into her hair and inhaled the scent of her. "Oh, God, Céleste if it were possible to die of desire I would have."

She felt her breath catch as he moved back to look at her, the heat in his eyes enough to scald her. He looked as desperate as he sounded, the usually cold eyes full of fire and dark with wanting.

"I suffered too, Alex, and far worse, for it was you who enforced it on me. It was your choice not mine."

"I wanted more for you, Céleste, I wanted a better man for you and more than I can offer you," he paused, shaking his head. "We will speak of all of this later. There is much I would say but not here, and not now."

She felt the pain in her heart as he confirmed everything she had come to realise in the past hours, but forced herself to laugh at him, outraged and amused. "So you can seduce me 'ere but not talk to me, *hein?"*

"Yes, *ma mie,"* he growled, returning to nuzzle at her neck. "No one can see us and Dorothea sleeps like the dead. Besides, don't tell me this doesn't appeal to your sense of adventure, you little minx."

She smiled, a slow curving smile as she closed her eyes and tilted her head back.

"You think you know what I like then?" she whispered.

"Yes," he said, and then bit her neck, just enough to make her gasp. "I think I do." Her breath caught as he tugged at one side of the low neck of her dress, just enough to reveal the ruched flesh of her tortured nipple. Reaching out he palmed her breast, caressing with his rough, calloused hand.

Almost dizzy with desire, Céleste was beyond the last thread of sanity. If he suggested taking her to the floor, right at this moment, she was very afraid she might be far gone enough to comply. She clamped her thighs together, trying to appease the frustrated aching that was impossible to ignore and finding her temper fraying at the male chuckle of amusement that fluttered over her skin. Furiously she thought every obscene word she could at him. Of all the places to begin his seduction! If he'd come to her room or waited until they were home she could have forced him to sooth her shattered nerves, to rid her of the all-consuming need that was as delicious as it was maddening. She gritted her teeth. *Well,* she thought, *two can play at that game.*

"I think, perhaps ..." she said, struggling for breath as he continued to stroke and caress her breast. "That I should give you some ... clues. In case you are wrong about that, and I did once see, at Madame Maxime's ... one of the girls ... She was laid out on a table, as though she was the dessert." His hand stilled at her breast and tension sang along the strong length of his thigh as Céleste ran her fingers up his leg. "And there was this gentleman, seated at the table and his head was bent, between her thighs ..." She paused, fighting for breath as the air seemed to crackle between them. His breathing had changed, as harsh and as laboured as her own. "He was feasting on her, and she was writhing and moaning with pleasure ..."

"Céleste," he said, his voice desperate.

"I 'ave often thought of it," she continued, her voice soft and breathless in the dark.

"Céleste, please ... don't ..."

"I have often thought about your mouth on me like this ..."

"Oh God."

"I 'ave thought about looking down and seeing your dark 'ead between my legs as you tasted me like this."

"Stop!" he pleaded, sinking his fingers into the coils of hair at the back of her neck and pulling with some force. "For the love of God stop or so help me I'll take you here and now and it will be the scandal of the century."

The two of them sat, in the darkness, their breathing out of control, their eyes intent on each other. "Swear you'll show me what I've been dreaming of when we get home and I'll be quiet," she whispered.

"Try and stop me," he growled.

Céleste bit her lip, trying to hold back her laughter as the ridiculousness of the situation caught her.

"Don't laugh, you little she-devil," Alex muttered, pulling her dress back up with sharp efficient movements. But the crosser he seemed the funnier it became. She covered her mouth to try and keep it in, but the more he glared at her the more difficult it was to suppress.

"Oh ... and poor Aunt Dotty," she gasped. "She would never 'ave recovered."

Alex's mouth twitched as he sat back, as far away from her as he could manage. "I believe I have previously mentioned to you ... your conversation is inappropriate for a young lady. I sent you away to deal with that," he grumbled, folding his arms, though she could see the amusement lurking in his eyes. "And stop looking at me like that, *ma mie,"* he added, keeping his eyes resolutely on the stage. "It's taking every ounce of self control I have to keep sitting here and not throw you over my shoulder and make off with you."

Céleste sighed, feeling at once warm and tense, happy and on edge with repressed desire.

"I'll be good, Alex," she said, with great solemnity.

"Hmph." He kept his eyes forward, his arms crossed and the tight-fitting material strained over the width of his biceps. "Oh, and by the way. You are going to be unwell during the interval and it will be necessary for us to go home. *Immediately."*

He cast a quick glance at her before returning his fierce countenance to the performance. *"Oui,* Alex," she said, smiling in the darkness.

Chapter 28

"Wherein lovers come so very close ..."

Alex endured the rest of the damned performance, got Dorothea and Céleste into the carriage, and then had the torment of being jolted through the dark streets with Céleste's amused blue gaze on him. He was in agony. His skin felt too tight for his body, the nerves stretched to breaking and every rub of cloth against his flesh was an acute ache that was driving him to insanity. That the source of that torment was just scant inches away from him was beyond unbearable. He didn't dare consider the retribution he was going to mete out to her either, as satisfying as it would be, for fear he would be unable to leave the blasted carriage. So he sat and he endured.

Finally the carriage rolled to a halt. With every scrap of patience remaining to him he helped the ladies down from the coach and helped Aunt Dotty inside, managing to paste a smile on his face and make appropriate noises as she chattered merrily about some old friend she had happened upon the day before and hadn't seen for years. By the time she finally bid him goodnight he was almost ready to weep with frustration.

He turned to Céleste and raised an outraged eyebrow at her when he saw she was about to ascend the stairs.

"Where the devil do you think you're going?" he said, catching hold of her wrist and aware that his voice was too harsh, too desperate.

She just smiled at him, her blue eyes wide and guileless. "Just to freshen up, Alex, don't look so worried," she said, clearly laughing at him. "I'll be back before you know it."

"Well if you're not, be warned, I'll be coming to fetch you," he grumbled. Dammit he'd waited for over a year, why was fate conspiring against him now? He dismissed the remaining staff, sending them all to bed, stalked to his office and reached for the decanter of brandy.

Pouring a small measure he downed it in one go, taking a moment to savour the burn before pouring another, larger amount and settling himself down to wait. A bare moment later he was on his feet and pacing. God where was she? Didn't she know what she was doing to him? With a snort of amusement he realised she was probably well aware and doing it on purpose.

He took a deep breath and tried to arrange his tangled thoughts beyond the basic fact of his physical need for her. Somehow, since the day The Bold Bessie had been torn apart in that dreadful storm, Céleste had become necessary to him. It wasn't just that he wanted her, that he wanted to taste her and touch her and lose himself in her. He wanted to know her, to know everything about her. He wanted to know what she thought, what she wanted, what she hoped for. He had thought at first that it was nothing more than desire, as she was simply the most beautiful woman he had ever known. But he couldn't deny now, that it was so much more than that.

She was as much a requirement to his well being as the air he breathed. He needed her the same way he needed water to simply exist, the feeling far more intense than any desire he had ever experienced. The word caught in his throat and made his chest tight but he didn't shy away from it. *Love,* he loved her. Good Lord, he would probably earn his place in hell if there wasn't a chair with his name on already, but he was going to have her. He would marry her and take her home to Tregothnan and spend the rest of his days making sure she never had cause to regret the decision. Though how she wouldn't in another twenty years or so when she was just forty and he pushing sixty. He grimaced and shook his head. That was a problem for the future and he had become selfish enough to disregard it. Maybe by then she would have grown tired of him and taken a lover ... His mind shied away from the thought. She wanted him now, and now was all he could consider.

The soft sound of the door opening caught his ear but he kept his back turned, trying to calm the disarray of his emotions. He didn't want her to see his desperate need for her. She deserved the sophisticated and accomplished lover she believed him to be, not some love sick fool who wanted to fall to his knees and make her promise to always love him, even when he was old and grey. But when he finally felt composed enough to turn towards her, any veneer of calm was stripped from him in the moment between one heartbeat and the next.

She had taken her hair out of the pins that had held it in place and it cascaded down her shoulders. Glimmering deep gold and a light, bright blond that put him in mind of ripe corn, it tumbled in heavy coils, almost, but not quite covering her breasts; and there was little else to keep his heated gaze from them. She was wearing a gauzy nightgown, the material of which was all but transparent and left little to the imagination. A delicate triangle of darker gold was clearly discernible at the juncture of her thighs, as was the faint blush of her nipples, peeking tantalisingly from beneath her hair. He caught his breath, quite unable to say a word.

She smiled at him, looking suddenly unsure of herself, a blush of colour at her cheeks that reminded him forcefully of the fact that she really was an innocent. No matter the things she had seen, no matter the explicit knowledge she might believe she had, in terms of her own experiences she came to him pure and unsullied and he felt the weight of that responsibility. For all that he wanted her, for all that his own body was screaming for him to take her, he would ensure this was everything she wanted it to be. There was a moment in which he acknowledged that, if he was truly a gentleman, he would marry her first. But he simply wasn't a good enough man for that, and he didn't have the strength to turn her away.

"Say something," she said, covering her chest with her arms and looking more and more uncertain as his stunned silence continued.

"I'm finding words in short supply, *ma mie,"* he said with a rueful smile. "You have stolen them." He moved toward hers, closing the distance between them slowly. As he stood in front of her he realised she was trembling and the fact made an intense burst of pain bloom in his chest. He hauled in a breath and reached out a hand, caressing her cheek. "I wish I had the right words for you, Céleste. If I had I would speak prettily of the oceans and the blue of your eyes, I would compare you to some ancient deity that stole the hearts of mortal men with a single glance, but I have never had that kind of gift. I am not a poet, but ... I have never known desire like this."

She looked up at him and the trust and love in her eyes almost overwhelmed him. "I don't need pretty words, Alex. I never 'ave. I just want you."

She reached up and wrapped her arms around his neck and he pulled her close to him, one hand still cradling her head as he lowered his mouth to hers. Infinitely tender, he kissed her with adoration and slow, seductive touches, deepening the kiss by increments, brushing his tongue against her lips, seeking entry. She responded with enthusiasm, mimicking his slow strokes as his kiss flamed with intensity, crushing her soft body against his harder one. She moaned into his mouth and he devoured the sound, holding onto his own desires with desperation as she moved restlessly in his arms.

"Easy," he murmured, pulling away and brushing his lips against her cheek, feathering butterfly kisses along her jaw, her forehead. "There is no rush, *mignonne,* I'm going to take care of you."

"Oh, but, Alex," she said, her voice breathless as she clutched at his neck. "I-I need ... I want ..."

"I know," he said, desperately holding himself in check. "I know what you need. Trust me, love." He sought her breast, caressing her through the sheer material as his other hand dropped to cup the delicious curve of her bottom, pulling her against him and insinuating one leg between both of hers. She gasped as the pressure of his hard thigh brought her the relief she sought and she clung to him, moving against him, seeking her own pleasure. "Oh, God, Céleste," he murmured, wondering how the hell he was going to keep control of the situation when she was temptation incarnate.

She was shredding his self-control and his body was coiled tight, like an over wound spring. Any moment the tension would become too much and he would break. He searched for the ties that held the flimsy garment in place, vaguely aware that he hadn't meant for this to happen in his study; he had planned to take her upstairs but now ... but now... He had never been so consumed by a woman, to the point where nothing else existed outside of themselves. The bloody house could burn down around them and they would be consumed in the flames without him ever noticing. The nightdress fell away with a hushed whisper of material and he looked down on her, his prize, his love, the source of so many sleepless nights.

"So beautiful," he murmured, hoping she could hear the reverence in his voice. "Perfect," he added, dipping his head to caress one sweet, pink nipple with his tongue. She sank her fingers into his hair, uttering soft, breathless sounds as she pulled his head closer. He teased and tortured the peak with lips and tongue and the occasional delicate graze of teeth, revelling in the little gasps and exclamations she made as he moved from one breast to the other, lavishing both with equal care.

He returned to her mouth, delving into the silky damp with deeper, fiercer, more penetrating kisses. She responded with abandon, giving herself over entirely to this new experience, trusting in him completely, and quite obviously at the mercy of her own body. He knew she had no idea yet, what to do with such an overwhelming cacophony of sensations and he sought to reassure her, to calm her, but she was like quicksilver in his arms, desperate and hot with need. He slid one hand over the lush curve of her waist and hip, traversing her stomach and dipping lower as he sought out the little thatch of curls, parting her tender flesh with care and holding her tight as she jolted in his arms.

He drew back from the kiss and stood watching, her mouth opening in a little O of surprise as he discovered the silken peak and stroked just a fraction higher. Caressing with feather light touches she gave a little gasping cry and her eyes drifted shut as she submitted to his touch, her head tilting back.

Oh God, he was never going to last. His body was harder than it had ever been, throbbing with need that bordered on the most exquisite pain. He allowed his head to drop, lavishing hot kisses over her throat, seeking her mouth and kissing her again as she sighed and shifted with impatience for more, faster. She was rushing towards the peak without yet understanding that he needed to lead her on a slow voyage to a higher destination. Her desire was only too obvious and he hauled in a breath as his fingers dipped a little lower and found her drenched and pliant. With more tenderness and patience than he had been aware he possessed he teased the slick opening, carefully sliding one finger inside and caressing. Her breath came ever faster and she clutched at his clothes, her skin flushing pink as he pleasured her with slow, sure strokes.

"That's it, *mignonne,"* he whispered against her ear. "That's it." He murmured to her, endearments and sweet words that he never would have believed could pass his lips as she trembled and moaned.

"I-I can't stand up, any longer ..." she cried, reaching up to hang her arms around his neck.

With a low chuckle of amusement he picked her up and carried her to a wingback chair by the fireplace. Settling her down, she collapsed, breathing hard and looking at him with anxious blue eyes.

"Oh, but don't stop," she complained, reaching forward and pulling at his shirt. "I don't want you to stop."

"I wouldn't dream of it," he said, grinning at her and getting to his knees. "But perhaps you should catch your breath."

She scowled at him, her sweet face full of consternation. "Are you laughing at me?" she demanded with suspicion.

"No," he assured her, taking her hand and kissing the palm. "I would never do such a foolish thing."

"B-but ..."

"Hush, *mignonne,"* he said, soothing her before she could begin. "I'm going to give you what you want, but there is no need to be in such a rush. I promise you won't miss a thing."

He took a moment to remove his jacket and waistcoat, leaving them in a crumpled pile on the floor. With care he arranged her on the chair, pulling her hips closer to the edge and pulling her mouth to him for a deep and searching kiss. She twined her arms around his neck, her fingers in his hair, caressing and pulling lightly as his hands cupped and stroked the generous curve of her breasts. His mouth trailed down once again, not wanting to miss an inch of skin. Every part of her merited equal devotion and he was only too happy to worship her with slavish fealty.

She squirmed beneath him as he dipped his tongue into the shallow round of her belly button, giggling and gasping and making him smile against her skin. The sound of her laughing, the closeness and the trust required for so soft and intimate a moment between them made something bloom in his chest, a feeling of such absolute rightness that he wondered how he could ever have considered seeing her marry another. It was insanity, an idea so utterly foreign to him now that he couldn't conceive of ever having considered it for a moment, let alone going to such lengths to make it happen. What a bloody fool he'd been. She grew still, however, as he eased lower, slower, parting her thighs as her breathing hitched, careful not to abrade her delicate skin with the faint prickle of his stubble.

He pressed a kiss to the silky flesh that ran beside the dense little nest of golden curls.

"Is this what you want, *ma mie,"* he said, breathing the words against her swollen flesh, smiling as goosebumps ran over her and set her to trembling for him.

"Oui, Alex, please, please, *s'il te' plaït ..."* she pleaded with him, utterly breathless.

Only too happy to oblige he sought the place where she needed him with a gentle caress of his tongue, rewarded as her hips lifted off the chair and he was forced to hold her still. He grasped her hips firmly with both hands, using his elbows to keep her legs wide as she wriggled and squirmed, overpowered by sensation.

"Alex, Alex," she murmured his name, half pleading, half demanding, restless and unsure of what it was she was seeking as he brought her closer.

"Hush," he said gently, stopping to kiss his way along her thigh. "You know where to go, love, I know you do. You found your pleasure all by yourself when you slept beside me at Allaire."

She gasped and covered her face as she realised he had known all along. *"Mon Dieu!"* she cried. "You were awake!"

"Yes, *ma mie,* I was awake, and in such agony that you cannot comprehend."

"Oh, I am so embarrassed," she mumbled from behind her hands.

"Love, I don't see how you can be bearing in mind my current position," he replied, suppressing the urge to chuckle for fear of offending her. "But nonetheless, my point is that you know where I am taking you, so stop trying to grasp at it. We will find it together, you and I." He kissed her curls, smiling at her as she dared to peer at him from between her fingers.

With a devilish grin he held her gaze and lowered his mouth once more and swept his tongue over her. She arched beneath him with a sound that made his own body tighten in response and made him fear that he would not get through the next moments without losing control. With every ounce of determination he fought to keep his focus on her, putting his own desires to one side as he gave himself over to her complete gratification. Focusing on the source of her pleasure he licked, softly, unwaveringly, building the tension in her body until she was taut, suspended on the edge of a precipice she had only glimpsed at before. And then she fell, over the edge, into a pleasure so deep that the sound of her made him groan against her scorching flesh. He stayed with her, easing her through the peak and on into a subtler, softer swell of contentment as pleasure continued to ripple through her and she quivered beneath his mouth.

He sat back and surveyed the results of his work with satisfaction. Laid back against the dark green velvet of the chair she was flushed, her porcelain skin pink with the excesses of pleasure, her eyes dark and hazy. She sighed, her lovely limbs arranged in a posture of utter abandon. A creature of pleasure and sensuality, she put him in mind of tales of succubi. Those female creatures who fed on men's lust and sex, for she looked so completely sated and replete, stretching with the luxurious manner of a spoilt cat.

He prowled forward, leaning over the chair and suckling at her breast, savouring her deep moan of contentment.

"Do I take it I met your expectations, love," he murmured as his hands moved restlessly over her heated skin, eager for his own pleasure now, any patience having long since deserted him.

He was replied with a long, heartfelt sigh. "I-I," she began and then just gave up and smiled at him. *"Oui,"* she said, and then pulled his head down, kissing his mouth and his nose and his eyes, covering his face in hot little kisses and punctuating each one with a breathless, *"Oui, oui, oui."*

He pulled her against him, holding her fiercely. "Oh, *ma mie,* I have never in my life wanted anyone as much as I want you. I need to be inside you or I fear I'll go mad."

"I'm yours, Alex, I always 'ave been. You only 'ad to take me." She looked up at him and something in her eyes troubled him.

"What is it?" he asked, "why do you look like that?"

She blinked and smiled at him, a little too brightly. "Like what, Alex? I am only so 'appy to be with you like this. Nothing else matters, only ..." She hesitated and he frowned, cupping her face with his hands. He didn't want to see that anxiety there, that worry. What was she worried about?

"Only?" he pressed, needing to reassure her that whatever it was he would make it right.

"Only ..." she repeated. She took a breath, as though she was trying to muster the courage to go on and said, "Only, must I be one of many? I--I know that you keep many mistresses, but ... but could I be the only one. *S'il te' plaït?"* she whispered, looking up at him as though she was making some unreasonable demand. "I don't think I could bear it if I had to share you."

Chapter 29

"Wherein dreams and reality collide and our heroine chooses between them."

He stared at her in utter shock, bewildered and uncomprehending. She believed he wanted to take her as his mistress? And not only that, but that she would be one of many? His heart hammered in his chest as he fought to organise his thoughts. After everything he had done to keep her safe, to give her a chance at a better life, she would throw it all away to be ... *his mistress?* He sat back, away from her and ran an unsteady hand through his hair. He was torn between fury and shock. He could hardly believe that she should value herself so cheaply, after having fought to keep her honour intact for so long and in such appalling circumstances. The knowledge that she loved him enough to give him everything, with so little required in return, made his heart ache. He was overflowing with such love and gratitude that he felt he would burst with it and yet, *Goddammit!* Why would she not see that it was him who should be grovelling at her feet. It was him who should be begging for scraps from her table.

"Alex," she said, her voice trembling. "Please ... don't be angry with me."

"Angry?" he repeated, dazed. *"Angry?"* He shook his head, *get a bloody grip man.* But before he could form an answer, a desperate hammering sounded at the front door.

They both gasped, shocked by the sound, so late at night, and the fury of the pounding, as though someone wanted to break down the door.

Alex was on his feet in a moment. The whole bloody household would be woken and curious if that continued, and with Céleste naked in his study.

"Stay there," he commanded, his voice rather harsher than he'd intended but dammit, was the world determined to drive him to the edge tonight?

He ran out the room, closing the door firmly behind him and went to find out what manner of insanity awaited behind the front door. Though such a visit, at such a late hour, never boded anything good.

He wrenched the door open in fury and ground to halt in astonishment to see the trembling figure of his mistress on the door step.

"Alex," she said, her large brown eyes full of tears. "Please, I had to see you."

"Lydia!" he replied in shock. "What on earth?" He grasped her arm and pulled her into the house. Unwilling as he was to have her here, worse would be having her discovered on his doorstep at this hour, causing a scene. With an anxious glance to assure himself that the study door was still closed, he led her quickly to the drawing room, closing that door also. "What is this about? Is something wrong?"

To his astonishment she threw herself upon him, weeping copious tears. As most men, Alex did not like women crying over him, they were to be avoided at all costs, and yet he wasn't a monster. If the woman was in trouble he would help her if he could.

"What is it?" he asked, trying to keep his tone gentle and patient with difficulty when his emotions had already been run ragged over the past hours.

"I can't be without you, Alex," she wept, burying her face against his chest. "I can't, I can't bear it."

Alex frowned. This was not at all like Lydia. She had never, in all their time together professed anything but an appreciation of his wealth and his skills in the bedroom. It was why the relationship had lasted so long. She was never inclined to jealousy unless she suspected one of his other light o' loves had a stronger grip on his purse. His heart had never been something she'd sought. He held her by her wrists and pushed her a little away from him. Something here did not ring true.

"You seemed little moved when I explained the situation to you before," he said, keeping his tone neutral. "In fact I had heard rumour my position was already filled."

She pouted and pulled at her wrists, forcing him to release her or leave bruises upon her flesh.

"Oh," she said, putting her hands to her bosom. "A woman has to find her place in the world, my Lord. Who else will pay my bills?" she wailed, loud enough to be heard upstairs. "But you alone are in my heart. Please, darling, say you won't give me up. Come back to me and let it be like it was before."

"Keep your voice down, dammit," he said, turning away from her. Nothing about this made the least bit of sense to him. "I left you enough money to keep you financially secure for some considerable time, with or without any other contributions."

She shrugged, and the soft look in her eyes was unconvincing. "I told you, Alex, it isn't the money. I love you."

He looked at her, staring into those dark eyes, and knew she was lying. Before he could accuse her or try and comprehend her motivation she darted past him and flung open the door, heading out into the hallway.

"Oh, Alex, yes, I'm so relieved nothing will change if you take another mistress!" she crowed, her words loud and only too clear. "I was worried one of us would go, and to reward you I will arrange for your other ladies to visit me. You liked that didn't you? All of us together for your pleasure?" He ran to her and grasped her arm, sickened as he realised just what she was playing at.

"Shut your mouth, you little bitch!" he swore, dragging her to the front door. "I know who did this, and why dammit. Sindalton put you up to it didn't he? He's your new paramour and he paid you to come and cause trouble for me."

"Put me outside that door and you'll know what trouble is," she said, her voice low and spiteful. "And yes, it was his Grace, and I was only too happy to comply. How dare you throw me over for that little nobody! They say you found her in the gutter."

Alex raised his hand, never before in his life had he wanted to strike a woman but in this moment it took a great deal of will power to turn away from her. He tried to marshal his thoughts. There was no possible way she could know the circumstances in which he had found Céleste. She was just mud-slinging, to see what stuck. He looked up and to his horror saw Lawrence, Henri, and his aunts standing on the upstairs landing, their faces full of shock.

"What do you want?" he demanded of her, turning his back on them. "Name your price and then get out of my house."

She looked up at him, her beautiful face unbearably placid. "Another five thousand pounds," she said, glancing up at the faces on the landing as Lawrence tried to herd the women back to their rooms.

He gritted his teeth. "And if I don't I suppose you'll spread your vitriol in everyone's ear about an innocent girl who's done nothing to you."

"Oh but she did do something to me," she said with a pout. "She took you away, but yes, of course you are quite correct."

Alex cursed her and gritted his teeth, the money hungry bitch. "Very well. You'll have it first thing tomorrow, but hear this, once this is in your filthy hands that's an end to it. Try this again and I'll destroy you beyond anything you can imagine, and don't think you can beat me in this, Madame. The word of an earl will always weigh heavier than that of a whore, no matter his reputation."

She laughed, sounding unconcerned and amused, but he could see his words had struck home from the fury in her eyes.

"As you wish, my love, but there will be two other small services before this matter is ... put to bed." She moved closer to him and he took a step away. She laughed again. "Oh but, Alex, all I want is a kiss goodbye."

He looked at her in disgust, the thought of touching her now made his stomach turn.

"I wouldn't touch you with a ten foot pole, Madame," he replied, investing his words with every ounce of vitriol he could summon, which from the look on her face was plenty. He hadn't needed to actually strike her.

"Do it, or I'll ruin her," she spat back at him. "I won't stop until everyone knows she's a whore. She'll never be able to show her face again."

He grasped her by the arm, holding tight enough to leave a mark. "Why?" he demanded. "Did Sindalton ask for this too?"

"Oh, no," she said, her voice low and seductive once again. "This is entirely my own piece of work. He merely wanted to illustrate to the chit what kind of man you really were to clear the path for him, everything else is my doing, my revenge for the way you tossed me aside like you'd done with me."

"Tossed you aside?" he growled, furious beyond all reason and wanting nothing more than to throttle the damn woman. "You've never had any desires further than a claim to my money and I gave you more than enough to show my appreciation. You'll get nothing more."

She shrugged and smiled at him. "Very well, then, I'll tear her reputation to pieces like a cat toying with a mouse, just a little bit at a time, until she's destroyed *even* if you destroy me in turn."

"Fine," he bit out, towing her back to the drawing room. "Have it your own way."

"Oh, no," she hissed, digging in her heels. "Right here, right now, or no deal."

With fury simmering in his veins he grabbed her and pressed his mouth against hers, shuddering as her arms wrapped around him and she pressed her body close to his. He submitted as she forced her tongue into his mouth and then pushed her away from him in disgust, spitting the foul taste of her onto the floor.

"Now get out," he said, his voice dangerously low.

"No, I don't think so," she said softly, as if nothing had happened between them. "The last thing you will do for me is to send for your carriage and escort me home. I had mine leave me at the corner to save you from scandal of seeing it outside your door at this hour, assuming you would want to play nicely. I knew you would. If you do this, you will never hear from me again, and I will leave your pretty little comtesse alone for good."

"Your word, Madame," he bit out, wondering when this bloody nightmare would be over.

She nodded and held her hand out. "You have my word, Alex."

"Don't call me that," he said, refusing to even touch her hand. "You will address me as your Lordship."

She gave a deep curtsey, her eyes full of mockery. "Of course, my Lord."

He turned to see the servants had come out to see what the commotion was. "Get to bed, the lot of you," he hissed, sending everyone scurrying, but pointed at one of the men. "Not you. Get the carriage brought around immediately." He turned back to Lydia. "You will wait in the drawing room," he instructed before barking at one of the footmen to fetch his coat.

With desperation he glanced at the study door. He needed desperately to see Céleste, to explain what had happened and that he would never want or need a mistress once she was his wife. But he didn't dare. There were too many people awake and he didn't want to risk drawing attention to her while that bitch was in the house.

Resigning himself to the inevitable he walked Mrs Morris to the carriage and escorted her home.

***

Céleste shivered and clutched Alex's jacket closer around her. She could still smell the scent of him, lingering upon the fine wool weave. It held a subtle mixture of expensive cologne, and something undefinable but unquestionably masculine, and purely him. She inhaled, allowing misery to overtake her. In all her life she felt she had never been more miserable in this moment. Even when the bastard Pelletier had her she'd been too consumed with fear and anger at her situation to feel such a profound sense of loss. Had she really hoped for too much? She had accepted she would never be wife to him. Some penniless foreign countess was hardly a brilliant match for the Earl of Falmouth, but she had hoped that he held sufficient regard for her that to be his only mistress, at least for a little while, wouldn't be so much to hope for. But Mrs Morris had ended that dream.

It had been hard to make out anything much of what was said. The study door was thick and heavy and little sound filtered through. But she had heard the woman laughing, relieved that the addition of another mistress didn't mean she was out of a job, and promising to invite the other women to join her in entertaining Alex. Céleste's stomach roiled. Is that what he hoped for? Not only that she should share him with his other lovers, but that they would share him in the same bed?

She blinked back hot tears of humiliation. She had heard muttered words after that joyful utterance and had been consumed with jealousy. Quite unable to resist, she had cracked the door open, just a fraction, and seen Alex and the dark-haired beauty entwined in a passionate kiss. Quite unable to bear any more she had closed the door quickly and leaned against it until her knees gave out and she crumpled to the floor, where she still remained.

It was too much to endure, the knowledge that she was nothing more to him than a pleasant dalliance. She would need to join forces with other women to hold even that small amount of his attention. Well she would have given away her honour for him and him alone because she loved him beyond reason. But she wasn't so lacking in pride that she could bear that. So what now? Sindalton would call on her tomorrow and she was almost certain he would offer for her sooner or later. The *on dit* was that his family were putting pressure on him to marry before the year was out. But if she married the duke she would be committed to inhabit the same world as Alex. They would inevitably meet at the same events, and she would have to endure gossip about whatever mistress he had taken up with next and she didn't think she could endure that for any price.

Hearing sounds at the front of the house she stole over to the windows and peered through a tiny gap in the curtains. With her heart breaking she watched Alex walk down the steps and get into the carriage after his beautiful mistress and knew now where she was ranked in the order of his affections. That he would leave her this way, naked and alone in his study, to escort another woman home ...

With a cold, numb feeling stealing over her she knew that she could never accept that little from him. She couldn't marry someone else, but she'd not be a whore, not even for him. She needed to go away. Somewhere no one would find her. At least for a little while, until her broken heart could stand to return to people who had become so very dear to her. She wondered if the aunts would ever forgive her? They and Henri and Lawrence and sweet baby Elizabeth, and her dearest Aubrey; they had become her family and the loss of them was a bitter blow. But they had all been deceived as even Henri had believed he loved her at heart. He truly had been trying to be kind to her all this time, trying to make her understand that she could never be anything but a brief amusement for him, and she had been too foolish to heed his warning.

But going away and never seeing him again ... the pain of that was such that she could hardly draw breath. A knife blade to her heart could surely have hurt no less than this, and yet that at least would be swift and therefore kind. This pain would endure for the rest of her days.

But she had suffered loss before, she reasoned. When Papa had died she had thought his loss unbearable, and then Maman had taken her own life and Marie had left her finally alone. With each loss she had thought she would die of misery, and yet she had lived. Clinging to life with a grim determination to endure, despite the wretchedness of her circumstances. Well this time she would leave prepared. She would not starve again, nor put herself in the hands of men. Men were not to be trusted. If one she had put her faith in so entirely could let her down in such a way, then there was no hope for them. She would never trust another man as long as she lived.

She wiped her eyes and forced herself to her feet, reasoning that the house would fall quiet again soon. She ran to Alex's desk and the locked box where she knew he kept an amount of cash, having seen him handing his steward money earlier in the day. She also knew the key was in his waistcoat. She ran and searched the discarded article for the tiny inside pocket and palmed the key. Opening the box she took all the notes, counting out the grand sum of five hundred pounds. That would have to be enough, it was certainly more money than she could ever have dreamed of before she met Alex. Closing the box and returning the key to his heavy, silk waistcoat she took a moment to carefully fold it and slip his jacket from her shoulders. Shivering at the loss of it she held it to her nose and inhaled, imprinting the scent upon her memories, knowing it would be all she had left to her.

It didn't take long to pack her things. There was little point in trying to haul her beautiful dresses with her, and she'd have little use for such finery anymore. Instead she packed a few of her more practical dresses, including a simple dimity gown she used when she was playing with Bandit in the garden, and things that would keep her warm when the weather turned. The idea of being cold again was not something she could countenance. She swallowed hard at the idea of leaving Bandit behind but she didn't feel she could take the little dog from his home and the life he was used to, and she was sure baby Elizabeth would love him as her own as she grew. She tried to hold back the tears but they seemed to slide down her face no matter how hard she tried to stop them. She took with her the locket Alex had given her for her birthday and a number of small mementos, but left the silver-backed brushes that Aunt Seymour had given her that had been Alex's mother's. Writing a note to say goodbye to everyone was harder. She didn't want them to blame Alex for her departure, but she didn't want them to hate her and think her ungrateful for all the kindnesses they had shown her.

In the end there were two short notes that she hoped would serve. She placed them on her pillow and arranged some cushions beneath the covers to make it look as though she was sleeping in the bed before taking a last look around the pretty room that had been hers since they came to London. With tears now streaming down her face unchecked she closed the door quietly, and headed down the stairs.

Standing alone, in the dark, outside the grand London residence in Mayfair, Céleste was forcibly reminded of how very small and insignificant she was. It was a feeling she was familiar with, but at least in obscurity she would not know what was said about her and her scandalous departure.

Taking a breath she drew the hood of her cloak up over her head, picked up her bag and began to walk in the direction of town where she hoped to find a chaise for hire. From there she would go to catch the mail coach. She only hoped she hadn't missed it as it was growing late indeed. She paused before turning the corner and took one last look at the elegant façade of Alex's home, and then she walked away.

Chapter 30

"Wherein hearts are broken."

By the time Alex returned home he was exhausted. Fury at dealing with a woman he had always admired had left him drained and his nerves frayed. That woman had proved to be such a vindictive and spiteful creature, and on top of the tumult of emotions that had battered his heart and his body earlier in the evening. He entered the house with quiet trepidation and went straight to his study, hoping foolishly that Céleste might have waited for him. Of course she couldn't have done. If anyone had discovered her she would have been mortified. But now he was in a quandary.

He was desperate to see her, to explain why Lydia had come to the house and to tell her that she was quite wrong. He wouldn't and had never had the slightest intention of keeping her as his mistress. Far from it. He wanted to fall on his knees and beg her to marry him. To beg her to overlook all the scandal, to withstand the gossip that would always follow her, to take the risk of marrying a man who may one day be too old and dull to interest her at all and make him the happiest of men. For he knew now that without her he would never again know what that emotion meant.

He hesitated outside of her door and gave a soft knock.

"Céleste?" He waited with his heart beating too hard in his chest and then knocked once more. To his frustration there was no reply. Likely she was sleeping now, he imagined, at least he hoped it was that and not that she was angry with him. The blasted Morris woman had made one hell of a scene and he needed to explain it all to her. But it would have to wait until the morning. He sighed and then smiled as an idea came to him.

He penned a short missive to his steward, instructing him that on rising he should go immediately to the proprietor of Rundell and Bridge, the jeweller at thirty two Ludgate Hill and instruct him that the Earl of Falmouth would be visiting at seven am sharp. He was also to make it clear Mr Rundell would be well compensated for the inconvenient hour of his visit. Satisfied that he had the very thing to hopefully smooth any ruffled feathers that Céleste might have, he took himself. Still, he prayed that his offer would meet with no objections once she understood his intentions.

***

The elegant Palladian style façade of Rundell and Bridge, jewellers to the crown, was emphasised by a grand entrance, flanked by Ionic columns. The interior, however, was sparse, if elegant, and served as a plain backdrop to display some of the most sumptuous and breathtaking jewellery ever made.

Mr Rundell greeted Alex with pleasure and lost no time at all in presenting him with the very best of his wares.

"I want something with sapphires," Alex said, casting a keen eye over silk-lined boxes and their array of dazzling treasure.

"Ah!" said Mr Rundell with an air of approval, disappearing to the back of the shop with a hurried step. "I have just the thing." He returned a moment later bearing a wide, deep blue leather box. "A very elegant piece," the man said with enthusiasm, opening it to reveal an exquisite necklace, nestled on a bed of ivory silk. "You see the flexible garland-like design? It is set with eleven cushion-cut emeralds weighing approximately twenty eight carats, spaced by scroll-work links, set with old mine and rose-cut diamonds also weighing approximately twenty eight carats, and mounted in silver and gold."

Alex nodded. "Yes, Mr Rundell, I concur, a very fine piece indeed. I will take it immediately. Would you also have three hair combs and a bracelet made to the same design please. I would like them delivered to me at your earliest convenience."

"Of course, my Lord! I felicitate you on your eye for beauty. I am sure the receiver of your gift will be quite overcome."

Alex smiled and touched a finger to a glittering stone that put him strongly in mind of a pair of wide blue eyes. "I do hope so," he said softly.

***

Returning home by half past ten, Alex was disappointed to discover that Céleste was apparently still abed, having left a note for her abigail that she was not to be disturbed before eleven. Eleven came and went. Although not unusual for her to sleep late after a night out, Alex demanded that the maid go and enquire if she was perhaps unwell.

A disquieting sense of unease had begun to slide under his skin and prickle the back of his neck. He hoped she had not taken to her bed in a fit of anger over what had happened last night, though he had to admit, she would be well within her rights to be furious with him and with Mrs Morris. Sitting in the bright drawing room, he smoothed his hand over the neat blue box and sighed.

He hoped he could convince her of the deep and heartfelt nature of both his apology and his ardent feelings for her. A scream from upstairs sent terror spiking through his veins and he leapt from his seat, taking the stairs three at a time until he stood in the doorway of Céleste's bedroom.

"What is it?" he demanded, taking in the sight of her abigail, white-faced and trembling and Henri with a letter in her hand and a look of devastation in her eyes.

"She's gone," Henri whispered, although she hardly dared to believe her own words.

"What?" Alex felt a rush of cold pouring over him like ice water as fear took a hold of him. He crossed the room and snatched a second letter addressed to him that Henri held out for him with shaking fingers.

Dearest Alex,

Please forgive my manner of leaving you, but I know if I were to stay we would both end our days unhappy. It's best that I go. I am sorry that I have run away, but it seems I am perhaps as young and childish as you first thought, for I cannot be one of many, Alex. I can't and I won't. I thought perhaps I could bear it, if I didn't know who they were or saw their faces. But I heard Mrs Morris speaking to you last night and I regret that the entertainments she spoke of were far too sophisticated for a country mouse such as I. I cannot share you, and never in so intimate a manner.

You have and will always hold my heart in its entirety, and so I could never consider marrying another. Please don't be angry with me and give my fondest love to everyone. I shall miss them all and will never forget everything they have done for me. But of course I shall miss you most of all, mon contrebandier.

Ever yours,

Mignonne.

P.S. I am afraid I have taken five hundred pounds from you, but I promise I will repay it, as soon as I am able to.

Alex let out a cry, a raw sound akin to a wounded creature and indeed he felt wounded, so grievously hurt and in pain he half expected to see blood pouring from some fatal wound.

"Oh, Alex, the poor child! Where would she go?"

He shook his head, trying to think past the shock. "Is there no clue in your letter?"

"No, nothing," she said, wiping her eyes. "She only says to forgive her and please to not think her ungrateful." She covered her mouth and sobbed. "Oh, Alex, we must find her!"

"Where's Lawrence?" he demanded.

"H-he ..." she stuttered. "He's taken the aunts to visit Aubrey."

"Find him," he said, trying desperately to keep a hold of his panic and think clearly. There was only one feasible way out of London, the Great North road. It was most likely she'd taken the Mail Coach. "We need to check all the coaching inns, see if she booked a passage and where to, and find out if Aubrey knows anything."

Henri nodded, sniffing. "I'll go right away and I'll instruct all the servants to hold their tongues. Not that they would talk. They all love her, everybody loves her so," she said, her voice breaking. "Does she not know this? Oh and there will be such a scandal if this gets out."

"It won't," Alex said, his voice certain. "She will be back here before anyone knows she's been gone."

"Yes," Henri reached out and grasped his arm. "Yes, you will bring her home, I know you will, but ... but why did she go, Alex?"

That question struck at his heart and the pain of it was so intense he didn't know if he could form an answer. "I discovered last night that she believed I only meant to take her as my mistress," he said, the words bitter in his mouth. "Before I could tell her I intended no such thing, that I love her and I wanted to marry her ... Mrs Morris ..." He could say no more and indeed needed to be away from here. He could waste no more time while his foolish, sweet Céleste was God knew where. And in whose company? He turned and strode from the room as Henri's words followed him out of the door.

"Oh, Alex, I am so very sorry."

He ran down the stairs, barking commands to his steward and yelling for his horse to readied immediately. He would find her, he swore to himself. He would find her safe and well before night fall, for if he didn't he would never forgive himself.

***

Céleste closed her eyes and endured the interminable jolting of the mail coach. She allowed her mind to take her back to another coach journey, with Alex sat beside her in the cramped Diligence as they left Madame Maxime's, heading to his brother's house at Bordeaux. So much had happened since then, she reflected. Her life had changed in ways she could never have conceived, and yet all the time she had been grasping at dreams. A dream that had been lovely and dreadfully beautiful, but as insubstantial as a cobweb, for when she had tried to take a hold of it she had found it without substance, too fragile to survive in a world she knew only too well was callous and cruel.

And so she would go back to where she came from. There at least she knew the place and the people, but none knew of her failed aspirations. She knew what to expect from a much smaller, simpler life, and hopefully with the money she had borrowed she could find a way to make a place for herself. There was enough to buy a house and live carefully for some considerable time if she was careful, and then she would need to consider how to earn a living. She determined to find Mimi and offer him a home with her if he would take it. At least then she would have a friendly face and someone to discourage the inevitable male visitors who would gather if they knew there was a single woman living alone and without protection.

She wouldn't allow herself to cry. She had already attracted the scandalised notice of the middle-aged couple on the seat opposite. The woman had just sniffed at her in disgust and turned her head away when she realised she was travelling unaccompanied, but the man's gaze had been rather more consistent and unpleasantly predictable.

By the time the coach drew up at The Red Lion in Dorset, she was stiff and tired, and heart sick. She wondered what was happening back home. Did Alex know she was gone? She wondered if he would come after her and knew that he would. He was too honourable to let her run away in such a fashion and do nothing about it. The idea made her chest tighten with anxiety. She couldn't let him find her. If he found her he would no doubt persuade her to come back home.

If she wouldn't be his mistress then he would find a suitable husband for her as he'd promised in the first place. But she wouldn't have it. She wouldn't have a man she didn't love have any say in her life, and she couldn't live in England with the ever present possibility, no matter how small, that she might one day stumble into Alex's path again and make a fool of herself. It was better to make a clean break. She'd give herself to no one and make her own way as best she could.

The pretty town of Shaftesbury overlooked the Blackmore Vale, and in other circumstances Céleste would have been enchanted by the beautiful countryside. Today, however, she saw nothing and spoke to no one, avoiding people's eyes as she stepped down from the coach and headed into The Red Lion. It was an elegant building and obviously profiting nicely from being on a busy coaching route. As such it was predictably busy with harassed employees scurrying back and forth bearing loaded trays, the enticing scents making Céleste's stomach twist. Though she was indeed faint from hunger, not having eaten since the previous evening, she thought it unlikely she would be able to eat anything. There would be a short stop here of forty minutes for refreshments though before the next leg of the journey commenced and she knew she had to make the effort or face the ignominy of swooning in public.

On searching around the packed eating parlour, however, she found to her dismay that there were no free tables. She jerked, startled by a soft touch of a hand over hers, and looked down to see a sweet-faced older lady looking up at her. With bright hazel eyes and cheeks that put her strongly in mind of overripe windfall apples, the woman had the kind of face that should belong to a fairy godmother.

"Come and sit with us, dear. Mr Harrison doesn't mind, do you Mr Harrison?" This last was addressed to her husband, a stout bald fellow with an improbable moustache.

Mr Harrison looked up from his steak pie, muttered something that sounded like agreement through the thick bristles of his upper lip and then reapplied himself with absolute concentration to his repast.

The older lady shifted on the bench seat, moving her own plate along as she went and practically pulled Céleste to sit down beside her.

"What a beautiful child," she sighed, looking at Céleste in wonder. "I said as soon as you walked in the door, didn't I, Mr Harrison? I said, what a beautiful young woman." She nodded to herself apparently needing no further comment from her husband which was just as well. "Oh, I'm Mrs Harrison, by the way and this is my husband, Mr Harrison, and isn't it a dreadful crush in here? Dear me, yes. Well now, we must get you something to eat, you look positively done in, you poor sweet thing."

In something of a daze and under the sway of the force of nature which was Mrs Harrison, Céleste was provided with food and a cup of ale and listened to her new companion chatter away while she ate. Happily Mrs Harrison didn't seem to need her to take any part in the conversation at this point, holding up her end of it and Céleste's quite admirably too, and prattled good-naturedly about her eldest son and her three daughters, *all married, dear,* and her recent trip to stay with her youngest daughter in Wiltshire.

It wasn't until she had finished eating that those bright hazel eyes were fixed on Céleste in a manner that made her believe Mrs Harrison wasn't as bacon-brained as she made out. She reached out and took hold of Céleste's hand in a motherly fashion.

"Now then, child, where are you going to?"

"To Plymouth, *Madame,"* Céleste replied, feeling a little uneasy under the woman's knowing gaze.

"You're going back to France?"

Céleste nodded and avoided her eye.

"You have family there I suppose?"

"Oui, Madame," she said, looking at her plate in case the woman detected the lie.

"Well now, it really isn't safe for you to be travelling all alone you must know this, my dear?"

Céleste swallowed and looked up but found nothing but concern in the woman's eyes. She smiled and shrugged. "I know, but ... but ..." Her voice trembled and she fell silent.

"Oh, my dear," the woman said, with such compassion in her voice that Céleste was very afraid she would begin to sob in the middle of a public place. "There, there, now child. Now where are you travelling to exactly?"

"Roscoff," Céleste mumbled, sniffing.

"Well then!" Mrs Harrison exclaimed, beaming at her. "You can get to Roscoff just as easily from Weymouth, and that is exactly where we are going. We live there you see, and so you must come along in our carriage with us. Mr Harrison won't mind, will you, Mr Harrison?" Not stopping for a reply from her husband who seemed disinclined to give one anyway, perhaps sensing there was little point, the woman beamed at her. "Well now that's all settled. Much nicer than rattling along in that nasty mail coach full of strange people. You come with us and we'll see you safely to Weymouth harbour."

"Oh, Madame, you are all kindness," Céleste replied with tears in her eyes, touched beyond measure.

Mrs Harrison began to sniff and blink rapidly at that and waved her hand. "Pho! Dear child, do stop or you shall have us both acting like a couple of watering pots."

And so with everything arranged quite nicely between them, Céleste was born off with Mr and Mrs Harrison, bound for Weymouth.

Chapter 31

"Wherein our hero tears the world apart."

Alex spent the rest of the day in a blur of activity. He began searching the coaching inns which were the principal departing point for the mail coach, and interrogating anyone he could get his hands on. Starting at the one closest to Mayfair he began at The White Horse on Fetter Lane to no avail, next The Saracen's Head Inn and after La Belle Sauvage back to Ludgate Hill where he had begun his morning with such high hopes. By the time he arrived at a very seedy place by the name of Blossoms Inn, in Cheapside, he was in such a pitch of temper and frustration that he very nearly murdered the manager of the fine establishment, when he suggested the girl might do right in trying to escape him. On reflection he realised he had reacted so because he felt there was no little truth in the man's words.

Exhausted and filthy from riding hell for leather between each inn, it was with relief that he realised his next destination was also in Cheapside. It was growing dark by the time he arrived at The Swan With Two Necks on Lad Lane. Between Wood Street and Milk Street, it was a huge and bustling place at all hours of the day and night.

Glossy black and maroon mail coaches, emblazoned with the Royal coat of arms in gold on their doors, lined up inside the central cobbled court yard. The yard was surrounded by tall, galleried buildings on all sides, offering overnight rooms for passengers, and horses were being led back and forth, brought up from stables underground. The place was alive with ostlers wiping down the glistening coats of twitching, sweating horses as a newly arrived coach was unloaded, and walking others around as they waited to be hitched to their carriages. Alex made his way through the throng, scattering people on all sides as they scurried to be out of the way of the towering, grim faced nobleman. Halting a weary and grime covered coach man bearing a whip he asked directions to the coach office and was directed to the left hand side of the yard, before they were both obliged to move hurriedly back as a team was sprung and a fully laden coach lurched forward heading for the tall archway behind them that led out onto the street. Turning as directed Alex discovered a large board stood outside the doors with all the destinations offered and he scanned them, wondering if it would jog any memory of some place that Céleste might head to, to no avail.

Searching out whoever had been on duty last night he was presented with a Mr Preston. A neat and precise man in his mid-fifties, Mr Preston informed him immediately and decisively that, yes, there had been a young woman, swathed in a dark velvet cloak and travelling alone, who boarded the midnight mail coach. She'd paid for the full journey to Plymouth. Alex was further informed that the coach would make stops every three hours for no more than a few minutes but that it would have arrived at The Red Lion in Shaftsbury in Dorset at around four pm, where the passengers would have had a brief stop for a meal before continuing onto Plymouth.

Plymouth! Dear God she was going back to France. If she left the country she could feasibly disappear without a trace. His heart grew cold at the thought but he grasped the man's hand. Thanking him for his help, he offered generous recompense for his time and asked that he might treat the matter with discretion.

"Oh, no my Lord," the man said with a kindly smile. "Tis a pleasure to help you. Believe me, I have a daughter myself and know what a worry they are. I hope you catch up with her safely."

Suitably chastened and feeling ever more the villain, Alex set off in pursuit of the midnight mail.

***

It was almost eleven at night by the time Mr and Mrs Harrison set her down outside a neat-looking boarding house close to the harbour at Weymouth. Apparently run by a very dear friend of Mrs Harrison, she assured Céleste she would be quite safe and Mrs Travers would wake her early to catch the packet boat.

Céleste bid a weary and tearful goodbye to the sweet lady who insisted on giving her their address and begging that Céleste should write and inform her that she had indeed reached her family safely. For Mrs Harrison was convinced she would not sleep a wink again until she was certain of such a fact.

Mrs Travers appeared to be a tall, sparse woman with an assessing gaze and Céleste wondered at the possibility of her being Mrs Harrison's dear friend. She seemed less sanguine about Céleste arriving on her doorstep without even an abigail to accompany her, but she was kind enough albeit in a brusk manner. Céleste was shown to a small room with whitewashed walls, a thin, hard-looking bed and, she was reliably informed, a lovely view over the harbour.

Provided with hot water and a curt goodnight, she was left to attend to her needs and turned in the little space feeling suddenly more alone than she ever had in her life before. She scolded herself soundly and began to give herself a talking to. After all, when Marie had died she had been in far worse straights. Completely alone, not a penny to her name. Now at least she had funds, and when she returned to Roscoff she would find Mimi and they would start a business of some kind. Perhaps a little boarding house like this one?

She huddled into the narrow bed, trying to tell herself it was an exciting adventure. That she would have no one to tell her what to do, how to live her life ... but soon enough her thoughts returned to Alex. She remembered the feel of his hands and mouth on her, the reverent way in which he had kissed her and shown her the path to pleasure. But of course that was just his skill as a lover. It was clearly why he had gained such a reputation among the ladies, gossip of such a type was ever in abundant supply and she'd had no illusions about the kind of man he was. But she hadn't been prepared for it to feel so very special, so very intimate, such a deep and close connection, for her at least. The idea that he had likely made many women feel much the same thing was more than her poor, wearied heart could bear, and after a day of trying to be brave she finally succumbed to tears, and she cried herself into an exhausted sleep.

***

The next morning dawned fair and bright, and Céleste stood beside the harbour, watching the bustling activity of fishermen and sailors, the unloading of merchant ships and the back and forth of small boats as they went about their day. Overhead the raucous cries of gulls, wheeling high above and harrying the fishermen as they brought their catch to shore, pierced her aching brain. She had slept deeply but not well and was overtaken now with the kind of bone deep fatigue that accompanies those afflicted by the harshest sorrow.

Instructed to wait for the packet boat which would begin boarding at nine o'clock sharp she discovered she had time on her hands. With over an hour to kill she searched out and found herself a sheltered spot, out of the way of the busy thoroughfare where she was likely to be set flying by a rolling barrel or an overloaded cart. From here too, she was out of the wind which snatched at her skirts and tugged at her bonnet. She was heartily glad of her foresight in wearing her simplest, blue striped sarsnet gown made high at the neck and with long, tight sleeves, rather than her usual pretty muslins, and also for the addition of her winter cloak and gloves. For despite the fact it was a glorious spring day the early morning breeze here was sharp indeed and she shivered, huddling into the thick folds of her cloak with relief.

From here she could watch the comings and goings of the harbour, and tried her best to keep her mind occupied and away from Alex and his possible thoughts or whereabouts, with little success. Her attention, however, was taken by a small flotilla of little boats returning from further up the channel.

A great East Indiaman was sitting out on the horizon, while the smaller boats scurried around it like servants at a King's feet. Céleste had often seen such sights in Roscoff. The big ships would attract the local fishermen, eager to trade with the sailors who offered small amounts of contraband, tax free, to add to their meagre wages. Of course this inevitably returned her thoughts back to her own *contrebandier*. Though she knew well his business interests were on a much grander scale than these little fishermen, who were simply hoping to scrape a living. She watched with a benign air as two men, perhaps father and son, returned to shore, hauling their boat onto the soft golden sands and offloading two small kegs, of what she suspected was French brandy. Smiling she turned her head and felt her heart skip when the flash of a red jacket in the distance brought her eyes firmly on the slow, but inexorable approach of three Revenue officers.

"Merde!" she exclaimed, returning her attention to the men, bearing a keg apiece as they made their way back up the beach. Suddenly frantic on their behalf she got to her feet and began to run towards them. They had just reached the edge of the beach and were stepping onto the walkway when she reached them, quite breathless and flushed in her anxiety to save them. They looked upon her in some surprise, clearly unused to being accosted by unaccompanied young ladies on the beach.

"The Revenue!" she squeaked at them. Their dilemma quickly became apparent to them and both men blanched. "Oh, put them down! Put them down!" she snapped, waving at the barrels. Perhaps too surprised to disobey they did as she asked, setting the barrels side by side, whereupon she sat on them and cast the voluminous folds of her cloak about to cover the small barrels. At this point she leaned back and moaned fanning herself. "Oh!" she cried in as convincing a manner as she could contrive, adding in an undertone to the startled men. "I've fainted, you fools, *aidez moi!"*

To her relief they caught on and the older man patted her hand as the other offered her a sip from a hip flask which she accepted gratefully even though she was shamming it.

She cracked open an eye to see the Revenue men cast a curious glance their way before continuing upon their path without a backwards glance.

"Oh, mon Dieu," she said, letting go of a breath. "That was close."

She looked up to see the two men staring at her, clearly torn between bewilderment and gratitude.

"Well, Madame, I don't know rightly how we should thank you," said the older man, scratching his head and looking at her in wonder. "That you should take it upon yourself to save two such as ourselves, well ... well I'm beyond words, that I am."

A short stocky man with a grizzled grey beard and blue eyes set under extraordinarily bushy eyebrows in a deeply tanned face, he looked genuinely flummoxed and Céleste couldn't help but laugh.

"It was my pleasure," she said. "I have a ... a dear friend who is occupied in a similar trade you see and ..." she shrugged but it seemed to be all that was required as the man beamed at her.

"Oh!" he said, his broad smile showing a row of uneven teeth. "Well in that case we're as good as kin. Now see, this is my son in law, Davy, and I'm Jack Webster. But everyone calls me Jacky." He held out a gnarled hand which Céleste shook with amusement. "But here, not that it's my business, but what's a little slip of a girl like you doing down here alone? It won't do you know, indeed it won't."

"Some shady folks down by the harbour," the son in law, Davy, intoned with a voice of deep foreboding. She had to look rather farther up for Davy, craning her neck as he was as long and thin as a fishing rod and about as substantial.

"Oh, well," she said, shrugging and recalling her own wretched circumstance with an unhappy start. In the excitement of rescuing them she had momentarily forgotten her flight and had felt eager to relay the whole tale to Alex, for how very entertained he would be!

How very stupid she was.

Seeing the emotions and the obvious misery that settled upon her face, Jacky's face darkened with understanding.

"Ah, like that is it? Where you going to, lass?"

"Roscoff," she said, looking at her shoes. "I am going 'ome."

"Waiting for the packet boat I suppose?" he added.

Céleste nodded and sniffed.

She looked up to see the two men share a glance and Jacky seemed to come to a decision. "Now look here," he said, his voice soft and concerned. "Why don't you come back with us. Davy's missus, my Meg, she lives with me and the wife. They'll look after you, and then, on the next tide we're Roscoff bound. Have to stop overnight at Jersey mind so won't be as quick as the packet, but you'll be safe and it will save you a penny or two."

"Oh," she said, blinking away tears. "You really are very kind, but ... but I couldn't impose ..."

"Impose!" Jacky barked in astonishment, before giving a heavy frown, his blue eyes momentarily disappearing under his thick grey eyebrows. "You just saved us from a Revenue and at the very least a hefty fine. It's the least we can do."

His face took on a look of understanding and he shooed his son in law away for a moment, crouching down to put his face on a level with hers. "Now, look, Miss ..."

"Lavelle," Céleste said, feeling awkward. "Célestine Lavelle."

"Well now, Miss Lavelle, I don't know what trouble you're in and I don't need you to tell me. But I know trouble when I see it." He hesitated before speaking again, but she could tell his words were heartfelt. "Davy's wife, my Meg, she got herself tied up with a gentlemen who really wasn't any good for her. A wrong'un he was and no mistake. Tried to lead her astray he did and ..." He shook his head and gave her hand a light pat. "I was lucky everything turned out as it should and that Davy is a good and kind-hearted fellow is all, but I'd like to repay the fates for that kindness and you for yours, if you'll allow it?"

"Oui, Monsieur Jacky," Céleste said with gratitude. "I will, and I thank you with all my 'eart."

***

Alex let out a cry of utter frustration, and ignoring the startled gazes of the people going about their daily business, he leaned back against the wall of the harbour master's office in utter misery. He hadn't slept, hadn't eaten, he was bone tired and out of his mind with worry. He'd arrived at the Red Lion close to ten the next morning and after a hair raising night ride. He thanked God there had at least been a bright moon and a clear night or he knew not what he would have done. On arrival it was confirmed that a single woman had indeed arrived on the mail coach, bound for Plymouth. Further than that no other information could be had as there had been such a crush of people, no one had time or interest to survey the goings on of a single customer.

But now on reaching Plymouth late that same afternoon, he was told that Céleste hadn't rejoined the mail coach at all. So now he had a dilemma. Her intention was clear enough, she was returning to France. But why then hadn't she continued her journey? Was this a deliberate step to hide her tracks or had something befallen her? His heart constricted at the idea. Please God, please let her be alright, please let me find her. He had repeated the heartfelt prayer over and over from the moment he had first read those heart wrenching words she had left for him. Oh dear Lord, why hadn't he told her that he loved her? Why hadn't he made his feelings plain?

Scrubbing his hands over his face he tried to stay focused. He was beyond tired, his eyes burning for sleep, his body sore and aching from so many hours in the saddle but he simply couldn't stop. He had to find her. At each stage of the journey he had sent word back to the family to inform them of his progress as well as leaving information at the inn in Shaftesbury and with the harbour master in case Lawrence was following his trail. He hoped that even now, Lawrence and whatever men he'd been able to gather were following close behind him for they clearly needed to widen their search. And so it was with a heavy heart that Alex remounted his horse and retraced his steps, back to The Red Lion.

Chapter 32

"Wherein a light is found in the most profound darkness."

August 1816. Tregothnan

"He's back!"

Henri looked up with a start as Lawrence flew into the room.

"Oh thank God!" Henri exclaimed, putting baby Elizabeth down to toddle unevenly around the room to her nurse maid as she ran to her husband and grasped at his arm. "Is she ...?"

Lawrence shook his head. "No, it appears not. One of the stable lads just ran round to tell me he's on his way up to the house but ... He's alone."

"Oh, Lawrence!" Henri put her hand to her mouth and blinked away tears. Her heart ached for her brother in law who had been living in the darkest depths of hell ever since Céleste had vanished from his life. Consumed with grief and guilt he would speak to no one and refused to be occupied with anything else but his determination to get Céleste back.

In his absence Lawrence had taken control of both his smuggling interests and the more legitimate business of running a vast estate such as Tregothnan. On his brief visits home it was all they could do to force him to eat and sleep a little before he left once more. Poor, poor Alex. "But it's been over five months now," she said, her voice trembling.

"I know," Lawrence said, pulling her into an embrace. "I know. But we both know Céleste is a resourceful girl and she grew up in such harsh circumstances. She's no softly bred pea-goose and she had some money, she'll be alright. I'm sure of it."

Henri looked up at him, and knew her eyes were full of the nightmares they'd all endured. Of all the terrible fates that could have befallen such a beautiful young woman, all alone in the world. The aunts were beside themselves, and had retreated back to Hertfordshire to await news as the family battled to hide the scandal by saying that Céleste had returned to France to seek out her lost family.

There had been no warm weather as the months passed, with frosts so late in the year, and so severe that people were calling it the year with no summer. It seemed as though Céleste leaving them had taken all the warmth and joy from their lives.

They both ran out into the entrance hall at the sound of the front door opening and Alex walked in.

Henri gasped as she took in the sight of him. His face was taut with worry and a thick black beard proved that it had been many days since he had seen a razor. Covered head to foot in mud and bringing with him the salt tang of the sea he looked indeed as though he had voyaged to hell and back.

He shrugged off his great coat while Henri shouted for a hot meal to be provided at once and they ushered him in front of the nearest fire and sat him down. Henri dropped to her knees and helped him pull off his filthy boots, caring nothing for the mud on her hands as Lawrence filled a glass with brandy and placed it firmly in his brother's hands.

Once he had taken a moment to drink and catch his breath they sat, waiting with horrified anticipation but not daring to force him to speak. In the end in was Lawrence who broke the silence.

"Did you find anything, Alex? Any sign?"

Alex shook his head and Henri felt a shaft of pain in her heart so severe she was obliged to seek Lawrence's hand for comfort.

"Nothing," Alex said, his voice ragged and rough, as though he'd forgotten how to use it. "No sign. Nothing." He ran a filthy hand through his hair which was far too long and completely dishevelled. "I went to Roscoff. Tore the damn town apart. The whore house is gone, boarded up and everyone vanished, though I did find Mimi. He'd not seen her, though he damn near killed me for letting her get away." He shook his head, his face utterly bereft. "I had half a mind to let him. If I thought I would never see her again ..." He stopped, his throat working as he looked away and stared into the fire.

Lawrence squeezed Henri's hand as she began to sob quietly.

"What then?" Lawrence asked, his voice soft.

"Then I went back to Allaire, checking at places along the route we took before. I had some idea that maybe she'd go to her family's old home, but there was nothing. No one had seen her. So I returned to Roscoff again with no more luck than the first time. Mimi wouldn't speak to me at all. I went back to Portsmouth, retraced my steps to The Red Lion, and stopped at every inn and boarding house on the way, I went from there to Weymouth but there's no record of her crossing on the packet boat.

I've been back to London, I've followed the mail route again and stopped at each possible place she could have alighted. I've asked everyone I could think of, been everywhere they might have seen her, and ... nothing." He rubbed his eyes and gestured for Lawrence to refill his glass. "And so I came back here, hoping ... maybe ..."

He met Henri' eyes and she shook her head. "Nothing, Alex, I'm so dreadfully sorry. Not a word."

Alex nodded and got to his feet. "I need to sleep. I have an early start in the morning."

"Oh but, Alex, no!" Henri objected, getting up and walking after him, tugging at his arm. "You must eat something first and I insist you stay here, at least a day or two. My God, you're exhausted."

Lawrence nodded, putting his arm around his wife. "Henri's right, Alex. You'll gain nothing by making yourself ill. At least stay a couple of nights to catch your breath."

But Alex just shook his head. "Instruct the stables to have my horse ready for me. Goodnight."

The next morning Alex was up early as he'd said and it was all they could do to force him to sit still and eat something before he went out again. Slightly cleaner but still unshaven, Lawrence reflected that he looked far more the pirate than he had ever done. He watched as his brother made his way through a thick steak as fast as he might, with the air of someone doing an unwanted chore.

They looked up as the butler, Pawly, entered the room with a silver tray bearing his lordship's correspondence.

"This has just arrived for you, my Lord," the old man said, as Alex took it up from the tray with a frown, breaking the seal.

He scanned the contents of the letter and sprang to his feet.

"What?" Henri asked in alarm. "What is it?"

"It's from the solicitor at Truro. He says he has been sent money to the amount of five hundred pounds by a person who wishes to remain anonymous in repayment of a debt.

"Céleste!" Henri cried, jumping to her feet and running to Alex's side to crane her neck and look at the letter. "Oh!" she said, clutching at his arm. "She's alright, she must be if she's returning the money to you. Oh thank God."

Both men were quiet and Henri frowned, looking at her husband in consternation.

"But how did she lay her hands on that kind of money?" Lawrence asked quietly.

Henri paled and sat down again hurriedly as Alex glowered at his brother and strode from the room. Lawrence leapt to his feet and ran after him.

"Where are you going?" he demanded as Alex snatched up his great coat and headed for the door.

"To see the solicitor and find out about my anonymous benefactor," Alex growled and slammed the door behind him.

***

The small but well-appointed offices of Egerton and Witham were set upon their ears by Alex's early morning arrival. The unhappy Mr Witham whose partner was sadly elsewhere looked up, apparently believing at first glance that there was a madman in his midst, intent on murdering him while going about his lawful business. It was at this point that the worthy Witham recognised at last the Earl of Falmouth.

"Have you lost your mind, my Lord Falmouth?" the poor man demanded.

Alex did nothing to dispel the man's terror at his state of mind, and in fact went out of his way to encourage it as he raised a pistol and levelled it at Mr Witham, the signatory of this morning's correspondence. He next demanded in a level voice, that Mr Witham produce all the information he had on the person who had been so kind as to forward such a sum of money to him.

A thin-faced man, with a back bowed like a whippet, Mr Witham cried like a maid and thrust the letter into Alex's hand whilst pleading for mercy. At this point Alex left the building, informing him as he went that he would pay Mr Witham handsomely for his inconvenience but that if a word of this got about he'd return and bring his pistol with him.

Alex stood in the street and stared at the letter once again, leaning upon his horse and finding that his hands were not quite as steady as they ought to be. He drank in the sight of the familiar hand which made his heart constrict and tears gather in his eyes. At last. Oh thank God, at last.

He pressed the letter to his lips and convinced himself that he could smell the scent of her upon the page. Returning his gaze once more to the sight of his beloved girl's handwriting he looked at the address on the correspondence, *Pleumeur Bodou, Roscoff.* How she had evaded him he could not understand, but at last he had a glimmer of hope that perhaps his nightmare was at an end. He would go to the address and throw himself upon her mercy, and pray to God she would find it in her heart to forgive him.

***

By late the next morning he was at Roscoff, having waited furiously for the tide and submitting with very bad grace to Henri and his valet's pleas to shave and make himself presentable. In the end he submitted, if for no other reason that he doubted his ability to persuade Céleste back into his arms after everything she had been through. And so he shaved and dressed with care, and took the precaution of bringing everything he could think of for Céleste's own comfort and any eventuality.

The journey was interminable though the winds were kind and they made excellent time, but his patience was at breaking point as his head was full of the bad dreams that had plagued him since that disastrous night. He had tormented himself considering all and any of the possible ills that could have befallen her, and now, when he was so close, he was almost quaking with a mixture of joy, anticipation and terror of what he might find. For if any had hurt his sweet girl, by the time he was done with them they would beg for the fate that he had delivered to Monsieur Pelletier and consider themselves fortunate to get it.

Hiring a chaise close to the harbour he was taken to *Pleumeur Bodou,* and on further direction was forwarded to a pretty stone house with far reaching views over the sea.

He approached on foot with his heart beating in his chest so hard he felt sick with anticipation and saw the figure of a woman playing with a child in the garden beside the house. Though he knew this was not Céleste, he hastened his step, eager to discover news of her.

"Bonjour Madame," he said, trying to contain his impatience as he greeted her and drew upon his best French. "Please forgive me the intrusion, but I was wondering if you might be able to help me. I'm looking for someone."

The woman, who had dark hair and a fierce expression, looked him over. Her brown eyes seemed far older than her face might allow and she seemed wary but resigned.

"Oui, I know who you are," she replied, sneering at him, her French accent far coarser that Céleste's more refined tone. "She's not here. So if you've come to upset her you can turn around and walk away again. We don't need men here. We don't want any of you. Devils every one, you are!" She spat on the ground at his feet with contemptuous look that he felt ill placed to object to.

"Madame," he said, praying she could see the contrition in his eyes. "I can't tell you that your opinion of me is totally misplaced, but please believe me when I tell you I would never, ever, intentionally hurt Céleste. And though I know I did and most grievously, I beg you to believe me that it was unintentional and not entirely of my doing. Please, I beg of you. Just tell me where I might find her, or when she'll be back. If she wants none of me I swear to God I'll leave and you'll never see me again. But I must see her, at least for a moment."

The woman seemed struck by the impassioned nature of his speech and bent down to pick up a little girl not much older than his niece who was pulling at her skirts. She kissed the babe, settling her on the generous curve of her hip and looked at him long and hard.

"D'accord," she said, her voice begrudging. "But if you upset her I'll send Mimi after you and he'll pay you back for every tear."

"Mimi is here?" he said, smiling as his heart lightened. He had found her. She was really here.

"Oui," the woman said with a sneer. "The only men welcome here are those who've lost their minds."

Alex laughed softly and nodded. "Well, *Madame,* I assure you that after the past months that description fits me only too well."

She smiled at that and nodded. *"Alors,* my Lord, you'll find her down by the beach. Tell her Belle sent you and that Mimi is standing ready to tear you limb from limb if required."

Alex bowed to her, acknowledging her words for the very real threat they were, before turning and making with all haste to the beach.

Chapter 33

"Wherein our two lovers make many confessions."

Céleste sat and stared out at the sea as she often did now. She buried her fingers in the sand feeling the surface warm from the sun, and the damp sand beneath far, far colder to the touch. Like she was, she thought. Her skin was warm and she seemed to live, but everything inside her was cold and shrivelled in on itself, crouching protectively around the pain in her heart.

She sighed and squinted out across the glittering sea. Though September was drawing on and the weather not so warm as it was, on a fine day she fancied she could see the coast of Cornwall and it made her feel in some small way closer to Alex. She pulled her cloak around herself and closed her eyes and allowed herself to remember him. To remember those cold grey eyes that would fill with warmth when he looked at her, the sound of his laughter when she had said something he found amusing, the feel of his lips on hers that one night when she had believed her dreams had come true. She blinked and scolded herself.

She had done enough crying. Crying and wishing didn't change anything, no matter how badly you wanted it to. She had been fortunate, she knew that, not least in her chance meeting with Jacky and Davy. They had become firm friends and their family had taken her in as one of their own. It was only misfortune that had seen them caught in a downpour on the journey to Jersey. More than five miserable weeks she had spent on the island there, feverish and more ill than she'd ever been in her life, and so weak in the aftermath that it had taken some time to recover. But Jacky had left her in the care of a distant cousin who couldn't have been kinder, and on coming to Roscoff he and Davy had become regular visitors, much to Belle's disgust, checking that everyone was alright and well provided for.

Yes, she had indeed been fortunate, for although life had dealt her some cruel blows in her short life, it had also put her in the way of people who had proved to be good and kind and honest, and for that she was grateful. Nonetheless Alex's dear face came to mind and she put her head in her hands and prayed for the pain to pass, prayed for the day when she could remember him simply with fondness and a sense of regret, rather than the turn of a knife in her heart when she thought about everything she'd lost.

***

When Alex crested the rise that led to the beach and looked across the sand his heart twisted in his chest and he was struck with a barrage of emotions that almost forced him to his knees. She was here, she was truly here! He had to stand for a moment to collect himself and simply drink in the sight of her. With her cloak pulled tight around her and her hair lose and flying around her face in the sea breeze, she looked both very young and terribly fragile and he gave his promise once more to God that whatever it was she wanted, even if it was no longer him, he would do everything in his power and more to ensure she was safe and happy and well for the rest of her days. And if by some miracle she still wanted him, he would spend the rest of his life ensuring that she found no cause to regret it.

He covered the space between them, his footfalls soft on the damp sand, the sound of his approach whipped away by the breeze, smothered by the soft wash of the waves on the shore and the gulls crying overhead. And so it was that when he said her name, she started and looked around in surprise.

She looked up at him, those wide blue eyes unblinking and astonished.

"A-Alex?"

He had promised himself he would not overwhelm her. He would behave calmly and allow her time to react to his presence, to shout or rage at him as she must want to, but in the end he could keep none of those promises. He fell to his knees in the sand and snatched her up, pulling her against him and holding her as tight as he dared without hurting her for fear that she was only a dream like so many others and he would wake any moment to find her stolen from him again.

"Céleste, Céleste," he mumbled, incoherent as he smoothed his hands over her sweet face, rubbing away tears that as yet he did not know were for joy or despair. "Oh, *mignonne*, what have you done to me? You have broken my heart and turned me into some feral creature that cannot eat, nor sleep nor think of anything but you. Why did you run away like that before I could tell you everything, before I could explain?" He covered her face with kisses, pulling her to him once again and trying not to weep as the horror of the past months caught up with him and shredded his emotions. He held her tight, silent for a moment, hearing her breathing just as ragged and uneven as his but reassured that she wasn't fighting her way out of his embrace but holding onto him just as fiercely.

He took a breath as she looked up at him, her expression a little shy and unsure as she reached up a hand to touch his face.

"Is it really you, Alex? *Vraiment?"*

"Oui, *mignonne,* it is truly me, though it's I that need reassuring," he said, leaning into her touch and smiling, cradling her face within his hands. "Swear to me I'm not dreaming," he pleaded. "Tell me I've truly found you, for if this is a dream I beg you don't let me wake. I cannot bear it, Céleste, I cannot bear another day without you. I know I am too old and too wicked and there are too many reasons ..." But he didn't finish the words as she pulled his head down and kissed him and he sank into her embrace. He kissed her with all the love and the tenderness that he had to give, needing to show her how very much she meant, how desperately sorry he was for everything that had happened.

When he finally released her she sobbed and buried herself in his arms.

"Oh, Alex. I dreamed that you would come."

"But surely you knew?" he asked, his heart aching. "Mimi is here, surely he told you I was searching for you?"

She nodded, averting her gaze from his. "He told me."

"Then why?" he cried. *"Mignonne,* why didn't you come back to me, or let me know where you were? Do you hate me so?" he asked, hardly daring to hear the answer for all that she had kissed him so sweetly.

She swallowed and shook her head. "I could never hate you, Alex," she said, smiling as tears rolled down her face. "Don't you see that's the trouble. I was afraid if you found me, you'd persuade me to ..." She flushed and looked away from him and guilt and anger blazed in his heart.

"To be my mistress?" he finished for her. She nodded and he bowed his head in shame.

"My God, Céleste, didn't Mimi tell you what I told him? Did he not give you the letter I left for you?"

She frowned and shook her head, perplexed as he cursed the damn fool. He had been sure he'd made his intentions clear enough. "He told me nothing, Alex, only that you'd come looking for me and then left again."

"I came twice," he said, begging her to see how hard he'd tried. "I came here and searched everywhere and he said he hadn't seen you. Then I went back to Allaire in case you'd returned to your family home, and then I came back here again and still he'd told me he'd seen no sign of you.

"Twice?" she repeated, reaching out and grasping his arm. "I didn't know Alex, truly. But ... but what did it say in the letter?"

He took a breath and looked into her eyes. "It said that I never had the slightest intention of making you my mistress, you foolish child. If you had but waited I was going to ask you to marry me."

Her mouth formed a little O of astonishment but she said nothing so he carried on.

"Ma mie, can you not see that I am in love with you? I have loved you from the first, and every day since has been a torment. I love you beyond reason and with a ferocity that scares me to death. I have lost my sanity and my heart these past months without you, my love, and though it's the most selfish thing I will ever do I am begging you to end this misery and marry me. Please, *mignonne,* say you will?"

His heart stood suspended in a void while she stared at him in utter shock, until a startled little laugh escaped her and she threw her arms about his neck.

"Oui, Alex! Oui! Oh yes, yes, yes I will marry you!"

Laughing with joy and relief he lost no time in tumbling her onto her back and kissing her until she was breathless.

***

It *was* like some kind of wonderful dream, thought Céleste, except that her dreams had never had quite such dizzying heights of happiness as she now felt. They sat huddled together on the beach, unwilling to move despite the fact the sand was damp and it was growing chilly. Alex just kept staring at her, touching her face and pulling her closer though she was sat in his lap. It was like she couldn't be close enough to him, or he was afraid she might disappear again. They talked in hushed tones about the past months, and as Céleste related her story he would punctuate her words by kissing her again.

"But I'd told her the day I came to London that it was over," Alex said, looking at her with his grey eyes full of guilt. "I told them all. I had no interest in any of them. There's no one but you, *ma mie,* you must believe that."

She nodded and touched a fingertip to his lip. "I do believe it now, I do," she said.

He sighed and shook his head. "It was that bastard Sindalton who put her up to it. My God, I'll have his head for it too, he won't ..."

"Non."

He looked at her in surprise. "Surely you don't defend him?" There was a tone in his voice that sounded a little like jealousy.

She shook her head. "Not defend him exactly, only ... I think he believed that ... that you were making me unhappy. The day at the theatre, when you came upon us, I'd seen you with Mrs Morris and I'd ...well, I'd been crying." She smiled and took his hand, pressing it against her cheek and turning her head to kiss the palm. "Don't look so guilty, I know now you were trying to avoid a scene, but I think he guessed why I was upset. I think he believed I would be better off with him as he would offer to marry me."

Alex snorted. "Out of the frying pan into the fire," he muttered, and Céleste chuckled.

"Is 'e a very bad man?" she asked. "I know 'e is supposed to be the most eligible man in England."

Alex glowered at her, his jealousy only too obvious and Céleste laughed and pressed kisses over his face. "Come now, *mon brave,* I 'ave only just forgiven you for being an earl, surely you don't think I want a duke?"

His face was still grave when he spoke again. "I know you're teasing, Céleste, but ... truly, are you sure? Are you certain you can be happy with me? I'm so much older than you. I keep thinking that when you're barely forty I'll be almost sixty and ..."

She kissed him, pulling at his head until he laid her down again and covered her body with his own.

"I'm sure," she whispered. "You're all I want, Alex. There could never be anyone else but you. I would rather be alone."

He sighed and she felt a little of the tension fall away from him as she burrowed into the warmth of his body.

"You're cold," he observed, rubbing his hands over her arms and back to warm her.

"A little," she admitted. "But I don't want to go back to the 'ouse yet."

He was quiet for a little while, and when he spoke his tone was cautious. "The girl at the house, Belle, was she ..."

"One of Maxime's whores?" she said, smiling at the hesitancy of his question. *"Oui*, Alex, she was." She looked up at him, wondering what on earth he must be thinking. "Annise and Clara are there also. I couldn't find any of the others." She smirked at the confusion in his eyes and covered her mouth as laughter began to build in her chest. "Oh, Alex, your face. Oh, *mon contrebandier,* I 'ave not become a Madame I assure you."

He had the grace to look appalled at the suggestion. "I never thought it!" he swore, as she laughed at him. "Céleste! I swear it never crossed my mind, only ... I am curious as to how all of this has been paid for. How did you raise enough to buy this house and repay the money you borrowed?"

She pursed her lips and stared up at him, pushing a lock of thick black hair off of his forehead. "Promise you won't be cross with me?"

He took a breath and then let it out on a huff of laughter. *"Mignonne,* I have the ominous feeling you are about to shock me to my bones, but at this moment, I can promise I won't be cross with you. You are here and you want to be with me despite everything. You could have murdered Prinny in his bed and I wouldn't bat an eyelid. Though I admit I hope it's nothing quite so dire as killing the Prince Regent as I would rather like to go home and marry you."

"Then I had better tell you quickly," she said, her serious tone bringing real anxiety to his eyes now. "Please let me sit up," she added. "I can't concentrate with you so close to me."

Too pleased by the comment to let her up right away, she sighed as his lips kissed a warm trail down her throat. "Hurry, then," he said, his voice husky. "For I have unfinished business with you, love."

She flushed a little and felt her heart pick up but he moved away and sat up, pulling her once more into his lap. Threading her arms around his neck she leaned her head against his and began to tell him of her voyage to Roscoff. Of Mr and Mrs Harrison and her meeting with two smugglers on Weymouth harbour.

She was about to explain her trip to Jersey when Alex stopped her.

"Wait, *ma mie,* are you telling me you stepped in and saved two smugglers from the Revenue by hiding their contraband beneath your clothing?"

She nodded and he groaned and buried his face against her neck. "You're right, you'd best tell me the rest quickly. Is it much worse than that?" He looked up and she could see real anxiety in his eyes

"Fi donc! I didn't get caught and neither did they, and I am here, *hein?"* She huffed at him. "I thought you might be proud of me."

"I am always proud of you, *mignonne,* but I would have a promise that you won't go hiding any more smugglers from the Revenue please. Well, except for me," he added with a rueful smile. His face fell as she bit her lip and looked at him feeling a little more nervous as to his reaction now.

"Oh God," he said. "You'd better get it over with. Let's have it."

Céleste swallowed and began to pluck at one of the buttons on his coat. "Well ..." she began, avoiding his eyes. "They took me to Jersey, as they usually buy their goods there rather than voyage all the way to Roscoff every time, as they only deal in a small amount of contraband. But on the way it rained very hard and I got very wet and cold and caught a chill. So I was poorly for some weeks."

"Wait." He held up his hand to interrupt her. "A chill would not keep you abed for weeks," he said, his expression full of concern.

"No, that is true, it ... it was a little worse than that I think, but I am quite recovered now."

Alex made a sound of distress and pulled her close to him, burying his face in her hair. "I'm never letting you out of my sight again."

"Please don't," she sighed, stroking the back of his neck.

"Go on," he mumbled his voice muffled against her hair.

"Well I was on the island for five weeks, which is why you didn't find me when you came 'ere before," she said. "And after that I came 'ere and bought this place with some of the money I took from you and invited the girls to come and live with me, where they would be safe and not 'ave to ... to ..."

He smiled at her, his eyes warm. "Yes, I quite see, love, carry on."

"So Mimi came too and we cleaned the place up and, oh, Alex, it is really quite charming. I would like to show it to you."

"And I look forward to that, only I want to know where the money came from, Céleste. If you bought this place and have been supporting yourselves too, how have you replaced what you took?"

"Oh, oui," she said, feeling her cheeks heat a little and wondering just how cross he was likely to be. She put her chin up, a little defiant, took a deep breath and decided to get it over with as quickly as she could. "Well, Jacky and Davy, they come by when they are in Roscoff and check we are all OK, and so I said to them they should spend more money 'ere where things are cheaper, so it was more worth their while, you see. But they 'ave no money and so ... and so ... " She said the next part in a rush of words to try and

soften the blow. "And so I said I would invest in their business and I bought them brandy and silk and lace and some tea and they sold it and ... they gave me a cut of the profits, and it worked so nicely that we carried on and ... and they 'ave found some other men to work with us too and so ... I've made enough money to pay you back and support the girls ... and a bit put aside as well." She hauled in a breath, after having rattled off her confession with such speed and glanced nervously at Alex who was staring at her, apparently speechless.

He cleared his throat and rubbed his hand over his face before taking a deep breath.

"Alex, are you quite well?" she asked and then bit her lip with anxiety as he didn't look well at all, in fact he looked dreadfully pale.

"Yes, *ma mie,* quite well," he said faintly though she noticed now that there was a muscle ticking in his jaw.

She frowned at him and put her hands to his face, forcing him to look at her. "You don't look well, you look ... you look ... like you're trying not to shout at me." She pursed her lips and crossed her arms. "You are cross aren't you? Alex, you promised!"

She huffed and looked away from him, only to turn back as she felt him begin to shake beneath her. Looking back she discovered that he was laughing silently, his big shoulders quivering with the force of it. A moment later and he could hold it in no longer and burst out laughing, gasping for breath as tears rolled down his face.

"Oh my God," he managed, apparently quite unable to stop. "You're a smuggler!"

She stared at him, not sure if she was relieved or cross that he found it funny but then he pulled her to him and kissed her soundly. *"Ma mie,* you never cease to surprise me and I pray you never do. You are simply the most extraordinary woman I have ever known." He sighed and shook his head. "My God, I do love you so."

"So you're not cross?" she asked, smiling at him.

"Not cross, no," he replied, his voice soft. "Though I hope you don't mind if I ask you to come back to Cornwall and marry me? I know it will likely be rather dull for you after all of your adventures but ... I would rather if you left this life behind you, if you think you can bear it?"

She gave a heavy sigh and pretended to give the matter great thought. "Well, it's true, I 'ave discovered I'm a rather good *contrebandier,"* she said with some gravity. "But ... I think I should like to marry you very much and life with you ... I think it won't be dull at all." She grinned at him and he chuckled.

"But, Alex," she said, putting her hand on his arm. "I would ask you the same thing. Please stop going on the runs. I couldn't bear it if you were 'urt or ..." She stopped as her voice grew thick and he leaned down and kissed her.

"As you wish, Céleste. I think perhaps, with you in my life, I will have no need to seek adventure to ease the boredom of my days." His smile quirked and his eyes glittered with amusement as he added, "Living with you will be quite adventure enough."

She huffed and smacked his arm playfully. "Odious man, are you comparing me to your smugglers?"

"No," he said, his voice serious now. "I am saying that nothing on earth makes my heart pound so fiercely as you, *ma mie."* The kiss that followed that statement kept them occupied for some considerable time, until Céleste shivered and Alex got up, pulling her to her feet.

"Come, you're freezing out here. Let's go back to the house and get your things. If we hurry we can catch the tide."

"Oh but, Alex ..." She paused and he looked down at her with a quizzical expression, taking her hand in his. "Well, it's just, Mimi and the girls. I 'ave promised them they will be safe 'ere."

"And so they shall, *mignonne.* I would not undo any of your good work. I am proud of you."

He slipped his arm around her waist and they began to walk back to the house. "Alex?" she said, her voice quiet.

"Yes, love?"

"Do we ... do we 'ave to go back 'ome right now?"

He paused and looked down at her, concern in his eyes. "Don't you want to?" he asked, sounding anxious all over again.

"Oh, oui!" she exclaimed, shaking her head. "Of course, only ... only ..." She blushed and he looked at her with curiosity in his eyes.

"Only?" he prompted.

"Only ..." She looked away from him and studied her feet. "Well, I was very unwell on the boat and ... and my room 'ere is really *très* comfortable. I 'ave bought a new bed you see and ..." She ground to a halt, blushing furiously and felt his hand slip beneath her chin, raising her head up to him and finding his eyes dark with wanting.

"What a wonderful idea," he murmured, dipping his head to brush his lips over hers. "If you're sure we won't shock the other residents."

"Well we might I suppose," she said with utter seriousness, pursing her lips and giving a little shrug. "But they'll just 'ave to put up with it."

Alex gave a bark of laughter and swung her into his arms. "Well now, let's see what we can do about that."

Chapter 34

"Wherein our reunited lovers are at last left alone and in the arms of bliss."

To Céleste's frustration Belle and the others were so full of excitement and felicitations for her that they insisted on drinking a toast, and then it was time for dinner and it would have been too embarrassing to refuse. Though from the knowing smirks on the women's faces they knew only too well she was anxious to quit their company. Only Mimi was quiet and she stole a moment to go and speak with him alone and reassure him that the house was theirs and that there would always be a place for him.

She understood, on talking to him, that he'd been afraid if the earl found her their little idyll would be at an end, and so he'd kept the information to himself. Although he'd caused her extra weeks of misery she found she couldn't be cross with him; her happiness was too complete for any amount of regret to be felt. As soon as she had assured him that nothing for him would change, he had beamed and hauled her into a rib-cracking embrace before shuffling off to leave them to their evening.

She turned back to the table and smiled when she observed that Belle conversed quite politely with Alex and that somehow he'd managed to charm the blade from her sharp tongue. Annise and Clara, though thrilled for her, seemed uncomfortable to stay in his company but Belle continued to surprise her. When she had found the woman, struggling to provide for herself and her baby she had been full of anger and spite and had not been the easiest person to help. But once she had seen Céleste was genuine in her desire to help give her and her daughter a better life, she'd come around, becoming her staunchest ally and even accepted her offer to teach her to read.

"Belle tells me you have been teaching them to read and write," Alex said echoing the direction her thoughts had taken. She felt a glow of warmth fill her chest at the pride in his eyes.

"Oui," she said, returning Belle's smile. "Though I am afraid I won't be able to continue if I am to return to England."

"Alors, don't you worry about that," Belle said, her voice softer than Céleste had ever heard it. "You've done quite enough. Giving us all a home, somewhere safe for me to raise my daughter, a place we can be at peace. We can never repay you for that."

Alex covered Céleste's hand and squeezed it. "I think perhaps a teacher could be found to continue those lessons."

She looked up with him and took in the sincerity on his handsome face with a lump in her throat. "You would do that?"

"Of course, *mignonne*. What you've done here is ... is quite extraordinary, and I think it would be a good thing to provide a safe place for women who find themselves in difficulties. A shelter from the storm," he said with a smile. "Where they can be protected from harm until they are able to find a place for themselves in the world."

She blinked up at him, finding herself lost for words, too overwhelmed with emotion for this wonderful man to give him the thanks he deserved. He stroked her face, his eyes full of the same force of emotion. "I sometimes wonder what would have happened to us both if my ship hadn't been lost that night and ..." He stopped as his voice became thick. "I would be proud to help you make a place for young women to run to when they are afraid and alone, Céleste. A place where you might have been safe if I'd never found you."

"Oh, Alex!" She threw her arms around his neck and clung to him, crying quietly as Belle discreetly left the table and went up to her own bed.

He held her until she managed to control herself and stop her tears. He looked down at her, holding her face in his hands and drying her wet cheeks with his thumbs.

"Are you going to show me this comfortable bed now, *mignonne."* he asked, his voice so full of love and tenderness that she feared she would cry all over again. So she just nodded, not trusting her voice and took his hand, leading him up the stairs to her bedroom.

He had to duck to walk through the low lintel over the door, but smiled as he looked around and took in the clean polished wood floor, granite stone walls and the two small windows which faced towards the sea. Céleste gave a private smile of her own, as she realised one of the girls had been up here and lit the fire and a lamp, and turned down the bed.

The fire flickered with salt blue flames, casting a lambent glow over them both as she turned, suddenly feeling rather unsure of herself and finding the room appeared much smaller than it ever had before, with Alex's huge presence filling the space.

"It's charming," he said, holding out his hand to her with a smile. She took it and allowed him to pull her closer. He rested his hands on her hips and looked down at her. "You're not afraid of me are you, love?" he said, a slight frown in his eyes as he watched her. She shook her head but didn't meet his eyes.

"Non, of course not but ... a little nervous I suppose." She stepped closer, burying her face against his chest and inhaling the familiar scent of him as he stroked her hair.

"There's nothing to be nervous about," he murmured, and she felt him drop a kiss on the top of her head.

"B-but the first time ... it 'urts I think?"

She looked up at him and found regret in his eyes. "A little bit, love, yes, but I'll do everything I can not to hurt you. I wouldn't hurt you for the world, Céleste. You do believe that don't you?"

Smiling up at him she nodded. "Of course, I trust you."

Slowly he lowered his head and brushed his mouth against hers, tender at first and then with growing need as he parted her lips and possessed her mouth in a tender and ravishing kiss. She slid her hand over his chest, leaning into him. Oh yes, this was what she had longed for, what she had needed for such a very long time, but it wasn't enough, not nearly enough. She reached up and pulled at his neck, encouraging him, wanting him to take more, faster, but he continued with the slow, sensuous assault on her mouth and her senses as his hands moved over her, dropping to cup her bottom and pull her firmly against him. She sighed into his mouth as she discovered him hard and ready for her and moved her hips restlessly against him. Her body was on fire and overwhelmed with sensation, eager to rush to that heady point that he had taken her to once before. He chuckled, breaking the kiss to run his mouth and tongue over her neck, setting her to shivering.

"Always in such a hurry, *mignonne*. Really there is no need. I have every intention of loving you all night."

She looked up at him with something close to reproach in her eyes. "But I want you ..." she said, trying not to sound as if she was whining and suspecting she had failed. "I want you so much, don't you ..."

His face grew serious and he put a hand to the back of her neck, his gaze intent. "Céleste, it is taking every shred of self control to do this right and not just throw you on the bed and take you. As it is I don't know how long I can restrain myself, so be a good girl and don't make it harder to do." Although she could tell he was in earnest there was a glimmer of amusement in his eyes.

She huffed at him, pouting. "And if I want you to throw me on zhe bed?" she demanded.

He chuckled and turned her around, applying himself to undoing the ties at the back of her dress and slipping it over her shoulder. "I promise you faithfully, next time I will throw you down on the bed and ravish you with utter abandon. Does that satisfy you, my little minx?"

"Alors, just see that you do," she replied with a haughty sniff that made him chuckle, his warm breath tickling the sensitive skin at the back of her neck and making her shiver. His hand searched through her hair, removing the pins and allowing it to cascade over her shoulders.

"So very lovely," he murmured, dropping a soft kiss on her bare shoulder as his clever hands made quick work of her undergarments. He turned her around and she heard his breath hitch and knew he had been truthful in what he'd said. He wanted her very badly. The thought, combined with the dark wanting in his eyes gave her confidence and she didn't blush as his heated gaze roved over her. He moaned and cupped her breasts, whispering sweet words against her skin as he dropped his head and kissed his way across the soft swells. As he took one nipple into his mouth, sucking gently and laving with his tongue she caught her breath and pulled his head closer. Her breathing became harsh and uneven as he continued his delicate ministrations, lavishing equal attention on the other breast. Suddenly he stood and swept her up, making her squeak in surprise.

"Are you going to throw me on the bed after all?" she asked, breathless.

"Not until I know the bed can take the punishment," he said chuckling and placing her down with rather more care. "I do not want to be searching out another place to make love to you at this point because you've broken the damn thing."

She bit back a giggle and instead watched with avid interest as he began to undress. He'd remained disappointingly clothed the only other time they'd been intimate and though she had seen him naked before he'd been unconscious at the time and that, she suspected, was rather a different thing. Her thoughts on this matter were confirmed as he stood before her, utterly and quite beautifully naked. She caught her breath and got to her knees on the bed, reaching out to touch him.

He stepped closer and stood patiently as she explored his body with wonder. Running her hands over the wiry hair on his broad chest and pausing to run her tongue over his nipples. She smiled, pleased as the skin puckered beneath her tongue and toyed for a moment, biting the tender flesh very softly. A low groan rumbled though his chest and she looked up at him in surprise. She went to give her attention to the other neglected nipple but was stopped as Alex's hands grasped her shoulders to move her back.

"Non!" she exclaimed. "Keep still, I 'aven't finished yet."

He made a soft noise of distress but she ignored him, batting his hands away and carrying on. Once satisfied that both nipples had been given great care, she slid her hands down his body, over the taut, ridged belly and coming to rest on the jut of his hipbones. She looked down, breathing out in awe and smiling as shivers ran over his skin in response.

Running her fingers over the hard length of him she found his skin astonishingly soft. "Are you quite sure it will only 'urt a little bit," she said, looking at the size of him doubtfully. He made a strangled noise but didn't answer as she smoothed her palm over him and back down again.

"No more," he said through his teeth, pushing her back among the pillows and climbing over her. Pulling her into his arms he kissed her and she wriggled closer to him, entranced by the contrast of his hot smooth skin. The rougher patches of hair on his chest and legs abraded her sensitive flesh and rasped against her breasts in the most tantalising fashion. His hands moved over her and she gasped as his large, warm palm slid over her stomach and lower, delicately parting her soft curls and seeking the small peak of flesh that made her hips rise off the bed and her breath hitch.

He continued to stroke her, with gentle, teasing touches until she was hot and writhing and then began a trail down her body with lips and tongue that made her shiver and gasp until he reached the source of her pleasure. She cried out as his mouth joined the delightful attack on her sanity and believed she really might lose her senses completely as his clever fingers slid inside her and were added to the erotic equation and brought her trembling and crying to an exquisite climax.

She was still gasping and twitching with delicious aftershocks rolling through her as he eased her legs further apart and settled himself between them. She arched again as the sleek skin of his hard shaft slid against her most delicate flesh, still throbbing from his attentions. Slowly he began to nudge his way inside her, teasing her with small, shallow thrusts, barely penetrating her as she sought to accept the strange and unaccustomed fullness. Her arms wrapped around the powerful width of his back, her fingers digging into his shoulders as he loved her. He murmured soft words of reassurance and she buried her face against the hot skin of his neck, kissing him and tasting salt on her lips. He nudged a little deeper inside and she gasped, arching beneath him.

"That's right, love, just a little more," he said, kissing the line of her jaw and the small hollow at the base of her throat as her head tilted back. "Oh, God, Céleste, you're so sweet, so perfect, love." The next moment he thrust hard and she caught her breath, surprised by the sharp pinch and more so with the swiftness it was gone. Little by little she felt her body accept him, acquainting itself with the feel of his larger, harder form twined so intimately with hers. Clinging to him with arms and legs she met his rhythm with the helpless thrusting of her own hips as her body's own instincts guided her.

Alex groaned and propped himself up on his arms, his heavy body moving carefully against the cradle of her own, driving harder and faster inside her. She slid her hands down his back, feeling the skin hot and damp beneath her fingers. Grasping at him as that powerful tug began all over again, gathering and pulling at her senses as she felt the heavy muscle and sinew sliding beneath her fingertips. Her breath came in short gasps, each punctuated with a strangled moan of desire which she was startled to discover was her own. But now she didn't care as the bright light of her peak was so close. She looked up to see Alex's eyes closed and his face one of stark concentration. She caught her breath as the gathering feeling got stronger and more insistent and his eyes opened, focusing on her for a moment and then widening as pleasure took him over and his body thrust deeper inside her as he shook helplessly with his own release. He held her tighter, desperate and primal as he took her mouth and she groaned and shattered in his arms, clinging to him as they searched greedily for every last quaking tremor of ecstasy.

Still breathless he moved to the side of her but kept her in his arms, pulling her with him until she was sprawled half over him, her head on his chest. Her heart was thundering still and part of her could hardly believe she had finally got what she had been longing for, for what felt like an eternity.

His big hand reached out and stroked her hair, and he shifted slightly, cushioning her head on the thick muscle of his arm so he could look at her.

"Are you alright, *mignonne?"*

"Mmmm," was the only coherent sound she could make, still not ready to go to the effort of forming words. Her limbs felt heavy and pliant and sleepily sated.

He chuckled and kissed her nose. "I'm going to take that as a yes."

"Mmmm," she repeated, snuggling against him and sighing with content.

"Go to sleep, love," he said, his voice a soft murmur in her ear. "Don't worry, I'll wake you again momentarily as I have no intention of wasting an entire night." He nuzzled her ear and nipped at the soft lobe making her giggle and squirm against him. "Best make the most of this bed after all; and you were quite right," he added, and she could hear the laughter in his voice. "It is very comfortable."

Chapter 35

"Wherein everyone is well pleased with themselves and the future is full of promise."

They were married in the private chapel at Tregothnan.

Céleste had been overwhelmed by both the warmth and love she received on returning to the family, and also by the manner in which she'd been resoundingly scolded by everyone, most especially Aunt Seymour, for breaking their hearts. Everyone who knew Seymour was forced to comment that they had never seen the old girl so moved as she hugged Céleste. Indeed Seymour thanked her profusely for coming home and for forgiving her idiot nephew, before chastising her roundly for giving them all such a nasty fright.

The day of the wedding dawned warm and clear, with the last bright glitter of summer surrendering to the loving touch of the softer, gentler gold of autumn. Everywhere the trees were touched with mellow tones of red and amber and the leaves fell in great swirling drifts, dancing with joyous sweeps of colour as they fluttered around Alex and his bride as they emerged from the church.

Dressed all in pale gold silk with the same fabric trailing a delicate flower pattern down the bodice and over-skirts and embroidered with pearls and gold lamé, she had walked the aisle. Alex had been moved to remark on seeing her enter the church that with her golden hair and the ripe colours of the countryside framing her petite figure in the Gothic doorway, she looked like the sun come to earth, with a fancy to walk a moment among mere mortals.

Céleste looked up at the man beside her before the alter and felt her heart give a sudden skip in her chest. He caught her glance and smiled at her, raising her hand to his mouth and kissing her fingers with such reverence her breath caught.

"Don't wake me up," she whispered to him, remembering his own words the day he'd found her again on the beach at Roscoff. How strange, she thought, to have found him on the beach all those months ago, and for him to have found her again along that same shoreline.

The earl ducked his head, his words as soft susurration against her skin."We'll dream together and leave the real world far behind us, and never return," he said and she sighed, wondering how long it would be before they could safely leave the wedding breakfast without appearing rude.

The ceremony itself had been mercifully brief with just the aunts, Aubrey and Henri and Lawrence in attendance. And now Aubrey was striding up to her and she found she was a little nervous in meeting once more her dearest friend, whom she'd not seen since before her hurried departure all those months before.

"M-my, Aubrey," she stammered, feeling suddenly appalled at how she had used his name to make Alex jealous. "It is so nice to see you, and looking so very well." She glanced up at her husband and he arched a brow at her, but to her relief his eyes danced with amusement. She sighed and knew she must face the inevitable. "I'm afraid I owe you an apology," she said, turning back to Aubrey, her cheeks reddening.

"I should say," he said with some indignation. "Couldn't you have found a shorter ceremony? Lord, stuck between m'grandmother and dear old Dotty sobbing for all she was worth. I'm clean out of handkerchiefs is all I'll say, so don't start acting like a watering pot for I can't help you."

"Non, I didn't mean that, silly boy ... I meant ... For telling Alex that you'd offered for me."

Aubrey grew pale and blinked at her, glanced at Alex who returned a bland expression, and then replied with some force, "You did what? Dash it all, you could get a man killed!"

Céleste bit her lip, torn between amusement at the alarm in his eyes and her very real regret at having been so deceitful. "I am most dreadfully sorry, Aubrey, truly. But 'e didn't kill you after all, so there's no 'arm done."

"Well of all the ..." Aubrey huffed and shook his head. "Never knew such a girl for getting into scrapes." He gave his cousin a serious look and wagged his finger at him. "Don't let her have an umbrella, that's all I say," he said obscurely. "Best bit of advice I can give you," he added.

"I'm in your debt, I'm sure," Alex said with some gravity as Céleste snorted beside him.

***

The family proceeded back to the house and the lavish wedding breakfast that awaited them and Alex bore it stoically as they were toasted and the merry party got ever merrier as the champagne flowed. In truth he was just as dazed as his bride and kept wondering to himself what the devil he'd done to deserve such complete and undiluted happiness. It was a thought he didn't dare to dwell on for very long as he was convinced it was nothing in this lifetime. But if retribution came in the next he'd take it and gladly, for an eternity in hell could not dissuade him from wringing every ounce of pleasure and joy from the hours since he had found his *mignonne,* and brought her safe home where she belonged.

He leaned over and interrupted her conversation with Aubrey as the two of them were bickering quite contentedly as they appeared wont to do.

"May I have a moment with my wife?" he asked his cousin politely.

"Lord yes!" said Aubrey, waving his hand in an impatient gesture. "Take her away and give my brain a rest."

"Bah!" Céleste replied and then glanced to assure herself Aunt Seymour hadn't noticed, relieved to find her too busy reprimanding Aunt Dotty for feeding Bandit from the table. "Odious creature!" she said, returning her attention to Aubrey. "If such a thing existed it would be tired indeed by the exercise."

"Devil a bit!"

"Children ..." Alex replied with a sigh, receiving a very black look from both parties as a result. "My Lady, if you would be so kind?"

With a haughty look at Aubrey she accepted the earl's hand and got gracefully to her feet and then quite spoiled the effect by turning and poking her tongue out at Aubrey and dissolving into laughter as he rolled his eyes at her.

She glanced up at Alex with a rueful smile. "Oh dear, I think I will make you a perfectly 'orrible wife, won't I?"

He chuckled and leant down to kiss her nose. "Perfectly," he replied.

"Where are we going, Alex. We can't go yet the meal isn't over."

Alex gave a heavy sigh. "No, I know that, we'll return presently as I suppose we must, but ... there is something I want to give you."

Céleste's eyes widened in surprise as he led her through the door to his study. "More presents? Surely not, Alex, really you don't need to. The beautiful sapphire set and the diamonds, your mother's pearls and all the dresses and shoes and ... oh, everything you 'ave done. I don't need anything more. Truly, I could not be 'appier. If it were even possible I would burst!"

"Well I think I shall have to take the risk nonetheless," he said, the corners of his mouth twitching slightly. "Though in truth, *ma mie,* this is not mine to give as it already belongs to you."

He watched as her smooth brow furrowed a little in confusion. "I don't understand."

Closing the door quietly behind them, he reached over and picked up a quantity of paperwork from his desk and handed it to her.

"Read it, love," he said, his voice gentle. She did as he bid her and he waited, sliding his arm around her waist and drawing her against him as she read the rather formal words on the heavy vellum pages.

"B-but what does it mean?" she whispered, looking up at him with her lovely blue eyes glittering.

"Just what it says, *ma mie*, you are confirmed as the Countess of Valrey and all properties and items that have ever belonged to your family are now, quite rightly, yours and yours alone."

She blinked and when she spoke her voice trembled with the force of emotion. "You did this, for me?"

"A very small thing, I assure you, but something I was glad to do."

"Oh, Alex!"

She wrapped her arms around him and held on to him so tight he was obliged to rescue the papers before they became creased beyond saving.

"There is something else," he added, almost apologetic as she shook her head and sniffed.

"Oh, no, Alex, I cannot take anything more it is too much," she said, sounding as though she was between laughter and a real bout of sobbing.

"But I have so wanted to show you this, *mignonne,* and I have saved it for today, surely you will not deny me?"

She laughed at the seriousness of his tone and shook her head again. "As you wish, my Lord, you know I could never deny you anything."

He stroked her cheek and leaned down, brushing a kiss against her lips. "You are too good," he murmured, turning her around so that her eyes fell upon a large item leaned against the wall and covered with a sheet. It looked rather like a painting. "It has been possible to locate some of the items which once belonged to your family. I'm afraid much of it is lost but there are a few items, paintings and furniture which have been recovered. This one in particular I thought you would like to have close to you." He walked over and carefully stripped away the sheet to reveal a heavy guilt frame and a portrait of a wonderfully handsome couple. The young man had a rather serious mien, though there was laughter in his eyes, and the woman was perfectly ravishing, with her golden curls and her wide blue eyes. Their body language and the air of tranquil happiness between them left even the most careless observer in no doubt that this had been a love match, and a very successful one.

Alex felt his own throat grow tight as Céleste covered her mouth with her hand and the tears that had threatened earlier finally overspilled the eyes so like those of the woman in the portrait.

"I thought I should never see them again," she whispered, staring at the picture and unheeding of the tears that fell down her cheeks.

"Well now you may look upon your parents whenever you wish to, and know that there was a time when their lives were happy and carefree."

She nodded, her face so full of emotion he found it hard to keep his own composure. *"Oui,* I should like very much to think of them in 'appier times."

He returned to her and stood at her back as she stared at the painting, putting his arms around her and holding her close. "You have no notion of the honour you have done me, I think, *mignonne,* by becoming my wife. But you see, I am taking your happiness very seriously. You must know that I would do anything so that you never have cause to regret this day."

She turned in his arms, her face one of great indignation. "Oh, Alex, how can you? You know very well that I 'ave loved you since the day I found you on that beach and I would 'ave married you and been the wife of a smuggler and counted myself blessed indeed. I didn't look to be a countess, twice over in fact!" she said, sounding bewildered by the turn of events. "But you could not possibly make me any 'appier. Just love me, *mon contrebandier,* and I will never, ever regret a single moment."

"You may have no doubts on that score, love. I intend to do just that for the rest of my days. But I am glad to have restored to you what was rightfully yours and ... perhaps one day we will have a daughter, and she will inherit your title just as a son will inherit mine."

She smiled and reached a finger up to trace the line of his lower lip, a tender touch that made desire glitter under his skin.

"A son and a daughter," she murmured. "I should like that very much. 'Ow many children do you think we should 'ave?"

He nuzzled his face against her hand, kissing the palm, his voice low and full of need. "As many as you like, enough to fill this dusty old house with chaos for years to come."

She nodded, her face serious. "Well, then," she said with a sigh. "I think perhaps we should waste no more time, there is that big empty nursery to fill after all."

He chuckled, low in his throat as he pulled her closer and feathered kisses over her face, her nose, the line of her jaw. "Quite right, my Lady. After all, we can't be seen to be neglecting our solemn duty." And with that he took her mouth and kissed his wife in such a way that there could be no doubt in her mind just how seriously he took his responsibilities; and after all, their guests could very well take care of themselves.

Fin

If you have enjoyed this book, please support me by leaving a review!

About the Author

Emma V Leech is currently the author of two series, Les Corbeaux: The French Vampire Legend and Les Fées: The French Fae Legend with much more to come. With the release of The Rogue and The Earl's Temptation she is taking her first foray into the world of Historical Fiction.

As an accomplished paranormal romance author, Emma won the world's largest online writing competition 'The Wattys' two years running, first with The Darkest Night, and then with her short story, A Dark Imperfection, A Les Fées Novella. Her third published novel, The Dark Prince has been touted as one of The Top 50 Self Published Books Worth Reading in 2015 and is #2 on the list of the Top 50 Indie Books in 2015 as well as being hailed as "An enchanting fantasy with a likable heroine, romantic intrigue, and clever narrative flourishes." by Kirkus Reviews.

Emma's novels have garnered attention worldwide, and fans who continue to clamour for more through email, Facebook, and Twitter.

When she's not writing she strives to live as far from the real world as possible. but otherwise she can be found in Darkest Dordogne, South West France with her husband, three children,

Scandal's Daughter

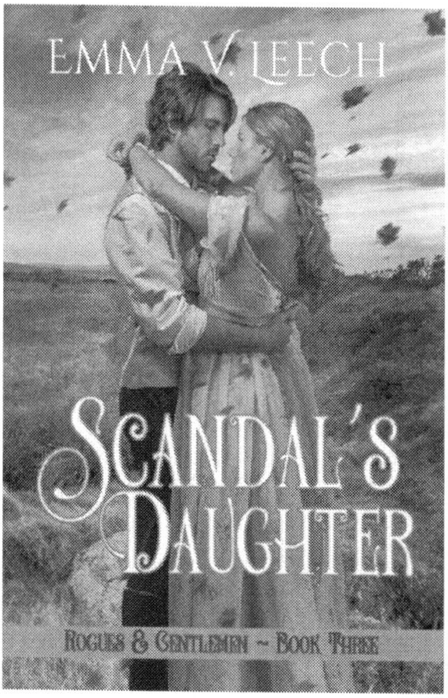

Coming May 2017!

Sebastian Grenville, The Duke of Sindalton, known as *Sin* to the ton, has had his fair share of scandal. His father's involvement in what became referred to as *'The Scandal of the Century'* plunged him into the spotlight at the tender age of twelve, and he's been there ever since. Egged on by his best friend, *Beau* - The Marquis of Beaumont, his life is one of dissipation and ease. But every duke needs an heir and everyone knows Sindalton is in the market for a wife.

Both men, bored to death by balls and matchmaking mamas, go to a friend's hunting lodge in Cornwall where Sindalton gets caught in a storm and heads for cover. Seeking shelter in a cave, the duke is delighted when he stumbles upon Miss Georgiana Bomford, the niece of the local doctor. But the feisty red-headed beauty is unimpressed by his attempt to entice her. Sindalton however is captivated, and intent on seduction, makes her the target of his all too tempting charms. But Georgiana is not who he thinks she is, and when they meet again in London, the scandalous past is in danger of repeating itself.

Other works

by

Emma V. Leech

Rogues and Gentlemen

The Rogue

The Earl's Temptation

Scandal's Daughter (May 2017)

The Devil May Care (June 2017)

Les Corbeaux: The French Vampire Legend

The Key to Erebus

The Heart of Arima

The Fires of Tartarus

The Son of Darkness (tba)

Les Fées: The French Fae Legend

The Dark Prince

The Dark Heart

The Dark Deceit (tba)

The Darkest Night (tba)

Novellas:

A Dark Desire

A Dark Tale

A Dark Design

A Dark Collection

Want More Emma?

I would love to hear from you. Please email me at TheKeytoErebus@gmail.com .

Or feel free to join my website for up to date news, short stories, photos and much more. Membership is always free! :

Emma V. Leech

I can also be found on:

Amazon Emma on Amazon

Facebook: Emma's Facebook

Twitter: Emma's Twitter

The Key to Erebus

Les Corbeaux: The French Vampire Legend

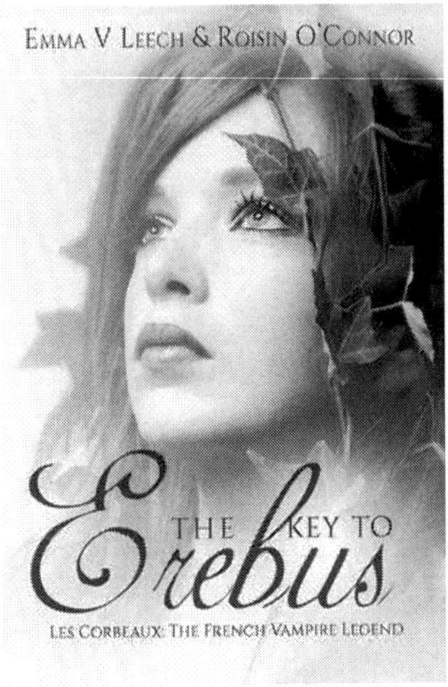

The truth can kill you.

Taken as a small child, from a life where faeries, sirens and mythical creatures are real and treacherous, Jéhenne Corbeaux is totally unprepared when she returns to France to stay with her eccentric Grandmother.

Thrown headlong into a world she knows nothing about she seeks to learn the truth about herself, uncovering secrets more shocking than anything she could ever have imagined and finding that she is by no means powerless to protect the ones she loves.

Despite her Gran's dire warnings, she is inexorably drawn to the dark and terrifying figure of Corvus, an ancient vampire and master of the Albinus family.

Jéhenne is about to find her answers and discover that, not only is Corvus far more dangerous than she could ever imagine but that he holds much more than the key to her heart…

FREE DOWNLOAD

Click to download The Key to Erebus from Amazon

The Dark Prince

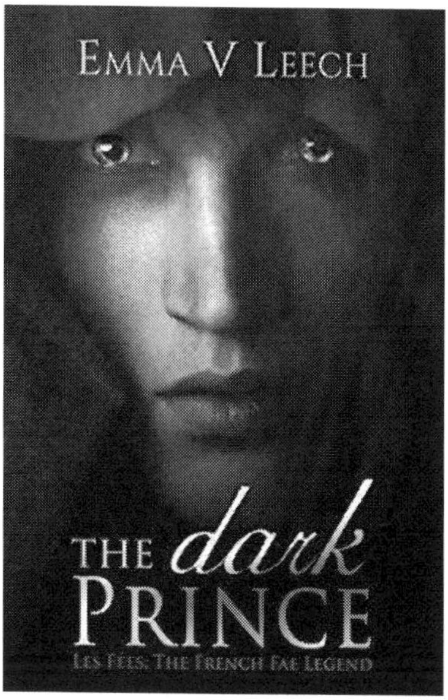

Les Fées: The French Fae Legend

The man of your dreams is coming ... or is it your nightmares he visits? Laen is Prince of the Dark fae, with a temper and reputation to match his black eyes, and a heart that despises the human race. When he is sent back through the forbidden gates between realms to retrieve an ancient fae artifact, he returns home with far more than he bargained for.

Océane DeBeauvoir is an artist and bookbinder who has always relied on her lively imagination to get her through an unhappy and uneventful life. A jewelled dagger put on display at a nearby museum hits the headlines with speculation of another race, the fae.

But the discovery also inspires Océane to create an extraordinary piece of art. Océane's lonely and romantic heart has created the story of The Dark Prince, but it soon becomes apparent that her story cannot be confined to the pages of a book. And it seems that her hero is far from the troubled, romantic figure she had painted, but something far more sinister

Acknowledgements

Thanks as always to my wonderful editor Gemma Fisk of FiskLit for being patient and guiding me through this adventure into Regency England!

To my wonderful BFF, PA, personal cheerleader and bringer of chocolate, Varsi Richardson Appel, for moral support, confidence boosting and for reading my work more times than I have. I love you loads!

To the betas! Varsi, Alejandra Avila, Varsha Shurpali, Veronique Glotin Phillips. Thank you so much for all your help and advice.

To all of the dedicated Dark Addicts and wicked Angels. Thank you all for your continued support and excitement over my work and for taking a chance on what for some of you is a new genre. You guys are such an inspiration and your enthusiasm keeps me excited to write for you. I'm always so happy to hear from you so do email or message me :) thekeytoerebus@gmail.com

To my husband Pat and my family ... For always being proud of me.

67453189R00202

Made in the USA
Lexington, KY
15 September 2017